'Compelling, thoughtful, emotionally intelligent'
Daily Mail

'One of my favourite writers'
Katie Fforde

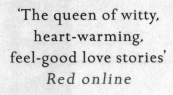

'Funny, romantic and brilliantly written'
***** *Heat*

'The queen of witty, heart-warming, feel-good love stories'
Red online

THE JOY OF
Jill Mansell

'The perfect romantic read to make you smile and dream of long summer days by the beach'
Woman & Home

'A fab, feel-good read' *Prima*

'Reading Jill is always such a joy!'
Veronica Henry

'A lovely uplifting read'
Good Housekeeping

Jill Mansell

is the author of over twenty *Sunday Times* bestsellers including
THIS COULD CHANGE EVERYTHING, THE ONE YOU
REALLY WANT and MEET ME AT BEACHCOMBER BAY. TAKE A
CHANCE ON ME won the RNA's Romantic Comedy Prize, and in
2015 the RNA presented Jill with an outstanding achievement award.

Jill's personal favourite amongst her novels is THREE AMAZING
THINGS ABOUT YOU, which is about cystic fibrosis and organ
donation; to her great delight, many people have joined the organ
donor register as a result of reading this novel.

Jill started writing fiction while working in the NHS, after she read
a magazine article that inspired her to join a local creative writing
class. Since she was first published in 1991, over eleven million
copies of her books have been sold worldwide. She is one of the
few who still write their books by hand, like a leftover from
the dark ages. She lives in Bristol with her family.

By Jill Mansell

The right of Jill Mansell to be identified as the Author of
the Work has been asserted by her in accordance with the
Copyright, Designs and Patents Act 1988.

First published in Great Britain in 2019 by
HEADLINE REVIEW
An imprint of HEADLINE PUBLISHING GROUP

First published in paperback in 2019 by
HEADLINE REVIEW

1

Cataloguing in Publication Data is available from the British Library

ISBN 978 1 4722 5200 5 (A-Format)
ISBN 978 1 4722 4846 6 (B-Format)

Map illustration by Laura Hall

Typeset in Bembo Std by Palimpsest Book Production Limited,
Falkirk, Stirlingshire

Printed and bound in Great Britain by Clays Ltd, Elcograf S.p.A

Headline's policy is to use papers that are natural, renewable and recyclable
products and made from wood grown in well-managed forests and other controlled
sources. The logging and manufacturing processes are expected to conform to the
environmental regulations of the country of origin.

HEADLINE PUBLISHING GROUP
An Hachette UK Company
Carmelite House
50 Victoria Embankment
London EC4Y 0DZ

www.headline.co.uk
www.hachette.co.uk

Jill Mansell

maybe this time

REVIEW

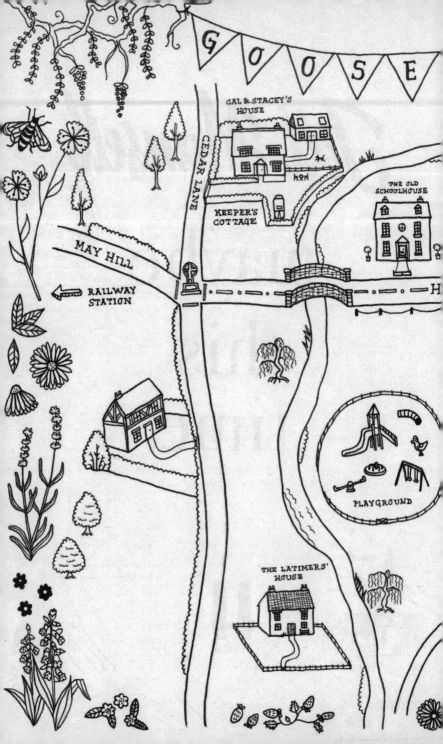

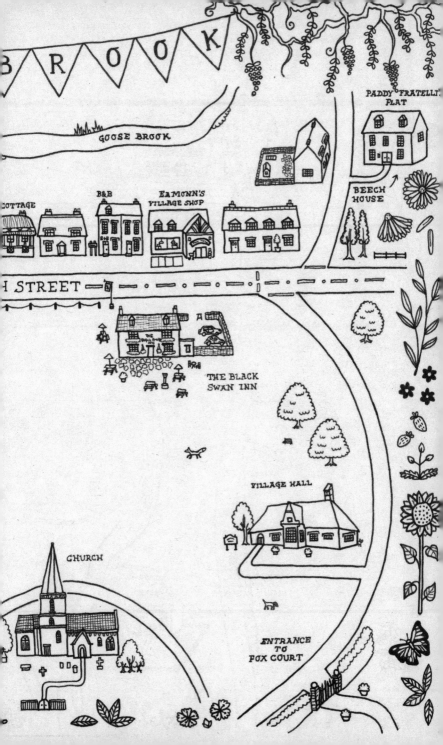

For Judi and Paul
with my love.

Chapter 1

So this was it then, the countryside. Well, there had been a few previous rural encounters over the years, but to a lesser degree. Whereas this definitely ranked as up close and personal.

Feeling intrepid, Mimi stepped down from the train and breathed in the mingled green scents of spring grass, new leaves, damp earth and the smallest hint of cow poo, presumably drifting across from the field visible through the lattice of trees on the other side of the track. A couple of black and white cows lazily lifted their heads in order to observe the train as it departed, before swishing their tails and returning their attention to the serious business of tearing up clumps of grass.

It had to be the world's tiniest station, very cute indeed, comprising a single track dotted with wild flowers and weeds, and a small stone shelter. It would probably faint if it ever saw the gigantic edifice that was Paddington. Making her way towards the rickety metal gate, Mimi realised she'd made a fundamental error in having assumed there'd be a friendly local taxi driver waiting outside to be of service.

The only other passenger to have disembarked, a sixty-something woman in a brown tartan skirt and brutally sensible lace-up shoes, said, 'Excuse me,' in a pained way, probably because Mimi was hesitating in front of the gate.

'Oh, sorry! It's just . . . I thought there'd be a taxi rank.'

The woman's eyebrows lifted. 'Seriously?'

'I've just come down from London,' Mimi explained. 'I mean, I knew this station would be small, but I didn't realise it wouldn't have . . . anything here at all.'

'Well, it doesn't. You live and learn.'

Helpful. Mimi tried again. 'OK, could you point me in the direction of the bus stop?'

The woman was now looking at her as if she'd landed from Mars. 'There isn't a bus stop. Because there aren't any buses.'

What?

'But that's just crazy. How am I supposed to get to where I want to go?'

Mrs Tartan Kilt took out her car keys and said impatiently, 'Where are you headed?'

Oh thank goodness. Mimi beamed with relief. 'Goosebrook.'

'Well in that case you need to turn left at the end of the lane, then just keep on going. Follow the signposts.'

And now, unbelievably, she was turning away, marching over to a filthy dark blue Volvo rakishly parked half on and half off the dandelion-studded verge. Having climbed behind the wheel and buzzed down the windows, she performed a nifty five-point turn and gestured for Mimi to move out of the way so she could drive off.

In desperation, Mimi said, 'Look, I don't suppose you could give me a lift, could you? I'd be *so* grateful—'

'Sorry, I'm going in the opposite direction.' She didn't sound sorry at all.

'But how am I going to get to Goosebrook?'

The woman gave a pitying shake of the head. 'You have legs, don't you? A couple of fully functioning feet? I know it's a radical idea, but I suggest you try using them.'

And she roared off down the narrow lane, just as the sun disappeared behind a cloud and the first fat drops of rain began to fall.

So much for friendly locals and the magic of the countryside.

An hour later, Mimi was making good, if sodden, progress. On the upside, at least she wasn't wearing high heels. But her ballet flats, with their wafer-thin soles, weren't the most comfortable either; she could feel every bump in the rough tarmac. And her overnight bag was making her shoulder ache; if only she'd brought along her red case with the wheels.

Oh well, she'd covered four miles and there was only one more to go. It had stopped raining, too. The sky was blue once more, birds were singing, the hedgerows were starred with primroses and there were sheep in the meadow to her right, some with newborn lambs gambolling in the sunshine—

Mimi stopped dead in her tracks, horrified by what she was seeing and realising at once what was going on. Just the other night she'd seen a report on TV about the recent spate of vicious attacks on horses in fields, and now it was happening right in front of her, but this time the victim of the attack was a sheep.

Shock and adrenalin surged through her body. She dropped her heavy bag, vaulted the low wall and charged down the slope towards the figure half hidden behind a clump of bushes, but not half hidden enough to disguise the fact that he was wrestling furiously with a sheep on the ground.

'Oh my God, *stop it* . . .' She gathered speed as she ran through taller clumps of grass that whipped around her bare legs. 'What are you doing? Get away from that sheep!'

The man was wearing jeans and a polo shirt; glancing up, he ignored her and carried on battling with the sheep, which was lying on its back, its little legs waggling furiously in the air as it struggled to escape.

'Stop it, just *stop it*!' Skidding to a halt a few metres away in case he was a lunatic with a knife, Mimi yelled, 'You leave him alone right now or I'm calling the police!'

The man abruptly released his hold on the sheep and rose to his feet, prompting Mimi to take a few more steps backwards. OK, she hadn't thought this through; what if he really was a lunatic?

'Let me take a wild guess.' As he spoke, he shook his wet hair out of his eyes and surveyed her, taking in the pink and white striped jacket, the short flippy white skirt and the silver ballet flats. 'You don't live around here.'

OK, the good news was that he wasn't wielding a weapon. He also had a nice voice, kind of drawly and amused. Still panting from her unexpected exertions, Mimi said, 'Just because I'm wearing silver shoes, you're assuming I'm some kind of . . . townie.'

'Partly true.' He nodded, conceding that she'd been right. 'Although one other clue was the way you called the sheep *him*.'

'Now you're just being pedantic. I was trying to stop you attacking it,' Mimi pointed out. 'There wasn't time to get out my binoculars and have a look at its private parts.'

4

This was evidently hilarious; the man was now biting his lip, doing his best not to laugh. He said, 'With this breed of sheep, if it were a male it would have horns. And it would be a ram.'

'Well, you weren't treating it very gently.' Sensing that she was fighting a losing battle, Mimi jumped as the sheep let out a long, baleful *baaaaaaaa*. 'There's no need to be cruel to animals, you know.'

'OK, let me explain. She's pregnant.' He nodded patiently. 'By the look of her, with twins.'

Mimi was appalled. 'All the more reason to be kind!'

He smiled. 'Her fleece is sodden with rain. She has a huge belly. When she lay down, she rolled onto her back and now she's stuck there, can't get up again. If she's left like that, she'll die. So if you want to help, come over here and give me a hand getting her back on her feet.'

The grass was wet and slippery, and the pregnant ewe was bottom-heavy and wriggly, but after a couple of minutes of tussling, heaving and baa-ing, they finally managed to get her upright once more.

The man who wasn't a knife-wielding maniac held the animal's bulky body against his legs, giving her time to regain her bearings. Then he released her and they both watched as she trotted off without so much as a backward glance to rejoin the rest of the flock.

'Not even a thank you,' Mimi remarked.

'I know. She won't write, she won't phone.' As they began to make their way back up the sloping field, he said, 'Still, you did a good job there, helped to save her life. Not bad, for a townie.'

'Thanks. And I'm sorry I shouted at you.'

5

'No problem. You meant well. Where are you visiting, anyway?'

'Goosebrook.' Wondering just how shiny her face was, but not wanting to get caught trying to make herself look better, Mimi surreptitiously gave her forehead a wipe with the sleeve of her jacket.

'Well that's where I live.' They'd reached the gate that led out onto the road, and Mimi saw now that a dark brown terrier was waiting there for him. As he unhooked the lead, which had been looped over the gatepost, the man said, 'This is Otto. I'm Cal.'

'And is this your flock?' She belatedly realised that he must be a farmer.

'No, they aren't mine.' He grinned. 'I just stopped to help out a young lady sheep in distress.'

Otto was up on his hind legs, nudging Mimi's hand with his nose, eager for attention. Rubbing his lopsided ears, she said, 'Hello, aren't you gorgeous?' then looked up at Cal. 'I'm Mimi. Well, Emylia. But mainly Mimi.' Now that she wasn't distracted by the sheep, she noted that his hair was straight and shiny, streaked white blonde by the sun. His brows and lashes were dark, the whites of his brown eyes very white. He had olive skin, an outdoorsy tan and an athletic physique.

'Mimi. Nice to meet you. So how long are you down here for?'

She couldn't help perking up a bit; whilst she'd been checking him out, had he been doing the same to her? Damn, though, she definitely wasn't looking her best. Aloud, Mimi said, 'Just a couple of days.'

'Staying in one of the holiday cottages?'

And now her heart was doing that uncomfortable speeding-up

thing it always did, even after so many years. She really should be used to it by now. She straightened her shoulders. 'No, I'm visiting my dad. He lives in Goosebrook.'

Cal looked surprised. 'He does? Who's your dad then?'

'Hang on a sec, I left my bag . . .' Turning before he could see the flush colouring her cheeks, Mimi ran back along the lane to where she'd flung her bag down in the dip where the grass verge met the dry-stone wall. She loved her dad to bits and she wasn't embarrassed by him, but there was always that tricky moment when other people discovered you were his daughter and you had to deal with whatever they might have to say about it.

The thing was, sometimes you weren't bothered about those people's reactions because they weren't important to you anyway. But at other times, when you met someone and instinctively liked them, it meant the pressure was on because you really didn't want them to come out with some response that was either rude or downright offensive.

Please don't let him do that.

Mentally preparing herself, Mimi hurried back to where Cal and Otto were waiting for her. She held up her bag – like an idiot – and said, 'Got it! Never a good idea to leave your overnight stuff in a ditch!'

Otto, eyeing her with bright-eyed interest, wagged his tail.

And Cal, also eyeing her with interest, said, 'Can I guess?'

'Um, if you like.' Did he really want to know what she'd brought down with her? OK, if he managed to tell her that her bag contained grey and white elephant-print pyjamas, a Fortnum and Mason fruit cake and half a dozen hardback thrillers, that would be seriously impressive and—

'Are you Dan Huish's daughter?'

7

Mimi stared at him. 'Yes! How on earth did you know that?' Because her father had told her only last night that no one in the village knew of her existence.

Cal shrugged and said simply, 'You look like him.'

'Oh. Really? I mean, I think I do a bit, but people don't usually notice. I'm more like my mum.'

'I'm observant.' He smiled. 'You have the same eyes. Green, deep-set. Similar face shape too. You have quite a bit more hair, though.'

'I definitely win that competition.' Mimi ruffled her mass of tortoiseshell hair, which always exploded out of control the moment it was exposed to rain.

'We didn't know he had a daughter. Is this your first time down here?' Cal hesitated, looked wary. 'Is he expecting to see you today?'

Touched by his concern, Mimi said, 'Are you worried I might be about to get a massive surprise? It's OK, don't panic. I do know Dad's gay.'

Chapter 2

Cal looked relieved. 'Phew, for a moment you had me worried. I suddenly thought he might be leading a secret double life.'

He was nice, Mimi could tell; he wasn't about to say anything bigoted or crass. 'Mum and Dad got divorced seven years ago, when I was fifteen,' she said. 'It was a shock at first, of course it was, but we got through it. And Dad met Marcus four years ago.'

'Marcus, that's it.' Cal nodded, clearly reassured there wasn't about to be some dramatic *EastEnders*-style showdown.

'And yes, they do know I'm coming down. Dad was going to meet me off the five o'clock train. But I left work at midday, caught the earlier one and thought it'd be fun to jump in a cab at the station so I could save him the trip.'

'A . . . cab?' Cal looked amused.

'Well I know that now. I just wasn't expecting it to be completely deserted. The countryside isn't my specialist subject.' Mimi shrugged. 'Anyway, never mind. I've had an adventure instead. And we're nearly there now. Oh wow, look at it . . . now that's what I call a view.'

As she'd been speaking, they'd reached the brow of the hill and now Goosebrook was revealed, appearing before them in all its bucolic spring-infused glory. The honeyed Cotswold limestone of the buildings was offset by the abundance of greenery and the bright colours of the flowers in the gardens. The church spire rose into the sky, the roofs of the jumble of houses and cottages were mottled ochre yellow and grey, and children and parents were visible on the village green in front of the church. There were a few shops – not many, Mimi knew – as well as a popular local pub called the Black Swan. And there too, snaking through the village and gleaming silver in the sunlight, was the brook itself, with the old stone bridge arching across it.

'It's a pretty nice place to live,' said Cal, as Otto strained on his lead to reach a butterfly that was taunting him, dancing around just out of his reach.

'Beautiful. Bit different from London.' Just breathing in the sparkling, unpolluted air was an experience. Then again, the lack of handy takeaways would take some getting used to. Personally Mimi wasn't sure she could survive without a Burger King on her doorstep.

'And how are your dad and Marcus settling in?'

'They love the countryside. And living here in the Cotswolds. I'm sure everything's going to be fine,' said Mimi. 'It's just that getting-to-know-people stage, especially in their situation. They want people to like them, but some of the villagers haven't been . . . you know, as friendly as they'd hoped. Not you, I'm sure,' she added hastily. 'It's just a few of the older people have been a bit stand-offish.'

Cal nodded. 'I'm sure they have. But it's not because of the gay thing.'

It was all very well for Cal to say that, but how could he know for sure? 'No? Dad and Marcus are so nice, though. What else could it be?'

'Just good old-fashioned tribalism, suspicion of strangers.' He shrugged. 'It's never changed. The general feeling is new people don't count as villagers until they've lived here for a good while. Because what's the point of bothering to get to know them if they're just going to up and leave again? Not saying it's right,' he added. 'Just that that's the way it's always been. And the older villagers especially resent the ones who buy second homes down here, then leave them standing empty for months on end. Which is what happened to Bay Cottage – your dad's place – before he and Marcus bought it. That's the reason they're wary . . . they don't want it happening again.'

'Fair enough. Well, that's good to know.' They moved to the side of the road as a van passed them, the driver exchanging a cheery salute with Cal. 'So how long before they count as proper villagers?'

'Not too long, only about thirty years.' He grinned at her. 'Maybe fifty years for the really suspicious ones. Are you sure I can't carry that for you?'

'I'm fine.' Mimi shook her head; the soles of her feet were burning and the weight of the overnight case was hurting her shoulder, but they were nearly there now. 'And thanks for the heads-up. I'll tell them what you said. They'll be relieved it wasn't the reason they thought.'

Mimi was relieved too; she felt like an anxious mum, reassured that her shy children would settle into their new school.

Cal said, 'Things will get easier, I promise. And I hope

11

they do stay. Who knows, we might see the three of you later in the pub.'

'Dad's not really a drinker.' At a guess, the fact that they'd been keeping away from the Black Swan hadn't helped.

'Well, they do food too. It's a sociable place. If they walked in through the doors,' said Cal, 'it wouldn't instantly fall silent like the O.K. Corral.'

His dark brown eyes were glinting with amusement. Mimi said, 'I'll tell them that too.'

'The more they join in, the better things will be. I do understand, though. It must be tricky sometimes.'

'It has been.' Mimi nodded.

'Not easy for you either,' said Cal. 'Especially if you were fifteen and it came as a bolt from the blue for you and your mum . . . unless they'd broken up years before. No, don't answer that, none of my business. Sorry.' He shook his head. 'Sometimes I ask too many questions without stopping to wonder if they're appropriate.'

Mimi had had enough practice by now to know that some people were desperate to hear all the salacious details, whilst others were simply sympathetic to her situation. Cal, she could instinctively tell, fell into the second camp.

Not that the details were remotely salacious anyway.

'It's fine,' she reassured him. 'Mum and Dad did their best to make it easy for me. Obviously I was devastated when they broke up and Dad moved out, but I didn't know the real reason behind it. So that bit must have been harder for Mum, because she did know, and when he'd told her it had come as a massive shock. Then about six months later, they sat me down with them and told me. And that was . . . well, weird. Pretty traumatic in one way, but then it kind of made sense, because I hadn't been able to understand why they couldn't stay together.' Mimi paused, still able to recall every moment of that rainy Saturday afternoon. 'I mean, I went through *all* the emotions. When you're that age, anything to do with the idea of your parents' sex lives is enough to make you want to throw up, so that aspect wasn't great. But on the other hand, he was still my dad and I loved him to bits.'

'It must have been hard to cope with,' said Cal.

'School was the worst. Some people were fantastic. And others were awful.' Mimi shuddered. 'Mainly the boys, who thought it was hilarious and couldn't stop making fun of me. Well, you can imagine the kind of crap I had to put up with.'

'Not ideal when you're that age,' said Cal.

'Teenagers can be brutal. You soon learn who your real friends are, I can tell you.' She pulled a face. 'It was definitely character-forming.'

'And I bet the worst culprits were the ones who were secretly battling with their own feelings.'

'Yes! Exactly that! The captain of the school football team was horrible to me for months, said some *really* mean things about Dad . . . and last Christmas I saw on Facebook that he was off to LA with his boyfriend. So I sent him a nice message saying I hoped they had a lovely time.'

'And did he apologise for everything he'd said at school?'

'Of course not. He might be gay now, but that doesn't magically stop him from being a massive prat.'

'Prats are boring.' Cal grinned. 'Tell me about you. Whereabouts do you live in London? Somewhere amazing?'

'Hmm, I wouldn't call it that.' Picturing the run-down building that had been all she could afford to share, Mimi imagined plonking it down in the centre of the ultra-rural scene surrounding them. 'It's a Victorian hovel in Bermondsey, rented out by a shyster landlord who's crammed twelve of us into a place big enough for six. But that's what it's like in the city if you aren't loaded, you kind of get used to it. You have to ignore the downsides, the rats and the tenants you'd rather not be sharing with, and just make the most of having somewhere to live. My friend Kendra has the room next to mine and she's great, so we mainly stick together. And it's a friendly enough neighbourhood. Bit different to this, mind.' She indicated the rolling hills and the bobbing fields of wheat or corn or whatever that green stuff was over to the left of them.

'Well we're friendly here too, I promise.' Cal sounded entertained. 'And how about work? What do you do?'

'I'm in PR.' Mimi paused, wondering if he was familiar with the term, because some sheep wranglers might not be.

But he inclined his head and said, 'Public relations. It's OK, I know what it means. And have you always done that? Do you love it?'

'Oh I do. I mean, I've always loved working, anyway.' Mimi glanced over at Otto, who had paused to cock his leg against a clump of dandelions. 'And I started early too. I used to do three paper rounds when I was at school, then I got into babysitting in a big way. After A levels I took a job in a travel agency, which was great, but after a while it began to feel a bit too office-based and restricting. So then I saw an ad for a position in PR and decided to give it a shot. Well, it was a revelation, it was just . . . perfect!' She found herself gesturing expansively to convey just how perfect. 'Because you need to be really organised and efficient,

14

which I am, and you have to think on your feet, which I love doing, and when things go wrong it's up to you to sort everything out and make it right again . . . ooh, and when you come up with a fantastic plan that works like a dream, you get showered with praise and the clients are thrilled with you for being so clever. It's just the best feeling in the world!'

Mimi heard the enthusiasm in her own voice and knew she was getting carried away again, but she couldn't control it, because when you really loved your job as much as she did, it was hard to be laid-back and super-cool about it. 'OK, don't laugh,' she said, because Cal was clearly trying not to. 'I know I sound like Julie Andrews in *The Sound of Music*, but when I wake up in the morning I honestly can't wait to get to work. I'd do it for free if I could afford to.'

'Probably best not to let your bosses know about that,' said Cal with a smile.

'I know, but what can I say?' Her hands were waving again, all by themselves. 'I was lucky, I found my perfect job. The more effort you put in, the more people appreciate you, and I'm addicted to praise. I mean, right now I'm still one of the juniors in the company, but I know I can work my way up and I can't wait. Are you still laughing at me?'

'Wouldn't dream of it. I think it's brilliant that you're so enthusiastic.' Mimicking her movements, Cal waved his hands as he said the word. 'And ambitious.' More gesticulating. 'And motivated.' He sidestepped out of reach as she pretended to take a swipe at him, and said, 'No, really, it's great.'

'I've found my dream job, and I'm good at it.' Mimi hoped she didn't sound overconfident. Since starting at the agency she'd had to learn to be confident in order to promote the

15

people and products she was being paid to promote. Growing up in a household where everyone was self-deprecating, it had been quite the learning curve; in addition, she'd needed to learn not to be shy about promoting herself. In their business, as her bosses were so fond of announcing, shrinking violets need not apply.

'And what do you do when you aren't working?' asked Cal.

'I think about working,' Mimi said honestly. 'I spend time planning brilliant campaigns and coming up with fantastic new ways to boost our clients' products and profiles.'

'What about a social life? Or is that it?'

He'd said it jokingly, but she shrugged and nodded. 'Pretty much. Kendra and I go out occasionally, but we're both as bad as each other. Right now, our careers take top priority.'

'Good for you.' Cal nodded approvingly. 'So no boyfriends?'

There hadn't been a boyfriend for months, which was no bad thing, given her abysmal track record. Life was so much easier and less fraught when you were single. She shook her head. 'What can I tell you? I'm a hopeless case, a work-obsessed spinster. Once my career's properly up and running, maybe I'll find someone. Except I might be ancient by then and look like a wizened old tortoise, and no one will want me. Which will serve me right.'

Cal was grinning at her. 'Oh I'm sure you'll find someone. For every wizened female tortoise there's a male tortoise who thinks she's irresistible.' He glanced round and said, 'Move onto the verge . . .'

A car was coming up behind them; Mimi stepped aside and looked over her shoulder, exclaiming as she recognised the dusty, mud-splashed blue Volvo. 'Who's that, d'you know?'

The Volvo sailed past, its driver pointedly ignoring them. Cal said, 'It's Henrietta Mercer. She lives at Fox Court. Why?'

'She got off the train at the same time as me. When I found out there weren't any taxis, I asked her for a lift.'

'Brave. And what did she say to that?'

'Told me to walk.'

He burst out laughing. 'Sounds about right. Just because you own the biggest house in the village, it doesn't automatically make you a charming person. And it certainly hasn't in Henrietta's case. So don't worry,' he added, 'it isn't just you.'

Mimi grinned, glad now that the flinty-eyed older woman hadn't agreed to give her a lift; she'd much preferred meeting one of the friendlier inhabitants of Goosebrook. Not to mention his human owner.

'What's funny?' said Cal.

'Nothing. I just made a joke in my head.'

'Oh? And am I going to hear it?'

He really did have an incredible smile; not overly flirtatious, but the joyous, inclusive kind that made you feel better for being on the receiving end of it. Just when she'd been so convinced she didn't need male attention, too. 'Maybe one day,' said Mimi. 'The punchline still needs work. Speaking of work, I haven't asked what you do.'

'I design garden buildings, bespoke summer houses. Only a small company, but it's great, working with clients to create something they'll love for years to come. Here we are, then. This is Goosebrook.'

They'd reached the main street now; the stone war memorial stood directly ahead of them in the centre of the village, with cottages and shops lining the road beyond.

'Beautiful.' Mimi paused. It looked like a film set.

'Well, we're going in this direction,' said Cal as Otto, tail wagging like a metronome, strained on his lead to head up the lane to their left. 'It's been good to meet you. Say bye, Otto.'

'*Woof*,' said Otto.

'Oh my God, I love that!' Bending down, Mimi ruffled his ears. 'Clever boy!'

'It's his party trick. Actually, it's mine too. Say it to me.'

'Bye,' said Mimi.

'*Woof*,' said Otto.

'*Woof*,' said Cal.

'You're both extremely talented.' Mimi kept a straight face. 'I'm impressed.'

He grinned. 'Right, we're off. Your dad's place is down there, just past the old schoolhouse. And we might see you over at the pub later, yes? See what you can do. It's pizza-and-quiz night tonight.'

He was nice. Sometimes you could meet a complete stranger and just know you really liked them. And he had an adorable dog too. Win-win. Experiencing that exciting zing of physical interest – all the more thrilling for being so completely unexpected, given recent events – Mimi said, 'Don't worry, I'll make sure it happens. Leave it to me.'

'You're here!' Marcus did a double-take when he pulled open the duck-egg-blue front door. 'We were meant to be picking you up from the station at five thirty, weren't we? Did Dan get it horribly wrong?'

'No, he didn't. Nothing went wrong.' Mimi resisted the temptation to blurt out that everything had gone right.

Instead, she gave him a big hug and said, 'I caught the earlier train and walked.'

'You got caught in that downpour too! Oh dear, look at your hair . . . and your mascara's all over the shop . . .'

Oh bum, was it? And in her head she'd imagined herself looking rain-swept, but in an attractively dishevelled kind of way. Shaking her head like a spaniel, she said, 'I met someone from the village and we had a lovely time rescuing a sheep—'

'Darling, let go of that strange man and come here. My turn for a hug.' Having materialised beside Marcus, her father wrapped his arms around her. 'It's so good to see you. We can't wait to show you everything we've done to this place – you're going to be so impressed.'

They were justly proud of all their hard work. Thirty minutes later, Mimi had been given the full guided tour of Bay Cottage, the home they'd spent the last three months lovingly restoring and redecorating. Now, installed on a high wooden stool in the kitchen with an enormous gin and tonic, she said, 'Listen, that guy Cal told me it's pizza-and-quiz night over at the pub tonight, and he said we should give it a try, so I told him we'd see him there later.'

'No need.' Already shaking his head, her dad opened the fridge and took out a selection of wrapped packages. 'Dinner's right here, we're doing all your favourites – seared king scallops wrapped in bacon, then fillet steak with tomato salad and asparagus.'

'And dauphinoise potatoes,' Marcus chimed in triumphantly. 'Followed by lemon tart with raspberry sorbet. Everything you love best.'

Oh, their lit-up faces. She couldn't ask them to put the

food back into the fridge – they'd arranged it as a huge treat, specially for her.

'And I get to sit here like the Queen whilst you two do all the hard work?' The ice cubes clinked as she lifted her glass. 'Well that sounds just about perfect.'

Later, as they ate the delicious dinner, Mimi ventured, 'Maybe we could go to the pub tomorrow night.'

'Ah, but we've managed to book a table at Le Champignon Sauvage in Cheltenham.' Her dad looked triumphant. 'It has two Michelin stars! You'll love it there, it's amazing.'

She nodded. 'OK, but when I was talking to Cal, he said people would find it easier to get to know you if they saw more of you. Popping into the pub every now and again might help a bit . . . I mean, that'd be nice, wouldn't it?'

'I don't know . . .' Her dad was already looking doubtful, shaking his head. 'They're still not sure about us. We don't want any awkwardness.'

Was this how it felt to be a parent, having to cajole a shy child into making friends with the other kids at school? Mimi tried again. 'Cal said they're just wary because you're new to the village and you might end up only spending the occasional weekend down here. He told me they don't care that you're gay, that's no problem.'

'Hmm, it feels like it might be a problem for some of them.' Marcus sounded unenthusiastic. 'It's all very well this guy saying it isn't, but we don't even know who he is.'

Mimi frowned. 'He guessed who I was, so he's seen Dad around. He recognised me because we have the same eyes.'

'Well we haven't been introduced to anyone called Cal,' Marcus said with an air of finality.

'But maybe if you called into the pub, you'd be introduced

20

to lots of people! And I bet loads of them are really nice,' Mimi pleaded. 'You just have to give them a chance to get to know you.'

'Easier said than done,' Marcus said drily. 'Especially when you overhear people muttering behind your back in the shop.'

'Are you serious?' Mimi was outraged. 'Show me who they are and I'll have a word with them. What a bloody nerve—'

'Shh, don't get upset. And please don't say anything to anyone.' Her gentle father, who hated confrontation of any kind, reached for her hand. 'We're fine as we are for now. Just let us settle in gradually and deal with things in our own way. It'll all work out in the end, I'm sure, and there's no hurry as far as we're concerned. We've got each other.' He exchanged a contented smile with Marcus. 'And that's what really counts, isn't it? There's plenty of time for everything else to fall into place.'

Chapter 3

It was the week before Christmas and snowflakes were tumbling like fat feathers from a pale sky as the National Express coach from London made its scheduled stop in Cirencester.

Mimi, recalling her last visit to the Cotswolds, silently congratulated herself on being much better equipped this time. She was wrapped up in warm clothes *and* her case had wheels. Which was just as well really, seeing as it was a full-sized one crammed with Christmas presents.

Plus, this time she'd checked beforehand and discovered there was a taxi rank – an actual *rank*! – in Cirencester's central Market Place.

But first some shopping needed to be done. There were still a couple more gifts she wanted to pick up, and Cirencester was looking both festive and gorgeous, with Christmas lights strung everywhere around trees and across the narrow streets. The shop windows were lit up as well, many of them decorated with fake snow that was now being rapidly overtaken by the real thing.

Mimi tipped back her head and closed her eyes, listening

to the dulcet tones of Slade booming from a passing car and revelling in the sensation of the tiny ice-cold kisses of the snowflakes as they landed on her upturned face . . .

'Oi, shift,' ordered an irritable man behind her. 'You're blocking the pavement.'

And a very merry Christmas to you too.

An hour later, the suitcase was becoming a bit of a liability. The shops and narrow pavements were crowded, the snow was coming down faster than ever and Mimi's empty stomach was rumbling like a cement mixer. Finding a pretty café on Black Jack Street, she ducked inside and grabbed the last tiny table by the window. Within minutes, with a cappuccino and a cheese and mushroom toasted sandwich in front of her, she heaved a happy sigh and took out her phone.

Kendra had sent her a text. *Are you there yet? Just saw the weather forecast on TV – looks like you're going to get some snow!*

Amused, Mimi took a photo from inside the café, of Black Jack Street with the shops opposite almost obscured from view by the rapidly falling flakes. She tapped out: *Happening already xxx* and sent Kendra the photo.

Moments later, in the middle of taking a massive bite of toasted cheese sandwich, there was a loud double tap on the window. Her head jerked up in surprise and there was Cal, waving at her through the glass.

Looking quite handsome, too.

Mimi hastily chewed her mouthful of molten food. The next moment the bell above the door rang out as Cal pushed it open and came into the café, snowflakes melting on the shoulders of his brown leather jacket and in his tousled blonde hair.

'Hello!' There was that magical smile, the one that instantly

23

put you at your ease, even if you were still struggling to swallow your cheese and mushroom toastie. 'Sorry, did I make you jump? Are you here with your dad . . . or anyone else?'

Mimi shook her head and swallowed at last. 'Hi. No, I caught the coach down from London this time. I've been doing a bit of last-minute shopping, but as soon as I've finished this I'm going to get a taxi to Goosebrook.'

'Well I'm heading back soon. Do you want to come with me?'

'Not if it means walking,' said Mimi, and he laughed, pulling out the chair opposite her and sitting down.

'Don't worry, I brought my car into town earlier for a service. It'll be ready to pick up in thirty minutes. I can give you a lift if you don't mind waiting that long. It'll save you a taxi fare.' When she hesitated, he added, 'It's OK, you'll be safe, I'm a good driver. Passed my test and everything.'

Mimi had only paused in order to marvel at the fact that she'd bumped into him again. Was this fate? She felt her pulse quicken, because sometimes these things did seem to happen for a reason. Basically, Cal was attractive, he had a winning sense of humour, and since their last meeting she'd occasionally thought of him, wondered about him and imagined what he might look like naked.

Well, you were allowed to think those kinds of thoughts inside the safety of your own head, even if you weren't officially in the market for a boyfriend.

'A lift would be great.' She smiled. 'Thank you.'

'Good. And you're here for a few days?' Cal glanced at the suitcase propped up against the wall behind her. 'I thought you'd have come down more often, but we haven't seen you again since that first time.' He tut-tutted. 'We were starting to take it personally.'

'I wanted to come down,' Mimi protested. 'But work's been crazy busy, and Dad and Marcus have been up to London a few times. Every time I rang and said I had a free weekend to come and see them, they told me they'd travel up instead. They still love being in the village,' she added, 'but they also like zipping back to London, getting to the theatre and catching up with their friends. Which is why I haven't been down. Still, I'm here now. How are things going for them? Are they settling in?'

'Like I said before, it's taking a bit of time. We do invite them to things but they're still wary.' Cal's brown eyes crinkled at the corners as he surveyed her across the table. 'Maybe now you're back we can make a concerted effort, get them to relax and join in.'

He really did care. Warmed by his attitude, Mimi said, 'I did try to get them into the pub last time, but they wriggled out of it. Look, if you're giving me a lift, the least I can do is buy you a coffee and something to eat. You can't just sit there with nothing.'

'I'm fine, don't worry.' He shook his head. 'They said the car would be ready by four. There's a couple of presents I still need to pick up before we leave, so . . .'

'Oh, sorry.' Mimi gestured apologetically. 'You go off and do whatever it is you have to do. We can meet up at the garage. Just tell me where it is and I'll find it.'

'Or you could come with me if you like. Help me choose what to buy. I'm only a man, after all.' Cal grinned as he sat back and watched her finish her coffee. 'All female expertise welcome.'

'Let's do it.' Why sit here on her own when she could spend the time being useful? Standing up and sliding her arms into the sleeves of her red coat, Mimi said, 'Who are the presents for? Your mum? Sisters?'

He shook his head. 'My daughter.'

'Oh!' Well, she hadn't been expecting that.

Already on his feet, he held the door open. Reaching to take the suitcase from her, he added easily, 'And my wife.'

Twenty minutes later, Mimi watched from across the shop as he flashed that incredible smile of his at the sixty-something woman behind the till. Just moments ago the woman had been stressed and irate, but now she was laughing and relaxed.

Because that was evidently the effect Cal had; he was one of those people who lifted the spirits of everyone he encountered. He was one of nature's mood-enhancers.

And he hadn't been flirting with her at all, Mimi now realised, chastened. So much for thinking he might have been. He was just as friendly towards the old man who'd slipped over in the snow and whom he'd stopped to help back onto his feet.

Cal's wife's name, she'd learned, was Stacey, and his daughter was Cora. At six years old, Cora was currently in the grip of a zebra obsession – evidently because they were like horses but stripy and *better* – and was desperate for Father Christmas to bring her zebra-themed presents so she could run like a zebra and look like a zebra. 'And sing like a zebra,' Cal added drily. 'But we're not sure how that's going to pan out.'

'So she already has a stuffed zebra toy?' Mimi double-checked.

'Oh yes. He's the one who started it all off. We bought him in the shop at Longleat.'

'And he's called . . .?'

'Kevin.'

She nodded. 'An excellent name for a zebra.'

'You wait till you meet Cora,' Cal replied with pride. 'She's one of a kind.'

After twenty minutes of diving in and out of shops, the task had been completed.

'If I say so myself, we've done pretty well,' said Mimi. On a stall in the craft market at the Corn Hall she'd found a soft cotton zebra-print scarf. In Accessorize, Cal had tracked down zebra-print fleece gloves. Finally, as they'd been passing a tiny shop that sold radios and electronic devices, Mimi had glanced inside and spotted a boxful of battery-operated microphones in an array of colours and patterns, amongst them zebra and leopard print.

'We have,' Cal agreed, 'but I'm not sure how thrilled the rest of us are going to be with this microphone by Boxing Day.'

'When I was eight, I was desperate for a drum kit,' Mimi remembered. 'Funnily enough, I never did get one – my parents told me the shops were all sold out. Right, where next?'

'Just one last thing, then we're done.'

They made their way back through the snowy streets towards the café where she'd first seen him through the now steamed-up window, then Cal led her down a narrow stone passageway to a craft studio. 'Stacey and I came here back in October. She fell in love with these mirrors, so I want to get one for her.'

It was a glassworks studio, small but bright with reflected colour and light. The mirrors he was pointing to had frames made from stained dichroic glass in vivid jewel colours.

'They're stunning,' Mimi marvelled.

'Which one would Stacey like best, though?'

She shook her head. 'You know her. I don't.'

'How about the red and yellow?' Cal indicated the rectangular mirror to the left of them.

Oh dear, it wasn't fair to choose something for a complete stranger, but Mimi said, 'If I'm honest, I prefer the other one.' The mirror she was pointing to was oval, framed in clusters of glass in shades of emerald, sapphire and violet, and had been finished with silver grouting rather than black.

'Really?'

Hastily she said, 'You don't have to choose it because of me.'

'No, I'm going to.' His tone was playful as he took out his wallet. 'Then if she really hates it, I can blame you.'

The mirror was bubble-wrapped and paid for, Mimi took control of her suitcase once more and Cal carried the heavy, unwieldy parcel as they headed towards the garage where he'd left his car.

Chapter 4

Once the bustling streets of Cirencester were behind them, the snow settled more thickly on the road that would eventually lead them to Goosebrook. Having now grown used to the idea that Cal was married, Mimi said, 'Can I ask how old you are?'

'You may ask.' He turned down the music on the radio. 'I'm twenty-eight. I know, I look marvellous for my age.'

'And Cora's six. So you were pretty young when you had her.'

'I suppose so.' Cal grinned. 'So was Stacey. We were both twenty-one when we found out Cora was on the way . . . we called her our wonderful surprise. And now, whenever she's playing us up or being particularly stroppy, we look at each other and say, "There she is, that's our wonderful surprise." Whoops, hold on tight . . .'

The car's wheels had gone into a minor skid, causing Mimi to hang on to her seat belt as they slid sideways down an incline. Once he'd expertly steered them to safety, Cal continued, 'I mean, I'm sure everyone else thought it was a disaster, that we'd messed up big-time, but we'd actually been together for a year by then. We knew how much we liked each other. No, not liked, we were crazy about each other.' He slowed down once more as a van approached them. 'What can I tell you? It was love, and we decided to go for it. Make the best of a dodgy situation and see if we couldn't prove everyone wrong.'

'Wow.' Mimi was impressed. 'And that's what you've done.'

'Hasn't always been easy.' Cal paused, concentrating as he steered past the van and a flurry of snow briefly obscured the windscreen. 'We bought a tumbledown cottage and worked night and day to get it done up before Cora arrived. That was pretty chaotic, I can tell you. Then, once she was here, we discovered what chaos was really like. But we stuck it out.' He shrugged. 'Cora changed our world; we couldn't remember what life was like without her. And Stace and I did some pretty speedy growing up. We were skint and shattered, but we still couldn't imagine not being together forever.'

'That's brilliant.' She actually meant it; was there anything better than a good old-fashioned romantic story with a confound-the-experts happy ending? Kind of disappointing that Cal was off the market, of course, but then again, she was the diehard career girl, concentrating all her attention on work. It was still nice, though, hearing his words and having your faith in love restored.

'It really is.' He nodded in agreement. 'We make each other laugh. Life's never dull. And we've got ourselves the most amazing daughter, who's half girl, half zebra.'

'Who could ask for more?'

'How about you? Work still going well?'

'Going brilliantly, thanks. I've been promoted since I last

saw you. I'm no longer the most junior member of staff. I have my very own client list!'

'Congratulations. Well deserved, I'm sure.' His brown eyes sparkled. 'And what's happening with the social life? Found yourself a tortoise yet?'

'My love life, you mean?' Mimi did a comedy shudder. 'Oh, I'm a walking disaster when it comes to boyfriends. Show me someone who'll end up treating me like dirt, listing all my faults in public and sleeping with other girls behind my back, and you can guarantee I'll think they're the one for me.'

'Really?' Cal looked genuinely intrigued. 'Why?'

'I have no idea. I promise I don't do it on purpose. My friend Kendra says I have unerring bad-boy radar.'

'And what happens when you meet someone who isn't a bad boy?'

'The kind who doesn't forget to turn up for dates, you mean? Who treats you nicely and actually remembers to buy you a card on your birthday? Honest answer?' Mimi waved a hand. 'I'd probably be really suspicious and wonder what he was playing at. Well, either that or assume there was something wrong with him.' She didn't tell him the real reason, was deliberately flippant. Flippant was good; it was the way she'd always dealt with her situation.

But Cal said, 'Your dad's a nice guy, isn't he? I mean, I don't know him but you told me he was.' He glanced sideways at her. 'Was he a kind and thoughtful husband when he was married to your mum?'

And *boom*, there it was, the answer to her dilemma that no one else had ever come up with. Deep down in her subconscious, she'd been afraid to allow herself to become emotionally involved with anyone who was gentle, decent and thoughtful, with all the good qualities you could ever hope for in a boyfriend, because what if they turned out to be gay?

'You've got it.' She nodded at Cal. 'Well spotted.'

He shrugged. 'You're still young. Give it time, you'll get yourself sorted out.'

'You won't tell everyone in the village, will you? *Oh . . .*' Mimi gripped her seat belt as the tyres lost traction on the snowy road leading down the hill into Goosebrook. When Cal had the car under control once more, he drove slowly over the stone bridge and along the high street before pulling up outside Bay Cottage.

'Of course I won't tell anyone. And I know you don't know if you can trust me, but you can. I won't say a word.'

'Well, thanks. And for the lift too.' Unbuckling her seat belt, Mimi prepared to climb out of the car.

'I don't think they're home.' Cal was leaning forward, peering past her. 'There aren't any lights on in the kitchen. And no sign of their car either. Do you have a key to let yourself in?'

'No.'

'Go and ring the doorbell.'

She skidded up to the front porch and rang the bell. No answer; he was right. Back at the car, she shook snowflakes out of her hair and said through the buzzed-down window, 'They're not in.'

'Right.' Cal nodded. 'Well, the Parkers next door have got an old shed at the bottom of their garden. They probably wouldn't mind if you waited in there.'

What? Mimi stared at him and belatedly realised he was joking.

32

'Just for a second,' she told him, 'I believed you.'

He broke into a grin. 'Come on, time to introduce you to our pet zebra.'

Keeper's Cottage on Cedar Lane was decorated on the outside with multicoloured fairy lights along the eaves and around the porch. Inside, there were plenty more Christmas decorations, festive music was playing and the intermingled scents of simmering garlic, onions and tomatoes filled the air. There was also an overexcited six-year-old who took a flying leap off the back of the cobalt-blue sofa into Cal's outstretched arms.

'Dad, it's snowing! Eurgh, your face is all wet.' Having planted a kiss on his cheek, she dramatically wiped the back of her hand across her mouth.

'That'll be the snow.' Cal teasingly rubbed the side of his face against hers. 'Have you built a snowman yet?'

'You can do one with me tomorrow. Can we make a snow zebra?'

'That might be tricky, sweetheart. Their legs are quite thin; he wouldn't be able to stand up.'

'But you can try,' Cora insisted.

'I bet Mummy could do it,' Cal told her as his wife came into the living room.

'Mummy said you could do it better.'

'And Mummy's always right.' Stacey turned to Mimi with a grin. 'Hello! You wouldn't happen to be brilliant at snow zebras, would you?'

'This is Mimi, Dan Huish's daughter,' Cal explained. 'Remember the one who thought I was wrestling with a sheep at Easter?'

'I do remember. And I loved that you tried to rescue it.'

33

Stacey's smile was friendly; she was one of those people you instantly warmed to. 'How lovely to meet you at last. Are you down here for Christmas?'

'Just the next three days, then I'm off to my mum's place in north Wales.'

'I bumped into Mimi in Cirencester, offered her a lift back. But Dan and Marcus aren't home yet, so . . .'

'No problem. We have a giant pot of bolognese on the go, so you won't starve. And we can stay inside in the warm while Cal takes Cora out into the garden.'

'Yay!' Cora wriggled to be put down. 'Why are you called Me-me? That's a funny name.'

'I know it is. I'm Emylia really, but when I was little I couldn't say that, so I became Mimi instead.'

'I could call you You-you,' said Cora.

'This is getting surreal.' Cal clapped his hands together. 'OK, go and fetch your coat. Wellies, hat, gloves. Let's build a snow-something before it gets dark.'

In the cosy yellow kitchen, Mimi perched on a stool at the counter and drank tea whilst Stacey made garlic bread and splashed red wine into the pasta sauce.

'So did Cal manage to buy any presents?'

'A few little things for Cora. Zebra-y things.'

'Oh thank goodness. It's mad, isn't it? Last year she was obsessed with parrots. Now they don't even get a look-in. Who knows what it'll be next Christmas?' Stacey reached across to throw a handful of torn basil leaves into the pan. 'We should start taking bets. Cal's been trying to get her into *Star Wars*, but she's not having it.'

They watched through the window as Cal and Cora, out in the back garden, worked together in the snow to construct something that resembled a small pony lying down with a hangover.

'Look at her, our gorgeous girl,' Stacey marvelled. 'Love her to bits. You can't imagine the difference they make to your life. Ten years from now she won't care about parrots or zebras. It'll be all about boys and we'll be the panicking parents, tearing our hair out, desperate to wrap her up in cotton wool and hide her upstairs.'

'Ah, that's ages away. You've got so much to enjoy before any of that happens. She's adorable,' said Mimi.

'She's a star.' In the garden, Cora was now waving madly at them, keen to attract their attention so they could admire her magnificent handiwork.

'Did Cal buy anything for me today?' said Stacey when they'd dutifully gasped with amazement and applauded the snow zebra in the centre of the lawn.

'It's possible he did.'

'Have you seen it?'

'Might have,' said Mimi.

Stacey's blue eyes danced. 'Is it a mirror with a stained-glass frame?'

'You can't ask me that question.'

'Hooray, that means it is! I went into the shop last week to take another look at them. Aren't they just gorgeous?'

'I have no idea what you're talking about.'

'OK, there was a red and yellow one and a bluey-pinky one. And I liked both of them but the bluey-pinky one was my absolute favourite.' She peered intently into Mimi's eyes. 'So . . .?'

'You're terrible, you know that?' But Mimi couldn't keep a straight face. 'You'll love it.'

'Thank you, thank you. And don't worry, I won't tell him. It's just so brilliant to know I'm getting the one I really want. I thought Cal would probably go for the red and yellow.'

'He did try.'

'Well now I like you even more.' Beaming, Stacey said, 'Thank goodness you were there to put him right.'

Over dinner, Cal and Stacey made Mimi promise to do her best to get her father and Marcus along to the pub for tomorrow night's pre-Christmas party. She assured them that this time she wouldn't take no for an answer. Finally her phone rang. Her dad was home at last and had picked up the message she'd left on their landline.

'Darling, come on in.' He greeted Mimi with a hug before ushering her into the cottage. 'Sorry, we thought we'd be back an hour ago, but the traffic in Cheltenham was grid-locked.'

'If only there was some way you could have called to let me know you'd been held up,' said Mimi, who had bought him a mobile phone for Christmas. 'Anyway, doesn't matter, I've had a fantastic time at Cal and Stacey's. Their daughter is amazing, she's obsessed with zebras. And they insisted I stay and have dinner with them.'

'Ah, so that's the little girl who wears zebra-print clothes. We've seen her around the village. And her mum's the pretty one with the long dark hair.' Marcus nodded, remembering.

They'd lived here in Goosebrook for almost a year; it was time they got to know people properly.

'There's a small party at the pub tomorrow night.' Mimi braced herself. 'Cal and Stacey are going, and I said we would too.'

36

'Oh, now—'

'Please, Dad. They really want to get to know you. Everyone does,' she pressed on. 'It's your first Christmas down here, and now's the perfect time to meet the rest of the village.'

'But what if—'

'I know you were worried about some of the older ones, but they've had long enough now to get used to the idea of you being a couple. They think you're keeping your distance because you aren't interested in getting to know them.'

Her dad looked at her and sighed. Mimi held his gaze. Marcus said, 'She's right, Dan. It's time. We need to make the effort.'

'I suppose we do.'

Relieved, Mimi broke into a smile. 'We'll go to the party tomorrow evening, OK? If you really hate it, you can leave after two hours.'

'If anyone says anything offensive, I'm not staying,' her dad warned. 'We'll be out of there.'

'If anyone does, I'll sort them out myself,' Mimi promised.

Hopefully, no one would.

Chapter 5

Twenty-seven hours later, her father turned to her and said, 'I can't believe we've never done this before.'

'Told you.' Mimi gave his shoulder a squeeze, because he was visibly enjoying himself, so much more relaxed and happy than he'd expected to be.

'We should have come in here months ago. Everyone's been great.'

'Better late than never,' said Mimi. 'This is just the beginning. From now on, things are only going to get better.'

A minxy blonde who'd introduced herself earlier as Lois Blake rejoined them and raised her glass. 'And the more we have to drink, the better everything gets! Dan, are you going to dance with me next?'

'The thing is, I don't really . . . I'm not much of a dancer . . .'

'Ah but I am,' Lois said cheerfully, 'and luckily I'm brilliant at it, so as long as you stick with me, that means you'll be brilliant too.'

'Oh well then,' said Dan, 'if you insist.' And off they went, piling onto the crowded dance floor to join in with everyone else who was dancing along to 'American Pie'.

'Look at them. You've done it,' said Stacey.

Mimi grinned. 'Thanks to you.'

'Oh, rubbish. They needed a hefty nudge and you managed to get them here.'

'It's going to make a world of difference,' Mimi agreed. Over by the bar, Marcus was chatting happily to a tall man in a blue and white striped shirt. 'Who's that?'

'Felix? He lives at Fox Court. Cal tells me you had a brief encounter with his mother the first time you came down here.'

'The bossy woman who refused to give me a lift? Ah, right.'

'It's OK, she isn't here. Henrietta doesn't come to the pub.'

'And what's Felix like? The same as his mother?'

'No, thank God. He's adorable. Jolly posh, of course, but just so sweet with it. And everyone's loving the fact that Henrietta can't stand Lois, but Felix flatly refuses to stop seeing her.'

Mimi was surprised. 'So Lois and Felix are a couple? I didn't realise.'

'Oh yes. Kind of unlikely, I know, but they seem to balance each other out. Lois is pretty wild, quite the party girl, and Felix is quieter, but so lovely. He's crazy about her, which is driving Henrietta to absolute distraction.'

'She's stunning.' Mimi paused to take a drink. 'Lois, I mean. Not Henrietta.'

Stacey laughed. 'Oh God, I know. You can't blame Felix for being besotted, can you? And look at the body on her, it's just perfect. She puts the rest of us to shame.'

Mimi said, 'Don't do yourself down. You're stunning too.'

'Ah, but I can't compete with Lois.' Stacey patted her slightly rounded stomach. 'I never did manage to get rid of my baby pouch. Some people spring back into place, but mine stayed right where it was.' Her face softening, she added, 'Still, we got Cora as a result, so it was worth it.'

'Will you have any more, d'you think?' Mimi winced the moment the words were out of her mouth. 'Oh God, sorry, that's a terrible question. Don't answer!' This was what happened when you met someone, liked them instantly and felt as if you'd known them for months.

'It's fine. And yes, we'd love to have a couple more babies. We left a bit of a gap so we could concentrate on getting ourselves on our feet financially, but we've managed to do that now. So the plan is to start trying again as soon as Christmas is over.' Stacey grinned. 'Who knows, if we're really lucky, a year from now the next one could be here.'

They clinked glasses and Mimi, absolutely meaning it, said, 'Lucky baby.'

'Thanks, but we're the lucky ones. Ooh now, see who's just come in? That's Paddy Fratelli.'

Mimi followed the direction of Stacey's nod. Paddy Fratelli was standing by the door talking to a group of people he evidently knew well. He had slicked-back dark hair, foxy good looks and shrewd bright blue eyes that were darting around the pub, missing absolutely nothing. A knowing half-smile lifted the corners of his mouth and his white teeth were slightly crooked. Clocking Mimi, he glanced at her for a second before turning his attention back to his friends. He was wearing a blue shirt, fitted black waistcoat and narrow black jeans. From here, she guessed he'd be the type to use industrial quantities of aftershave. She watched as Lois, still on the dance floor with Dan, caught Paddy's attention and blew him an extravagant kiss.

'OK, one question,' said Mimi. 'Am I right in thinking he wears a lot of cologne?'

Stacey spluttered with laughter. 'I know what you mean, he looks as if he would. But Paddy's actually smarter than that – when you're that much of a womaniser, it makes far more sense not to wear any cologne at all.'

He and Lois glanced at each other once more; Paddy smiled as Lois playfully swivelled her hips as she danced. Mimi lowered her voice. 'Is there something going on between those two?'

'Honest answer? No, nothing at all. It's just a game they play, pretending to find each other irresistible. It's fun, it's harmless and nothing ever happens . . . well, apart from giving some of the villagers something to gossip about.' Stacey's eyes sparkled. 'So if you ever do happen to hear any whispers, don't get too excited because they aren't true. And I'm not just saying that because Lois is one of my best friends. She'd never cheat on Felix, she just wouldn't.'

Stacey was telling the truth, Mimi could tell. 'And Felix doesn't mind the flirting?'

'Oh God, no, he finds the whole thing completely hilarious. He says it makes him feel all the more of a winner because he's the one Lois goes home with. And Lois loves the fact that Felix isn't threatened . . . As I say, they're an unlikely couple to look at, but it works. And Paddy flirts with everyone he meets, so you never can tell what he's up to . . . Oh hi, Paddy! How are you, all right?' She beamed as the man in question materialised beside them.

'Hello, girls. Stacey, looking amazing as always. And your name is . . .?' Paddy turned his attention to Mimi.

'Emylia.' Somehow 'Mimi' seemed too intimate under the intensity of his gaze.

'Well it's a pleasure to meet you, Emylia. You're looking wonderful too.' Close up, his electric-blue eyes were almost hypnotic and his expression was playful. The next second he was addressing Stacey once more. 'And the gay guys are here, I see. So how did that happen?'

Mimi stiffened like a dog preparing to attack. Next to her, Stacey said, 'This is Dan Huish's daughter.'

'Really? Excellent.' Unfazed, he broke into a grin that revealed his crooked white teeth. 'We thought we weren't good enough for them.'

Stacey said, 'They were just shy. But now they're really enjoying themselves.'

'I can see that.' Paddy nodded comfortably as, with a flourish, Lois and Dan finished their dance together. 'Well, nice to see them joining in at last. And how about you, down here for long?'

And now, in this light, his eyes were vivid turquoise. It was almost impossible not to stare at them. Mimi blinked. 'Just a couple of days.'

'I can't believe we haven't seen you before.' Oh, that flirtatious charm.

Stacey said, 'Maybe she's been steering clear of men like you.'

'Touché.' Paddy nodded at their half-empty glasses. 'Can I get you two another drink?'

'Thanks, but we're fine. Cal's up at the bar.'

'You're still sticking with him, then? Not tempted to run away with me?'

'And join your harem?' Stacey laughed. 'You'd need to hire a double-decker bus to carry all those girls of yours off to wherever you're planning to take them. It's a generous offer, Paddy, but I think I'll stay with Cal.'

He winked at Mimi. 'Don't these faithful types just make you sick? You'd think they'd be ready for a change by now.'

By eleven thirty, Mimi had been introduced to pretty much everyone in the pub. Through the windows, the strings of Christmas lights in the houses opposite and the orange glow of the street lamps illuminated the snowy centre of Goosebrook. Inside, the atmosphere was convivial and relaxed enough for Marcus to clink his glass against Cal's and declare, 'I'm so glad we did this. It's all thanks to you and Stacey.'

Cal shook his head. 'Mimi was the one who dragged you down here.'

Unaccustomed to drinking, and by now onto his third bottle of lager, Marcus said, 'It sounds ridiculous to say we were too scared, but we were.'

'Not scared,' Mimi corrected him. 'Wary.'

'We were wary.' Her dad nodded in agreement. 'We shouldn't have been, but we didn't know.'

'We did try,' Felix announced. 'I saw you outside in your front garden, Dan, not long after you'd moved in. I walked across the green to say hello but as soon as you saw me heading towards you, you disappeared into your house.'

'I know. I'm sorry.' Dan shook his head. 'The reason we moved from our last place was because we'd had terrible trouble with bigoted neighbours.'

'Well you're here now,' said Felix. 'And if you ever get any trouble from anyone at all, you let us know and we'll sort them out for you. I say, just listen to me!' He rubbed

43

his hand over his tousled hair and beamed with pride. 'I sound like a vigilante. Quite gangster!'

Anyone less like a gangster than ultra-posh Felix was impossible to imagine.

'Unless your mother's the one causing the trouble,' Lois chimed in, 'then we should probably get someone else to do the sorting out. Honestly, though, she's a nightmare. Total witch.' She patted Felix's arm. 'Sorry to have to say it, darling, but she is.'

Felix shook his head. 'Ma's not such a bad old stick once you get used to her.'

'Well she can't stand me,' Lois retorted, 'so it's going to be a while before I get used to *her*. I mean, why does she have to be so difficult?' Her hands spread in disbelief. 'Everyone knows I'm completely adorable!'

'I know you are.' Felix dropped an apologetic kiss on her tanned forehead. 'And I keep telling her that too. Don't worry, my angel. Give her a little more time and she'll come around, I'm sure.'

'I love you so much.' Lois tilted her beautiful face up to his for a proper kiss. 'Will you still marry me if she doesn't?'

Mimi wondered if the amount of flirting that went on between Lois and Paddy might have reached Henrietta's ears and possibly had some bearing on the situation. She and Stacey exchanged a glance as Felix replied gallantly, 'Of course I will.'

'Eurgh, that's enough sloppy romantic stuff. Ignore them. *Anyway.*' Stacey changed the subject and turned back to Dan and Marcus. 'You're going to start getting invited to join in with things, just so you know. Now that you've stopped hiding away, there's going to be all sorts.'

'You might want to say no to the church bell-ringers' society.' Maria, who ran the pub, grimaced as she said it.

'The boules tournaments are great, though,' said Cal. 'Definitely join in with those.'

'And they'll want you on the committee for the summer concert on the green,' Stacey added. 'Especially when they find out you're both accountants.'

Felix, who had now finished kissing Lois, said, 'Don't forget the road rally challenge.'

'A road rally?' Dan looked doubtful. 'I'm not much of a racer.'

'It's a treasure hunt,' Cal explained. 'You can be a passenger, you don't have to drive.'

'And remember you don't have to do anything you don't want to do.' Stacey's tone was soothing. 'You can always say no.'

'But the more often you say yes,' Maria chipped in, 'the more fun you'll have.'

'Unless it's Terence Pugh's ancient history club.' Felix shuddered at the memory of what had clearly been a traumatic experience. 'Go along to that and I guarantee you'll have no fun at all.'

'Hang on, call the police, my glass is empty!' Lois waved her empty champagne flute wildly. 'Felix, this is an emergency, I need more Moët, more music and more dancing, stat!'

'Coming right up,' said Maria as the familiar opening chords of 'Ziggy Stardust' began to flood out of the speakers, provoking cheers from the rest of the pub.

'And I hope we'll see a bit more of you down here too.' Materialising at Mimi's side, Paddy rested his hand oh-so-lightly on the small of her back. 'Now the awkwardness is all sorted. It'll be nice to get to know you better.'

45

Mimi smiled, because he was the type who appeared to be flirting even when he wasn't trying – it evidently came as naturally to him as breathing. 'I live in London and work all hours. It isn't easy to get down here, but I will when I can.'

'Well I hope you do,' said Stacey. 'And I definitely want you on my team at the next quiz night. Cal, I promised the babysitter we'd be home by midnight. We mustn't be late.'

'Plenty of time for one more drink.' Felix expertly uncorked the bottle of Moët and gestured for Stacey to hold out her glass for a refill. Beaming, he turned to Mimi. 'And for us to have a dance, don't you think?'

'Oh come on, that's not fair.' Paddy held out his hands in protest. 'I was about to ask her to dance with me.'

'You snooze, you lose,' said Felix with a grin. 'My turn with Mimi. You can make do with my gorgeous girlfriend instead.'

At ten minutes to midnight, Maria bellowed, 'Right, that's enough debauchery for one evening, don't you lot have homes to go to?' and hustled everyone out of the pub. The snow had stopped falling now, the moon was a gleaming white crescent in the sky and the stars were out. Crunching across the virgin snow on the pavement, Mimi breathed in a lungful of icy air and searched in her pockets for her gloves. One was missing.

'Here.' Catching her up, Paddy said, 'You dropped it when you were putting your coat on.'

'Thanks.' She took the missing glove from him and wondered if it really had fallen out of her pocket on its own.

'If you fancy a nightcap, my place is just down there, where the road forks off to the left.' Paddy was pointing into the misty darkness at the end of the high street. 'It must be a bit of a shock to the system, coming down to Goosebrook when you're used to the nightlife in London.' His teeth gleamed white as he fell into step beside her. 'We tend to make our own amusement around here.'

'I'm sure you do.' Everyone was preparing to make their way home now, calling out to each other as they said their goodnights. 'And thanks for the offer, but no thanks.'

'Ah well, that's a shame. Still, we'll bump into each other again.' Resting his hand on her coat sleeve, he turned her to face him. 'Enjoy the rest of your stay, and have fun. Well, as much fun as it's possible to have without me being involved.'

'I'll do my best.' Mimi couldn't help being entertained by his manner.

'Merry Christmas, Emylia Huish.' Leaning closer, his warm lips brushed her cold cheek.

'You too.' Mimi smiled, perfectly aware that he was only doing it to make some kind of point to Lois, who was just behind them with Felix.

'Put her down,' shouted Stacey, arm in arm with Cal.

'I've just made this girl an offer she can't refuse,' Paddy announced with a grin. 'And she turned me down flat. Can you believe that?'

'Of course she did,' Stacey told him. 'I warned her about you hours ago.'

'I can always rely on you to ruin my night,' Paddy said good-naturedly. 'Well, that's it, I'm off home with my confidence in tatters. Bye, all. And if you change your mind,' he told Mimi, 'just come over to Beech House and knock three times on the blue door. I'll let you in.'

'You told me to knock four times,' Cal said jokingly.

'No need to be jealous, lover boy. That's so I know who's going to be there when I open the door.'

For a split second there was an awkward pause as everyone realised this was one of those off-the-cuff comments at which Marcus and Dan could take offence. The next moment, Marcus patted the back pocket of his jeans and said, 'The ones he likes best already have their own key.'

Amid the explosion of laughter, Mimi exhaled with relief. Stacey came over and gave her a hug, murmuring in her ear, 'I think it's safe to say you can stop worrying about them now. Everything's going to be fine.'

'I'm just so *glad*.' Her eyes prickling with hot tears of joy, Mimi said, 'Are you around tomorrow?' Because sometimes you met someone and hit it off with them so brilliantly that you knew you'd made a new friend for life.

'Oh I wish we were, but we're off to Stratford. Cal's great-aunt was going to drive down to see us, but the snow's freaked her out so now we have to trek up there to visit her instead. Will you still be here on Sunday?'

Mimi pulled a face; there was an event she had to attend. 'I have to head back first thing. I'm working in the afternoon.'

'Sod's law. Ah well, definitely see you next time you're down here.' Stacey gave her another enthusiastic hug. 'It's been so lovely to meet you. Have a fantastic Christmas.'

'You t-too.' Mimi's teeth had begun to chatter with the cold. 'OK, I'm officially frozen. We need to get home now.' Waving goodbye to Stacey and Cal, she said, 'See you soon!'

Chapter 6

On the crowded concourse at Paddington station, Mimi concentrated all her attention on the departures board, silently willing the *Delayed* sign to be replaced by a slightly more helpful time of departure.

Ah, but it was typical, wasn't it, that the more you were looking forward to being somewhere, the less likely it was that the train would get you there in time.

At this rate she was going to miss the treasure hunt completely.

A middle-aged man in a hurry dragged his heavy suitcase in front of her, running the wheels across the pale suede of her new ankle boots and not stopping to apologise. Mimi sighed and took out her phone, which had begun to ring. It was Kendra.

'Hey, I just had a text from my brother inviting me along to a private party at Hush tonight. Do you fancy being my plus one?'

'I can't, I'm heading down to Goosebrook.' Mimi peered up at the departures board once more. 'If the damn train ever gets here.'

'Well the party sounds fantastic, so I thought I'd offer you first refusal. If you change your mind, let me know within twenty minutes otherwise I'll call someone else. There's going to be loads of celebs there,' Kendra added persuasively, because her brother worked for a successful record label. 'And the food's always amazing.'

'Thanks, but I'm still going to try and get down there . . . Oh, it's happening!' Miraculously, the sign on the board had changed; the train was now marked as waiting on Platform 5 and other travellers were already streaming like lemmings towards it. 'I need to grab a seat. You have fun and I'll see you tomorrow . . . I'll hear all about it when I get back.'

An hour later, Mimi was fantasising about marrying a billionaire and never having to catch a train again in her life.

'Mummy, why are some people nice and some people not nice?'

'I don't know, Barnaby. It's all part of the rich tapestry of life.'

'Mummy, what's tapestry?'

'It's kind of like sewing, darling.'

'Like when the button came off my shirt and we took it to the sewing lady in the shop to put it back on?'

'Exactly, Barnaby! Well done!'

'And it cost fifteen pounds but you said don't tell Daddy.'

'Mind that drink, darling . . . Oh, whoops! Say sorry to the lady.'

'I don't want to say sorry. The train did it, not me. Anyway, she's standing too close.'

Mimi glanced down at the small boy who was glaring at

50

her for having the temerity to be standing too close to him. He stuck his tongue out at her, then said in his high-pitched voice, 'Mummy? Give me a yoghurt.'

'Here you are, darling. Now do be careful with it.' Barnaby's mother returned her attention to the phone in her hand, missing the moment Barnaby deliberately dropped the messy yoghurt lid onto the floor at Mimi's feet.

'Mummy, I don't like that lady.'

'Oh darling, you mustn't say that.'

'She isn't smiling and she's too close to our table. Tell her to go away.'

Mimi, swaying as the train rattled over the tracks, tried not to breathe in the overpowering smell of the cheap deodorant worn by the man squashed into the aisle next to her in the hopelessly overcrowded carriage.

'Just give Mummy a rest for a few minutes,' murmured Barnaby's mother, wholly engrossed in scrolling through her Twitter feed. 'Why don't you play on your new iPad?'

Would that keep him quiet? Of course not. The iPad was duly switched on, the boy selected a game that was played to the accompaniment of uber-irritating loud music that sounded like saucepans being crashed together, and Barnaby's mother dealt with it by plugging herself into a pair of earphones.

Which was nice for her.

'Oh for fuck's sake,' sighed Deodorant Man, next to Mimi.

Barnaby's head shot up like a meerkat. He grabbed his mother's hand, pointed at Mimi and yelled, 'Mummy! That lady just said FUCK.'

'I didn't.' Mimi in turn pointed to Deodorant Man. 'It was him.'

The middle-aged woman squashed up against Mimi's right side said, 'But we were all thinking it.'

The boy continued to stare at Mimi. He dipped his spoon in his pot of yoghurt and slowly licked it, whilst the saucepan-crashing music continued to blare out of the iPad. Returning his attention to the game, he managed to knock the almost full pot off the table so that it landed at Mimi's feet and splashed blackcurrant yoghurt liberally over her new suede boots.

'Oh Barnaby,' murmured his mother when she finally noticed what had happened. 'That was silly, wasn't it?'

Mimi took a slow, steadying breath, then realised the train was slowing down too.

'Sorry, ladies and gentlemen,' came the genial voice over the tannoy, 'but we're having to stop for a bit. Looks like signalling problems up ahead. I'll be back to tell you what's happening once we know more.'

Mimi closed her eyes, because now she definitely wasn't going to reach Goosebrook in time to join in with the treasure hunt. She'd really been looking forward to it, but they were going to have to start without her.

So much for swapping work events this morning in order to get down there in time, and having to spend the entire hideous journey on her feet because there were no seats on this stupid train. So much for being forced to endure nightmare travelling companions too.

Not to mention missing the glitzy party back in London.

Could things get any worse?

'Mummy, *Mummy*.' Barnaby's voice rose as he shook his mother's arm. 'I think I'm going to be sick.'

Three interminable hours later, the train eventually

reached Kemble station, five miles outside Cirencester. There had been no reply to the texts Mimi had sent her dad to let him know about the delays, but he was probably far too busy tearing around the countryside to stop and look at his phone. Anyway, it didn't matter. She had no idea how long these treasure hunts lasted, but this one had to finish soon. And they'd already arranged to leave a key for her under the blue flowerpot next to the front door.

At least she was here now. And things were finally looking up; there was a taxi waiting at the tiny rank next to the car park. Behind her, Mimi heard a familiar voice trilling, 'Come along, Barnaby, we want to get to that taxi before someone else grabs it . . . Hurry up, darling . . .'

'Noooo, Mummy, stop, I left my iPad on the train!'

Karma at last. Increasing her pace just to be on the safe side, Mimi reached the taxi and opened the back door. 'Goosebrook, please.'

Still no reply to the texts, and her phone battery was now perilously low so she didn't bother trying again. After so many hours standing on the train, it was a luxury to sit down. Her stomach rumbled with hunger; what a treat it was to know that when she reached the cottage there'd be a fridge full of amazing food.

'That's a pain,' said the taxi driver when they reached the road to Missingham and found it closed, sealed off with incident tape and no entry signs and guarded by a police officer. 'Something going on down there. We'll have to take the long way round.'

'I wonder what's happened?' Mimi peered out of the window as they passed the turn-off.

'Two of the big houses on the left were burgled last week. Maybe something to do with that.'

Mimi winced, because her dad was paranoid about break-ins and had taken some persuading to leave the spare key for her under the flowerpot. If burglars had found it and let themselves into the cottage, she would never hear the end of it.

Fifteen minutes later, they reached Goosebrook and Mimi paid the taxi driver. She lifted her case out of the car and gazed around, happy to be back and even happier to know that the contents of her dad and Marcus's well-stocked fridge were now just moments away. There was a cluster of people standing outside the shop further down the street, deep in conversation. As she looked at them, they stopped talking and turned to stare at her.

Not recognising them, Mimi made her way up to the front door of the cottage. If they were burglars, would they be able to see her retrieving the key from its hiding place? OK, they appeared to be old age pensioners so housebreaking probably wasn't uppermost in their minds. But she still found herself hesitating, because under a flowerpot was such a cliché . . .

She turned at the sound of another vehicle coming down the hill towards them, and saw that it was Marcus's car. As it drew closer, Mimi saw that he was alone. When he pulled up, she also noted that he didn't park exactly parallel to the kerb. *Tut tut, Marcus, it's not like you to be so careless.*

The driver's door opened and he climbed out. 'Did someone tell you?'

'What?' said Mimi.

'Have you heard?'

He was gazing at her intently. Goodness, she'd had no

idea the treasure hunt was something he'd take so seriously. 'I haven't heard, I only just got here. Did you win?'

Marcus didn't reply. Instead he moved towards her, and suddenly she saw the expression on his face, the desolation in his eyes. And that was when Mimi felt the world tilt and slide into slow motion. Something was terribly, horribly wrong, so wrong that she didn't even dare to think it. His skin was the colour of putty and he was trembling as he reached out to her and gripped her hands.

'I've just come from the hospital . . . I had to get back here to tell you. It was an accident, the car hit a tree. Your dad was in the back seat . . .'

No, don't tell me, don't say it, I don't want to hear this.

'I'm so sorry, sweetheart . . . There wasn't anything they could do.'

It can't be true, this isn't happening.

But as Mimi stared dry-eyed at the shoulder of Marcus's pale blue sweater, she saw a smudge of dried blood and somehow knew that it wasn't his own. Shaking her head in disbelief, she croaked, 'Is he . . . is he dead?'

Just say no, please just say no.

But Marcus, his strong arms tightening around her as her knees began to buckle, said, 'Yes. Oh Mimi, I'm sorry, he is.'

The accident that ripped so many lives apart had happened on a sunny Sunday afternoon in March.

The first brief newspaper report stated:

Three people died and a fourth sustained injuries yesterday when a car left the road near Missingham and crashed into a tree.

The second, a day later, said:

> The people killed in a car crash on Missingham Lane
> have been identified as Edward Mercer, 68, Daniel Huish,
> 49, and Stacey Mathieson, 28. The fourth occupant of
> the vehicle, 27-year-old Lois Blake, remains in a critical
> condition at the Great Western Hospital in Swindon. The
> road is expected to remain closed whilst investigations
> into the collision continue.

Mimi woke with a start and stared wide-eyed at the ceiling,
her stomach plummeting at the realisation of where she
was. If only she could have been back in her tiny bedroom
in the flat in Bermondsey, that would mean it hadn't been
real . . .

But the ceiling in her flat was off-white and cracked,
with swathes of cobwebs in the high corners. The one she
was looking at now was freshly painted and pristine, signalling that she wasn't there, she was here. Which meant she'd
had that dream again, the one where she was rereading
the piece about the crash in the local newspaper, but this
time her father's name wasn't on the list of victims and
her heart leapt with joy as she turned to Kendra and
exclaimed, 'Oh thank goodness, it's OK! He wasn't in the
car after all!'

Weighted down with grief, she slowly levered herself out
of bed. It was the third time this had happened in less than
forty-eight hours and she couldn't understand how it was
possible to have a dream like that which so cruelly raised
your hopes then brought them crashing down again.

Because her lovely, kind father, the very gentlest of men,

no longer existed on this earth, and she still couldn't take it in, because it was just so impossible and unfair.

Oh Daddy, where are you? Where have you gone?

It was five thirty in the morning. Still dark outside. Downstairs in the kitchen, Mimi switched on the kettle to make a mug of tea she didn't even want to drink. Yesterday she must have made at least twenty, simply in order to have something to do.

She drank a glass of cold water, left the kitchen and went back upstairs. Marcus was in the master bedroom, the one he'd shared with her dad. All was silent, but who knew if he was asleep? In the bathroom, Mimi sluiced her face with more water and brushed her teeth. Dressing in jeans and a grey sweater, she took one of her father's padded nylon jackets down from the coat rack and left the cottage.

Outside, an owl was hooting somewhere in the trees to the left of the village green. She concentrated on every step she took, watching her booted feet as they crunched across the frosted grass. The darkness was abating now, the sky a lighter shade of charcoal than before. If all she allowed herself to think about was the grass and the owl and the rhythmic sound of her own footsteps, it meant she couldn't picture the last moments of her father's life, when cheerful normality had abruptly turned to chaos and carnage.

It was after her fourth full lap of the village green that the first orange glimmers of sunrise began to appear in the sky and she heard the sound of rapid breathing behind her. She turned and dropped to her knees on the grass as Otto skidded to a halt in front of her, his tail wagging joyfully.

Sometimes being greeted by a dog who wasn't about to inundate you with questions was just what you needed. Mimi buried her face in his neck and let him lick her ear, his paws scrabbling against her knees as he strained to reach her.

She stayed like that for a minute, then opened her eyes and looked up at Cal. The expression on his face was unbearable. He looked as if he'd never learned how to smile.

'I still can't believe it's happened.' Her voice was hoarse.

He nodded bleakly. 'I know. I suppose we're still in shock.'

'I keep having this dream where my dad's still alive . . . and then I wake up.' She shuddered at the memory of it.

'Me too. This isn't a coincidence, by the way.' He gestured to explain his presence. 'I knew you were out here. Felix called me ten minutes ago.'

'To tell you I was walking around the green?'

'To let me know how Lois is doing. He just got back from the hospital.'

'Oh, of course. Sorry.' Mimi remembered a car passing her. Grief made you selfish; engulfed as you were in your own pain, it was hard to remember that others were suffering too. 'How is she?'

'Not good. They're preparing her for more surgery later this morning.' The shadows beneath Cal's eyes were a sludgy shade of violet. 'But she's still alive, at least.'

The ensuing pause was filled with unspoken words and emotions. They looked at each other and Mimi wondered if they were both thinking the same thing: he'd lost Stacey and she'd lost her father, and you might have to be polite on the surface and pretend to be glad that Lois hadn't been killed, but deep down wouldn't anyone secretly wish their loved one could have been the one to be spared instead?

58

And if that was a shameful thing to have to admit . . . well, too bad.

Because sometimes life *was* just unbearably unfair.

Mimi gathered herself. 'How about you?'

'Well, I guess I'm still alive too. Doesn't feel much like it at the moment, but I suppose we have to carry on. Not really any other choice.'

Mimi blinked hard, her eyes sore and dry. As terrible as her own loss was, Cal's must be worse. Beautiful Stacey, the love of his life and the mother of his daughter, was gone forever. Everything she'd ever been to them had been wrenched away. At the age of six, Cora had lost her mum, leaving Cal to deal with her grief as well as his own.

By unspoken consent, they made their way across the green to the wooden bench beneath one of the chestnut trees. Cal's phone went *ting* and he checked the message on the screen.

'My sister,' he said. 'She's staying with us. I asked her to let me know when Cora wakes up so I can get back there.'

'And has she woken up?'

'No. She just texted to tell me Cora's still fast asleep.'

They sat in silence for a couple of minutes, watching as the sky lightened and began to glow white in the east behind the church spire. Next to her, Cal was turning his phone over and over in his hands like a magician building up to a card trick.

'I heard it happen,' he said finally.

'You heard the accident?' Confused, Mimi said, 'You were *there*?'

Cal had been in a different car along with Marcus, Felix

59

and Maria from the Black Swan. According to Marcus, they'd been miles away when the accident occurred.

Cal shook his head and indicated the mobile in his hand. 'We were on the phone. Stacey called to tell me they'd just solved the fifth clue.' He paused. 'Do you want me to tell you this?'

Mimi shivered. 'Yes.'

'OK, she asked me how many we'd solved and I said four, and she laughed and called us a bunch of absolute losers, then the next moment there was a screech of tyres and a scream and a thud.' He took a steadying breath. 'That was it. After that, nothing. I don't think I'll ever stop hearing it. It's like an endless loop playing in my head.'

'Oh God . . .' Mimi was now hearing it too, not wanting to picture how it had happened but unable to blank it out.

'Sorry, I shouldn't have told you.'

'No, I'd rather know.' She laced her icy fingers together in her lap. 'At least it was quick.'

And then they were lost in their own thoughts once more. Mimi knew from Marcus that the treasure hunt had been Lois's idea, an afternoon of harmless fun, with the participants dividing up into groups and travelling in separate cars around the local area while they solved clues and tracked down a list of the items that needed to be collected in order to win the game.

She also knew that for all the pride and delight she'd taken in having been the one who'd persuaded Marcus and her dad to integrate themselves into the community, they would both still be alive today if she hadn't done it.

'I wish I'd never brought them down to the pub that night before Christmas.' The words caught in her throat as she uttered them.

Next to her on the bench, Cal reached down to take the stick Otto had brought for him. He hurled it so that it cartwheeled through the air, then sat back. 'It was my idea that Stacey and I should travel in separate cars. She chose your dad for her team and I chose Marcus for mine, so they'd feel more included.' He breathed out, puffing a white cloud of condensation into the cold morning air. 'If we'd stayed in couples, Stacey would still be alive.'

By this reckoning, Marcus and her father would both be dead. As they watched Otto retrieve the stick, Cal murmured, 'Sorry, I didn't mean . . .'

'It's OK, I know. We can think about all the if-onlys, but there's nothing we can do to change any of it.' Mimi swallowed; if her train down here hadn't been delayed, she'd have been in one of the cars too.

A new text arrived on Cal's phone; he glanced at it and rose to his feet. 'Cora's starting to wake up. I need to get back.'

And with Otto bouncing along at his heels, he was off at a fast pace, his daughter his number one priority now.

Mimi stayed where she was and slid her cold hands into the pockets of her jacket to warm them up. Her fingers encountered a piece of paper and she drew it out, expecting to see a petrol receipt. But it wasn't a receipt, it was a page torn from a notepad containing a shopping list. The list, she knew, had been attached by a magnet to the front of the fridge and added to at different times, which was why some of the items were in Marcus's handwriting and others in her dad's.

She smoothed out the unevenly folded paper and read:

Unsalted butter
Cherry tomatoes
Shoe polish – black
Peach yoghurts
Raspberries
I love you
Camembert
More Camembert
Liquid soap – not that awful purple bottle
Olive oil
Sweet potatoes
I love you more
Eggs
You couldn't – not possible
Cabernet Sauvignon
Well I do

A tear dripped off Mimi's chin and landed with a tiny splash on the bottom of the list. Oh, they'd been so lucky to have found each other.

How was Marcus going to manage without her dad, his soulmate?

When something this arbitrary and cruel happened, could you ever really get over it?

And if so, how?

Chapter 7

Four years later

'Hooray, you're home.' Kendra pushed back her chair with relief. 'I was about to turn into a desiccated husk.'

Mimi kicked off her heels and dumped the bags of shopping on the table, next to the laptop Kendra had been working on for goodness knows how long. 'What would you do if I didn't bring food back and cook it?'

'Shrivel up completely and die of starvation, I suppose.' Kendra tilted her head and drained the can of Coke that was probably her third or fourth of the evening. Left to her own devices, she would exist on a diet of crisps, toast and wine gums. Preparing meals simply didn't feature on her radar. On the upside, at least she always did the washing-up.

'You're hopeless,' said Mimi.

'I know. What are we having?'

'Chicken and bacon fettuccine, Caesar salad, lemon ice cream.'

'Ah, Rob's favourites. Are you making it to remind you of him, or does that mean he's coming over later?'

'He's got the opening of the boutique hotel in Chiswick,' Mimi explained. 'But he should be here by ten.'

'I'm starving now! We don't have to wait that long, do we?'

'You can have yours early.'

'Well thank goodness for that.' Kendra stretched and yawned extravagantly. 'I'll probably be asleep before he gets here. I'm shattered.'

But a bottle of wine was opened and they carried on chatting while Kendra finished off the pitch for a lucrative new account for the web design company she worked for and Mimi made the sauce for the pasta. They'd known each other for six years now, having first met when they'd both been sharing that terrible house in Bermondsey with ten other people. Then two years ago Kendra's great-uncle had died, leaving her this tiny top-floor flat on Ladbroke Road in Notting Hill. When Kendra invited her to move in with her, Mimi had been over the moon, because who in their right mind would turn down such an offer? They were friends who got on well together, they didn't annoy each other, and now they'd upgraded to Notting Hill. You couldn't ask for more.

At five to ten the doorbell chimed and Kendra said, 'That'll be the Greek god. Want me to let him in?'

Mimi was busy sieving boiling water out of the pan of fettuccine. 'Could you?'

'Greek god, is that you?' Shouting through the intercom, Kendra grinned when Rob replied, 'Yes it is.'

'Prove it.'

Mimi smiled to herself, because it was so nice that the two of them got on well together. When two single girls shared a flat, sometimes you had to grit your teeth a bit and pretend to like each other's boyfriends, but Rob and Kendra loved to bicker and tease and had a great brother–sister relationship.

It made life so much easier.

'You're wearing those shoes again,' Kendra complained when she'd buzzed him in. 'I told you, they're too pointy.'

'Luckily, I don't care what you think. I like them and my beautiful girlfriend likes them, and that's all that matters.' Rob came up behind Mimi, wrapping his arms around her waist and nuzzling the nape of her neck while she finished draining the pasta over the sink.

'Fine then, look like a throwback from the nineties, doesn't bother me.' Kendra poured him a glass of wine. 'OK, I'll leave you two in peace now. I'm off to bed.'

'Lightweight. Aren't you staying to eat with us?'

'Like a big old gooseberry, you mean? While you and Mimi get on with your lovey-dovey canoodling?' She pulled a poor-me face. 'I'm a sad singleton and it would just make me cry and cry.'

'Plus she already had hers two hours ago,' said Mimi.

Rob laughed. 'Excellent. And thank goodness, now we can do our lovey-dovey canoodling in peace.'

But once Kendra had disappeared into her bedroom, he said, 'Actually, is it OK if we don't canoodle? It's been a long day and I'm knackered.'

Ah, the relief; they'd been seeing each other for six months now and it was good that they could be honest. 'Me too,' Mimi said. 'It's fine. How did the launch go?'

'Good, good. Apart from one of the waiters dropping a tray of canapés in the fountain out in the courtyard. And there was a decent press turn-out. The clients were happy. What about you?'

'Not too bad. Couple of dodgy moments, but I managed to smooth things over.' A year ago, Mimi had gone to work for Morris Molloy PR, the agency set up and managed by Rob Morris in the heart of Soho. It wasn't the most sensible move, to become romantically involved with your boss, but sometimes these things happened; the attraction was just too powerful to resist. After a simmering few months of working together and not doing anything about the growing chemistry between them, they'd given in to temptation. And so far it was all going well. Rob was great to work for, dynamic and confident, and he was a great boyfriend too. All in all, the last six months had been pretty much perfect in every respect.

'Go on then, break it to me gently,' said Rob as they sat down to eat. 'What kind of dodgy moments?'

Mimi had spent the day with one of their trickier clients. CJ Exley was a hugely successful thriller writer who liked to be adored by his public and didn't take kindly to criticism. Having met him first thing off the plane at London City airport, she had taken him on a whirlwind tour of TV and radio stations, signing events and an interview with the *Telegraph* before getting him onto his flight back to Palma, Majorca.

Well, pouring him onto it, considering the number of vodkas he'd knocked back during the course of the day.

'A woman at one of the signings told him she'd bought all his books in car boot sales, which went down as well as you'd expect,' Mimi said drily. 'He called her a cheapskate. Then some other guy piped up during the Q&A to say he thought CJ's first couple of books were far better than the last few and didn't it bother him at all that his writing was becoming more clichéd and formulaic?'

Rob whistled. 'And he's still alive?'

'There's a possibility his body parts got packed into a suitcase and flown back to Majorca. At this very moment CJ could be tipping them into the Med.' She smiled. 'No, I reminded him that he sells millions more books now than he did back then, so clearly millions of people know better than one rude guy who's only jealous because he never found a publisher for his own work.'

'Well done, crisis averted.' Rob refilled her glass. 'In his head, CJ does like to think he's the hero of his own books.' He paused to consider the possibilities. 'Although brawling with a fan in a bookshop would generate a fair amount of publicity.'

'Maybe not the best kind,' said Mimi.

'Not for him.' Beneath the table, Rob gave her a playful nudge. 'I'm thinking of the agency. It wouldn't be bad publicity for us.'

The sound of a text arriving on her phone woke Mimi up from a deep sleep, purely because she was so unused to it happening. Following her dad's death, when her sleep had been so fractured and elusive, she'd got into the habit of switching off her phone before bed so the random notifications didn't disturb her any more than her own anguished thoughts did.

The difficulties had subsided after the first eighteen months but she'd kept up the practice. Except this evening she'd forgotten to do it. Reaching out, she groped around on her bedside table and opened one eye. The text was from Marcus, who knew she kept her phone turned off at night and wouldn't be expecting a reply. All it said was: *Give me a call in the morning xx*

See? Messages sent in the middle of the night were never worth waking up for. Rolling onto her back, Mimi turned her head to look over at Rob and saw that his side of the bed was empty. He must have gone to the bathroom.

Five minutes later, when he still hadn't returned, she pulled a dressing gown around her and went to see if he was OK. Had he been taken ill? He couldn't have fallen asleep on the loo, could he?

But no, the bathroom door was open, the bathroom empty. Nor was Rob on the sofa in the living room, or in the kitchen . . .

Baffled, Mimi rechecked the bedroom and even peered under the bed. She was about to wake Kendra – who *really* didn't appreciate her beauty sleep being disturbed – when she spotted the unlocked latch on the sash window that opened onto the fire escape.

It was a warm night; had Rob gone up to the roof terrace for some fresh air? Had he gone *down* the fire escape? But no, his wallet and phone were still in the bedroom . . .

Then Mimi's heart jolted as she remembered a story he'd once told her about how he'd gone through a sleepwalking phase in childhood. Had he sleepwalked his way out onto the fire escape? Was he up on the roof right now, wandering close to the edge of the terrace without realising how high up it was and how much danger he could be in?

Oh God . . .

She hauled the sash window open, scrambled over the

ledge and crept up the flight of metal steps. The urge to call out his name was strong, but she also knew not to startle a sleepwalker. In his state of confusion, the very worst could happen . . .

And when Mimi reached the roof terrace, she saw that the very worst *was* happening, but not in the way she'd imagined. Now she was the one in a state of confusion, because over there, dimly visible in the shadows on the padded garden sofa, were what appeared to be two people, and whatever it was they were doing, it definitely wasn't sleepwalking.

Still struggling to make sense of the situation, she moved closer. They weren't having sex, but they were kissing passionately, bodies entwined.

They were also far too occupied to notice her standing there, although it seemed unbelievable that they couldn't hear the frantic tom-tom thudding of her heart.

Because the man was Rob, and it just wasn't something you expected to witness, the sight of your own boyfriend wrapped around another girl.

As for the rest of it, her brain skittered away from the growing terrible realisation . . . No, surely not . . .

But Mimi knew she needed to get a grip and make some kind of decision here. Because there was no longer any getting away from it: the girl wasn't some stranger she'd never met.

It was Kendra.

Chapter 8

A wave of nausea surged up into Mimi's throat. She took a step backwards to steady herself and her bare foot made contact with an empty drinks can. As the tinny clatter caught their attention, she saw them freeze, then spring apart like opposing magnets.

Her best friend.

'Oh shit,' Rob muttered under his breath.

'Well this is . . . interesting,' said Mimi. The nausea was lessening, which was good; for a minute she'd actually thought she might throw up.

'OK, sorry.' Kendra swung her legs down so she was in a sitting position, and used her left hand to pull up the strap of her thin pink camisole top. Her right hand, Mimi noticed, was at her side, tightly clasping Rob's.

Mimi braced herself. 'Sorry for doing it? Or sorry for getting caught?'

'OK, you weren't supposed to find out,' Kendra said calmly. 'But now that you have, it's better that you know everything.'

'What does that mean? What's *everything*?' Mimi's knees

were shaking because this whole situation was just so utterly surreal. Here they were at two in the morning, on a balcony rooftop in Notting Hill. The lights of London twinkled away all around them; music was drifting up from a car in the street below. The scent of summer-warm tarmac mingled with the garlicky cooking smells from the late-night takeaway on the corner. She'd always loved spending time up here on this magical terrace with its stunning views across the roof-tops of the city she loved.

Well, up until now.

'We didn't want to hurt you,' said Kendra.

'Which is why you pretended to be tired, then crept up here while I was asleep.'

Kendra shrugged. 'But that makes sense, doesn't it?'

'Are you *serious*?' As she stared at Kendra in disbelief, Mimi realised this wasn't the first time it had happened. They were still holding hands, joining forces against her.

Rob said, 'Let me explain—'

'No,' Kendra interrupted, 'let me do it. And don't look at me like that,' she pleaded with Mimi. 'I'm your *friend*. I'm not a bad person and we didn't mean for this to happen, of course we didn't. But sometimes you click with someone and there's no way of stopping it. We tried to ignore it, but it just wasn't possible. Every time we saw each other, the chemistry built up and up, until we just couldn't . . .'

'. . . help ourselves,' said Rob.

'And how long has this been going on?' Mimi gestured at them, sitting side by side on the garden sofa.

'Only a couple of weeks.'

'Rob, leave this to me.' Kendra shook her head. 'It's been two months,' she said gently. 'We weren't expecting you to

71

wake up tonight. You know what you're like – once you're asleep, you're out like a light.'

'So it's my fault?' Mimi was incredulous.

'No, no, you don't understand, it's nobody's fault. And we kept it a secret because it seemed like the sensible thing to do. Rob and I were crazy about each other, but what if it didn't last? We thought we should give it a go first to see how things worked out. Then if the feelings wore off quite quickly, we could just call it a day and carry on as if nothing had ever happened. That way, you'd never need to know about it and everything would be fine!'

What were they expecting, a round of applause? 'And if the feelings didn't wear off?'

Kendra shrugged again. 'Well, then Rob would break up with you. But only once we were completely sure.'

Mimi surveyed the two of them, her boyfriend and the girl who for the last few years had been her best friend. Kendra still appeared to be convinced that they'd only done this because they had her best interests at heart.

It was like one of those elaborate prank shows on TV where the innocent person can't make sense of the unreal situation they suddenly find themselves in. Except there was no camera crew hiding behind the chimney pots on this rooftop.

'And before you ask,' Kendra went on, 'we *are* sure.'

'Great,' said Mimi.

'Oh sweetie, you're upset. I know you don't mean that.'

Mimi shook her head. She might be lots of things right now, but weirdly enough, upset wasn't one of them. She looked at Kendra. 'Oh I really do. I think you and Rob completely deserve each other. It's like you're a perfect match.'

★   ★   ★

The next morning Mimi heard Kendra leave for work on the dot of six thirty, as always. By seven, shards of sunlight were streaming in at an angle through her bedroom window and she'd run through the events of last night a hundred times in her head. Some of her imagined ripostes and one-liners had been so brilliant it was a shame she wasn't able to hit rewind and inflict them on Rob and Kendra without the five-hour delay.

If this had been a film, though, she could have come up with them straight away. Or climbed back in through the sash window and locked it, leaving the pair of them stuck outside the building for the rest of the night.

She could have flushed Rob's precious phone down the loo.

Broken every piece of crockery in the kitchen cupboards and flung cornflakes like confetti around the whole apartment.

Taken scissors to every dress in Kendra's wardrobe.

Pushed the two of them over the parapet and watched them plummet to the ground . . .

OK, prison food was horrible; maybe not that.

Prawns, though. Prawns stuffed into the deep cracks between the floorboards so the whole flat would smell as if it were harbouring dead bodies . . . wouldn't that be good?

There was a knock at the door. Opening it, Mimi saw Rob standing there, showered and dressed in one of the dark suits he always wore when he had an important business meeting to attend. She'd heard him leave last night, and now he was back.

'Look, I really am sorry.' He gave her his trust-me look. 'I never meant for any of this to happen. If I'm honest, I

73

can't see it working out for me and Kendra.' He smiled fleetingly. 'She's not even my type. It was one of those things that just happened out of the blue.'

'Two months ago,' Mimi reminded him.

'It was her idea, not mine.'

'You're wearing too much cologne.' In the space of a few hours, Mimi was discovering, she'd gone right off it.

'Am I? Thanks, I'll sort it out. I just wanted to drop by and check you're OK.'

'Never better, thanks.'

'You look fine, anyway. I didn't know if you'd have been crying.'

Mimi shook her head. 'No, none of that.'

'Well, that's good. I'm glad. So, we're all adults, no reason why we can't be civilised about this, is there?' And now he was giving her his closing-the-deal smile, accompanied by the rapid nod.

'We're adults,' said Mimi. 'No reason at all.'

'I knew you'd understand.' Rob glanced at his sleek watch. 'OK, busy day ahead, better get moving. I can give you a lift into work if you like?'

'Bit early for me. I don't have my first meeting until nine thirty. I'd rather walk in,' Mimi told him.

Visibly relieved to have the situation under control, he made to leave. 'Excellent. I'll see you later. No need for awkwardness in the office,' he said cheerfully. 'We can do this.'

She gave him a grown-up smile. 'Of course we can.'

She watched from the bedroom window as Rob emerged from the house and made his way along the pavement to where he'd parked his car. She conjured up a mental image of herself running him over in an army tank, then for good measure flattening that pretentious vintage Porsche of his too.

Then she turned away and surveyed the contents of her room, considering what to do next. Life was about to get complicated and she still hadn't worked out a plan. On the downside, this was the time when you'd normally throw yourself wailing into the arms of your best friend, who would sympathise and be on your side and agree that your ex-boyfriend was a cheating bastard who definitely didn't deserve you.

And if you lost your best friend because she turned out to be a two-faced liar with no morals and zero conscience, you'd automatically expect your wonderful boyfriend to console you and help you through the trauma of it all.

Well, she didn't have either of those options, which was a shame.

On the upside, witnessing their dual betrayal with her own eyes had definitely helped. A lot. Instead of being distraught, the cord had been cut in an instant, as if a razor-sharp guillotine had come crashing down. Because when relationships ended, the worst thing you could hear was the *it's not you, it's me* line or the *it just isn't working, is it?* excuse.

Which was fine when you weren't bothered anyway, but awful to hear when it was coming from someone you actually liked, and usually meant they'd moved on to someone else. Leaving you dumped and disappointed, and only able to imagine the happy couple together . . .

Whereas this time she hadn't needed to imagine them; it had all been happening right there in front of her, telling her everything she could possibly want to know.

It really was impossible to be distraught when you were furious.

At eight thirty, a text came through from Kendra: *Hi, angel, all OK? I'll be home around six, so let's have a drink and a proper chat then. Dinner on me this evening — tell me what you fancy and I'll order it in xxx*

Mimi texted back: *How about the special menu for two from that nice Indian place on Kensington Park Road?*

In no time, Kendra replied: *Consider it done. Glad everything's going to be OK. Love you xxx*

Mimi conjured up a mental image of a rhinoceros smashing its way through the swish glass doors of the web design company where Kendra worked, its beady eyes gleaming as it eventually located her cowering behind her desk . . .

OK, stop that. She had more important things to do and not much time to do it in.

At nine twenty-five, Mimi called Jess who worked on reception at Morris Molloy and told her she wasn't able to make it into work today, so Rob would need to cover her schedule.

'Oh noooo, you poor thiiiiing,' cooed Jess, who loved her elongated vowels. 'That's going to make things difficult for Rob, isn't it, at such short notice? But you're never off sick, so it must be really baaaad.'

'It's been a bit of a rough night,' Mimi confided. 'I think something must have disagreed with me.'

Chapter 9

Mimi hung up and was about to switch her phone off when she remembered Marcus's text.

'Hello!' He sounded delighted to hear from her. 'It's OK, I know you're rushed off your feet, it's just that I'm up in London today and if you happened to be free after work I thought we could maybe meet for dinner. But don't worry if you can't make it.'

'Oh Marcus, I'd love to.' It was so nice to hear his friendly voice. 'What are you doing up here?'

'One short meeting at midday with a client, that's all. I thought I might squeeze in a visit to the Summer Exhibition beforehand. When shall we get together, then? What time would suit you best?'

'Um . . . any time you like . . .' To her horror, Mimi realised her throat was tightening up. She tried to swallow and realised she was having a bit of a moment, some kind of delayed reaction to the events of last night.

'Mimi? Are you still there?'

'Y-yes.'

'Is everything OK?'

'Not really.' She gave herself a mental shake. 'Kind of the opposite.'

'Where are you?' said Marcus.

She stared blindly at all the clothes she'd pulled out of the wardrobe, despite not having enough cases to pack them in. 'I'm at the flat and I have to move out of here today and I don't even know where I'm going . . .' Her voice had gone all high-pitched now, like a cartoon chipmunk's.

'Stay there,' said Marcus. 'I'm on my way.'

Mimi did her angry, protracted and wonderfully cathartic bout of sobbing in the shower before getting dressed and defiantly applying eyeliner and lipstick so she didn't look like a complete wraith.

Marcus had always been good with hugs. He was smartly turned out, beautifully kempt as always, and smelled delicious too. When one of your parents met a new partner and subsequently died, how often did the child of the dead parent lose touch with the partner? When the person who connected the two of you no longer existed, and you lived a considerable distance from each other, wasn't it easier to drift apart?

Mimi was glad they'd managed to avoid that happening. For the first year or so, all she and Marcus had really had in common was their grief, but they'd both made the effort to stay in contact. Gradually they'd formed a genuine friendship that had survived his move to Cannes in the south of France. They might not see each other often these days, but the bond had remained unbroken and she was grateful for that.

Today's hug was especially enveloping; it was strong and secure, just what she needed right now.

'Go on then,' Marcus prompted when they broke apart. 'Tell me everything. What's happened?'

She told him, and the worst part was how unsurprised he was by the actions of both parties.

'You only met Kendra twice. And not even for very long,' Mimi protested.

'Long enough to know the kind of person she was.'

'But how?' It was confusing and somewhat humiliating to discover she'd managed to miss the signs that had evidently been so obvious to him.

'OK, I didn't know for sure. But I had an inkling.'

'Rob too?'

Marcus hesitated, then nodded. 'Honestly? Yes. And if you think back to when you first started working for him, you thought the same. I remember you telling me he was a smooth character who always liked to get his own way.'

'I did think that for weeks, and then he won me over. I told myself he was a good person underneath. God, I'm useless.'

'You aren't useless. Right, so what's happening?' He stood back and surveyed the state of her bedroom. 'What's the plan?'

'All I know is, I'm not staying here. And I won't be going back to Morris Molloy either.' She indicated the emptied wardrobe and chest of drawers, and the mountains of her belongings piled up on the bed. 'I want to be out today, so I need to shift some of this stuff into storage. There's a couple of friends who'd let me sleep on their sofas for a night or two until I find somewhere. I was going to go and visit Mum, but she's got her new chap and her place is *so* tiny.' Her mother's flat in north Wales had only one bedroom, and the thought of imposing herself on the two of them would be too much to—

'Mimi, you don't have to put anything in storage. Let me help you pack this lot up, and I can take it back with me to Goosebrook.'

'Really? Oh thank you so much, that'd be a huge help.' Grateful for the offer, she said, 'I can run down to the corner shop and buy some strong bin bags so we can make a start. I really want to be out of here before either of them comes back.'

'Look, I know you'll probably want to stay in London,' said Marcus, 'but if it's crossed your mind for even a second that it might be nice to move out of the city . . . well, you'd be welcome to come down to Goosebrook.'

Mimi was incredibly touched by the offer. 'Do you mean that?'

'Of course. My God, more than welcome. The spare room's yours for as long as you like.' His voice softened. 'Did you think you couldn't ask me?'

'I just thought I might be a nuisance. I wouldn't want to be in your way.'

'Right, well that's sorted.' He rubbed his hands together in a can-do fashion. 'We're going to load up the car, get ourselves out of here and head home as soon as my meeting's done and dusted. Spend the weekend down there while you decide what you want to do next. How does that sound?'

He was so kind, so thoughtful. When her dad had found Marcus, he'd chosen well. Mimi said gratefully, 'It sounds like just what I need.'

'Good,' said Marcus. 'And you can stay as long as you want. I promise you won't be in the way.'

It had turned into one of those days when an awful lot happened. Together she and Marcus had cleared every sign of herself out of Kendra's Notting Hill apartment, driving away in a car that was bursting at the seams with her belongings. Next, Mimi had waited in a coffee shop while Marcus met with his client in Holland Park. Then, because she knew he'd been looking forward to the Summer Exhibition, they spent two hours at the Royal Academy viewing the artworks and choosing their favourites.

After that, they'd left London behind them, crawling through heavy traffic at first but speeding up once they hit the motorway and headed west. Wiped out by last night's lack of sleep, Mimi had dozed in the passenger seat to the accompaniment of Puccini's *Madame Butterfly* spilling from the speakers.

When she woke up almost two hours later, she briefly switched on her phone and saw the messages stacking up from both Kendra and Rob.

Well, good. And it was seven o'clock, so presumably Kendra had arrived home from work with the food delivery she'd ordered to assuage the tiny amount of guilt she presumably did feel.

No doubt she'd be happy, though, to share it with Rob when they realised her erstwhile flatmate wasn't planning on coming back to eat it.

Mimi smiled, glad she'd asked for the set menu of king prawns and beef vindaloo. Poor Rob, he didn't like seafood *or* sauces with chillies in, couldn't cope with anything hotter than a tikka makhani.

What a wimp.

Now they were approaching Goosebrook, making their way down the winding lane into the village as the sun, sinking lower in the sky, shone into their eyes.

It was Friday evening, the last week in July, and a cricket match was in progress on the village green. The players were all dressed in their whites, contrasting with the bright colours worn by those watching the match. Some were in deckchairs, others sprawled on rugs on the grass, whilst the rest occupied the wooden benches that belonged to the pub.

Marcus pulled up outside Bay Cottage and they climbed out of his car. Bees buzzed, butterflies danced and the scent of honeysuckle hung in the clean balmy air. Over on the green the thwack of leather on willow was followed by the ball soaring up and over the boundary for a six, prompting a cheer to go up from the spectators.

'That's something you don't get to hear in the south of France,' Marcus said.

'Are you happy to be back?'

He nodded. 'I am. Cannes was glamorous, but you can't beat this place. Everyone's been amazing.'

Mimi was glad for him. In the aftermath of the accident, the villagers had rallied around; barely a day had passed without containers of home-cooked food being left on the doorstep, even though the very last thing Marcus had wanted to do was eat. He'd been grateful for their efforts and their kindness and concern, but after a while the emptiness of the cottage had grown too much for him to bear. Caring neighbours were all very well, but the absence of Dan proved to be painful beyond belief.

Desperate to escape, he had rented out the cottage on a long lease and decamped to a tiny apartment just off the Boulevard de la Croisette. Living there had been an experience; the weather had been wonderful, and taking long daily strolls along the beach had given him plenty to look at, but he'd soon discovered that there was no quick fix, no magic wand that could be waved. He continued to miss and grieve for his beloved Dan. No amount of glittering azure sea and silver sand could heal a broken heart.

He'd stuck it out for three years, though, realising that the unbearable loneliness would lessen in due course; there was a grieving process that needed to be gone through, stage by stage, and one day he'd be happy again. And now, he had admitted to Mimi, life was becoming easier. It had also been the right time to return to Goosebrook, which had gone through something of a mourning process itself and was only now coming out the other side.

Having spotted his car from their positions around the periphery of the cricket pitch, people were waving to attract his attention, beckoning him over to join them.

Marcus raised a hand in acknowledgement. 'Let's get your stuff into the house first. Then you can decide if you're up to socialising.'

Mimi wondered if Cal was over there among the cricket-watchers. It would be good to see him again. And the others too, of course. She said, 'Oh, I'd like to say hello. I'll be fine.'

Chapter 10

Ten minutes later, they headed back out and across the green. On closer inspection, there was no sign of Cal. But Felix and Lois were sitting on one of the wooden benches and Felix instantly leapt to his feet.

He greeted Mimi with a hug. 'How nice, and what a surprise. We did wonder if you'd be down, now that Marcus is back . . . Here, have my seat . . . no, I insist. Lois, isn't it great to see Mimi? And doesn't she look well?'

Lois embraced Mimi. 'Lovely to see you again. And you are looking well.'

'So are you,' Mimi told her, because what other response was there?

Lois's smile was dry. 'Well, hardly. But never mind.'

Mimi nodded. They hadn't seen each other since the accident. When she'd come down for the funerals of her father and Stacey, Lois had still been in hospital, battling to recover from her injuries. The lone survivor of the crash, she'd sustained multiple severe lacerations, bone fractures and internal injuries to her spleen and pancreas. Her left leg had been amputated below the knee. They'd managed to save

84

the left arm, but the scarring was clearly visible, as it was on her face and neck.

'It's OK, you can have a proper look. I'm used to it. If you had scars, I'd want to see yours.'

Mimi saw the way Lois's eyelid had been bisected and carefully repaired; as had the deep gash that ran diagonally from the right side of her forehead to the left side of her chin. There was other scarring on her upper chest, visible above her white vest top.

'You're still beautiful, though,' she told Lois. 'You're still you.' It sounded like a platitude, but she meant it.

'Yeah.' Lois grimaced. 'I know. I'm the lucky one. At least I'm still here, alive and kicking with my good leg, and being the bane of my mother-in-law's life.'

'Really?'

'Oh yes. Are you kidding? She strongly disapproved of me seeing her precious son from the word go. Then the accident happened and her ex-husband was the driver, which made the whole situation that much more awkward.' She paused to indicate to Felix that she'd like another drink, and waited while he and Marcus made their way into the pub behind them.

Mimi waited too. She hadn't come to Goosebrook for Edward Mercer's funeral, because why would she? Divorced from Felix's mother many years earlier, Eddie had been living it up in Monte Carlo, enjoying every aspect of the expat lifestyle. An enthusiastic gambler and drinker, he'd evidently been far happier not being married to Henrietta. On that fateful weekend four years ago, he'd come back on a whim to see Felix. Delighted to join in with the treasure hunt, he had volunteered to be one of the drivers and the teams had been picked.

Eighty minutes later, a wild boar had shot across the road directly ahead of them. Reacting instinctively, Eddie had yanked the steering wheel to the left as the boar ricocheted off the bonnet, and the car had smashed at high speed into the trunk of an ancient oak tree.

Eddie, Dan and Stacey had been killed outright, as had the wild boar. The emergency services had managed to cut Lois free from the mangled wreckage and airlift her to hospital, where she'd remained for the next three months.

At the inquest, Eddie Mercer's body was confirmed to have been free of alcohol and drugs.

'Henrietta can't stand me,' said Lois. 'She's convinced I only married Felix to get my filthy grasping hands on his money. She thinks Felix only asked me to marry him because he felt guilty about what happened. She says if there hadn't been an accident, Felix and I would have broken up long ago.'

Since bluntness and honesty appeared to be the order of the day, Mimi said, 'And do you think so too?'

Lois shrugged. 'It's a possibility. She's right about Felix feeling guilty and responsible by proxy. Let's face it, I'm not the catch I once was.' She glanced down at her prosthetic leg. 'I didn't marry him for his money. I'll admit, though, I did wonder if anyone else would still want me.'

'Oh you can't have thought that. Thousands of men would want you. *Millions*,' said Mimi.

'But I don't want *any* men, I want the same level of man I had before. I don't want to settle for someone I wouldn't have looked twice at before the accident. Sorry, I know what I sound like and you must be thinking I'm a spoiled selfish bitch because your dad died and I didn't, so what do I have to moan about?' Lois exhaled audibly. 'But it's kind of hard, trust me, getting your head around the idea that you can't do the things you used to do, or attract the kind of men you used to attract.'

Mimi had heard from Marcus that the marriage was rocky, but it was heartbreaking to hear the reasons from Lois herself. 'It must be so difficult,' she said.

'It's awful. And even worse feeling guilty about it too. Anyway, here they come with the drinks; let's change the subject. How are things with you?'

Under the circumstances, it seemed only fair to say it. 'I just found out this morning that my best friend has been shagging my boyfriend, who also happens to be my boss.'

Lois's eyebrows shot up. 'Seriously?'

'Oh yes.'

'That makes me feel better. Sorry, but it does. Thank you.' Reaching for the glass Felix was holding out to her, Lois clinked it against Mimi's tumbler. 'Cheers!'

Forty minutes of conversation later, Mimi said, 'The girl over there with the blonde curls . . . is that Cora?'

'Where? Oh yes, it is. I suppose she's grown up a bit since you last saw her.'

Mimi nodded; back then, Cora had been a chirpy six-year-old obsessed with zebras. Now, taller and thinner, wearing a plain white T-shirt and a pair of cut-off denim shorts, she was lying on her stomach on the grass, propped up on her elbows and gesturing with her hands as she chatted away animatedly with her friends. She was ten now. If it was hard losing your father in your twenties, imagine how much more agonising it must have been to lose your mum when you were just six.

'How's she doing?' Mimi asked Lois.

'Pretty good, all things considered. Cal's been amazing with her.' Lois shooed away a hovering wasp. 'Mind you, the hormones are about to kick in; he'll have that to deal with next.'

This was true, and a daunting enough challenge for any parent. Mimi watched as the wasp circled her glass like an old man taking a walk around his garden pond. 'And how's Cal coping?'

'Fine on the outside. On the inside . . . who knows? You'd think after four years he'd have found someone else, but no. There hasn't been anyone. Well, unless there has been and we just haven't heard about it. Always a possibility.'

'He's not around this evening?'

'Working, I think.' Lois lowered her voice and murmured, 'Look at Felix watching Maria. See the look on his face? D'you think something's going on between them?'

Startled, Mimi followed the direction of her gaze. Maria was collecting empty glasses, and laughing at something Felix was saying. 'I don't think so. It's just a normal kind of look.'

'You're probably right.' Lois shook her head. 'God, I hate being like this. I'm pathetic.'

Mimi checked once more. 'There's nothing going on there, I'm sure of it.'

'Then again,' said Lois, 'you had no idea your boyfriend was carrying on with your best friend. So what would you know?'

Mimi grinned. 'Touché.'

They left not long afterwards, heading back to the cottage. In the kitchen, Marcus began putting together something for supper. Upstairs, Mimi got on with unpacking her belongings, stowing her clothes in the wardrobe in the spare room that – if she decided to stay down here in Goosebrook – would become *her* room.

As she was stuffing underwear in the top drawer of the chest of drawers, she heard a car pull up outside, then a voice call out, 'Cora!'

Even if the name hadn't made it obvious, she would have known who it was. Cal's voice was instantly recognisable, even four years on. Crossing the bedroom and pushing the window open further still, Mimi leaned out to get a look at him and saw that he was out of his car, beckoning to his daughter.

Then Maria said something to Cal and pointed in the direction of her window, prompting him to turn and look up at her. He raised a hand in greeting and Mimi automatically did the same, realising too late that she was still holding her underwear.

Hoping he wouldn't notice, she released her grasp, expecting the items to land on the inner windowsill. But no, the turquoise bra with extra-extra padding and the navy knickers that were designed for comfort rather than seduction sailed through the air and landed on one of the rose bushes below.

Bugger.

By the time she'd galloped downstairs and wrenched open the front door, Cal was there on the doorstep with her mismatched bra and knickers in his hand.

'Thanks.' She took them from him with a rueful smile.

'No problem. Just for a moment there I felt like Tom Jones, getting underwear chucked at me.'

'If I'd been doing it on purpose, I'd have thrown nicer ones.'

Cal's eyes creased at the corners with amusement. 'How long are you down here for?'

Mimi shrugged. 'No idea, haven't decided yet.'

'Well, it's good to see you again.' He took a step back. 'I have to get Cora home now, but if you'd like to come over for a coffee tomorrow morning, just turn up. We'll be there.'

Chapter 11

Mimi rang the bell, then realised it wasn't working. The front door had been left on the latch though, so she pushed it further open and called out, 'Hello?'

No response. She hesitated for a second, then made her way into the cottage and through to the living room. There was the cobalt-blue sofa that, last time, Cora had used as a launch pad to leap into her father's arms. DVDs were scattered on the rug in front of the TV, next to a plate sprinkled with toast crumbs. Up on one wall was the mirror with the stained-glass frame that Cal had given Stacey that Christmas. And there was a framed photo of the three of them together standing in pride of place on the mantelpiece.

Mimi moved closer. At a guess, the photograph had been taken at around the same time; there were out-of-focus Christmassy colours in the background. Cora had one arm curled around her mum's neck and the other hand clutching Cal's knee. Her expression was full of joy and mischief as she sat between her parents, secure in their love.

'*Woof woof,*' barked Otto, bounding into the living room and making Mimi jump. Thank goodness she hadn't been holding the glass photo frame. She looked at the dog, whose tail was wagging wildly, and heard rapidly approaching footsteps behind him.

'Hello, are you Mimi? Yes, I think I remember you now.' Up close, Cora had a light dusting of freckles across her tanned face, and bits of grass stuck in her hair. 'Sorry, we were outside and the doorbell's broken. Dad said you were coming over. I'm Cora.'

'I definitely remember you.' Bending to greet Otto and rub his ears, Mimi said, 'The last time we met, you were mad about zebras.'

'That's for babies. I was only young then.'

Mimi smiled at her air of world-weariness. 'Right. Well, I did knock at the front door . . .'

'That's why it wasn't locked, so you could let yourself in. Dad's out in the shed, if you want to come through.'

Cora led the way into the kitchen and out into the garden, pausing en route to help herself to an ice lolly from the freezer and ask Mimi if she'd like one too. She added helpfully, 'It's OK, they're made of fruit juice so they're good for you.'

They crossed the lawn and Cora opened the door to the shed, which was bigger than Mimi had expected and hadn't been there when she'd last visited.

'Dad, she's here.'

Cal turned and said, 'Thanks, sweetheart. Her name's Mimi.'

'I know it is, you already told me.' Cora rolled her eyes and gave Mimi a complicit smile. 'And before you ask, I did offer her an ice lolly but she said no. So anyway, me and Otto are going over to Lauren's now, is that all right? Don't forget you're taking me into town this afternoon to buy my new trainers.'

'How could I forget?' said Cal.

'And not those orange ones you saw in the supermarket.'

'The fluorescent orange ones? They were my favourites.' He winked at his daughter so she knew he wasn't serious.

'Bye, Dad. See you later.' Cora took a loud slurp of her lolly, gave him a kiss, waved at Mimi and ran out of the shed with Otto at her heels.

'Sticky.' Cal's tone was rueful as the door swung shut and he rubbed at the place on his cheek where she'd planted the kiss. 'Anyway, hi. So that was Cora.' He sat back on his stool and said, 'What d'you think?'

'I think you're doing a fantastic job. She's great.'

His expression softened. 'She is. I've been lucky. Not saying we haven't had our moments, but she's doing all right.'

'So are you, by the look of things.' Mimi gestured around the shed, which was actually more of a studio. 'These are amazing. I mean, Lois mentioned it last night, she said you'd started doing this, but I had no idea . . .'

Because propped up against the whitewashed wooden walls of the shed were canvases of varying shapes and sizes. Some were blank, still waiting to be used, but most were finished portraits. More to the point, they were *good* finished portraits of people Mimi was instantly able to recognise. She did a double-take as she spotted one of Prince Harry in his polo gear.

'Oh my God, do you *know* him?'

'No.' Clearly entertained by the way her voice had just spiralled up to a squeak, Cal said, 'It's called making the best of what you have. I start by pinning up a dozen or so photos of the person I've decided to paint and work from them to create a composite picture. It's more like having them sitting for you than just making a straight copy of one photograph. And it's cheaper than paying someone to sit for hours while you use them to practise on. Here, like this.' He reached around and lifted a board off the shelf behind him, bearing several photos of Cora with her mischievous elfin face captured at a variety of different angles. Then he pointed to a portrait on the wall. 'And that's the finished result. Because Cora doesn't mind having a few photos taken but she can't sit still for longer than five minutes.'

'And do you sell them?'

'No, no.' He shook his head. 'Still learning. I only started to give myself something to do in the evenings after Cora had gone to bed. Watching TV was leaving me with too much time to think. I was doodling one day while I was on the phone, waiting to see Cora's teacher. She saw the doodle and asked me if I was a professional artist, which made me laugh. But that night I grabbed a few sheets of printer paper and started sketching with a pencil. Four hours later, I had twenty fairly terrible sketches, but I'd enjoyed making them.' Cal shrugged. 'I also realised I'd been so occupied I hadn't once thought about Stacey or felt sorry for myself.'

'That's amazing.'

'It really was.' He nodded in agreement. 'It takes all your concentration. You can't think about anything else when you're drawing and painting.'

'And at the end of a few hours, you've created something incredible. You must be so proud,' said Mimi. 'I mean, to think you had all this talent and didn't even know it. You do realise people would pay to have their portraits painted by you?'

'Or they'd feel obliged to.' Cal shook his head. 'The last thing I want is to become one of those charity cases, for people around here to feel they had to support me. Like when you go along to the school Christmas fair and end up buying those cupcakes the kids made themselves. Except it'd be worse, because you can't buy a portrait for fifty pence and chuck it in the bin when you get home.'

'But—'

'No, no way. I couldn't stand having people feeling sorry for the not-very-good artist because his wife died.'

'Except you're *not* not-very-good,' Mimi protested.

His gesture was dismissive. 'Not good enough. I'm still practising. Hopefully I'll get better, but I don't need the pressure of having to meet expectations. I'm just doing it because I enjoy it.'

'OK, I'll stop nagging.' She glanced around the shed at the portraits, an eclectic mix of well-known actors, people who lived in the village, famous musicians (Mick Jagger over there, propped up on a stool, looking like a skinny Shar Pei) and random characters off the TV. 'What happens to the ones that don't work out? Do you bin them?'

He broke into a grin. 'No one's asked me that question before.'

'I'm asking it now.'

'They're behind the others. I leave them there for a few weeks, then get them out and start a new portrait, see if I can make a better job of it second time around.'

'And can you?'

'Yes. That's how I know I'm improving.'

95

'Show me your worst one.'

'You really want to see?'

'Of course I want to see!'

Cal wiped his hands on his paint-smeared jeans and crossed the shed. He searched behind the stacked canvases, flipping through them like giant playing cards before pulling one out. 'OK, this is my most disastrous. In my defence, it was one of the first ones I ever did. I haven't even made a second attempt at this one, it's just so awful.'

He turned it around and Mimi studied the portrait in muted acrylics.

'OK,' she said finally. 'Well I know who it is, so it can't be that bad.'

'Who is it?'

'Benedict Cumberbatch.'

'Nope.'

Oh. She narrowed her eyes and looked again. 'Is it that guy from Emmerdale, the one who—'

'No.'

'Fine then, I give up. You win. Who is he?'

'Dame Judi Dench,' said Cal.

Mimi nodded. 'Of course. I see it now.'

He laughed. 'Come on, I promised you coffee. Time for you to tell me how things have been with you.'

In the shade of the mulberry tree, Mimi settled herself on the cushioned swing seat and stirred the coffee Cal had just handed her. He sat down in the chair opposite. 'What a hideous thing to have to go through. All I can say is you're well rid of the pair of them.'

'OK, I only told you because you'd have heard about it anyway.' Mimi pulled a face. 'It's pretty embarrassing, whingeing to someone about the rotten thing that just happened to you when they've been through stuff that's a million times worse.'

'Tell me about it. I've spent the last four years asking people how they are and getting that reaction. It's like having all the trumps in Top Trumps, every time.' His smile was rueful. 'I just wish that sometimes I could lose.'

Two hours later, Mimi found herself in the passenger seat of Cal's car with Cora and Otto sitting behind her, while Cal drove them into Cirencester and complained about the music his daughter had downloaded onto his phone.

'It's really good, Dad,' Cora patiently explained. 'You just don't like it because you're old.'

'I'm thirty-two,' Cal protested.

'That's what I just said.'

'See what I have to put up with?' He glanced across at Mimi. 'Brutal.'

Mimi looked back at Cal. 'What's it like to be thirty-two?'

He grinned. 'Exhausting.'

As Cal had evidently discovered years ago, it was nice to have something to keep your mind occupied. Every time Mimi's mind wandered back to the situation she'd so abruptly found herself in and her stomach began to clench with muddled emotions, Cora came out with something that made her laugh. She was bouncy, interested in everything and a great asker of unexpected questions.

'Mimi, do you miss your dad?'

Mimi twisted round in the passenger seat to meet her gaze. 'I do. I miss him a lot.'

'Do you think you miss your dad as much as I miss my mum?'

'Honestly? I think you probably miss your mum more. Because you were only six when it happened. At least I was a grown-up.'

Cora nodded and wrapped an arm around Otto beside her. 'Yes.'

A minute later, she said, 'Mimi?'

'Yes?' *Oh crikey, what was coming now?*

'Will you help me choose my trainers?'

'Of course I will.' Mimi nodded reassuringly. 'Shopping's what I'm best at.'

Cora was visibly relieved. 'Good. Because Dad tries his hardest but sometimes he gets it wrong.'

Cirencester was crowded with tourists, but they managed to park and made their way on foot into the centre of town. Cal picked up his latest order of acrylic paints and red sable brushes from the shop on West Market Place, then they embarked on the search for the perfect trainers.

'See what I mean?' whispered Cora, when her father held up a pink and yellow pair with flashing lights in the soles. 'Dad, no. Put them down.'

'I can't believe it,' Mimi murmured in her ear. 'You were right.'

'What are you two talking about?' Cal protested. 'They're brilliant. They flash when you walk.'

'If you like them so much,' said Mimi, 'you buy a pair for yourself.'

But twenty minutes later, they found a pair that Cora fell in love with, midnight blue and scattered with tiny white stars, with a plush red inner sole. They weren't expensive but they were comfortable and just what she wanted. Having tried them on, she gazed at her reflection in the mirror and beamed with delight. 'These, Dad. Can I have them, please? They're the best trainers ever.'

'Well that was painless,' said Cal as they left the shop. 'Shall we find something to eat now?' He gave his daughter's curly blonde ponytail a tweak. 'How about that place on Black Jack Street with the blackberry ice cream?'

And Mimi remembered the snowy day four and a half years ago when she'd been sitting in the steamed-up café and he'd spotted her quite by chance through the window.

But as they were about to make their way over there, Cal's phone beeped with a message. He stopped to read it, then frowned and looked at his daughter.

'What?' said Cora.

'It's a text from Charlotte's mum. She's offering to pick you up and take you to Georgia's party.'

Cora's eyes lit up. 'Great. When is it?'

'Well apparently it starts at three o'clock. Today.' Cal checked his watch. 'And it's two thirty now.'

'*What?* I didn't know it was today!'

'But are you sure you've been invited?'

'Of course I have!'

'It's just that I haven't seen an invitation,' said Cal.

Cora gazed around wildly, in search of an answer. Suddenly it came to her. 'It might be in my school bag. Georgia gave them out on the last day of term before we broke up.'

'So that means we didn't reply to say you'd be going.'

'Oh I did say I'd go.' She nodded, remembering. 'Definitely.'

Cal exhaled. 'And where's the party being held?'

'At the water park. We're doing zorbing. It's going to be brilliant!'

'Sweetheart, you should have mentioned it before now.'

99

'I forgot.'

'And these are the situations no one ever warns you about,' Cal told Mimi.

He called Charlotte's mother, thanked her for the offer and explained that they'd be heading to the water park from the other direction. Then, putting his phone away, Cal said, 'OK, we have five minutes to buy you a swimming costume, a towel and a card and present for Georgia.'

Cora let out an anxious yelp. 'Can we do it in five minutes?'

'If we don't,' Cal told her, 'we'll be late.'

Chapter 12

'Are we late?' Cora asked breathlessly as they swung into the busy car park.

'Only two minutes. We're here, everything's fine.' In a rush, they all leapt out of the car. Peering around like a meerkat, Cora exclaimed, 'There they are! I can see them!'

Cal handed her the silver gift bag containing the multi-coloured bangles they'd picked up in Accessorize, and the card she'd written in the car. 'Have fun. We'll be on the terrace outside the café.'

'All right, but you have to promise not to watch me.'

'Sweetie, there are hundreds of people here. Everyone's going to be watching you.'

Cora clutched her rolled-up beach towel. 'Well promise not to laugh if I fall over. And definitely don't cheer either.' As she raced off to join her friends she called over her shoulder, 'And don't take any photos!'

Cal shook his head. 'Something else you aren't warned about, how embarrassing you suddenly become. Well,' he amended, 'you do get warned, but you don't realise how it feels until it starts happening. Look, sorry about dragging you here like this. Can you bear to put up with me for another couple of hours? Because if you're desperate to get home, I can drop you and come back.'

'I'll put up with you,' said Mimi as they made their way over to the café's terrace. 'It's just a shame you couldn't have brought me somewhere half decent.'

He smiled, because the view was spectacular. 'Have you been here before?'

'Only once, and that was a couple of weeks after the accident. Marcus drove me out here to see it. It was March and freezing cold; the ducks were sliding all over the ice. It was still nice, but this is just so different. It's incredible.'

Last time the sky had been steel grey, the trees had been bare and her eyes had been so swollen from crying that it had been hard to appreciate the stark wintry beauty of the water park.

But today . . . well, it just seemed surreal that such a glorious place could exist in the middle of the countryside. Altogether, there were one hundred and fifty lakes occupying an area of over forty square miles, with a range of activities for everyone to enjoy. People came here for swimming, kayaking, rowing and picnicking. On the larger lakes you could go speedboating, wakeboarding, jet-skiing and para-skiing. Others were for fishing, sailing or paddleboarding. On dry land there were adventure playgrounds, cycle tracks and crazy golf.

And on this particular stunning lake, which had the largest inland beach in the country, were the water zorbs.

Cal found them a table and went to buy a couple of coffees. Mimi settled into her chair and surveyed the scene – a cloudless blue sky, clear turquoise water as smooth as glass glittering in the sunshine, and a crescent of silvery sand. Families sunbathed and young children played on the beach, whilst others splashed in the shallow section of the lake. Green trees lined the distant shoreline on the other side, birds swooped and sang overhead, and in the water, lined up alongside a wooden jetty, bobbed the transparent zorbs.

What a place to spend a summer's afternoon. Just beautiful. Mimi took out her phone and switched it on out of habit, saw the stacked-up messages from Rob and Kendra and hastily turned it off again before memories of her old life could ambush her. It was easier not to think about everything that had happened; such a gorgeous setting didn't deserve to be sullied.

Oh God, though. *Kendra*. To lose a boyfriend was one thing, but losing your best friend was worse.

At that moment a burst of laughter went up from a group of women at a nearby table and Mimi's heart gave a jolt because the woman sitting with her back to her was wearing a flowery yellow jacket identical to the one Kendra had bought a few weeks ago and worn practically non-stop ever since.

Apart from when she was ripping off all her clothes in order to have sex with Rob.

'Everything OK?' Cal was back with a loaded tray. 'You look . . . unsettled.'

'I'm fine.' Mimi nodded in the direction of the woman. 'I just saw someone wearing the same jacket as Kendra and for a split second I thought it was her.'

He turned to look. 'The yellow flowery thing?'

'That's the one. It's from Topshop, though, so that means

there are thousands of . . .' Her voice trailed off, because the owner of the jacket had swivelled around to glare at them.

'Excuse me?' Her eyes wide with outrage, she pointed an accusing finger at Cal. 'How dare you call my jacket a flowery *thing*? It's not a *thing*, I'll have you know, and I demand a full apology.'

God, was she serious? How terrifying. Mimi held her breath.

'What can I say? I'm a fashion philistine.' With a grin, Cal raised his hands in defeat. 'I'm sorry.'

'Apology accepted, I suppose,' the woman said. 'But I should warn you, I may have to come up with a suitable punishment.' And now she was unfurling herself from her chair, approaching their table. 'Hello, Cal, how are you doing? Haven't seen you for a couple of weeks.' She kissed him on both cheeks and gave his arm an affectionate stroke. 'You're looking so well.'

'I'm good, thanks. Della, this is Mimi Huish. Mimi, this is Della Day-Johnson, Charlotte's mum.'

Ah, right. So that was the connection. 'Hi!'

'Hello, so nice to meet you!' Della's smile was like car headlights on full beam as she did a lightning up-and-down sweep. 'Do you have a daughter here at the party too?'

'She doesn't,' Cal explained. 'Mimi's a friend of mine.'

'I see. How lovely! Well, here we all are.' Della gestured behind her to the large table around which the other mothers were gathered. 'You're very welcome to join us. The more the merrier, that's what I say!'

'Thanks,' said Cal, 'but we'll stay where we are. I have to . . . um . . .'

'We have some private business we need to discuss,' Mimi

cut in when he paused in search of a plausible excuse. 'Cal's helping me out with something.'

'Of course, of course. Well if you change your mind, you know where we are. And don't forget what I've told you before.' Della waggled an index finger at Cal. 'If you ever fancy a drink or a bit of company, it's open house over at our place. And Cora's always welcome for a sleepover.'

She returned to her friends and Cal sat down with his back to them. Amused, he murmured, 'What are they doing now?'

'All leaning across the table, whispering like crazy to each other. About you, I should think.'

'And you too. They'll be wondering where you've come from and what's going on.'

'They're going to be disappointed when they discover the truth. Actually,' Mimi amended, 'they won't, will they? Because right now they think I'm your girlfriend. They'll be delighted when they find out I'm not.'

'We should hold hands.' His eyes danced. 'Don't worry, we won't. I wouldn't embarrass you.'

'I'm guessing you're quite the centre of attention at the school gates.' Of course he would be, given his looks, charm and availability. He was by any standards a catch.

'I generally pretend to be busy on my phone,' Cal admitted. 'It's easier.'

'And is Della single?'

'Divorced. Keen to move on to husband number two.'

'She likes you.'

'I know.' He sighed. 'I know she does.'

Mimi marvelled at how easy it was for them to discuss their personal issues. 'Has there been anyone else since the accident?'

See? Like that! The words just came out as if it were the most natural question in the world.

'No.' Cal paused. 'And I know it's been over four years. I know everyone thinks I should have got over it and found someone by now. But it just isn't happening. Every time I meet someone new, I compare them to Stacey and . . . well, they don't measure up. And that's when I feel myself losing interest, because why would I want someone who isn't as good as her?' He sat back and watched as an ant crawled over the back of his hand. 'It all seems a bit pointless and I'd rather not bother. Shit, listen to me. This is cheery stuff, isn't it? Bet you're glad you came out with us now.'

Mimi said, 'I am glad. I love it here.'

'Dad! DAD! Look at me, watch me!' Down on the jetty, the group of girls were all in their swimsuits, ready to climb inside the floating zorbs. Cora was bouncing up and down, waving madly to attract Cal's attention.

'You told me not to watch,' he shouted back.

'I've changed my mind! Watch me and take lots of photos! This is going to be *great*.'

For the next forty minutes there was much photograph-taking and videoing of the overexcited group of girls shrieking with laughter as they flung themselves around inside the zorbs and raced each other across the shallow water.

'Looks like they're having fun,' remarked a male voice behind Mimi while Cal was down on the beach videoing Cora and her friends. Turning in surprise, she found herself gazing up into the distinctive electric-blue eyes of Paddy Fratelli.

'They are. Hello, fancy seeing you here!'

106

'Not that much of a coincidence.' He grinned and she realised he was wearing a sea-green polo shirt bearing the logo of a water-skier on it. 'This is where I work.'

Of course. With his wiry, athletic build and deeply tanned skin, he looked completely at home. Mimi said, 'I should have realised. What is it you do here?'

'I'm a water sports instructor over on one of the other lakes. Water-skiing, wakeboarding, parasailing . . . basically, anything you want to learn, I'll teach it.' There it was, the playful twinkle in his eye as he said the words, designed to win over every female who crossed his path. He raised a hand in greeting at the tableful of mothers who'd spotted him, and said to Mimi, 'Heard you were back. So is this a flying visit or are you planning to stay for a while?'

'Staying for a bit, I think, while I decide what to do next.'

'Well for what it's worth, the guy was an idiot and you're better off without him.'

So word was spreading fast on the mean streets of Goosebrook; Lois must have told him about her situation. Mimi said, 'Thanks,' and marvelled at the irony of his remark, seeing as sleeping with other men's girlfriends was apparently one of Paddy's hobbies.

His mouth twitched. 'And if you ever need any help getting over your heartbreak, you only have to ask.'

'That's very kind of you. But I'm not heartbroken.'

'OK, but if you change your mind . . .' Breaking off, Paddy nodded cheerfully as Cal returned to the table. 'Hey, how's Cora doing? Enjoying herself?'

'Having the best time,' said Cal.

'Well, I need to drop off these keys and get back to work. I'll see you guys around.' He jangled the keys and left via

Della's table, saying, 'Bye now, ladies, enjoy the rest of your day.'

'Paddy, could I squeeze in an extra water-ski lesson next week, or are you completely booked up?' This came from one of the glamorous mothers sitting with Della, sipping pale pink Prosecco from a mini bottle through a straw.

'Text me and we'll fix something up.' Paddy briefly rested a hand on her bare shoulder. 'I'll always make time for you.'

All eyes were on him as he left the terrace. The glamorous mother fanned herself with a menu. 'I can't imagine why I keep having these lessons.'

'Especially when your husband's away working in Dundee.' Della smirked.

Cal caught Mimi's eye. 'He hasn't changed.'

'I noticed.'

'What was he saying to you?'

'Oh, just offering to mend my broken heart.'

'So noble of him. And do you think you might take him up on that?'

'I don't know. I'll probably give it a miss.'

'Good, glad to hear it.' After a moment, Cal added hastily, 'OK, that doesn't sound right. I meant I'm glad for *your* sake. I didn't say it because I meant . . . Oh shit, sorry . . .'

Amused by just how out of the flirting loop he was, Mimi said, 'Don't worry, I know what you meant.'

'Dad, did you see me? I *loved* it. Zorbs are so cool!' Cora came hurtling up to them, dripping water and with her beach towel flying behind her like a Superman cape.

'And we loved watching you.' Cal gave her a wet hug.

'We're having a picnic down on the beach now. Then everyone goes home after that.'

'We'll wait here and have something to eat,' said Cal.

'This is a brilliant day.' Cora beamed at them both and raced back to rejoin her friends.

'It has been pretty good.' Cal nodded in agreement and asked a passing waitress for a couple of menus. 'Are you hungry?'

And miraculously, after the traumas of yesterday, Mimi discovered that her appetite had returned. 'D'you know what? I could murder some chips.'

Once the food had arrived, she said, 'I've decided, by the way. I'm going to stay down here for a while. And before you ask, no, it has nothing to do with Paddy Fratelli.'

Cal nodded. 'I think that's the right decision to make. You could do with a break, and it'll take a while to get over what's happened.' He squeezed mayonnaise onto the side of his plate. 'If you can bear to sit for me, I'd love to paint you at some stage.'

'I'd like that.' A kernel of warmth began to unfurl inside Mimi's chest. 'We could do it next week if you want.'

'Ah well, that's not—'

'Dad, Dad, Katy just invited me for a sleepover at her house in three weeks but I said I had to ask you because I don't know when we get back from holiday.'

Cal shook his head. 'We'll still be away then. We won't be home until the end of August. Say sorry to Katy but you can't make it.'

'OK, but I won't say sorry because I'd rather be on holiday anyway!'

The kernel of warmth faded in Mimi's chest. When Cora had skipped off once more, she said, 'When are you off on holiday?'

'Monday.' Cal popped a chip loaded with mayonnaise into his mouth.

'Oh nice!' *Not nice at all.* 'So you're away for a month? Wow.' She spoke extra brightly to conceal her dismay.

'I know, and my company builds summer houses for a living. Hardly ideal workwise.' He shrugged. 'But it's something we started doing after Cora was born, and it became a tradition we didn't want to break. Sometimes you just have to go with what feels right, you know? My sister lives on the Gower coast in Wales, so we spend every August there with her family. Cora gets to run wild with her cousins and she adores her aunt and uncle, so it's great for all of us. And Otto gets to race around with his dog cousins too. We all love it.'

Mimi nodded, although she didn't love it one bit. Ridiculous though it seemed, she would miss him while he was gone. Her brain was still in a state of flux over the Rob and Kendra bombshell, but being in Cal's company had been making everything so much easier to bear. Their friendship was effortless and just what she needed right now. And yes, of course it was selfish to be thinking about her own needs, but you couldn't help the thoughts hidden away in your mind.

At least he didn't know she was having them.

'It sounds perfect,' she told him with a relaxed smile. 'Just what you need. You'll have an amazing time.'

Oh well.

He'd only be gone for a month.

Chapter 13

The text said: *What's happening?*

It was from Rob, of course. He'd sent dozens over the course of the last week, so many that Mimi's heart no longer did a dolphin leap each time a new one arrived.

'Another one from the boyfriend?' said Lois, which just went to show how monotonously often it had been happening.

'Ex-boyfriend,' Mimi automatically replied.

'I'm just going to call him the bastard from now on. Why's he still doing it, though? You'd think the message would have sunk in by now.'

'I'm great at my job and my clients will be missing me. Rob wants me to go back to work and he never likes to take no for an answer.'

'*Utter* bastard.'

'He built the business up from nothing. It's his pride and joy.'

'And you loved working there too. Uh oh . . .' Lois shot her a sideways look as they headed into the churchyard. 'Does this mean you're tempted to go back?'

111

Mimi trailed her hand over the silky wild grasses growing up against the dry-stone wall to the left of the ancient iron gate. She picked a stem of something with silvery leaves and purple flowers. 'I'm not going back. But I do miss the job.' There weren't too many openings for her kind of PR work in this corner of the Cotswolds. 'If I'm staying down here I'm going to need to find something else to do.'

'I can ask around if you like. Want me to text him back?'

Amused, Mimi said, 'Feel free.'

Lois seized the phone and began texting at the speed of light. *Hi, I'm just looking after Mimi's phone for a bit. You're the bastard ex, am I right?*

The next moment the phone began to ring. Pressing reply and putting the call on speaker, Lois said cheerfully, 'Ah, hello, bastard ex!'

'Look, I made a mistake. I've admitted it and apologised. What else can I do? It didn't even mean anything,' said Rob. 'Kendra thinks it does, but she's got it all wrong. None of this was ever meant to happen.'

'Oh I know! It's a real shame, isn't it, when you get caught out like that? For no reason at all! And you missed out on a good one there, I can tell you.'

Rob hesitated. 'Who am I speaking to?'

'Hi, I'm Lois, a friend of Mimi's.'

'OK. Look, could you ask her to call me? It's urgent and I need to—'

'She isn't coming back to the agency, if that's what you're wondering.'

'But—'

'No, I mean it. She's already had a better offer.'

'What?' Rob's tone was dismissive. 'She can't have.'

'Except it happened. Sometimes it's just a matter of being in the right place at the right time, isn't it? Can you hear that noise in the background? That's her new boss's stunt plane,' said Lois as a two-seater flew overhead. 'I'm just looking after her things while he takes her up in it to show off his aerobatic skills . . . Oh, I can see Mimi waving to me . . . Honestly, I can't tell you how thrilled we all are that she's moved down here, it's so brilliant having her around . . . Aargh, I wish you could see this, they're going into a barrel roll now! Rather her than me!'

'Sounds like fun,' said Mimi once Lois had ended the call and handed the phone back to her. 'I've always wanted to try a bit of loop-the-looping.' She twirled the stem of the plant she'd picked a couple of minutes earlier. 'This is pretty, what's it called?'

'Oh my God, *drop it*,' Lois shouted, staggering backwards. 'That's deadly nightshade, it'll kill you!'

What? Mimi let out a bat squeak of fear and threw the plant over the wall in a panic before realising that Lois was doing her best not to laugh.

'Ha, sorry, couldn't resist. The look on your face!' Lois grinned. 'Don't worry, city girl, it wasn't anything poisonous – just willowherb.'

'I'm going to have to learn about these plants if I'm staying down here.' Mimi was still wiping her perspiring palms on the sides of her jeans. 'This countryside is a dangerous place.'

They wandered between the gravestones, some ancient and covered in lichen, others shiny and more recent. Lois showed her the tall, imposing memorial to Henrietta's family, carved with names going back centuries.

113

'That's where Henrietta will go.' She pulled a face. 'Must be getting pretty crowded down there by now. She'll have something to say about the state of the place when she gets to see it, I'm sure.'

Mimi looked at the most recently added name, that of Eddie Mercer, Felix's father. There was no mention of how he'd died; just the dates of his birth and death.

'Will Felix be buried there too?'

'I guess so. It seems to be the done thing.'

'And you?'

'What, in with that lot? No thanks. I'd rather be cremated and have my ashes scattered in Puerto Banus.' Lois's eyes danced. 'If Henrietta outlives me, she'll probably tip them down the nearest loo.'

They carried along the overgrown path and Lois pointed out some of her favourite gravestones.

'See this one? In memory of Rose Valentine, best and most beloved mother of Daisy, Daffodil, Zinnia, Petunia and Fred.' She clapped her hand to her chest. 'I always wonder if Fred secretly wished he could have had an exotic name too.'

'Oh!' Mimi exclaimed, moments later. 'Here lies Malcolm Gainsforth . . . and his wife Elspeth . . . and his second wife Mavis. I bet at least one of them wasn't too happy about that arrangement.'

Minutes later, they came to Stacey's grave. Newer than most, the white marble headstone gleamed in the sunlight, and in front of it stood a white pot of miniature red roses.

Mimi silently read the silver-engraved wording on the stone: *Stacey Mathieson, adored wife of Cal, mother of Cora. Loved by all who knew her.*

114

'She really was loved,' said Lois, bending to brush fallen leaves away from the base of the stone and swiftly pulling up a couple of weeds that had poked their way between the glistening white marble chippings. 'Cora chose these, did you know? She called them Mummy's diamonds. Sorry,' she added, wiping her eyes with the back of her hand. 'But if you ever want your heart broken, just come along to this graveyard and watch a seven-year-old washing a bucketful of chippings in soapy water so they'll stay sparkly for her mum.'

Mimi shook her head; the mental image was unbearable.

'I can't believe I still miss her so much,' Lois continued. 'We only knew each other for a year. But sometimes you meet someone and just instantly get along with them, don't you? And that's what happened with me and Stacey.' She sat down with difficulty, folding her good leg over the prosthetic one. Then she patted the dry grass beside her, indicating for Mimi to do likewise, and rested her other hand easily on the headstone so that Stacey was included in the conversation. 'She and Cal were in the pub the very first time Felix took me down there, and she was so welcoming and friendly. Then a couple of days later in the shop, she heard Henrietta telling someone I was nothing but a tart and a gold-digger. So Stacey chimed in and said, "But how can you possibly know that when you haven't even met her yet?"'

Mimi could just picture Stacey mounting the challenge. 'And what did Henrietta have to say about that?'

'She announced that she'd seen me from a distance and it was pretty obvious what kind of a person I was.' Lois shook her head. 'Basically, the sight of me told her everything she needed to know. I was a blonde in a short skirt who

115

wore high heels and plenty of make-up. But Stacey said she'd met me and I was lovely, just what Felix needed. And word got back to Felix that she'd stuck up for me big-time. Well as soon as I heard about it, I loved her even more.' She paused to give the headstone an affectionate pat. 'We had so much fun after that, we really did. Such laughs . . . Oh, did you ever hear her doing her imitation of Henrietta singing?'

'What? No.' Mimi was intrigued. 'What kind of singing?'

'OK, Henrietta was invited along to be the guest of honour at the infants' school end-of-term concert and all the children were so excited to be performing on stage in front of their families. Stacey said it was the sweetest little show – well, the kids were only tiny, so you can imagine what it was like – but afterwards she overheard Henrietta telling the vicar it was a shame half the kids were tone deaf.'

Mimi was appalled. 'That is so mean!'

'Stacey was longing to have a go at her. She didn't, though, didn't say a word. But the next week on karaoke night at the Swan, she dressed up as Henrietta and sang the song from *Titanic* in an off-key Henrietta voice. Oh, it was just the most brilliant impersonation. She brought the house down; it was spot-on. I'm not as good as Stacey was, but I'll try and show you . . .' Stiffening her spine and transforming her features into a haughty, horsey Henrietta face, Lois stretched out her arms and in an ultra-posh high-pitched voice began to warble the opening lines of 'My Heart Will Go On'.

'Oh my God, you can do it,' Mimi gasped, enthralled. 'You sound just like her!'

'Come on, you can do it too. Tilt your head back and look down your nose, that's the secret.' Waving her arms in encouragement, Lois urged Mimi to join in, and together the two of them continued, reedy and deliberately out of tune, until they reached the final line, before high-fiving each other and collapsing with laughter. Then Lois accidentally snorted, which made them both laugh even more. They were rocking back and forth, by now completely hysterical, when an all-too-familiar voice sounded behind them.

'This is a graveyard, not a comedy venue. Is it too much to ask that you show some respect for the dead?'

Together, they turned. Henrietta stood there, looking about as disapproving as it was possible to be. Her shirt collars were pointed up at angles, she was wearing a tweed skirt and brogues, and at her heels stood a slinky Burmese cat whose tail swished slowly from side to side as it regarded them with feline *froideur*.

Lois said, 'We weren't disrespecting the dead, Henrietta. I was just telling Mimi a funny story about Stacey. She was my friend and I loved her. We're still allowed to laugh, aren't we, when we talk about our friends?'

'There's a time and a place,' Henrietta retorted.

'If you heard us singing,' said Lois with a touch of defiance, 'it was one of Stacey's favourite songs.'

From the way Henrietta was narrowing her gaze at them, Mimi suspected that she had indeed heard their singing.

'Well, I'll leave you to it. I'm sure Cal would be delighted to know you've been having so much fun at his wife's graveside.'

She stalked off down the path with the Burmese slinking

along beside her. When she'd disappeared from view and they were alone again, Lois said, 'See what I have to put up with? Honestly, that woman's the bane of my life. Where's a big old bunch of deadly nightshade when you need it?'

Chapter 14

There was no getting away from it: the job situation – or rather the non-job situation – was turning into a bit of a slippery slope. Having made a list and embarked on a blitz of applications on Monday, Mimi had discovered that the current market was even trickier than she'd imagined.

It was her own fault for wanting to continue in PR. There had been only three positions available within a twenty-five-mile radius, and the interview for the first had got off to a dodgy start when she'd reached Malmesbury and called into the café next door to the office on the high street.

'Hang on, I'm confused,' said the chatty middle-aged waitress when she'd ascertained the purpose of Mimi's visit. 'How can Alma still be interviewing people when she's already given the job to her sister?'

'You daft wazzock,' the other waitress retorted. 'No one's supposed to know about that. Her husband told her she had to advertise to try and get someone better, so she's just going through the motions to shut him up.'

'Oh,' said Mimi, downcast.

'Me and my big mouth. Sorry, love. I shouldn't have told you. Don't mention it to Alma, will you? She's a nightmare if you get on her wrong side.'

Mimi went for the interview anyway, in case it was all an elaborate double bluff to test her in some way. An hour after returning to Goosebrook, she received a text from Alma spelling her name wrong and breezily informing her she wasn't right for the position.

Presumably because she wasn't a blood relative.

The second job, upon closer inspection, turned out to be less of a prestigious PR position and rather more of a trudging-the-streets-going-door-to-door affair, trying to convince people to sign up to buying a range of eye-wateringly expensive anti-cellulite creams.

Interview number three, at an advertising agency in Oxford, seemed to be going really well until the Spanish girlfriend of the man interviewing her stalked into the office, took one look at Mimi and demanded to speak to him outside. When he returned three minutes later, he heaved a sigh and said, 'Did you hear any of that?'

The flashing-eyed Spanish girlfriend hadn't bothered to lower her voice. Mimi nodded. 'Most of it.'

'She's the possessive type.' He shrugged apologetically. 'Jealousy issues, you know? If I'm going to hire a female, it has to be an ugly one. And let's face it,' he gestured at Mimi, 'you're the opposite of ugly. She'd make my life hell if I took you on.'

Through the closed door, his eavesdropping girlfriend bellowed, 'That's because you sleep with all the pretty ones, you cheating bastard!'

Yikes. Mimi reached for her handbag, keen to leave before

the other girl came bursting back in with a loaded Beretta. 'Well, good luck with—'

'I know, I'm sorry, she's an absolute nightmare.' Rising to his feet on the other side of the desk, he shook her hand and lowered his voice to a supposedly seductive whisper. 'But look, I'm always free on Tuesday afternoons if you ever fancy meeting up for a couple of hours. That's when she gets her nails done.'

By done, he presumably meant filed to razor-sharp points, all the better to attack her rivals with. Poor woman, thought Mimi, no wonder she was pathologically jealous.

Anyway, that delightful encounter had happened yesterday. And now, to top it all off, she had drastically lowered her expectations and was *still* not being offered a job.

It was sheer frustration that had driven her to apply for a kitchen job in a café in Cheltenham, because any work was better than nothing.

'Honestly, I'm a really hard worker,' she protested. 'I wouldn't let you down. I'm great at washing up!'

But the skinny café owner was already shaking his head, his mind clearly made up. 'You say that now, but look at you.' He pointed with a nicotine-stained finger at her tailored white shirt and smart pencil skirt. 'You ain't the kitchen-helper type, not for more'n a few days, at any rate. Soon as you get yourself a better offer, you'll be off on yer toes and I'll be back to square one, havin' to advertise all over again. See, what I'm really after is some old dear who's desperate for a bit of cash in hand who'll stay for the next year at least.'

He clearly didn't have a lot of time for political correctness. It was also one of the grottiest cafés Mimi had ever encountered. Oh well, she didn't want the stupid job anyway.

But she wanted *some* kind of job, and so far none had been offered. They were halfway through August and she was running out of options fast.

Now, arriving back in Goosebrook following today's unsuccessful interview, Mimi drew up outside Bay Cottage and parked behind a gleaming black Mercedes. Idly wondering who it might belong to, she peered in through the tinted glass and saw a smartly dressed man sitting behind the wheel reading a book.

When she let herself into the cottage, she caught a waft of distinctive cologne – Aventus by Creed – and realised who had travelled down here to see her.

The question was: why?

'Hi.' Marcus appeared in the hallway and greeted her with his warning face on. 'You have a visitor.'

'Well that makes me sound like some posh old bat out of *Downton Abbey*,' bellowed CJ Exley, materialising behind Marcus.

'Hello, CJ.' Mimi greeted him with a polite kiss on each cheek. 'This is a surprise. What are you doing here?'

'Well I'm not planning to declare my undying love, if that's what you're hoping.' Up close, the cologne was stronger than ever. He was wearing a crimson polo shirt with a gigantic Ralph Lauren logo on the chest, his favourite Hugo Boss jeans and deck shoes by Chanel, because if it wasn't designer, CJ wasn't interested.

'I'll try to hide my disappointment,' said Mimi, which caused him to beam with delight.

'And *that's* the reason I'm here. Because you aren't afraid to take the mick out of me. Bloody sycophants, sick of the lot of them! Anyway, what happened with you and the agency? And are you quite sure you don't have any vodka tucked away somewhere in this house?'

Evidently not for the first time, Marcus said patiently, 'We don't. I'm afraid we're a vodka-free zone.'

'Huh, you don't know what you're missing.' CJ gazed down with disappointment at his half-drunk cappucino.

'I left the agency,' said Mimi.

'Well I know that. Called them up, didn't I, and tried to book you for a job. Your man Rob said you wouldn't be able to do it and tried to fob me off with Mary Poppins instead.'

'Brenda,' murmured Mimi. 'She's very efficient.'

'So I told him to fuck off. I said I didn't want her, I wanted you. Which was when he had to tell me you'd moved on, but he wouldn't say where.'

'Go on,' Mimi prompted.

'So I called back an hour later, told the squeaky woman on reception that I'd found your driver's licence in my suitcase after our last trip and said I needed to get it back to you. That was when she told me you'd broken up with lover boy and hightailed it out of London. She didn't have an address, but said she'd overheard someone saying you'd gone back to the village your dad moved to before he died.'

'Right.' Mimi nodded; during a previous author tour he'd asked about her family and she'd told him about the accident.

CJ shrugged; uncovering information was his stock-in-trade. 'So I did some googling, found out the name of the village . . . and here I am.'

'I can see that. But what I'm wondering is why.' He was after something, clearly. And he definitely didn't have her driving licence.

123

'I need a PA.'

Inside, Mimi's heart did a small leap, half optimism, half wariness. Because on the one hand CJ would be a living nightmare to work for, but then again . . . it was a job.

'What's happened to Willa?' She'd never met CJ's long-suffering personal assistant, but had liaised with her on the phone on many occasions while they'd been putting together itineraries for publicity tours.

'Willa's let me down.' CJ shook his head in disgust. 'She left yesterday.'

'Am I allowed to ask why? Or has she just had enough of working for the world's trickiest employer?'

'I'm not tricky.'

'OK then, let's call it temperamental.'

'She's gone off on extended sick leave, if you must know.'

Mimi was appalled. 'Oh no, poor Willa! What's wrong with her?'

'She hasn't had a nervous breakdown, before you start thinking that. She's suffering from hyperemesis.' He grimaced. 'Like a fountain. It's not pretty, I can tell you. It makes *me* feel sick just knowing it could be about to happen again at any second and she'll have to rush off to the bathroom—'

'Hang on,' Mimi interrupted. 'Why's she being sick all the time?'

He sighed. 'Reckons she's pregnant.'

'You mean she *is* pregnant.'

'I suppose. Bloody inconvenient.' CJ tutted at the temerity of his employee. 'I thought she'd be working all the way up until it popped out, but no, the puking's put the kibosh on that. She's buggered off back to her mum's place in Sheffield, leaving me up the creek without a paddle. And that's why

I'm here.' He fixed her with an irritated gaze. 'I need someone to organise me and I can't be doing with interviewing strangers. I need someone who isn't going to get on my nerves or burst into tears if things aren't going their way. I thought of you and planned on hiring you through lover boy's agency, but—'

'Could you please stop calling him lover boy?' said Mimi.

'How about dickhead?'

She shrugged and nodded. 'That'll do nicely.'

'But then I found you'd left, which was even better.' CJ spread his hands. 'You aren't working, so you're free to come with me.'

'Who says I'm not working?'

'I called into the pub before coming over here. Woman who runs it told me you hadn't had any luck yet with finding a job. How'd it go this morning at the café?'

'None of your business,' said Mimi.

'Didn't get it, then.' He looked smug. 'Come on, stop trying to play hard to get. I'm making you an offer you can't refuse. Who in their right mind would say no?'

'You told me yourself that before Willa came along you'd had seven PAs walk out on you.'

'Did I tell you that?' CJ looked surprised. 'Must've had a drink or two.'

'That's an understatement,' said Mimi.

'It frees up my mind, makes the words flow when I'm on a deadline. I write better after a couple of sharpeners.'

'And yell at people better too. If I came to work for you, I wouldn't put up with any yelling.' She lifted an eyebrow. 'Just so you know.'

'Is that a yes?'

Of course it was a yes. Aloud, Mimi said, 'It's a cautious maybe. How much would you pay me?'

CJ took out one of his business cards and scrawled a figure on it with the flashy fountain pen he always used at book signings. 'More than you'd earn working in that cockroach-infested café.'

This was his way of letting her know he'd weaselled the name of the café out of Maria, then checked out the less-than-flattering reviews on TripAdvisor.

'Where would we be based?'

'Puerto Pollensa, northern Majorca. Officially you'd be covering Willa's maternity leave, but who knows if we'll see her again? So I'd need you up until next March at least. If she decides not to come back, you could be permanent.'

'Let's not get ahead of ourselves. How soon would you want me to start?'

'Well I'm off to LA tomorrow for a fortnight. I'll be back on the thirty-first of August. We can fly out to Majorca together the day after that.'

Mimi glanced over at Marcus, who was leaning against the Aga observing the exchange with interest. 'What d'you reckon?'

'Me? I think if you turn it down he's not going to have time to find a replacement. Which I'd say puts you in a pretty strong bargaining position,' Marcus replied in his deceptively mild way.

'That's a very good point,' said Mimi.

'Oh for crying out loud. *Fine.*' Uncapping his flashy fountain pen again, CJ crossed out the first offer and scrawled a higher figure across the card. 'Bandits, the lot of you.'

'That'll do nicely.' Mimi reached out and shook his hand. 'You're on.'

'At last.' He broke into a grin. 'Made me sweat a bit there.'

'Eww.' She let go of his hand, then smiled. 'If Marcus hadn't said that, I'd have done it for the lower price.'

'Yeah? Well I'm just glad you went with the second one. I'd have paid more.'

'Damn, I *knew* it,' said Marcus.

'Too late, the deal is done. Come on then.' CJ was already heading for the door. '*Now* can we go over to the pub and get a drink?'

Chapter 15

It was midday on the last day of August and Mimi was in the village shop stocking up on emergency supplies of Marmite and her favourite chilli sauce, just in case they didn't have them in Puerto Pollensa.

She heard a familiar bark outside and felt her heart do a froggy leap. She'd been waiting for days for Cal and Cora to arrive back in Goosebrook, but they'd evidently decided to squeeze as much holiday out of the month as humanly possible.

'Sounds like Otto,' said Eamonn, who ran the shop. 'Yes, here they are. Welcome home, you two! Did you have a great time?'

They'd been away for a month but it felt like longer. Mimi had been quite shocked to discover just how much she had missed Cal's presence in the village; it felt emptier when he wasn't around. But the break had clearly done them both good. Cora's hair had grown longer, blonder and more wildly curly, and her blue eyes were bright in her heart-shaped face. Cal, wearing a pale yellow cotton shirt and faded jeans, was more deeply tanned than ever, his sun-streaked hair making his eyes appear darker brown by comparison.

He grinned at Eamonn. 'The very best, thanks.'

'Well we missed you.' Eamonn moved out from behind the counter. 'But I'm afraid we missed Otto more, so you'll just have to chat amongst yourselves while I head out and say hello to my favourite boy . . .'

'I'll get some food,' Cora announced as the door swung shut behind Eamonn. 'Dad, can I choose my yoghurts?'

'Go ahead.' Cal looked at Mimi. 'How have things been with you? All OK?'

'Great.' It was so lovely to see him again.

His gaze flickered in the direction of her wire basket and he did an exaggerated double-take. 'Wow, what's going on here?'

Mimi looked too, and laughed. 'Don't worry, I'm not pregnant.'

'No? Well that's good to hear. When Cora was on the way, Stacey was obsessed with Worcester sauce; had to drown every meal with the stuff. We were getting through three bottles a week.'

'That's so gross.'

'It was horrible to watch. Anyway, what's the situation with the ex? Seen him at all?'

'God, no.'

'Or her?'

Kendra. 'Not her either.'

'Dad, can I get doughnuts for me and Lauren?'

'Go ahead. Although you're both going to be chatting so much you won't have time to eat them.'

'I need to tell her everything about our holiday,' Cora

explained to Mimi. 'And then I have to hear all about Lauren's holiday in Cornwall. But it's OK, we'll manage; we can talk with our mouths full.'

'How about work?' Cal raised his eyebrows at Mimi. 'Any joy?'

'Actually, yes. I'm starting as a personal assistant tomorrow.'

'Excellent! Where's that, in Cirencester? Cheltenham?'

'Majorca.'

Cal said, 'Oh,' and for a split second she saw a flicker of disappointment mixed in with the look of surprise. Which was nice, but also kind of frustrating, because what she really longed to know was if he'd miss her as much as she'd be missing him. 'Well, good for you.'

'Puerto Pollensa,' said Mimi, as Eamonn came back into the shop.

He nodded. 'Excellent.'

'That's why I'm stocking up on these.' She placed the basket on the counter. 'To take with me.'

Eamonn, who was perfectly well aware that she was off tomorrow, said with a wink, 'And there was me thinking you were up the duff.'

Outside the shop, Mimi greeted Otto while Cal helped Cora to divide up the snacks.

'Right,' Cora announced once the task was complete. 'Me and Otto are off to Lauren's. And you have to do some work, yes?'

Cal nodded in agreement. 'I'll be out for a while. Be home by six, OK?'

They watched as Cora skipped off down the pavement towards Lauren's house with Otto trotting along beside her, clearly interested in the doughnuts in her bag.

'Not the best timing.' Cal finally turned to look at Mimi. 'Just as we get home, you're leaving.'

Mimi felt a fizz of adrenalin. 'It wasn't deliberate.'

He smiled slightly. 'Glad to hear it. So what are you up to now? Do you still have a ton of packing to do?'

'All finished, because I'm so super-efficient. Well, apart from these.' She held up her bag containing the jars of Marmite and bottles of chilli sauce. 'And a trip to the dentist this afternoon.' She looked rueful. 'I had a bit of a toffee-based incident with one of my molars last week and Marcus said I really had to get it sorted before I left for foreign parts, so he's booked me in to see his dentist in Tetbury.'

'What time?'

'Four o'clock. Why?'

'I'm heading over to Tetbury this afternoon to meet with a client at three. I can take you if you want.'

'Oh! Marcus said I could borrow his car . . .'

'Don't worry then, that's fine.' Having seen her face fall, Cal held up a hand. 'It was just a thought.'

It was the knowing she wouldn't see him again for a while that had caused Mimi's face to fall. Hastily she said, 'No, no, I'd love that. I just thought you might be tired after driving back from Wales . . .'

'Oh I think I can probably manage a few miles more.' Cal flexed a bicep, Popeye-style. 'Shall I pick you up in an hour?' He paused, glancing at the unenthralling contents of the plastic carrier in his hand. 'Or we could head over there now and get lunch. If you fancied it.'

Oh I definitely fancy it.

Stop it, smutty girl.

Aloud, Mimi said, 'Perfect.'

Once they reached Tetbury, they found a restaurant and, much like Cora and her friend Lauren, caught up with each other's news. Mimi heard all about Cal and Cora's adventures on the sweeping, spectacular beaches of the Gower coast with his sister and brother-in-law and their dogs and children. In turn, she relayed the latest goings-on in Goosebrook and told him about her series of unsuccessful job interviews.

'Then CJ came along and gave me the hard sell, and I can't tell you how impossible he's going to be to work for. He's actually a brilliant writer and his books are incredible, it's just that personality-wise he's a bit of a nightmare. But once you've been turned down for a washing-up job in a skanky café, you kind of realise you can't afford to be too choosy.' She gestured with her fork. 'If it didn't involve working for CJ, it'd actually be a dream job. It's just a shame it couldn't have been someone else.'

'CJ Exley.' Cal nodded. 'I know the name. I think I heard him being interviewed on the radio the other week. He sounded normal enough.'

'That's because he had Willa there to keep him in check. Trust me, he's rude, he's an incredible show-off, he thinks he's irresistible.' Mimi was ticking off the list of non-attributes on her fingers, 'Oh, and he absolutely *hates* having to sit down and get on with writing his books. Trying to keep him under control is like wrangling a ten-year-old with ADHD. He likes to hint that he worked for MI5, but there's no way that ever happened.'

'How do you know?'

'Because every time he meets a pretty girl, he says, "Keep it to yourself, darling, but I know my stuff – I used to work for MI5 as a spy!" And he *winks* when he says it.' Mimi shuddered. 'Like this.' She gave Cal a lecherous wink. 'Honestly, he thinks he's James Bond.'

'I need to see what he looks like.' Taking out his phone, Cal pressed some keys. 'Maybe you'll start off hating each other, then as the weeks go by your feelings will change and you'll end up falling madly in love, like in a rom-com. OK, don't look at me like that.' He laughed as he shook his head. 'My sister made me sit down and watch one with her last night. Apparently that's the way it always happens in that kind of film.'

'Well it definitely isn't going to happen to me.'

Cal studied the photo of CJ he'd found online. 'He doesn't look too bad. You couldn't call him ugly.'

'That's his publicity shot. Three per cent truth, ninety-seven per cent Photoshop.'

'So you're quite sure you're not going to fall in love with the nightmare James Bond character?'

Cal's tone was playful, but she couldn't help wondering why he seemed so interested. Mimi's breath caught in her throat and her brain started to wish she wasn't off to Puerto Pollensa for the foreseeable future. She said, 'I promise.'

Chapter 16

'You don't have to stay in the car,' Cal said when they reached the address at three o'clock. 'I'm sure they'd love to show you the finished result.'

He was right. The Carters were a chatty couple in their sixties who couldn't have been happier with the bespoke summer house Cal's company had constructed at the bottom of their large south-facing garden.

'I'm absolutely furious,' Marion Carter announced as she led them across the sitting room and out through the French doors. 'To think we could have had one built twenty years ago and we didn't. All that time we lived without one and had no idea what we were missing.' She clutched Cal's arm. 'It's the best thing we ever did! We're spending more time in it than we are in the real house . . . we just love it to bits!'

Against the layered backdrop of trees, well-tended shrubs and bright flowers of a well-loved English country garden stood the recently constructed summer house, hexagonal in design, with a silver-grey Victorian lead roof and the doors flung open. The outer walls were painted palest pink, the windows glittered in the afternoon sunshine and inside there were strings of cotton bunting, elegant lights and two comfortable lilac and blue striped sofas.

As they entered the summer house, Marion's smile widened. 'I sit in here and read . . . and do my knitting . . . and we listen to music. The cats adore it too.' She lovingly stroked the pale blue silk cushions on the sofa nearest to her. 'And look, we've installed one of those mini fridges to keep our drinks cold! It's our favourite place to spend time.'

'So no problems with the installation?' Cal double-checked.

'Oh my goodness, none at all – did you seriously think I was asking you over here so I could make a complaint? No, quite the opposite.' Marion's eyes sparkled in the sunshine. 'My sister was entranced when she saw what we'd had done, but she has one of those gardens you can only get to through the house, plus she's completely phobic about having strangers in her home. So although she'd love one of these, it just wouldn't be possible. Except it's her seventieth birthday in a fortnight and her daughter's whisking her off on a cruise, and we thought maybe we could arrange to have a summer house installed while she's away as a surprise.'

'Look, it's a nice idea.' Cal was already shaking his head. 'But if your sister's so opposed to letting strangers into her home, I don't know if I'd feel comfortable sneaking in behind her back . . .'

'Oh, it's OK, we wouldn't dream of asking you to do that,' Marion assured him. 'I wouldn't do it to Barbara, she'd have a complete meltdown, poor darling. No, we've come up with a rather marvellous plan . . . here, let me show you.' Her husband handed her an iPad and she started scrolling through the photos. 'It was so thrilling, sneaking out and taking these in secret, I felt like a spy! Anyway, here's Barbara's garden and there's where we think the summer house should go . . . what do you think?'

'I think that looks like the best spot.' Cal was studying the photos, nodding slowly. 'But if we can't gain access through the house, I don't know how we'd manage it. It'd be tricky to drop the parts in by parachute.'

'We went over and spoke to the woman who lives *there.*' Marion angled the iPad and pointed to a rooftop partially obscured by trees. 'That's the road behind Barbara's and their gardens back onto each other. We'd seen her before, because she was often out in her garden, and she'd always seemed very nice, so we paid her a visit and explained our situation. And she was wonderful, we were so lucky. As soon as we asked the question, she said yes. She's happy for everything to be brought in through her back garden. All we need to do is take out one fence panel *here*' – she pointed again, to the right-hand side of the photo – 'and fix it back in place again afterwards. Well, I say *we*. I mean you.'

'It'll be a lot easier than doing it by parachute,' said Cal.

'And when Barbara gets back from her cruise, it'll all be done and dusted. Do you think you can manage to squeeze it in before the end of September?'

He smiled at the look of anticipation on her face. 'For you, we'll make sure we have it finished by then.'

Marion clapped her hands. 'Oh, you're a star, thank you so much!' She turned to Mimi. 'You've got yourself a lovely man there. Just make sure you hang on to him, OK? Don't let him go!'

'We aren't together,' Cal said hastily. 'Just friends.'

'Oh, I'm sorry. That *is* a shame.' Marion turned her appraising gaze to Mimi once more. 'Why not?'

As they made their way back to the centre of Tetbury, Mimi said, 'I can't wait until I'm that age. I'm going to go around saying anything I like, whatever crosses my mind. The more embarrassing it is, the more fun I'll have.'

Cal nodded. 'It's like being five years old again. One time, I was in the supermarket with Cora and she said, "Dad, that lady over there has a baby in her tummy and when the baby finds the hole it's going to come out!"

'Oh no.'

'She said it really loudly.'

'Oh *no.*'

'It was pretty awkward.' Cal's mouth twitched. 'The woman wasn't even pregnant.'

Fifteen minutes later, Mimi was upstairs in the dental surgery vigorously brushing her teeth before being called through for her appointment. A flash of sunflower yellow caught her eye through the frosted glass and she nudged the window open a few inches to see if it was what she thought it was.

Yes, there was Cal in his bright shirt, having settled himself at a table outside the café opposite. He'd ordered a coffee and was scribbling notes in his work diary as he simultaneously spoke on his mobile.

There was something about observing someone whilst they weren't aware of it. Mimi finished brushing her teeth, then peered around the side of the window again. No longer on the phone, Cal was now stretching his long legs out in front of him, stirring his coffee and engaging in conversation with the ancient owner of an equally ancient Jack Russell.

As he spoke, he reached down to scratch the dog's throat affectionately, and Mimi, watching from across the road, found herself lifting her own chin a fraction, wishing she were the little dog.

OK, when you found yourself secretly spying on someone from a dentist's bathroom and fantasising about being a geriatric Jack Russell, it definitely meant something.

Not to mention getting those squirly sensations going on in the pit of your stomach every time they smiled at you. And feeling your heart speed up every time you wondered what it would be like to kiss them.

Mimi swallowed. It was time to face facts. She definitely had a crush on Cal Mathieson.

Through the closed bathroom door, she heard the dental assistant enter the waiting room and call her name.

The dentist, once he'd examined her, said, 'And you're off abroad tomorrow, I hear?'

'Nnnggggh.' His gloved hands were still in her mouth.

'Well I'd say you got yourself here in the nick of time.' He sounded delighted. 'And you're in luck, because the next patient's cancelled. So we can get you all sorted out in one go!'

Chapter 17

It was over, finally. Mimi settled the bill and marvelled that something so horrible could cost quite so much. If life was fair, surely she should be the one getting paid for enduring that amount of torture.

Anyway, she'd been a grown-up and at least it was done now. She left the dental surgery and crossed the road to the café.

'I'm tho thorry . . .'

Cal looked up from the newspaper he'd been reading. He broke into a grin. 'Thorry?'

'Thorry it took tho long.' In her head, she was pronouncing the words with perfect clarity, but they weren't coming out that way. 'Ny 'ithdon dooth . . .' Mimi shook her head, because it was just too complicated to try and explain that her wisdom tooth had been growing at a bizarre angle, pressing hard against the tooth next to it, which was the one that had cracked down the middle, so the drill-happy dentist had repaired the broken tooth and yanked out the wisdom tooth, showing her the spoils of his plundering with a cheery 'Look at the roots on that!'

'You poor thing.' Cal was torn between sympathy and amusement. 'Your face is so swollen.'

'Feelth thwollen . . .' She cupped her jaw, wincing at the new shape of it.

'It's going to hurt later.'

'Thankth.'

'I'd ask if you wanted a coffee, but it's probably safer if you don't have one right now.' He drained his own cup and rose to his feet. 'Come on, we should get you home.'

And in the car on the way back to Goosebrook, because her ability to speak was hampered, Cal told her about the twists and turns in his life that had led to him running the company set up by his grandfather.

'I'd always wanted to be an architect,' he explained. 'I got a place at Bath to study for a BSc in architecture and started in the September. It was great, I loved it . . . then six months later my grandad had a stroke. It wasn't that severe, but it affected the right side of his body so he couldn't work any more. And he was distraught, because he'd spent the last thirty years building up the business. So he asked me to take it over because he just couldn't bear to see it sold to strangers.'

Mimi murmured, 'Oh . . .' because at least she could make a sympathetic noise without sounding like a complete Neanderthal.

'There wasn't anyone else he could ask,' Cal continued. 'And I loved my grandad. I didn't want to leave the course, but how could I turn him down? Since I was fourteen I'd been working with him during the school holidays. I owed him so much. So I gave up uni and took over the running of the business. And then I met Stacey. Well, you know the rest,' he said. 'Maybe I'd secretly wondered about one day going back and finishing the course, but it never did happen. Cora happened instead. Which we never regretted, obviously, although it came as a bit of a shock to the system when we first found out.'

Mimi tried to say: *Must have been scary*, but it came out as 'Nuthdadeehthcarghh.'

'Well, quite.' Cal grinned. 'Whatever that was, I completely agree with you. And OK, I didn't end up doing what I'd originally planned, but it didn't matter any more. Our priorities had changed. I concentrated on the business and built it up, and we bought the cottage and did that up too. Life was pretty busy, but it really couldn't have been better. We had Cora, and each other, and we were just . . . happy . . .'

His voice trailed away, because they both knew what had happened to change that.

'Cowth,' said Mimi as they rounded a bend in the road and saw the herd of Friesians ahead of them, slowly making their way from the field where they'd been grazing down to the farm for milking. Tails swished, flies were lazily dispersed and the farmhand behind them made a vague gesture of apology at the hold-up.

'Bet you didn't have to put up with this sort of thing in London,' said Cal.

'Nuurgh.' *God, listen to me.*

'Well there's no way past them, so we can either spend the next ten minutes crawling along at cattle speed or pull in here and wait.' As he said it, a cow at the back of the herd lifted her tail and splattered the road with poo.

'Let'th thtop,' said Mimi.

Cal parked the car in the next gateway and switched off the engine. Overhead, cotton wool clouds scudded across a

141

clear blue sky. Wild flowers and tall grasses swayed in the light breeze and bees buzzed like tiny drones as they darted from one flower to the next. Suddenly hyper-aware that Cal's tanned, muscular forearm was mere inches from her own, Mimi experienced a wild urge to reach for his hand, touch it with her fingers, feel the warmth of his blood beneath the skin.

Just as well he couldn't know what renegade thoughts she was thinking. Oh, but she'd missed him so much while he'd been away. And now that it was her turn to leave, she was going to miss him all over again . . .

'So anyway, I know the last few years have been hard.' Cal resumed the story he'd begun. 'But life goes on. And it does get better, thank God. Last year was an improvement on the year before, and this year is better than the last one. I used to think I'd never get over losing Stacey, but it's happening. I'm used to her not being here. I'm surviving without her.'

Mimi nodded. 'That'th goo.'

'I used to want to yell at people when they told me I'd meet someone else,' he continued drily. 'But I can cope with that now, because I suppose I want it to happen too. Whereas before I couldn't bear the thought of it.'

Another nod. As he gazed ahead through the windscreen, Mimi studied his profile in detail, taking in the way his sun-streaked hair fell across his forehead, the set of his jaw, the high curve of his cheekbone. Earlier, she'd observed him from a distance and now she was doing it close up. Suddenly Cal turned his head and looked straight at her, and the expression in his dark, thickly lashed eyes caused a fountain of butterflies to explode inside her ribcage.

'I was looking forward to painting you,' he said. 'We seem to have missed our chance. Maybe some other time, when you come back.'

Mimi had seen *Titanic* enough times to know that sometimes you just had to seize the moment. Look what had happened after Kate Winslet had told Leo's character to paint her like one of his French girls. Spurred into action, she said impetuously, 'Or we could do it tonight . . .'

Except it came out as: 'Orghhgudurghduergh.'

Of all the times to completely forget your mouth was numb and your tongue felt like a car tyre and you couldn't speak.

'What was that?' Cal frowned. 'You sound like Chewbacca.'

Maybe it was just as well he hadn't been able to understand. Mimi shrugged and shook her head, indicating that it really didn't matter.

'Oh you poor thing.' A flicker of a smile lifted the corners of his mouth as he studied her face. 'It's going to be agonising once the anaesthetic wears off. You're even more swollen now than you were when you came out of the surgery.' As he spoke, he moved closer and carefully moved a single strand of hair out of her field of vision. 'There, is that better? Sorry, it was about to go into your eye.' He paused, then lowered his hand a few inches and touched the side of her inflamed jaw. 'Can you feel that?'

Oh dear Lord . . .

Mimi did her best to swallow without making a gulpy noise. She shook her head a fraction. 'Nurgh.'

'How about this?' He moved his hand and she sensed that his fingertips were now brushing her cheek.

Another tremulous shake.

143

'You can't feel this at all?'

Mimi looked at him and silently shook her head for the third time. Was he remotely aware of the havoc he was causing in her body? Because she knew he was touching her lower lip now. And whilst it wasn't intended to be a seductive gesture – it was, she knew, purely in the spirit of exploration – she was beginning to feel very light-headed indeed.

Seriously, this much adrenalin overload couldn't be good for you.

If she were to close her eyes now, Cal could bend his head and kiss her on the mouth and she wouldn't even be able to tell it was happening.

Apart from the fact that she could sense him, and smell the faint clean scent of his cologne, and hear the regular sound of his breathing.

Silence.

More silence . . .

'Hey,' murmured Cal, and her eyes snapped open once more. Had it happened? Had he done it? Had he just kissed her and she'd completely missed it? He raised an eyebrow. 'Did you just fall asleep?'

'Nugh.'

He grinned, then reached past her to open the glove compartment. 'Here you go.'

Bemused, Mimi took the mini packet of Kleenex he was offering her. A split second later she realised why, and a shudder of mortification zapped down her spine.

Oh, the glamour.

'Thorry.' What else could you do but laugh? Even if it did involve gurgling yet more saliva and sounding like the

Elephant Man. When you were a hostage to excessive drool, it simply wasn't the time to be fantasising about taking a friendship to the next level.

'No need to apologise.' Cal's smile broadened. 'It's been fun. More fun for me than for you, admittedly. But this is a day I don't think either of us will forget in a hurry.'

You're not kidding. Mimi pulled a face and nodded mutely in agreement.

'Well, the cows will have reached the farmyard by now.' He checked his watch. 'The lane will be clear. And I need to be back before Cora gets home.'

Mimi nodded. Who knew how long it would be before they saw each other again? She dabbed at her mouth in case the drool had restarted and said, 'Let'th go.'

Chapter 18

'You're late,' said CJ when Mimi found him at the airport bar.

'No I'm not. I'm early. More to the point, so are you.' Checking his watch, Mimi saw that he'd reset it wrongly following his last flight; oh well, at least it meant they wouldn't miss this one. Expertly she reset the time, then nodded at the gin and tonic in his other hand. 'Speaking of early, is this a good idea?'

Ask a silly question.

CJ said, 'It's an excellent idea. Airport rules. When you're flying, it's allowed.'

He had a point; all around them, people were knocking back wine and downing pints of lager, despite the fact that it was nine fifteen in the morning. Mimi hopped onto the stool next to him. 'What time did you wake up?'

'Haven't been to bed yet. What can I get you to drink?'

'Flat white, please.'

'Coffee? Boring.'

'Someone has to look after you.' Just to remind him, Mimi said, 'It's kind of the reason you're paying me.'

146

'Turn your head.' CJ narrowed his eyes, made a twizzling gesture with his index finger. 'This way.'

She swivelled on her stool to face him and he did a double-take. 'Jesus, what happened? Who did that to you?'

'Someone with a big pair of pliers.'

'You're kidding. Was it your ex? Did you see him last night?' Outraged, CJ said, 'If you want me to have him dealt with, just say the word.'

This was evidently the trouble with being a crime novelist; your brain instantly conjured up the worst-case scenario. Tempting though it was to have Rob dealt with by a hired assassin, Mimi said, 'That's sweet of you, but it was my dentist.'

The flight was uneventful. CJ fell asleep before they'd even taken off and mercifully didn't snore. Once they'd passed through customs and left Palma airport, Mimi found them a taxi. As they travelled across the island, she went through the long list of instructions Willa had emailed her.

Honestly, it was going to be like looking after a delinquent chimpanzee.

'What's that?' CJ leaned over to try and get a look.

'Willa's rules for nursemaiding an author who doesn't like to do his job.'

'I hate writing. I love having written. Who said that?'

'You just did.'

He tutted. 'I mean who said it first? It's a quote. Look it up.'

'Please,' said Mimi.

'What?'

'If you're going to ask me to do something, it would be nice if you said please.'

'But I'm paying you. That means I don't have to.'

'It's called manners. Being polite. You pay me *and* you say it.'

CJ shook his head in disbelief. 'Don't worry. It was probably Ernest Hemingway, the miserable sod.' He closed his eyes for a few seconds, then snapped them open again. 'Arthur murdered his brother when he was eighteen.'

'Sorry?' Was he talking about one of Ernest Hemingway's relations? Or was Arthur someone he knew?

'It needs to go into the book.' CJ jabbed a finger at the phone in her lap. 'Come on, make a note. He killed his brother and made it look like an accident during a skiing holiday in the French Alps . . . no, wait, not there, let's do it at Lake Como. They were in a boat and he used fishing line as a garrotte.' Pause. 'Would fishing line do the job?'

'Maybe too thin and slippery.' Mimi was busy taking down everything he said. 'You'd need to get a proper grip.'

'He can slit his throat then. With the knife he was using to gut the fish. Find out what kind of fish live in that lake and if the knife would be serrated. But someone saw him do it. The gardener. Or the aunt. Are you getting all this?'

'Of course.' She'd been warned by Willa that this was how the creative process happened in CJ's case; plot details and vital snippets of dialogue could be blurted out at any moment and it was her job to save them, like a goalkeeper being bombarded from all angles by penalty shots.

'Even though I didn't say please?'

'I decided to let you off. Just this once.'

He winked at her before closing his eyes once more and sleeping the rest of the way to Puerto Pollensa. When they arrived, he lifted his head. 'Here we are then. Your home for the foreseeable future.'

'It wasn't Ernest Hemingway.' Mimi had looked up the quote while he'd been out for the count. 'It was Dorothy Parker.'

CJ said with a grin, 'I know. She was a miserable sod too.'

The nice thing about being a hugely successful thriller writer was the lifestyle it brought you. Mimi had already seen photos of the property online, but in real life it was even more impressive.

'Well?' CJ spoke with a touch of pride as she gazed at the dazzling white villa surrounded by manicured gardens overlooking the bay. 'What d'you think?'

'I think it's the kind of place I could never afford to stay in if I was on holiday. When I was growing up,' said Mimi, 'caravan parks were as good as it got.'

'When I was a kid, a holiday in a caravan was beyond our wildest dreams. We used to borrow a tent from our neighbours and spend a week camped out in Nan's back garden in Warrington.'

'Was it awful?'

'Are you kidding? It was the most brilliant adventure and we loved every minute, even when rats got into the tent and chewed holes in the airbed. But that was when I was seven and kept spiders in matchboxes for pets. Wouldn't want to do that now I'm old and rich.'

CJ wasn't *old*-old; he was only forty-three. But he was definitely rich-rich.

'Do you think you'd be a different person now if you hadn't become a writer?' It was something Mimi had wondered ever since their first encounter.

'You mean would I be more content? Poor but happy?' He looked appalled at the very idea. 'Not a chance in hell.'

'Actually, that wasn't what I meant. I wondered if you'd still be the way you are.'

CJ stared at her. 'You mean stroppy, bossy and selfish?'

'And rude,' Mimi reminded him. 'Don't forget rude.'

'If I was poor, I'd be bloody furious. And far more obnoxious than I am now. You'd better believe it.' He gave a bark of laughter. 'That's why I've hired you, and why it's in your best interests to keep me writing these damn books.'

The modern two-storey villa had been designed to make the most of the views of the sea and the mountains. The ground-floor apartment that had been Willa's was connected to the rest of the house but had its own separate entrance, which opened out onto the terrace.

'Here you are, this is yours. The housekeeper's been in, got everything ready for you.' CJ showed her the compact but spotless kitchen with its well-stocked fridge, the made-up bed, and the snowy bath towels in the white marble bathroom. 'Not too shabby, eh?'

From the small living room Mimi had a view of the glittering turquoise pool. For a moment she remembered sitting with Cal in the car yesterday, holding her breath as he'd leaned across and gently brushed a strand of hair away from her numb, swollen cheek. Today he was still in Gloucestershire, where, according to the weather app on her phone, it was now chucking it down with rain. Whilst here she was, in the lap of sun-splashed luxury, with the multi-millionaire CJ Exley.

She exhaled. She would so much rather be in Goosebrook with Cal, but work was work. And who was to say he would want her back there with him anyway? They were friends, she knew that much for sure, but the romantic overtures had only ever existed inside her own head.

Because when a man spoke as honestly and movingly as Cal had about the wife he'd loved and lost, it was hardly the done thing to hurl yourself at him, wrap yourself around him like a needy koala and eagerly offer yourself up as a replacement.

'You aren't saying anything.' CJ was looking offended. 'What's the problem? Not good enough for you?'

'Of course it's good enough. It's great.'

'I know, it's fucking amazing. I just hope you appreciate how lucky you are to be here.' He gave her a nudge to let her know that this time he was joking. 'Right, I'm going to take you to my favourite restaurant later, to show you I can be nice sometimes. I'll leave you to unpack and settle in. Make sure you're ready by seven, OK?'

At exactly seven o'clock, dressed in a white cotton frock and pink sandals, Mimi rang the bell and waited for CJ to come to the front door.

Nothing.

She called his mobile and heard it ringing inside the house.

Eventually, peering in through the living room window, she spotted him slumped across the ivory suede sofa with his eyes closed and his mouth hanging open.

Was he dead?

Dead drunk?

Who knew?

At the back of the villa, she found a small unlocked window and managed to squeeze through it.

'Wha . . . whassup?' With a groan, CJ half opened his eyes.

'I saw you through the window, thought I'd better check you were still alive.'

'Just about. What's the time?'

'Time for you to take me out for dinner, to show me you can be nice sometimes.'

CJ groaned again and rolled over. 'I'm not hungry. You go.'

Because sitting alone in a restaurant was always a delightful way to spend your first evening in a new country.

Mimi looked down at him, wishing even more fervently that she could be back in Goosebrook with Cal. Her empty stomach rumbled. Aloud, she said, 'Fine, I will.'

Chapter 19

It had been a somewhat rocky start. But as the days passed, they settled into a routine of sorts. The beauty of the coast-line and the perfect weather made it easy for Mimi to rise early each morning and go for a run along Puerto Pollensa's famous Pine Walk, followed by a swim in the crystalline sea. Once CJ was out of bed and had finished eating his break-fast on the terrace, it was her job to somehow trick him into getting some work done, whilst he did everything in his power to avoid doing it.

'You're a harridan,' he grumbled, when she switched off the Wi-Fi so he couldn't idle away the morning on the internet.

'I'm only a harridan because you're a hopeless case.' Mimi didn't take the insults personally. 'Your publisher needs a hundred thousand words by December and you need to buckle down. Now, I've typed up everything you wrote yesterday and here are the notes you fired at me last night.' She'd printed everything out for him, because CJ was a dinosaur who wrote his books by hand. 'If you need a coffee or a snack, don't get up, just call me and I'll bring it to you.'

Because she'd rapidly learned that if he went to make a coffee for himself, he'd then either go for a wander in the garden, or switch on the cinema-sized TV and become instantly engrossed in *Homes Under the Hammer.* 'You're not leaving this office until you've written a thousand words.'

'Nag nag nag.'

'The sooner they're done, the sooner you can stop for lunch.'

CJ heaved a sigh and looked down at the fat A4 writing pad on his desk. 'I hate this.'

'I know, but you won't hate it once you get going.'

He gazed mournfully past her. 'Is Eddie blind in his left eye or his right?'

'He's blind in his right eye.' This was the new character he'd introduced three chapters ago. 'And his name's Eric.'

'Just testing you.'

'Of course you were. Time to get busy now.'

'Right. I'm going to make a start. You can close the door behind you.'

Mimi held out her hand, palm up. Reluctantly, having thought she might forget to confiscate it, CJ took out his phone and passed it over.

'Thank you. *Now* I'll close the door.'

While he was in his office, Mimi set up her laptop in the kitchen and began working her way through all the tasks that needed addressing. She tackled a long list of emails, then replied to the day's fan mail. In order to run CJ's social media accounts she'd had to learn to write in his voice, albeit a more avuncular and friendly voice than the real one, because telling people to fuck off if they dared to point out mistakes or criticise his books wouldn't be doing him any

154

favours. A couple of years ago, whilst briefly allowed to write his own tweets, he'd got himself embroiled in a ferocious altercation with a boxing champion that had ended up being splashed all over the *Daily Mail* online.

She spent the next two hours responding to messages from CJ's readers, adding content to his website, setting up a competition and uploading photos from a literary festival he'd attended in Brazil.

At midday, she took him a coffee and a plate of fruit.

'How many words?'

He raked his fingers through his already raked-up hair. 'Thirty-four.'

'Seriously?'

'Trust me, I've counted them enough times.'

Mimi said, 'You're going to be stuck here for the next week.'

'I'd be OK,' CJ exploded with frustration, 'if I just knew what's meant to happen next.'

'Get on with it,' said Mimi.

Two hours later, she quietly pushed open the door to the office to see if he'd fallen asleep.

'One thousand four hundred words.' CJ was triumphant as he gestured grandly at the sheets of A4 paper littering the floor, all covered in his terrible, barely legible writing.

'Are they good words?'

'The very best.' He was a changed man; the tension in his neck and spine had visibly subsided and he actually looked happy, at peace with himself, as if the weight of the world had floated off his shoulders. Spreading his arms wide, he said simply, 'I worked out what needed to happen next.'

'Brilliant.' Mimi gave an approving nod. 'Would you like me to bring you another coffee?'

He recoiled in horror. 'I wouldn't like that at all. The words are done. I thought we'd go out and celebrate.'

Willa had warned her about this before she'd started, and Mimi had grown proficient at heading CJ off at the pass, but still he persisted in trying it on, like a puppy in search of treats.

'Listen, you're in the zone.' She used her coaxing voice. 'If you stop now, you won't start again. You're behind schedule and you know how much you hate that feeling, so doesn't it make more sense to keep going while you're on a roll and see how much more you can get down on paper?'

'But—'

'Words in the bank.' Mimi stared him down. 'You know it makes sense.'

'You're heartless.'

'Thanks.'

'Worse than Willa.'

Mimi shrugged. 'Or you could say I was better than Willa.'

'I hate you. Remind me again why I took you on?'

'To look after you and make sure you write your books. Because if you don't,' said Mimi, 'you'll mess up your publisher's schedule and they'll start to resent you, then they'll refuse to renew your contract and *then* the royalty cheques will stop rolling in and you'll have to sell this villa and find a proper job, except you're basically unemployable . . . oh, and you won't be getting any attention from pretty women any more either. You won't see them for dust.'

'Bloody hell.' CJ shook his head. 'Now I *really* hate you.'

'We could go out for dinner tonight if you want.'

He looked pained. 'I'm hungry now.'

'No worries.' Magnanimous in victory, Mimi said, 'I'll make you some cheese on toast.'

Later that evening, in a buoyant mood because his word count for the day had ended up hitting the magical three thousand mark, CJ said, 'Thanks for today. I don't hate you any more.'

'Until tomorrow.'

'Well, obviously, goes without saying. But I need you there. I just do.'

He did. Some authors, Mimi knew, couldn't wait to leap out of bed and switch on their computers each morning, all ready to start work; they loved every minute and happily rattled off thousands of words, oblivious to the passage of time and not even wanting to tear themselves away at the end of the day. Whereas CJ, at the opposite end of the eagerness spectrum, would do almost anything to avoid the task in hand. Employing someone to force him to work might sound extreme, but it was really no different from those reluctant exercisers who paid a fortune for personal trainers to come to their home, bully them out of bed and beat them with sticks until they'd done their quota of planks and star jumps.

She wasn't a luxury item, she was a necessity.

'Whatever works for you,' Mimi told him.

'And how are you liking it out here? Is it bearable?'

They were sitting outside one of his favourite beachfront restaurants with lights reflecting off the satin-calm water whilst locals and late-season tourists made their evening promenade along the Pine Walk behind them.

Mimi paused. 'This place is great.' And it was, but there was no denying that it would be nicer if CJ weren't the only person she knew here. Working all day up at the villa and having no one to talk to other than him was a bit—

'Eddie hijacks the helicopter and shoots the pilot with the gun he stole from Maria's grandfather.'

Mimi dutifully wrote it down. 'You know, you could make these notes yourself. You'd just need to dictate everything onto your phone and let me transcribe it afterwards.'

'Tried it. Kept pressing the wrong buttons. Anyway, don't complain.' He sat back, assessing her. 'So you're going to stick this out, are you? Not planning to bugger off back home and leave me high and dry?'

'I'm not going to bugger off home,' said Mimi. 'And his name's still Eric.'

'Couldn't we just change it to Eddie?'

'No. You had an Eddie in your last book.'

Twenty minutes later, while CJ was away from the table visiting the bathroom, a text arrived on her phone from Lois.

Hi, hope all good with you. Just letting you know I'm getting out of Goosebrook for a while. Looks like me and Felix are headed for a break. We need some space, anyway. Sorry, bit pissed, don't really know what to do. Miss you. X

Mimi looked over at CJ, held up on his way back to the table by a family of British holidaymakers who'd recognised him. Crossing her fingers, she hoped he'd be nice to them.

When he rejoined her several minutes later, CJ said, 'See? I was polite.'

'Well done you.'

'Bloody well done me.' He gave a snort of derision. 'They buy one paperback and share it around the seven of them.'

'It's what families do. Some people can't afford to buy seven copies.'

'They kept telling me I was their favourite author.'

'Isn't that brilliant?' Mimi nodded encouragingly.

'Not really. They thought I was Ian Rankin. Don't laugh.' CJ scowled. 'It's not funny.'

'It kind of is, though. And his books are fantastic.'

'Not as fantastic as mine.'

This was debatable.

'Listen to me. Next time you're interviewed on TV, talk about what just happened.'

'Are you crazy?' CJ was so appalled he almost spilled his drink.

'It's endearing to tell a story against yourself,' Mimi assured him.

'I don't want to tell a story against myself. That just makes me look like a big loser. I want to tell stories that make me sound *great*.'

'Everyone will love you for it, though.'

'Everyone will think I'm a complete fucking failure.'

Mimi said, 'Trust me, one of us is an expert when it comes to public relations. And it isn't you.'

'Hmm. We'll see.'

Which meant there wasn't a snowball's chance in hell of it happening. Some people simply weren't capable of doing self-deprecating. Not for the first time, Mimi idly wondered if this particular character trait had something to do with CJ's upbringing, but she already knew from experience that he didn't speak about that. When questioned, he glossed over his childhood, claiming it was simply too uneventful to discuss. Not much money but plenty of fun, that was as far as he'd go, as much detail as he was prepared to impart. Basically, he always maintained, because people's childhoods were always so bloody boring to hear about.

'Would you like me to change the subject?' said Mimi.

'Please do, because there's no way I'm going on TV to make a tit of myself.'

'Am I allowed to have a friend come out to visit me?'

CJ's eyebrows lowered. 'Are you talking about someone dropping by for a quick cup of tea?' He mimed lifting a cup, little finger daintily held aloft. 'Or is this someone coming to stay with you in your apartment?'

'Stay,' said Mimi.

The scowl deepened. 'Is it that bastard ex of yours?'

'*What?* No!'

'Oh. Who, then? New bloke?'

'No bloke at all. It's my friend from Goosebrook. She's going through a bad patch with her husband and could really do with a break.'

'Does that mean she's going to be crying and wailing the whole time?'

'God, listen to yourself,' Mimi declared. 'Such empathy. She won't cry all the time, OK? And if she ever does cry, I promise you won't have to witness it. She's my friend, not yours. You don't even have to speak to her if you don't want to.'

'Fine then.' CJ shrugged. 'She can come and stay.'

'You're such a ray of sunshine.'

'She'd better not throw herself at me, that's all.'

'She's married. And you're no George Clooney,' Mimi retorted.

'Ah, but I'm me. CJ Exley, worldwide best-selling author. The moment she claps eyes on the villa, I'll magically become more attractive, you wait and see.'

'No offence,' said Mimi, 'but I don't think you will.'

While CJ was ordering another bottle of wine, she texted Lois back: *Want to fly over and stay with me for a bit?*

Within seconds, Lois's reply flashed up: *That would be amazing. YES PLEASE!!! How soon can I come?*

Chapter 20

Eighteen hours later, Lois arrived on the doorstep.

'Mimi, hoorayyyy! Oh my God, you're a *lifesaver*.' She flung her thin arms around Mimi. 'Thank you so much, you have no idea how desperate I was for something like this to happen. I didn't even realise it myself, I just knew I had to get away . . . and look at this place, it's like paradise!' Taking a step back, she held Mimi at arm's length. 'Look at you too, all glowy and gorgeous. Are you having the best time ever? Have you met someone? Ooh, is he a flashing-eyed Spaniard?'

'I haven't met anyone.' Amused by Lois's train of thought, Mimi said, 'Haven't had time. Too busy working.'

'And how's it going, having to spend so much time with the stroppy author? I want to hear all the gory details . . . is he still a complete monster?'

Behind her, the partially opened window of CJ's office was flung wide and CJ bellowed, 'Yes, he *is* still a complete monster, chiefly because he has to put up with other people being rude and fucking ungrateful when he's generously allowed them to stay at his luxury fucking villa.'

Whoops, Lois mouthed. She turned to CJ. 'Hi, sorry about that, but you have to admit your reputation precedes you.' She made her way over to him and thrust her outstretched hand through the open window. 'Anyway, I'm sure you can't be as bad as everyone says. But if you'd rather I booked myself into a hotel, it's no problem at all. I can do that.'

They shook hands. 'What happened to your face?' said CJ.

Mimi closed her eyes. Why did he have to be like this?

'Just my face?' Lois gestured to the scars on her neck, across her chest and down her arm. 'I have plenty more I can show you, if you're interested.'

'Tell me, then.'

'Car accident.'

'Ah.' CJ nodded, belatedly putting two and two together. 'You're the one who got out alive.'

'You do have a way with words,' said Lois.

'Mimi didn't tell me it was you, that's all.' His gaze flickered over her jeans, noting the prosthetic foot. 'So you're leaving your husband, I hear. Not rich enough for you?'

She held his gaze. 'If anything, too rich.'

'You don't look heartbroken.'

'That's because Mimi warned me I wasn't allowed to cry in your presence. This is my brave face. Look,' said Lois, 'am I staying here or getting a hotel room? Because I need to know—'

'Don't be such a drama queen.' CJ's tone was curt. 'Of course you're staying.'

'Thanks.' Lois indicated the oversized case standing on the drive where it had been deposited by the taxi driver.

'Now, does Mimi have you locked in that room or do you think you could come out and give me a hand with this?'

'Bit different to home,' said Lois.

Mimi smiled. 'Definitely not so many sheep.'

They were sitting on the beach, dry sand sifting through their toes. The sun was setting behind them, turning the mountains across the bay rosy pink, and tantalising smells of seafood and garlic from nearby restaurants filled the air.

'You've only been here a month. It seems like so much longer.' Lois flipped back her blonde hair and propped herself up on her elbows to watch the last swimmers in the mirror-like water. 'I've missed you.'

'I've missed you too. It's weird only having CJ for company.'

'Weird? Torture, more like.'

'At least I get paid to put up with him.' Mimi changed the subject, because Lois was longing to talk about her marriage, she could tell. 'So what's been going on with you and Felix?'

'Urrrgh.' Lois let out a wail of frustration and threw herself flat on the sand. 'This is going to be so boring for you. I hate moany people and I hate being the moany one, but is it OK if I have a really selfish moan? Could you bear to listen, if I'm quick about it?'

'Hey, you've come all this way. Take as long as you like.'

'Right, you know the kaftan you sent me for my birthday? Hot pink silk with violet crystals around the neckline?'

'Yes . . .' Had it shrunk drastically in the wash?

'I loved it,' Lois said simply. 'I still love it to bits. I've worn it practically non-stop . . . it's so *me*.'

'Well that's great! I bought it in a little boutique not far

164

from here, so we can go and look at the rest of them tomorrow.'

'D'you know what Henrietta gave me?' Pause. 'A mustard and grey tweed skirt.'

'Oh,' said Mimi.

'But you know what? It's Henrietta and that's what she's like, so I didn't let it bother me. And at least I knew I had a fantastic present to come from Felix, because a while back he'd said something about not knowing what to get me and I'd seen this amazing pair of Tiffany sunglasses in a magazine . . . I mean, really expensive but it was love at first sight. So I told him to look at page seventy-eight in *Red* magazine and he was delighted not to have to worry about it any more.'

Mimi couldn't help noticing that Lois wasn't wearing sunglasses from Tiffany. 'And . . .?'

'So then it was time for Felix to give me his present and it was in a great big box, but I just thought he'd wrapped the sunglasses up in a dressing gown or something to make me think he hadn't bought them for me. Except it turned out he really *hadn't* bought them for me. Instead, he got me the most horrible coat you've ever seen in your life. It was egg-shaped and modern, the colour of baby poo, with these bizarre hand-knitted brown bobbles sewn randomly all over it. It was everything I hate in a coat – and I mean everything anyone in their right mind would hate in a coat – and there was Felix looking all pleased with himself.'

'But why?' Mimi was baffled. 'Why did he buy it for you?'

Lois sighed. 'Because he looked at page eighty-seven instead of seventy-eight.'

'Oh no! So it was a complete accident. He didn't do it on purpose.'

'I know, I do know that. And he was mortified when he realised he'd got it wrong. But . . . oh, and now I'm going to sound like a spoilt brat whining about not getting the present she wanted, but it's really not that.' From her prone position on the sand, Lois stretched out her hands in despair. 'I just don't understand how he could look at that photo in the magazine and think for one second that I'd ever want to own a coat like that. It felt like he doesn't know me at all . . . or he just doesn't care enough to think it through and check that there hasn't been some kind of mistake. I mean, if he'd turned to page eighty-seven and seen an advert for a motorbike or an electric trouser press or a lifetime's supply of incontinence knickers, would he have gone ahead and ordered those too? D'you know what, I think he would. Anything so he could stop having to worry about it and get the boring present-buying business out of the way.'

Oh poor Felix. Mimi said, 'I think some men just panic because they're scared of getting it wrong.'

'You're defending him, like everyone else does. They're all on his side. Because they like him and feel sorry for him being stuck with me.'

'Oh now that's not true.' Turning sideways to look at her, Mimi saw a tear leak out from beneath Lois's Ray-Bans and disappear into her ear. 'And there's more to this than a bad coat.'

'Damn, I don't have a tissue . . .' Sitting up slightly, Lois used her wrist to wipe the side of her face.

'I've got some.' Mimi scrabbled in the bottom of her bag for the cellophane pack she always carried. As she found it, a shadow fell across the sand.

'Blubbing already?' said CJ.

'Are you stalking us?' Lois snapped back.

'I looked out of my bedroom window and saw you out here on the beach. Hardly counts as stalking. In fact you'll be amazed to know that I came down here to invite you both to have dinner with me.'

She regarded him with suspicion. 'Why would you want to do that?'

'To make up for being rude earlier,' said CJ. 'To show you I can be nice when I set my mind to it.'

'And?' prompted Lois.

He looked amused. 'Perspicacious. I like that in a woman. OK, and because I'm a writer, which means I'm interested to hear about your situation.'

'You mean you're bloody nosy,' grumbled Lois. 'Which restaurant would you be taking us to?'

'It's called Stay.'

She nodded approvingly. 'I've been reading up about it on TripAdvisor. OK.'

By eight o'clock, they were seated at CJ's favourite table outside the restaurant. Over drinks, he heard the story of the bad coat.

'Did you return it to the shop?'

'I would have done, but Truman did a wee on it.'

'Truman. Who's that, the family butler?'

Lois raised an eyebrow. 'My mother-in-law's cat. I think Henrietta speaks to him in cat language and instructs him to do things that will make my life more miserable.' She shrugged and cast a fleeting glance at the people seated at the next table. 'Anyway, the coat can't go back. I'll have to

167

get it cleaned then take it to the local charity shop. Bit of a waste of five hundred quid, but there you go.'

'I googled you earlier,' CJ announced.

'You did? Why?'

'Why does anyone google anyone? To find out more about them. There are some pretty amazing photos of you online.'

'I wouldn't call them amazing,' said Lois. 'I'm a mess.'

CJ took out his phone and showed her the screenshot he'd saved. 'This one, taken before the accident. You and your future husband together at a charity ball.'

Lois glanced at it, then looked away. 'Oh well, that's when I *was* amazing.'

He showed Mimi the photo of Lois, utterly fabulous in a scarlet Jessica Rabbit dress and sapphire-blue stilettos. Her blonde hair was pulled back from her face in a high chignon and she was laughing, whilst Felix, next to her, looked on with open adoration. CJ said, 'Let me guess, you don't wear your hair up any more. You keep it covering as much of your face as possible.'

Lois poured more wine into her glass. 'Well spotted, Sherlock.'

'And you chose to sit in that chair because it's where people are less likely to notice you.'

'You're lucky. Sometimes I sit in restaurants with a brown paper bag on my head.'

'You haven't run away from your husband because he bought you the wrong birthday present,' said CJ.

'Haven't I?'

'When the two of you first got together, you were the adored and Felix was the adorer. You were the stunning, extrovert party girl and he couldn't believe his luck because he'd never been out with anyone like you before. Basically, you had the upper hand. Then the accident happened and everything changed. You nearly died, you went through a tough time in hospital and you lost—'

'My looks,' Lois countered evenly. 'My leg. My confidence. It's not rocket science.'

'I was going to say you'd lost the balance of the scales being tipped in your favour. How you feel now is how Felix felt before the accident.'

'Except he was rich,' Lois pointed out. 'Which meant he always had girls interested in him even if it was for the wrong reason. *You* should know all about that,' she added pointedly.

'Of course I do. It's the way the world turns. It's also the reason I'm single.' CJ pushed the rocket leaves on his plate to one side. 'Before the accident, were you faithful to Felix?'

She bristled. 'Yes.'

'You didn't sleep with other men?'

'No!'

'Did you flirt with them?'

Lois blinked. 'Maybe sometimes. A bit.'

'Hey, I've seen the photos.' He tapped his phone's screen. 'Trust me, I can tell. And it's not a criticism either. If I looked like you did back then, I'd flirt too.'

Mimi watched as Lois managed a rueful smile. Somehow, against all the odds, CJ was managing for once not to be offensive.

'I loved to flirt,' Lois admitted. 'It brightened my day, made me feel great. It was like a fabulous harmless drug, my favourite hobby . . . you meet an attractive man and just get that zingy feeling. There's nothing else like it.'

169

'What about men who weren't attractive?' said CJ.

'They didn't give me that zingy feeling.'

'So you wouldn't bother to flirt with them.'

'No, I wouldn't.'

'Would you have flirted with me?'

'Honestly? No.' Lois shook her head. 'Sorry.'

'No worries.' CJ dismissed the apology. 'And when was the last time you flirted with someone?'

'Well, that would have been on the day of the accident.'

With a jolt, Mimi realised the extent to which Lois's life had altered. 'Not even Paddy?' she said.

Lois put down her fork. 'Are you kidding? Especially not Paddy.'

'Who's that?' said CJ.

'The good-looking one who used to flirt with me the most. But who now treats me like some fragile spinster aunt, because why would he even want to be seen playing flirty games with someone who looks like this?' She shrugged as she said it, which only made the underlying pain all the more apparent.

'Tough,' CJ conceded. 'You know what you need to do, don't you?'

'I'm sure you're about to tell me.'

'Lower your standards,' said CJ. 'I mean, big-time.'

'That's fantastic advice.' Lois nodded. 'So reassuring. I feel miles better now.'

'But you're not being realistic, are you? I'm just giving you some practical advice. Being honest.'

'You're just being horrible,' said Lois.

'Hey, give me a break, I'm making an effort here. More of an effort than I usually make.' He gestured towards himself. 'If you need someone to practise on, feel free.'

170

'*Practise* on?' Mimi covered her eyes and groaned. This was too much.

'I mean flirting,' said CJ. 'I don't sleep with other men's wives.'

'Even so,' said Lois, 'no thanks.'

Chapter 21

The following afternoon, CJ was heading out to meet up with a couple of expat friends who lived in the hills above Pollensa Old Town. As he left the villa, he waved and called out, 'You have fun, girls. Behave yourselves.'

When the waiting taxi had borne him away, Lois said, 'That man's a piece of work.'

Mimi shrugged. 'I did warn you.'

'Anyhow, now he's out of the way, I can have a swim.'

They were lying on the yellow padded sunloungers beside the pool. They might be into October now, but the temperature was still up in the high twenties, perfect for sunbathing. Even Mimi, with her naturally pale skin, had managed to build up a light golden tan. She watched as Lois peeled off her top and jeans to reveal the pink bikini underneath, then sat down at the edge of the pool and removed her prosthetic leg. Leaving it on the side, she eased herself down into the clear water and did a dolphin dive beneath the surface before setting out for the far end of the pool.

The taxi, racing back in through the entrance gates, screeched to a halt at the top of the driveway before Mimi was able to put down her mug of tea and scramble off her sunlounger. She called out, 'CJ's back,' but Lois, still swimming underwater, was unable to hear a thing.

To reach the front door, CJ had to make his way past the pool. 'Can you believe it?' he said. 'Left my damn phone upstairs.'

The next moment, like a seal, Lois popped her head out of the water at the other end of the pool. Spotting CJ, she let out a spluttery yelp of dismay and ducked back beneath the surface.

Which entertained CJ enough to cause him to stand and wait until the need to breathe brought her back up again.

'What's the problem?' He grinned at her.

'I don't want you looking at me.'

'See this beach?' He indicated the endless stretch of sand beyond the perimeter wall. 'I'm used to seeing girls in bikinis.'

'But they aren't covered in scars,' said Lois, 'and they probably have the usual number of legs.'

'Is this why you only swim when I'm not around? Because you don't want me to see your leg?'

'Not just you. Anyone. I don't love looking like this,' Lois said defensively. 'It doesn't feel great.'

'Have you ever watched the Paralympics? The athletes competing in the swimming competitions? They aren't bothered by the way their arms and legs look. They don't care, they just get out there and go for it.'

'I know they do, and good for them, but I don't feel that way about my leg and I'm allowed to be self-conscious and not want people staring at it.'

'Which is why you always keep it covered up.' CJ nodded.

'Don't lecture me. You can't have any idea what it's like.'

'How about your husband? Has he kissed your leg and told you it's beautiful?'

'Of course he hasn't.' Lois visibly recoiled. 'Because it isn't beautiful, it's a mess.'

'In your opinion,' said CJ.

He collected his phone from the villa and left for the second time. Lois had the rest of her swim in peace. Then she climbed out of the pool and rejoined Mimi. With her prosthetic leg fitted back into place once more and her Ray-Bans covering her eyes, she lay back on her sunlounger and said, 'He wants us to have a baby.'

'*What?*' Mimi yelped, stunned. 'CJ?'

'Oh my God, no! I'm talking about *Felix*.'

Mimi burst out laughing. 'When you said it, I was just thinking about CJ, but your option makes more sense.'

'Can you imagine having a baby with CJ?' Lois pulled a face and reached for her iced water.

'Never mind that. Can you imagine having one with Felix?'

Lois heaved a sigh. 'I could. But I don't want a sticking-plaster baby. We shouldn't have one just to try and keep our marriage together.' She paused. 'You know that thing CJ said about Felix kissing my stump and telling me it was beautiful? Do you think any man would ever really do that?'

Mimi looked at her; it was the question she'd been thinking about too.

'I don't know. Maybe.' What could she say? Felix evidently hadn't done it, so would it be cruel to say yes? 'Everyone's different . . . some people find it easier to deal with things like that. But honestly, it's not as awful as you think it is.'

174

How she longed to be able to lessen the turmoil in Lois's head. 'It's just a healed-over scar, maybe bigger than we're used to seeing, but not scary. After a while, you don't notice it or think about the way it looks any more. It's just a part of you.'

'I can't bear people looking at it. I don't even like seeing it myself. It's bearable at the hospital because the nurses are used to all sorts.' Lois gestured between Mimi and herself. 'And I can cope now because it's just the two of us and I feel safe with you. But no one else gets to see it.'

'Except Felix.'

Lois swallowed, shook her head. 'I wear a long nightie in bed. It stays covered.'

Mimi spoke tentatively. 'But what about . . .?'

'The lights stay off. He's never touched that part of my leg.' She didn't even like to say the word *stump*, Mimi realised. 'It's the thing we don't talk about.'

'But you should,' Mimi said gently. She felt for Lois.

'I just can't. Men can be squeamish. I don't want to hear Felix say he finds it grotesque to look at. And if he lied and said he didn't . . . well, then I'd know he was lying and that'd be even worse.'

'But he still loves you. You're married. He wants a baby with you.'

'Or he feels sorry for me, or he feels guilty because his father was the one driving the car.' Lois paused and sighed. 'Or he feels stuck with me and thinks a baby might help to take his mind off how trapped he is.'

It was the fourth day of Lois's stay. Mimi wanted nothing more than to ask her about Cal, but the subject hadn't arisen

175

and she'd forced herself not to be the one to oh-so-casually mention him first.

Oh, but she'd been longing to know what was going on in his life.

And now it looked as if she could be about to find out. Her mobile was playing its jaunty tune and the caller name flashing up on the screen was Cal. They'd exchanged numbers years ago, shortly after the accident, but he'd never phoned or texted her before, so she hadn't messaged him either.

Until today.

Her heart racing at three times the speed of the ringtone, Mimi pressed answer and said, 'Hello?' as if she'd been too busy to glance at the screen.

'Mimi? Hi, it's Cal. Is this a good time to call, or are you rushed off your feet?'

Oh, the sound of his voice, the beautiful *timbre* of it. She had to hold the phone away from her mouth in case she accidentally sighed with delight.

'Hi! Sorry, I was in the middle of something . . . No, it's fine.'

'Are you sure? Because I can call back later.'

'No, no, just dealing with a psychopath who's carved up a Russian double agent and fed his liver to the family cat.'

'As you do.' He was smiling now, she could tell. Mimi wondered where he was calling from; it was hard to picture someone at the other end of the phone when you didn't know if they were lazing in front of the TV or striding across the fields with their dog or reclining naked in a hot bath.

OK, he probably wasn't naked in the bath. But it was a nice idea.

Aloud, she said lightly, 'All in an afternoon's work. Mind you, deciphering CJ's handwriting keeps me on my toes. I thought he'd cut up a fiver and was frying the pieces in a pun whilst skating round the kitchen in a piddle of blood.'

And hearing Cal's laughter took her back to the hot bath scenario, listening hopefully for background sounds of splashing water.

'It's a tough job but someone has to do it.' The tone of his voice softened. 'How are things really? All going OK?'

'Not too bad. Puerto Pollensa's fabulous, the weather's brilliant and CJ's bark is worse than his bite.' Wriggling onto her favourite high stool in the kitchen, Mimi heard herself say brightly, 'Speaking of barks, how's Otto?'

Oh God, so lame.

'Otto's great.'

'And Cora?'

'Better than great.' The warmth and love for his daughter was plain to hear in Cal's voice.

'Of course she is.' Glimpsing her reflection in the screen of her laptop, Mimi realised she was grinning like an idiot; just as well they weren't on Skype. 'And how are things going with you?' She'd managed to get the tone right, thank goodness: friendly and interested, but not too interested. Not in an I-dream-of-you-every-night kind of way.

Well, it wasn't *every* night.

'All going pretty well, thanks.' Cal sounded cheerful. 'In fact something interesting happened yesterday. I've accepted my first painting commission.'

'What? That's amazing!' Mimi was genuinely delighted for him. 'I thought you said you weren't ready. What changed your mind?'

177

'Well, I suppose it felt like fate. A friend posted photos of a few of my paintings on Instagram and they were seen by some footballer's wife. The next thing I know, she was calling me up, asking me to do a portrait of her and her family. I said I wasn't ready to do that and she couldn't believe I was turning her down – she took it like a personal insult. Before I knew what was happening, she was pretty much telling me to name my price.'

'Wow.'

'I know, right? Talk about surreal. So I drove over to Windsor yesterday to meet up with her and the kids. Showed her some of my other work, half expecting her to back out. But she didn't. And we fixed up a couple of dates.'

'Oh *wow*,' Mimi said again, a bit squeakily.

Cal sounded amused. 'Ha, not that kind of date. Appointments to get the preliminary sketches done.'

'Well that's great.' *OK, get a grip.* 'Who's she married to?'

'His name's Darren May. He plays for—'

'Yes, I've heard of him. Gosh, this could be your big break.'

'Or my biggest humiliation if it all goes horribly wrong.' Cal's tone was rueful. 'We'll just have to see how it turns out. Anyway, so that's my news, but the main reason I'm calling is about Lois.'

'Ah, OK.' Of course there had to be another reason; he hadn't rung her number at long last because the urge to hear her voice again had become simply too overwhelming to resist.

'Felix asked me to speak to you. He wants to know what's happening with Lois, and when she's coming home.'

'Does that mean he's missing her?'

'Oh come on,' said Cal. 'Of course he's missing her.'

Ten minutes later, after wishing him luck with the commissioned portrait and discovering via Google that Darren May's wife Lara was very pretty indeed, Mimi ended the call. She sat back and tipped her head from side to side, aware that the nape of her neck was still prickling and damp with perspiration as a result of just speaking to Cal on the phone.

The door to the kitchen opened and CJ stood in the doorway with a crooked grin on his face and an empty whisky tumbler in his hand.

'Who was that?'

'None of your business. And isn't it a bit early to be hitting the Scotch?'

'It's last night's tumbler. I'd always wondered if holding a glass against a door actually did help you to eavesdrop on conversations.' CJ was blithely unrepentant. 'And guess what? It does. Come on, tell me who you were talking to.'

'Just a friend.'

'A friend you sound pretty keen on.'

Oh God, had she sounded keen? Mimi felt herself redden. 'He called to ask about Lois.'

'Is he interested in you, though?' CJ thought for a second. 'I suppose not, otherwise I'd have heard about him. Or he'd have been over here to visit you.'

This was mortifying, but all she could do was brazen it out. 'And if I was that keen on him, I wouldn't have moved out here to work for you, would I?'

'Touché.' CJ's wink told her he'd been teasing all along, which hopefully meant she hadn't made a fool of herself by sounding like a besotted fangirl on the phone to Cal.

She gave him her Cruella look and said coolly, 'I think

that's quite enough eavesdropping, don't you? Time you got back to work.'

'Whatever you say, boss.' Still chuckling to himself, CJ turned to leave. Just before the kitchen door swung shut, Mimi heard him whisper in a high voice meant to mimic hers: 'Hi! Wow! Oh wow!'

Bastard. Reaching for her laptop, she brought up more images of Darren May, his stunning wife Lara and their two wildly photogenic young children.

Cal wasn't hers; he never had been hers. Mimi knew that only too well, but a tiny flame of jealousy still flickered inside her ribcage. She was only human, after all.

On the reassuring side, at least Lara and Darren's bond appeared to be a famously secure one. And when you were married to a multimillionaire Premiership footballer, you were unlikely to risk everything for a fling with a just-starting-out unfamous portrait artist.

At least, let's hope so.

Chapter 22

There he was. Mimi's breath caught in her throat, because seeing him in real life was so much better than just picturing him in her mind.

She watched from her bedroom window as Otto, tail wagging madly, bounced through the fallen leaves as if he were on springs. Locating the orange frisbee Cal had just thrown, he grabbed it in his mouth and did a quick victory lap around the frosted village green before returning to drop it back at Cal's feet.

Mimi hastily wiped the glass with her sleeve, where her breath had misted it up. It was the fourth of November, just over two months since she'd last seen Cal, one month since they'd spoken on the phone. He was wearing a dark blue rugby shirt and jeans, and his blonde hair was less sun-streaked now. As she leaned her elbows on the windowsill, a quiver ran across her shoulders and down her spine, and she couldn't work out if it was due to the temperature in the air or the sight of Cal.

Oh, but look at those legs, that *body* . . .

The next moment, almost as if she'd said it aloud and he'd heard her, Cal turned and looked up at her window.

Mimi's heart went into instant gallop mode but she resisted the urge to duck down. Because that would be ridiculous and anyway he'd already seen her. His eyes widened and he held out his hands in disbelief. Which felt fantastic, because he looked genuinely delighted to see her. And now he was signalling to her to open the window. The last time she'd done that, she'd managed to throw her bra and knickers at him. On this occasion she managed it without mishap.

'Well this is a surprise,' Cal called up. 'Nobody told me you were back.'

'Nobody knows. Marcus picked me up from Bristol airport late last night.' Remembering with a jolt the way CJ had made fun of her after eavesdropping on their last phone conversation, Mimi deliberately didn't let her voice go high-pitched and over-keen. 'I'm just back for a couple of days. Time off for good behaviour.'

He laughed. 'Anything you want to chuck down to me?'

'Maybe not.' See? Not remotely eager or flirtatious.

'Are you decent?' said Cal.

Well I try my best. Aloud, she said, 'Sorry?'

'Clothes. I can't tell if you've just got out of bed or are already dressed. Because if you're dressed, why don't you join us? Look at Otto – he's missed you!'

Was this Cal being flirty? Or simply as charming-in-a-platonic-way as he'd always been? Because Otto might be gazing up at her with interest but he clearly wasn't on the verge of exploding with excitement. A happy tail-wag was as far as it went.

'Give me two minutes,' said Mimi, 'and I'll be down.'

Let's be honest, the answer was never going to be no. The greeting was more enthusiastic once she reached them. Otto barked with delight, scrabbled his front paws against Mimi's jeans and optimistically pushed his nose into her hand in search of treats.

Cal grinned. 'Told you he'd missed you.'

Yes, but what about you?

Mimi said, 'I've missed him too. Hello, pretty boy!' She knelt amongst the crackling leaves and found herself on the receiving end of a boisterous and wriggly welcome. A split second later, a small blur of movement shot across her peripheral vision and Otto was off, abandoning Mimi in mid-wriggle in order to hurl himself after the blur.

'Don't take it personally. It's squirrel–chasing season,' Cal explained as they watched him race across the grass.

'For three whole seconds I felt so loved,' said Mimi.

'Squirrels take priority. It just kills him that they can climb trees and he can't.'

Now that she was back on her feet, she could see the fine laughter lines fanning out at the corners of Cal's eyes. She was able to breathe in the scent of him, an irresistible mixture of toast and shampoo and the faintest hints of coffee and cologne.

'How's it been going with Lois and Felix?' she asked.

He made a so-so gesture with his hand. 'Lois is convinced Henrietta's trained the cat to spy on her. She says everywhere she goes, Truman's there, swishing his tail and giving her the evil eye.'

'I think it comes naturally to Truman to do that. It's kind of his speciality.'

'I know. Anyway, I told Felix what you told me and he's trying to make things better. He does love her,' Cal said with a sigh. 'And he's doing his best to get through to her.

But Lois doesn't help herself sometimes. I know it's not her fault, but there's so much going on there that neither of them can sort out and it doesn't make it easy for Felix.' His smile was rueful. 'At least she came back after flying out to see you. Felix was terrified she wouldn't.'

Mimi half smiled too, because Lois had taken some persuading. Otto presented her with his frisbee and she tossed it into the air. 'She doesn't know I'm back. I thought I'd surprise her.'

'Still enjoying it out there? You look well.'

'The weather's fantastic. I mean, it's the beginning of November, but we still have warm sunny days. Whereas here . . .' Mimi nudged the frosty grass with the toe of her boot and gave an exaggerated shiver. 'Bit chilly. Anyway, how did that portrait go? Was it a success?'

'Turned out OK, thank goodness. Finished it last week and took it over there a couple of days ago. Pretty nerve-racking, but Lara seemed to like it.'

Mimi realised she was watching him for clues; was it her imagination or had there been a momentary flicker of something in Cal's eyes, a hint of a secret in his smile, when he mentioned Lara's name? Oh God, *had* something happened between the two of them? Surely not, though; Lara was married – happily married, by all accounts – to Darren May.

But the unsettled sensation in her chest was expanding; once you'd discovered that your best friend had been carrying on a torrid affair with your own boyfriend, you kind of realised anybody could be doing anything right under your nose whilst you remained completely oblivious to it.

Anyway. Mimi gathered herself. 'Is she nice?'

'Who, Lara? Oh yes, she's great. Really friendly . . . well, you know. The kids were fine too, thank goodness. I didn't meet Darren because the painting's a surprise for their wedding anniversary. She's planning on giving it to him tomorrow, so we just have to hope he likes it as well.'

What did *really friendly* mean? Forcing the possibilities out of her mind, Mimi said, 'Ah, I bet it's brilliant. I'd have loved to see the painting. D'you have a picture of it on your phone?'

'I do.' Cal went to take his mobile out of his jeans pocket, then remembered and said, 'Except I left my phone at home on charge. Damn. Unless . . . well, if you wanted to come back with me now, you could see the photo on my laptop. Or if you'd rather, I can just text it to you . . .'

'I'm not busy. I'd love to come and see it,' said Mimi. 'Is Cora at home?'

'She is, although she's off to dance class soon. And she'd love to see you again too.' He whistled for Otto, who was still performing acrobatic leaps into the air at the foot of one of the chestnut trees whilst the squirrel taunted him from above. 'Come on, boy, let's go.'

When they reached the house, Cal said to Cora, 'Look who I found!'

'Hi!' Cora, dressed in pink tights and a black leotard, was busy criss-crossing the satin ribbons of her ballet shoes around her ankles, tying them neatly and tucking in the ends. She beamed up at Mimi from the floor. 'Oh, have you left your job? Are you back for good?'

And for a moment Mimi wished she could say yes. Because living back here in Goosebrook and seeing Cal and Cora on a daily basis would be so much nicer and more fun than working for a stroppy, self-centred writer who hated to write.

'Mimi's just back for the weekend,' said Cal. 'Now how are you doing, nearly ready? I'm just going to show Mimi the photo of the painting I did for Lara May, then we need to head off.'

'Dad, it's OK, Charlotte's mum called while you were out. She's on her way over here now to pick me up, then I'm going back to theirs afterwards. It's all arranged.'

'Really?' Cal looked surprised. 'Well that's nice of her, isn't it? That's great.'

The happy thought flitted through Mimi's mind that this now left Cal with a few hours unexpectedly free. Maybe he'd suggest they went out for lunch again.

'Charlotte's mum's taking us to the cinema, then afterwards we're going shopping.'

'Are you saying you'd rather do that than spend the day at work with me?' Cal clapped his hand to his chest in abject dismay.

'You mean sit in a boring office while you meet people and talk to them for *aaaages* about summer houses? Even though it's winter?' Cora flashed a grin at Mimi. 'Yes, Dad, I'd rather go to the cinema and watch a film with Charlotte and her mum.'

'Ah well, nice to know one of us has a social life,' Cal said good-naturedly. 'I suppose I can manage on my own.' He opened his laptop and gestured for Mimi to join him at the dining table, cluttered with Cora's efforts at jewellery-making. 'Sweetie, you need to clear all this away before you go.'

Having seen Mimi start at the word *sweetie*, Cora giggled. 'Mimi thought you were telling her to clear the beads away.'

Which was a tad awkward. Mimi said, 'My dad used to call me sweetie too. And when I was little he was always telling me to tidy up my stuff.'

'Mum used to call me beanie.' Cora held up her finger and thumb, an inch apart. 'Because when I started growing in her tummy she said I looked like a bean.'

'Here we are,' Cal announced and Mimi stood behind him as the finished portrait filled the screen.

Coming up alongside her, Cora said, 'I think it's good because they're all so smiley.'

'That's exactly it.' Mimi nodded; it was true. The likenesses were there, but more than that it was the atmosphere of warmth and happiness that the portrait had managed to capture and convey. It was informal, colourful and immensely cheering, everything you could want in a depiction of the people you loved most in the world.

'No wonder she's happy with it,' said Mimi. 'It makes you want to live inside the painting. It's just perfect,' she told Cal. 'When he sees this, he's going to be bowled over. How could he not love it?'

The next moment, Otto jumped up and started barking. They heard a car pull up outside, followed by doors banging and the sound of female voices.

'We're here!' Finding the door on the latch, Charlotte's mother let herself in and joined them in the living room. 'Oh, hello, I've seen you before, haven't I? Back in the summer at the water park. Cora tells me you're working in Spain now. How wonderful! Della Day-Johnson, how d'you do?'

Mimi shook her outstretched hand and smiled at Charlotte, who'd appeared behind her mother. Della was wearing a

187

cream fake-fur coat and her hair was the expensively streaked kind that swung like a curtain. She was tall and slender, wearing a high-necked honey-coloured sweater, matching narrow trousers and leopard-print ankle boots. Her make-up was expertly applied and her perfume was gorgeous.

'Hi, I'm Mimi.'

'I know.' Della beamed. 'Cal told me about you. Back for long?'

Mimi shook her head. 'Just a couple of days.'

'Well, enjoy the cold weather! Right, you two, let's go. Cora, have you got your change of clothes? Cal, do you want to come over and pick her up around seven? You're very welcome to join us for dinner – I've already made my world-famous lasagne, because it's Cora's favourite. In fact you *must* stay, I insist. Do we all think he should do that, girls?'

'Yes!' chorused Cora and Charlotte with childish enthusiasm.

Nooooo, wailed Mimi, but only in her head.

'And if you have a couple of glasses of wine and can't drive home, you're most welcome to stay in the spare room. How about that, Cora? Does it sound like fun? You and Charlotte can have another sleepover!'

Talk about obvious . . .

'Yayyy!' Cora and Charlotte hugged each other as they jumped up and down.

Mimi marvelled at Della's over-the-top tactics.

'And now we really should be leaving,' said Della. 'Mustn't be late for ballet. Cal, you have a good day at work and we'll see you this evening. Lovely to meet you, Mimi. Bye, Otto!'

'*Woof,*' Otto barked, performing the party trick that had so entranced Mimi the first time they'd met. It was weirdly disappointing to hear him doing it for Della, who beamed her approval and said, 'Oh you're such a *good* boy, aren't you!'

When they'd left in Della's car, there was a moment of awkward silence before Cal said, 'Well, I suppose I need to get to work.'

What was going through his mind? Something, but Mimi couldn't begin to decipher it. And it was a real shame he wasn't free for the rest of the day, but that couldn't be helped.

She said, 'I must go too. Have fun this evening over at Della's.' Teasingly, she added, 'At least you're getting dinner cooked for you. Always a bonus.'

'There is that.' Cal smiled wryly and reached for his car keys.

'She's definitely still keen on you.' Mimi couldn't help herself; she had to say it. 'I mean, you've probably noticed, but just in case you hadn't. The way she was looking at you and being so super-casual, bit of a giveaway.' It was only fair to warn him.

Cal nodded. 'It's fine, I can deal with it.'

Of course he could. He'd had enough practice, fending off the less-than-subtle advances of the other mothers at the school gates.

'Right, I'm off. Thanks for showing me the painting. Will you be going to the fireworks display tomorrow night, or do you have to stay here with Otto?'

'Oh, Otto isn't bothered by fireworks,' said Cal. 'He loves them. We'll definitely be there tomorrow night.'

'I'll see you there then.' Reaching the door, Mimi turned and said brightly, '*Bye*, Otto!'

But Otto was too busy noisily slurping water from his blue china bowl to notice.

It was surprisingly galling to be snubbed by a dog.

Chapter 23

The fifth of November, and the weather was kind. No rain had fallen in the last fortnight, the air was crisp and cold but not agonisingly so, and excitement was in the air along with the smell of bonfire in the cordoned-off centre of the village green.

People had come from neighbouring villages for miles around to witness the fireworks display that was due to start at seven. Mimi stuffed her hands into the pockets of her red coat and watched the crowds gather around the crackling bonfire as sparks flew up into the star-studded night sky. Marcus and Felix were both busy serving on the stall that had been set up to sell hot dogs and burgers. Extra staff had been laid on in the pub to cope with increased demand. Small children were racing around, shouting with excitement. And down the high street came three familiar figures that caused Mimi's breath to catch in her throat. Cal, Cora and Otto had arrived.

As they made their way onto the green, Cora said, 'Dad, I want to show Mimi my new hat!'

Mimi's heart swelled as Cora ran over to her with Cal

and Otto following behind. It expanded further still when Otto jumped up and barked an enthusiastic welcome as if yesterday's snub had never happened.

Otto, do you like me more than you like Della? One bark for yes, two barks for no . . . come on, you can do it . . .

'Hi, Mimi, look at my hat,' Cora said eagerly. 'D'you like it?'

'Of course I do, I love it! It's the best hat I've ever seen!' Mimi gave the pink velvet kitten ears attached to the crown a playful tweak.

Cora beamed. 'I love it too! Charlotte's mum bought it for me yesterday. She bought me an orange one and Charlotte a yellow one so we both have the same!'

'Perfect,' said Mimi. 'And did you have a good time at the cinema?'

'Oh it was great. Charlotte's mum bought us big drinks *and* a bucket of popcorn. I ate so much popcorn I thought I was going to be sick, but I wasn't. Charlotte's mum is so much fun!'

Cora's eyes were shining. For a moment Mimi was too afraid of the giveaway emotions in her own eyes to look at Cal. The temptation to tell Cora that she could be fun too was intense. Nor could she bring herself to ask if they'd stayed for a sleepover.

'Dad, there's Lauren and Ben over there, can I watch the fireworks with them? Is that OK?'

'I think I can probably manage on my own,' said Cal, and Cora was gone, haring across the grass to join her friends.

'She's growing up.' His tone was rueful. 'Once I used to carry her on my shoulders during firework displays. Then she got older and would hang on to me, squeezing my hand every time a rocket exploded. And now she'd rather watch the display with her friends.' He smiled and patted his heart.

The next moment, just as Mimi was debating whether to offer to squeeze his hand or climb onto his shoulders, they both heard a male voice behind them say, 'There he is, that's him. That's Mathieson.'

Swinging round, Mimi realised with a jolt that the couple heading directly towards them were Darren May and his wife Lara. Darren, tall and wiry and wearing a khaki waxed jacket over his jeans, wasn't looking amused. Lara, hurrying along behind him in high heels, was saying, 'Darren, *don't* . . .'

'I've seen the pictures she took of you on her phone,' Darren announced without preamble. 'What's been going on between you and my missus?'

'Excuse me?' Cal remained outwardly calm but a muscle was twitching in his jaw. 'I don't know what you're talking about. Nothing's been going on.'

'You came over to my house while I wasn't there. You took a whole load of photos of her and the kids.'

'Your wife hired me to paint a family portrait. That's how it's done,' said Cal. 'Seriously, that's all that happened.'

'And why did she need to take photos of *you*, hey? Tell me that.' Producing a phone in a pink leather case, Darren waved it at him. 'Bloody loads of them.'

'Darren, I take photos of everyone, you know I do,' Lara protested. 'We were just having fun, it didn't mean anything. The kids were there the whole time—'

'Yeah, I bet you had fun,' said Darren. 'You know Terry Carter's wife's a professional portrait artist, do you?'

'Well, yes . . .'

193

'But instead of getting her to do it, you had to choose this guy instead, even though he's never sold a painting before in his life.'

'I saw some of his work on Facebook and I *liked* it.'

'Funny how he just happened to be a good-looking bloke though, isn't it?' said Darren. 'I wonder if you'd've been quite so keen if he'd been some ugly old grandad.'

'But it's OK for you to go to that physio at the club,' Lara shot back. 'Not the ancient bald guy, oh no. You always have to end up being looked after by Helga, don't you? I wonder why *that* is?'

Mimi's eyes widened. *Whoa, it's all coming out now . . .*

'I get looked after by Helga because she doesn't hurt as much as Tom and she doesn't tell bloody awful jokes.' Darren swung round and addressed Cal once more. 'Just give it to me straight, tell me the truth. Are you shagging my wife or aren't you?'

'No he *isn't*,' said Lara, visibly mortified.

'I'm really not,' Cal told him, 'and I never have.'

'So why's she spent the whole day talking about how fantastic you are?' Darren was still on the attack. 'Because I'm telling you now, she hasn't stopped. It's been Cal this and Cal that all afternoon, like a teenager with a crush—'

'I'm here, I'm here,' panted a voice as the sky suddenly exploded with colour and light and the crowd gathered for the firework display sent up a collective *Ooh!* of delight. Turning, Mimi saw Della with her daughter, hurrying across the grass towards them, waving her arms to attract their attention.

What on earth . . .?

Then again, the most surreal aspect of all was the fact

194

that one of the most successful Premiership footballers in the country was currently standing on Goosebrook village green but everyone else was too entranced by the fireworks to even realise he was here.

Cal was looking surprised to see Della too. As she reached them, he said, 'What's going on?'

'It's all gone wrong,' Lara cut in, clutching Della's arm. 'He still doesn't believe me.'

'OK, let me get my breath back a minute. Cal, where's Cora?'

'Over by the swings, watching the display.'

'Darling, you go and join her.' Della gently pushed Charlotte in the direction of the playground area to the left of the bonfire. As soon as Charlotte had run off, she put her hands on her hips and fixed her gaze on Darren May.

'Right, listen to me. Lara isn't having an affair with Cal.'

'You're her friend, so you would say that.' Darren shook his head. 'You should have heard her today. I'm not making it up.'

'I know you aren't, and I'm sorry,' said Della. 'It was my idea and I thought it was a good one. Turns out it wasn't.'

'What was your idea?' Cal was clearly baffled by whatever was going on.

'OK, Lara was worried about Darren, she thought there was a chance he could be getting involved with whatshername, the Swedish physio with the huge boobs. So I told her she should make him realise what he stood to lose if he played away, let him think the same thing could happen to him . . . because if Lara *did* go off with someone else, Darren would be devastated.'

'Hang on.' Darren pointed an accusing finger at Della.

'Who says you aren't the backup plan? What if you and Lara came up with this idea so that if I ever twigged what was going on, you could trot out this whole story to put me off the scent?'

Exasperated, Cal said, 'Nothing *has* been going on.' He turned to Della as yet another explosion of rockets lit up the night sky overhead. 'Are you telling me you put those pictures of my work on Instagram so Lara could *pretend* to like them?'

'No . . .'

'But you told her she should commission me to do the portrait not because my work was good but because of the way I looked?'

It made sense, it made perfect sense. Enthralled, Mimi held her breath and watched as the colours of the bursts of fireworks were reflected in Cal's eyes. This was excellent news; if anything was guaranteed to ensure that absolutely nothing ever happened between Cal and Della, it was this.

'No, no, that's not true.' Vigorously Lara shook her head. 'I saw your work when Della posted it on Instagram and fell in love with it straight away. And that was before I even knew what you looked like.'

'So you got a nice surprise when you found out.' Darren clearly remained unconvinced. 'I still don't—'

'OK, stop.' Della raised a manicured hand and said firmly, 'It's your wedding anniversary and you've so much to be grateful for. You have two beautiful babies and a wife who loves you to bits and who *isn't* having an affair with a good-looking artist.'

'But how . . .?'

'How do I know that for sure? I'll tell you, shall I? It's because I'm the one seeing Cal.'

196

It was a mic-drop moment, punctuated by a series of explosions in the sky like the rat-tat-tat of gunfire. The world turned electric blue, red, violet and gold, and the assembled crowd went, 'Ooooooh!'

Della had reached for Cal's hand and was giving him a little smile. The word currently going through Mimi's mind was more of a *nooooo*.

'It's fine, it's time people knew anyway,' Della announced. 'It's not as if we were planning to keep it a secret forever.'

The sensation in Mimi's chest was similar to when you got squeezed too enthusiastically by someone who didn't know their own strength. At the same time she knew she had to look merely surprised by the announcement and hopefully delighted for the happy couple.

'I suppose not.' As he said it, Cal glanced across at Mimi and her heart skipped a beat, because how had she not known? He exhaled and his breath hung visible in the still air. By way of explanation he added, 'It's just the girls . . . they don't know.'

'But it's been over six weeks now.' Della's tone was confident. 'It's time we told them. And it's not as if they're going to be upset about it, are they? Charlotte thinks you're great and Cora adores me! You wait, they're going to be so happy when they find out. They'll be thrilled.' To seal the deal, she planted a kiss on Cal's mouth, then turned to bestow a dazzling grin upon the rest of them. 'Almost as thrilled as I am. From now on we won't have to hide how we feel about each other. Plus, we'll be able to have a lot more sleepovers!'

Darren and Lara had listened in silence to Della's announcement. Now, Darren turned to his wife and blurted

197

out, 'I swear on the kids' lives I'd never do anything to hurt you. Nothing's ever happened between me and Helga, but if she bothers you I'll never go to her again.' He held Lara's face between his hands. 'I love you so much. You don't have to worry about losing me because that's never going to happen.'

'Oh Darren, I'm so sorry I tried to make you jealous. I was just so scared, I didn't know what to do.' Lara's voice cracked with emotion. 'I love you too, more than anything else in the world.'

Mimi, stuck between the two couples, felt like more of a gooseberry than she'd imagined possible. Awkwardly, above the sound of the firework display building towards its noisy finale, she said, 'Well, glad everything's been sorted out.' She flashed a bright smile at Della and Cal. 'Congratulations! And now I'm going to go and find Lois . . .'

'Thanks,' said Della. 'Bye.'

Otto, who'd been happily watching the fireworks, thumped his tail against the ground and said, '*Woof!*'

'Bye, Otto!' Mimi said.

But Otto was once more engrossed in the fireworks.

'Aah.' Della gave her a sympathetic look. 'That's such a shame. He always does it for me.'

'I don't know,' said Marcus. 'I just don't know. None of this makes any sense to me.'

Mimi's teeth were chattering and her fingers and toes were numb, but she felt obliged to stay outside with him and carry on peering into the depths of the car's engine in the vain hope that it might suddenly spring into life.

The temperature had plummeted since yesterday evening's

198

firework display; overnight a heavy frost had fallen, casting a thick layer of white over the village. Well, over the entire country, which was why when Mimi had called the car rescue service, they'd warned her that all their operatives were out on calls and it would be a good couple of hours before anyone could get out to Goosebrook.

Likewise, the mechanics at the local garage had already been inundated with requests for help and were currently occupied dealing with a van that had skidded into a ditch on the main Cirencester road.

Marcus, the brilliant accountant, shook his head. 'Numbers make perfect sense to me. Car engines make no sense at all.' He waggled a couple of oily leads. 'Are these spark plugs? Do they look like spark plugs to you? Bloody hell, of all the times for this to happen.'

A car was coming down the high street behind them. Mimi experienced a rush of adrenalin when she turned and saw that it was Cal and Cora, then hoped her nose wasn't unattractively red with cold before remembering that both reactions were now irrelevant anyway.

Cal drew to a halt and buzzed down the driver's window. 'Problem?'

No, no problem, we're just admiring the engine.

'Car won't start,' Marcus sighed, 'but it's not the battery, so that means we don't have a clue. And the rescue people can't get here for ages and Mimi has a plane to catch, so I guess you could call it a problem.' He held up one of the black leads and said, 'Any idea if this is a spark plug?'

'Plugs plug into things,' Cora announced, scrambling out of the passenger seat. 'So that definitely isn't a plug, is it?'

For a moment Mimi thought Cora was getting out of

199

the car in order to inspect the engine and fix the fault, but no such luck. Instead, she raced off down the pavement and vanished into the shop.

'Well I just need to drop Cora off at school.' Cal addressed Mimi. 'If you want to jump in, I can give you a lift to the airport.'

Which was a kind offer but not really ideal under the circumstances, seeing as last night she'd tossed and turned for hours, tortured by thoughts of Cal and Della together. Opening her mouth to say thanks but no thanks, Mimi was beaten to it by Marcus, who practically hugged him. 'Are you sure? Cal, you're a lifesaver, that would be amazing. Thank you *so much*.'

'Look,' said Mimi as they left Goosebrook, 'you don't have to do this. I can get a later flight.'

Cora, who was cramming a bottle of fruit juice and a packet of cheese biscuits into her lunchbox along with her sandwiches, said, 'Marcus told us you'd already tried that but this evening's flight was full.'

'Well, yes it is, but I could have flown tomorrow.'

'Marcus said CJ needed you back there today,' Cal pointed out.

Honestly, all she'd done was nip back inside the cottage for a quick wee.

'OK, you're right. Thanks.' Mimi twisted round to Cora. 'And how did you enjoy the fireworks last night?'

'They were good.' Lunchbox sorted to her satisfaction, Cora finished zipping up her school rucksack. 'Did you know Dad's got a girlfriend?'

Here we go . . .

'Really?' She glanced at Cal's face in profile, noticing that the tip of his ear had turned pink.

'Yes, and it's Charlotte's mum. They told us last night.'

'Wow,' said Mimi. 'And how do you feel about that? Are you happy?'

Cora shrugged. 'It's cool. She buys me loads of things. And she's fun too. I like her.'

'Well that's great.' Mimi smiled as warmly as she knew how.

'She said we can have lots more sleepovers now.'

I'll bet she did.

Mimi valiantly carried on smiling. 'Fantastic!'

Once Cora had been dropped off at the school gates, Cal headed for the motorway that would take them to Bristol. Mimi had by now been smiling so much her cheeks ached.

'So, Cora approves. That must be a relief.'

Cal kept his attention on the road ahead. 'It is. I had planned on keeping things quiet for a while longer, but . . . well, last night happened and there was no going back. Plus, Della felt it was time we went public anyway.'

'You did well to keep it under wraps for as long as you have.' *Did she want to know or didn't she?* Forcing herself to sound cheerful, Mimi asked the question she would ask any friend under those circumstances. 'So how did you two get together?'

No sexual details, please . . .

Cal said, 'Remember when we paid a visit to the Carters in Tetbury? And Marion Carter wanted us to build a summer house in her sister's garden but there was no direct access?' He waited for her to nod before continuing, as if she was likely to have forgotten it. 'Well, I paid a visit to the neighbour

201

behind the sister's house who'd agreed to let us go through her garden . . . and it turned out to be Della.'

Of course it did.

'Amazing!' Mimi feigned delight, because what else could she do? Wailing *Oh no!* and bursting into tears wouldn't go down well at all.

'I know! What were the chances? So we took down the dividing fence and started work in the client's garden. And the weather was fantastic in early September, so Della was there spending a lot of time outside too. She also kept us supplied with cold drinks and snacks. It was brilliant.'

I'll bet it was. Mimi was only too readily able to envisage Della, tall and blonde and deeply tanned, wearing a minuscule bikini that showed off the results of her daily workouts in the gym. She imagined Della stretched out on a sunlounger, her skin gleaming with bronzing oil, then emerging from the kitchen carrying a tray of drinks clinking with ice cubes, enjoying the attention and the gratitude of Cal and his team of visibly impressed workers.

'Then on the last evening, after the job was finished, she invited me to stay for something to eat,' Cal went on. 'She said she'd enjoyed seeing me every day and would miss having me around now that it was over. And I suppose that was when I realised . . . well, quite how much she liked me.'

Had he honestly needed it to be spelled out to him? Talk about a hopeless case. Mimi pictured Della in a strappy summer dress, wearing full make-up and with every inch of her golden body primed and ready for seduction.

'How did you know for sure?' Because she was a masochist and had to ask.

Cal shrugged. 'She told me.'

Simple as that. Was she jealous? Mimi exhaled; of course she was jealous, wildly so. But at least no one else was aware of it.

Thank goodness.

'And it all went from there,' she marvelled, as if nothing could be more perfect. 'That's brilliant! I'm impressed you managed to keep it a secret.'

He nodded. 'I had to. We needed to make sure it wasn't going to cause any problems for the girls. I knew Cora and Della got on well together, but it's still tricky, figuring out what's going to work. If I were seeing someone Cora wasn't keen on . . . well, there's no way I could do that to her. Then again, if it was someone Cora absolutely adored, I had to be really sure the relationship wasn't just going to be a flash in the pan. Because imagine raising her hopes then dashing them again, letting her think she's on her way to getting a stepmum . . . until the next thing you know, it's all over.' He paused in order to concentrate on overtaking a couple of lorries. 'I did give it a lot of thought, you know.'

'Of course you did. You have to.' Mimi was now feeling sick at the idea of Della becoming Cora's stepmother. Images of the wedding taking place in Goosebrook's fourteenth-century church filled her relentlessly overactive imagination. Della, looking stunning in a column of ivory silk, standing on the steps of the church with Cal in a beautiful dark suit and their respective daughters, the beaming bridesmaids in purple because that was their favourite colour . . . Oh God . . .

'And I know Cora and Charlotte are good friends,' Cal went on, 'but Charlotte isn't her *best* friend. I couldn't do that to her; it would be too traumatic if Della and I ever broke up.'

'Plus, her number one best friend is Lauren,' Mimi pointed out, 'and I can't really see you and Lauren's mum getting together.'

Cal grinned, because Lauren's mother was a cheerful farmer's wife in her early fifties with frizzy hair, more than the usual number of teeth, and six other children besides Lauren. Endlessly hard-working, she was seldom seen wearing anything other than muck-splattered wellies and a brown boiler suit. He said, 'She's fantastic, but how would I cope if she turned me down flat?'

At that moment his phone went *ding*, to indicate the arrival of a message. The phone lay face down in the well between their seats.

'Can you take a look and see who it is?' said Cal. 'Just in case there's a problem at work that needs sorting out.'

It wasn't a problem at work. Reaching for the phone and turning it over, Mimi said, 'It's from Della.'

Cal said, 'OK, don't worry,' but by then it was too late. Without even meaning to, Mimi's thumb had brushed against the glass and the photo of Della had already filled the screen. Della, wearing a low-cut translucent black lace bra so that her beautiful pillowy breasts were shown off to their best advantage. Her lipstick was crimson, her hair sexily dishevelled, and the message beneath the photo said: *Missing you! Here's a little reminder of what you can look forward to tonight!!!* Followed by a row of hearts, lipstick kisses and shooting stars.

'God, I'm so *sorry*.' Mimi let out a yelp of panic and threw the phone back into the well. 'I didn't mean to do that!'

Chapter 24

'Do what?' Cal's attention was still fixed on the road ahead.

'I opened the message! Completely by mistake! It was an accident!'

'OK.' He grimaced slightly. 'What does it say?'

It had all happened in a split second. Mimi's scalp was still prickling with mortification, her palms damp with sweat. 'Um . . . she misses you and can't wait to . . . er, see you tonight.'

Cal nodded. 'Well that's OK. No need to be embarrassed.'

'I shouldn't have opened it, though.' Because he was going to find out anyway, Mimi said, 'There was a photo too.'

'Ah.' A brief pause. 'Thought there might be.'

'I'm sorry.'

'Me too. Was she naked?'

'No!'

He looked relieved. 'Well that's something.'

'But she wasn't wearing a sweater and jeans either.'

'OK, I can guess.' Cal heaved a long sigh. 'Look, I probably shouldn't be saying this, but I don't know who else to ask. Della keeps sending me these photos of herself and I wish she wouldn't, but I have no idea how to stop her without making things awkward. If I tell her not to do it any more, she's going to be offended.' He gestured helplessly. 'This is going to make me sound a hundred years old, but it's never happened to me before. Stacey and I didn't . . . go in for stuff like that. So for it to be happening now . . . God, it just seems so weird. But I don't want to hurt her feelings. Della thinks it's a fantastic thing she's doing for me. It's not her fault I'm finding it a bit cringey.'

Mimi's heart went out to him, at the same time as giving a secret squeeze of *Schadenfreude* because Della's efforts evidently weren't as welcome as she thought they were.

'You aren't a dinosaur, you've just been off the market for over a decade. That's the equivalent of a century in olden-days dating. Technology's changed everything,' Mimi reminded him. 'People used to snigger at the idea of dating agencies and personal ads in the paper. Now everyone's on Tinder.'

'Paddy told me I should give Tinder a go.' Cal shook his head. 'I just couldn't bring myself to do it.' He looked at her. 'Are you on Tinder?'

'No point, not while I'm out in Puerto Pollensa. Anyway,' she swerved the subject back around to him, 'I think you should tell Della that someone accidentally saw her photo and just say it was a bit embarrassing so maybe she shouldn't send any more. Don't tell her it was me,' Mimi added hastily. 'Pretend it was the vicar, or Henrietta, or someone like that. And explain how awkward it was.'

'I could try that.' Cal nodded, but he was sounding doubtful. 'Although she'll probably just tell me to put a lock on my phone.' Another pause, while he signalled and took the turning off the motorway. 'Does everyone do it now? Send photos like that? Is it just . . . *normal*?'

'I think probably a lot of people do . . . I don't really know. They have cameras on their phones, so they use them. But not everyone does it.' Seeing that Cal was glancing sideways at her, she added, 'I never have.'

He visibly relaxed. 'That makes me feel a lot better.'

'Good.' And now it was the turn of Mimi's phone to burst into life. She saw the name and pulled a face. 'Hi, CJ, how are you?'

'How am I? Sick of people expecting me to arrange things that it isn't my bloody job to arrange. Have you landed yet?'

Oh joy.

'No, I haven't landed yet because it's only ten o'clock and my flight doesn't leave until midday. Are you picking me up from the airport?'

He snorted. 'What am I, your personal taxi service? You can get the bus.'

'Yes, thank you,' Mimi said brightly. 'I've had a lovely break.'

'*What?*'

'Oh sorry, I thought you were asking me if I'd had a nice time.'

'You're hilarious,' CJ growled. 'Also, I emailed you two hours ago and you haven't replied yet.'

'Marcus's car wouldn't start.' Mimi marvelled at his impatience. 'The rescue services weren't able to come out. Someone else is kindly giving me a lift to the airport and when I get through to departures I'll deal with my emails. I'm sure it can wait until then.'

'I suppose it'll have to. Who's giving you a lift?'

'A friend. His name's Cal.'

'Cal, Cal. Dead wife.'

For God's sake. Mimi squashed the phone hard against her ear, but CJ's booming voice was still audible; Cal must have heard it. 'He's driving the car,' she said.

'And is he the one you've got a crush on?'

What? Where had that even come from? 'No, definitely not. Not at all.' Clammy with horror, Mimi repeated firmly, 'No.'

'I'll see you later.' CJ barked with laughter. 'Bye.'

Mimi hung up and closed her eyes. He was an absolute nightmare.

'What did he say?'

She looked across at Cal, unable to tell for the life of her whether or not he knew.

'Couldn't you hear him?'

Cal shook his head. 'No.'

Was this true? Or a double bluff to see if she'd say it?

'He wanted me to write a Q&A on his behalf for the *New York Times*. Because he can't be bothered to do it himself.' The lie sounded convincing, as well it might; it was a favour he'd asked her to do for him last month. 'Well he can take a running jump.'

'Right.' Cal nodded. 'So he's still a pain to work for, but you're going to stick it out.'

'It's a job and it pays well. It'll look good on my CV.' Mimi corrected herself. 'It's going to look *miraculous* on my CV. And it's only for a few more months. I can cope with CJ for that long.'

'Good for you.' After a moment Cal said, 'And when it's over, I suppose you could go anywhere, London, abroad . . . anywhere at all . . .'

How was she supposed to respond to this? She imagined saying: may as well, seeing as I'd kind of hoped something might happen between you and me, but clearly that now *isn't* going to happen . . .

No, no. No way.

'I'll go wherever I get the best offer.' Mimi plastered her confident-career-girl smile firmly in place. 'And once those agencies see how long I've survived working for CJ, they're all going to want me. Trust me, I'll be in demand.'

Cal half smiled. 'I'm sure you will.'

They reached the airport and parked up in the express drop-off area.

'Honestly, thank you so much for this, you saved the day,' said Mimi as Cal hauled her carry-on case out of the boot and locked the car. 'Oh, you don't have to come in with me.'

'Let's just make sure the plane hasn't been delayed. The last time I dropped someone here, the flight was cancelled. Come on, it won't take two minutes to check.'

They had to walk single-file along the covered walkway. Cal was in front, pulling her case, and Mimi followed just behind him. Because she was only human – and how often did you get this kind of opportunity? – she studied his rear view. The ends of his blonde hair curved over the collar of his brown suede jacket, which tapered from his broad shoulders to hip level. Then there was the back of his faded jeans with the outline of his wallet visible through the worn right-hand pocket. He truly did have the best backside she'd ever seen, and his long legs as he strode along were just . . . well, equally hypnotic to watch. Some men were just able to walk in that particular way; it was mesmerising to witness—

'All right?' Cal paused to glance over his shoulder and Mimi almost cannoned right into him. 'Sorry, just checking I hadn't lost you.'

And the easy way he said it, coupled with the expression in his eyes, sent a rush of adrenalin through her body. Because he *had* lost her.

Worse still, he'd never had her.

She nodded, hiding the tangled emotions behind a bright smile. 'Don't worry, I'm here.'

Then they reached the main concourse – no delays on the board – and it was time for Mimi to head up to departures. It was sheer bad timing that she and Cal found themselves at the foot of the escalator, launched into what felt like the end credits of *Love Actually*. To her left, an Italian couple in their thirties were superglued to each other; to the right, a French girl and her boyfriend were enthusiastically kissing and murmuring endearments, whilst just behind them an older man was clutching his partner, saying tearfully, 'I'm going to be counting the minutes until I see you again.'

And now a teenage couple were exchanging final frantic kisses whilst a middle-aged woman ascending the escalator bellowed, 'Stop it now, Victoria, for goodness' sake. That's *quite enough*.'

More kissing, then Victoria peeled herself away from the love of her life and sulkily followed her mother up to Departures. Which was something to be grateful for, but still left the other couples competing for most romantic goodbye of the year.

Mimi, standing in front of Cal, said, 'Well, thanks again for the lift.'

Oh God, could I sound any more British?

'My pleasure,' murmured Cal.

His pleasure. Just the way he said it was bringing the little hairs up on her arms. Surveying him from this angle was even more breathtaking than viewing him from behind. Plus, the smell of his aftershave was so delicious that the moment she reached duty-free, Mimi knew she was going to have to find some and spray it all over herself.

Oh, he'd been saying something. Flustered, she said, 'Sorry, missed that. Couldn't hear you over the sound of all the kissing.'

'I said, when are we likely to see you again, any idea? Will you be back for Christmas?'

'I don't know, hopefully I'll get a few days off.' It was distracting to say the least, having the French girl to the right of her exclaiming, '*Oh mon ange, je t'aime, je t'aime beaucoup!*'

'Well, let's hope you do. Right, I'll let you go.' Cal inclined his head slightly towards her and Mimi froze, realising he was about to kiss her. Sensing her reaction, he promptly froze too, and for a split second they stood there suspended in time, before Mimi tilted her cheek up to his and he responded, his lips brushing against the side of her face, and this time it wasn't completely anaesthetised so at least she was able to feel it.

Even if it was possibly the world's clunkiest cheek-kiss, followed by that awkward moment when you both tried to pretend it hadn't been clunky at all.

'OK! Bye, lifesaver!' Mimi grabbed the handle of her case.

'Bye.' Cal's answering smile made her long to try again but get the kiss right this time.

She couldn't do that, though.

Halfway up the escalator, after twenty seconds of imagining Cal's eyes lingering on her rear view just as hers had earlier been fixed on his, Mimi twisted round to smile and do a tiny farewell wave.

But he wasn't watching her. Instead he was turned away, fishing in his jeans pocket, hurrying to answer his ringing phone.

Which kind of told her all she needed to know.

Moments later, as they queued to go through security, the jovial man next to Mimi said, 'Cheer up, love, might never happen.'

Except it had.

Chapter 25

December arrived. Puerto Pollensa had wound down for the winter. Many hotels and restaurants had closed their doors for the season and most of the sun-seeking holiday-makers had moved south to the year-round warmth of the Canary Islands. The golden beaches were now largely empty and Mimi was able to jog along the sand without having to worry about bumping into dawdling tourists.

Out-of-season Majorca was still pretty great, though. The warm sunny days might be less frequent than before, but she was settling in and enjoying herself. The British expats who'd made the place their home were friendly and sociable, and she'd got to know many of them. On Wednesdays, the weekly market was held in the town square, which was a central meeting point lined with bars and restaurants. She'd been greeted with enthusiasm, invited along to social events and urged to try cycling trips and windsurfing. For a few weeks she'd even been persuaded to join a local art group, which had only increased her admiration for Cal, having proven to herself that she really couldn't paint at all.

She still had plenty of work to keep her busy, too. With fewer people around and less to distract him, CJ was actually sitting down and getting a lot more work done. When the writing was going well, his mood improved, and Mimi, picking her moments with care, was able to persuade him to agree to appear at various literary festivals and other events in the new year.

And then one evening, quite without warning, she found out more about CJ than she'd ever expected to know.

It started when she emerged from the shower in her apartment and heard loud music playing next door.

Except CJ had only left an hour earlier to go out to dinner with his latest girlfriend, so it was weird that he should be back this early.

On the other hand, if burglars had broken into the villa, it seemed unlikely that they'd be blasting out Wagner's 'Ride of the Valkyries' at maximum volume.

Mimi finished drying herself, then pulled on cotton pyjamas and a towelling dressing gown. She called CJ's mobile and got no reply. Opening her French windows, she stepped out onto the terrace and peered up at the villa just as a shoe sailed over the balcony outside CJ's bedroom and landed with a splosh in the heated pool.

Seconds later, a second shoe came cartwheeling through the air, missing the pool by inches and landing on the tiled edge.

'*Fuck.*'

It was CJ's voice. Mimi called out, 'What's going on?'

'I bloody missed, didn't I?' He gestured irritably. 'Go and sort it out.'

She made her way over to the pool and picked up the

still-dry shoe. The underwater lighting made it possible to read the label stitched inside.

'It's a Louboutin.' Mimi held the classic black patent stiletto in her hands and admired the shiny red sole.

'Chuck it in the water,' CJ bellowed above the music as it reached a crescendo.

'Oh, but they're beautiful. And they cost a fortune.'

'*DO IT.*'

He wasn't in a mood to be bargained with; sometimes you could just tell. Mimi dropped the stiletto into the water and watched it sink to the bottom. Maybe she could secretly rescue them later.

'Now get out of the way,' CJ roared, moments before a handbag landed with a splash in the deep end.

She spread her hands. 'What's going on?'

'Nothing.'

'Well something's upset you.'

'That's where you're wrong.' CJ shook his head vehemently. 'I'm not upset. I've just been proved right. *Again.*'

'Would you like to talk about it?'

'Not bothered. Can if you want.'

This meant he did. Mimi said, 'OK, but you're going to have to turn that music down. It's making my ears hurt.'

Wagner was switched off. CJ made his way downstairs and Mimi joined him in the living room, where he poured her a small brandy and himself a larger one.

'Go on then, tell me.' She tucked her bare feet under her on the grey suede sofa. 'It's to do with Laura, yes?'

'Top of the class.' He took a slug of the brandy.

'What happened?'

'We were having dinner and talking about girls who are

gold-diggers. And she was telling me how disgusting they are and why they should realise there's more to life. So I said I'd met my share of gold-diggers over the years and Laura said she could never be like that, it was so shameful and undignified. Then I mentioned it was the small gestures that made the difference, like if I paid for a meal, it was nice if the other person took care of the tip. At that point, I left her at the table to visit the gents. And when I got back, Laura said she'd take care of the tip tonight, even though she couldn't really afford it, but she wanted to do it to prove to me that she wasn't like those other girls who'd taken advantage because I had money.'

'Right.' Mimi nodded cautiously.

'Except what she didn't know was that I'd deliberately left my wallet sticking out of my jacket pocket, and my jacket hanging over the back of the chair. I'd also double-checked how much money was in there.' CJ paused. 'When I opened the wallet to pay for the meal, there was two hundred euros missing.'

'Oh God.' No wonder he'd resorted to Wagner.

'So I waited until Laura put a fifty-euro note down on the table as a tip, then picked it up and showed her where I'd scribbled my initials in the corner. You should have seen her face.'

'What did she say?'

'Nothing. I'd caught her bang to rights. I also told her I knew she had three more fifty-euro notes in her bag, also signed by me. Then I said it was a real shame she wouldn't be getting those fancy shoes she'd admired when we were in Palma the other day. And that was when she called me an ugly old bastard and told me I was crap in bed. Then she snatched the fifty-euro tip off the saucer and stalked out of the restaurant.' He gave a bark of laughter. 'Well, I suppose she needed it for the taxi back to Alcudia. I don't imagine Laura's much of a bus person.'

CJ might be laughing, but it had to have hurt. Mimi said loyally, 'You're not ugly.' Then she added, 'You're not old either.' Well, not *ancient*.

'And I'm not crap in bed,' he said dismissively. 'Just in case you were wondering.'

She put down her brandy glass. 'If you counted your money and signed the notes, you must have had your suspicions.'

CJ nodded. 'Oh yes. I think it might have happened a couple of times before. But you know what I'm like with cash.'

Mimi did. He was forever stocking up from the ATM and leaving his wallet lying around. She said, 'I'm sorry.'

'Better to find out now than six months down the line.' He snorted. 'Or six years.'

'Still not very nice, though.'

'What did you think of her?'

The last time someone had asked her that question, Mimi had given them her honest opinion, only to see the couple get back together again a week later. Which hadn't been ideal. But hopefully this time Laura's boat had well and truly sailed.

'OK, you aren't *old* old, but there was a fifteen-year age difference,' she reminded CJ. 'Laura's very beautiful, she has an incredible body and she is quite keen on the finer things in life.'

'She also thinks Margate is in south Wales,' CJ interjected.

'And is convinced that *Keeping Up with the Kardashians* is the greatest TV show ever made.'

'I'm just saying, the way she looks is her side of the bargain. If you didn't have a ton of money, she probably wouldn't be interested in you. You do know that,' Mimi told him. 'It means girls like Laura aren't necessarily the most . . . trustworthy. They aren't the ones you end up with if what you really want is a happy-ever-after kind of relationship.'

'You see, you think you're right.' CJ pointed his drink at her. 'But in fact you're only half right. Because you're saying a plain girl who doesn't have a banging body wouldn't mess me around, and I don't agree with that. In my experience, anyone can do it. So if it's going to happen anyway, you may as well go for the best-looking ones. And as long as you don't expect it to last, you won't get your heart broken when it ends.'

Shocked, Mimi said, 'Do you really believe that?'

'Of course I do. If you don't let yourself get involved, you won't get hurt. It makes life a lot easier, trust me.' CJ nodded to prove he was right. 'Look what happened to you with that idiot you used to work for. Bet you wish you'd never bothered with him, don't you? Just one more cheating bastard amongst all the rest of them.'

'Not everyone is a cheating bastard,' Mimi protested.

'And if you believe that, you're even more gullible than I thought. Cheating, lying, twisting the truth for their own ends . . . oh, mark my words, they all have their own agendas.' He paused to take another gulp of brandy. 'Look after number one, that's all you can do. Because you can be damn sure everyone else is. And you can guarantee every last one of them will let you down in the end.'

Wow. It was the most he'd ever opened up to her. Even more extraordinarily, as CJ rose to his feet to refill his suddenly empty tumbler, Mimi was almost certain she glimpsed a tear in his eye.

If it had been there, he'd dashed it away by the time he sat back down. But, sensing that a mental barrier was showing signs of wavering, she said, 'What if your soulmate's out there waiting for you, except you're too scared to let yourself believe she exists?'

'I'm not scared. I'm being practical.'

'But people can fall in love and be happy together for the rest of their lives.' Mimi spread her hands. 'How long did your longest relationship last?'

'Three months. And when you were growing up, I bet you thought your parents were happy together. Until your dad upped sticks and found himself someone else.'

Which was fair enough, but how interesting that he'd mentioned her family. The brandy was warming her stomach, relaxing her enough to ask a question she might not otherwise have asked.

'What about *your* family? Were your mum and dad happy?'

CJ blinked. For a second she thought he was going to ignore the question and change the subject. Then he said, 'No, I wouldn't call them happy. In fact, I'd say their marriage was a humiliating farce. Ooh.' He widened his eyes, mimicking avid interest. 'That's exciting, isn't it? What are you going to do now, channel Dr Freud?'

'You never talk about them,' said Mimi.

'For good reason. It's not something I particularly like to spend my time thinking about.'

'OK. We can change the subject if you want.' She shrugged.

219

'I just thought, you know about all the rubbish things that have happened in *my* life . . .'

CJ sat back and stared at the ceiling for a couple of seconds. Then he said, 'My father adored my mother. And in return she treated him like dirt. He always seemed to prefer my older brother to me, which made me all the more desperate for attention. We used to hear them arguing sometimes, but it didn't happen too often because most of the time Mum did whatever she wanted and he let her get away with it. Then when I was eleven I found out he wasn't my biological father. Mum had been having a fling with our next-door neighbour when she found out she was pregnant with me. But he wasn't interested, so she stayed with my dad and they both pretended I was his.'

'Oh CJ.' Now Mimi realised why'd he'd been keeping his head tilted back. When he looked at her, his eyes were glassy.

'Yeah, well.' He shrugged. 'I'd never liked our next-door neighbour anyway. He used to smirk at me and I couldn't figure out why. Then one day I asked Mum if I could go on a school trip and she said no, so I said I'd ask my dad instead. And she laughed and said, "Good luck with that, but if you're talking about the one who's upstairs painting the bathroom, he isn't your dad." Which was one way of finding out.' The pain was only too evident in his voice. 'I don't know why she did it, completely out of the blue like that. I didn't know how to react. She was furious about something, presumably. Then she told me to go upstairs and ask him, so I did, and he looked pretty shocked too. But he said it was true.'

It was heartbreaking. Picturing CJ at eleven, stunned and confused, Mimi murmured, 'You poor thing.'

220

'So I went up to my room and lay on my bed and thought about it, and in a weird kind of way it made sense. Then I started to fantasise about who my real dad could be, and I thought maybe he was someone incredibly rich and successful, with tons of money, who would really love me when he found out I was his son. And after that, no one said anything for a while but the whole time I was busy building up the fantasy. It was great, I could imagine all these scenarios. I even made a list of possible fathers in my diary.' As he said it, CJ mimed holding a pencil and writing down the names. 'David Bowie was on there. And Steve McQueen, because my favourite film was *The Great Escape*. Then there was Kevin Keegan . . . Freddie Mercury . . . Rod Stewart . . . If I say so myself, it was a fantastic list. Anyway, I'd hidden the diary under my bed, but Mum found it. When I came home from school the next day, she threw the diary down in front of me and said, "Don't get your hopes up, lad. Your real father's Frank from next door. And he couldn't give a toss about either of us."'

'Oh no.'

'So that was it, dream shattered.' CJ wiped his eyes roughly with the back of his hand. 'Frank was a layabout who didn't work but always had enough cash to buy himself a few drinks. It was obvious that my mother had told him I knew, because he started smirking more than ever every time our paths crossed. And that Christmas he jokingly told me not to expect anything from him because he didn't believe in wasting money on presents. It was like a joke to him.'

'What a pig,' said Mimi. 'That's *so* cruel.'

CJ shuddered. 'I hated everything about him. Smug, cocky bastard. Even worse, every time I looked in a mirror, I could see I was starting to look like him, which made me feel sick. Anyway, I left home at seventeen and moved down to London, lived in a squat and worked on a building site. Went back a year later when Mum was taken ill, and heard that Frank had dropped dead a month earlier; had a massive coronary in the bookies just as one of his horses came in at eight to one.'

Mimi said, 'I'm so sorry.'

'Don't be. I'm fine. He didn't leave me anything, obviously, but I wouldn't have wanted it anyway. Mum died a few years after that, and Dad followed her six weeks later. Couldn't live without her, despite everything she'd put him through. And that was when I vowed I was never going to be like that. My life would be different. No way was I going to take any shit from anyone ever again. And I've stuck to that. I have all of this.' CJ gestured around the villa's palatial living room. 'Paid for with my own money. My life is better than theirs was, and no one's going to hurt me because I won't let it happen.' He tossed back the last inch of brandy in the glass. 'So there you go, now you know the whole story and you're going to keep it to yourself. Plus,' his tone grew even more steely, 'you'll end up sleeping with the fishes if you ever tell anyone you saw me cry.'

Chapter 26

'So you're coming home for Christmas? Go on, go on, you know you want to,' Lois wheedled over the phone. 'God knows, *I* want you to. And Cora was asking the other day if you'd be back. So did Paddy, now I think of it. See?' she concluded brightly, 'That's loads of us!'

Well, a grand total of three.

Mimi hadn't decided what to do for Christmas. Marcus's elderly father was growing increasingly frail and Marcus would be heading up to Newcastle for what could be their last Christmas together. The idea of returning to Goosebrook in his absence had seemed strange at first, but if she was honest, it was where she most wanted to be.

'Go on then, you've twisted my arm,' she told Lois, and heard a whoop of delight at the other end of the line. 'I'll book my flight for Christmas Eve.' Touched by the thought of others asking after her, she added, 'You can tell Cora I'll see her soon.'

Lois said playfully, 'I shall, and I'll mention it to Paddy too.'

Mimi smiled, because Lois had taken to teasing her about

Paddy, pretending there was a potential relationship there waiting to happen. Whereas in reality, and pointless though it still might be, she was far more interested in Cal. By way of a diversion she said, 'Any ideas of a small present I could buy for Cora?'

'Hmm, let me have a think,' said Lois. 'Maybe something to keep her warm, seeing as they're heading off the day after Boxing Day for a skiing holiday in Austria.'

Oh.

Oh.

An hour later, an email popped up on Mimi's laptop from CJ's US editor, Carmen.

Hey M,

Can I ask you to show these edited pages to CJ and confirm that he's happy with the small changes we've made before they go off to the printers?

Thanks so much!

Also, I'm belatedly attaching a couple of photos that my husband took in August when we came to visit PP – we're currently knee-deep in snow here in NYC so I thought CJ might like a reminder of happier, sunnier times!

Mimi had heard from CJ that Carmen and her husband had flown over to Europe back in the summer, and had incorporated a visit to Puerto Pollensa into their trip. The photos had been taken here, out on the terrace, at the end of what had presumably been a long and enjoyable lunch. The table was awash with glasses, wine bottles and plates containing remnants of food. There was CJ, tanned and shiny with perspiration, raising his glass to the camera alongside Carmen, equally tanned but far less shiny in a white shirt and trousers and a wide-brimmed straw hat. To the left of them sat Mirielle, who ran a boutique in Alcudia and had briefly been CJ's girlfriend last year. And at the other end of the table was a young woman in a blue sundress, whose dark-blonde hair was held back from her face in a high ponytail.

In the first photo, everyone was smiling broadly for the camera. The second one, taken when they'd stopped posing, showed the rest of them laughing together while the girl in the blue dress, wielding a pen, wrote something in the notebook on the table in front of her.

It was Willa, Mimi realised. Probably scribbling down a line of dialogue CJ had just blurted out. Never having met Willa or seen a photo of her before, she'd always imagined her to be dark-haired and curvaceous. On the phone, her voice was quiet but efficient.

The door to the office swung open and CJ stuck his head round. 'Sorry to interrupt when you're busy looking at your holiday photos, but any chance of a coffee for the worker?'

'I'll bring you one.' Mimi beckoned him over and pointed to the screen. 'Look, Carmen just sent these.'

He came to peer over her shoulder. 'Back in the summer. I remember.'

'Is that Willa?' She tapped the screen.

'Of course it's Willa.'

'No need to snap. I've never seen a photo of her before. She looks nice.'

'And there's Mirielle.' CJ grimaced. '*Not* nice.'

Mirielle, it transpired, had been simultaneously carrying

on with an athletic young Majorcan who ran a boat that took tourists out on dolphin-watching trips.

Mimi said, 'Can I send a copy of these to Willa? She might like to see them.'

'If you want. After you've made me my coffee.'

'How many words have you done today?'

'Fifteen hundred. Because I'm a complete hero.'

'Glad to hear it.' Mimi beamed. 'Now get back to work.'

Once she'd taken CJ his Americano, she sent the photos on to Willa along with a friendly message asking how she was doing and hoping all was well.

Five minutes later, Willa's reply popped into her inbox:

Hi Mimi,

Many thanks for these! I remember Carmen and Steve's visit very clearly – they were great fun. (I wouldn't fit into that blue dress now.)

And I'm feeling fine, thanks. Bit tired, but apparently that's par for the course. Mum's spoiling me, which is nice! Are you heading home for Christmas or staying in PP?

Hope CJ isn't working you too hard, anyway. How's he doing – is he seeing anyone at the moment?

Thank you again for the photos.

Willa x

Glad to hear all's well with you, and how lovely that your mum is spoiling you. I've just booked my flight home on Christmas Eve – hooray! CJ still hasn't decided whether to stay here or zip over to London to visit Anna and Tom – you know what he's like about making decisions. (And no, he's having a girlfriend break at the moment. The last one turned out to be another gold-digger, surprise surprise.)

Mimi paused, wondering if Willa was aware of the details of CJ's traumatic childhood. There had been no further mention of it since the night he'd confided in her, and he'd blocked the one or two attempts she'd made to suggest that it might help if he talked things through with a professional. Anyway, it wasn't her place to mention it—

'AAARRGH,' CJ bellowed from inside his office, making her jump. She heard his chair scrape back, followed by a crash of china on the marble floor.

'What is it?' she called out.

'FUCKING MONSTER SPIDER ON THE WALL. GET IN HERE AND DEAL WITH IT!'

He was such a wuss when it came to insects. Mimi typed: *Whoops, have to go, spider emergency. Happy Christmas! M x*

Coffee had splashed everywhere including across CJ's desk and writing pad where he'd flailed his arms in panic and sent the cup flying. It took Mimi twenty minutes to catch the poor traumatised spider and put it safely outside, then clean up the mess in the office while CJ recovered in the living room with a stiff drink and an episode of *Line of Duty* on Netflix to calm his nerves.

When order had finally been restored and she returned to her laptop, she saw that Willa had replied to her hastily signed-off message with a row of spider emojis.

Mimi grinned and wondered if she'd get the chance to meet her one day. Willa sounded great.

Chapter 27

It was Christmas Eve at last. Mimi had risen early to make sure the journey to the airport went smoothly, without them having to turn back because CJ had forgotten to pack something vital.

She was cramming the last of the wrapped presents into her case when she heard her phone beep with an incoming message.

'If it's work, don't answer it,' CJ ordered. 'I'm not doing anything for anyone. For the next seven days I'm on holiday and they can all take a running jump.' He looked out of the window as a car pulled up on the drive. 'Taxi's here. Want me to take your case out for you?'

Mimi pretended to faint. 'Sorry, did you just offer to do something useful?'

'I'm in a good mood. No more slaving over a hot notepad for the next week. Better still, no more being bossed around by you.'

'In that case you can definitely take my suitcase,' said Mimi. 'Let me just check the rest of the villa, make sure everything's switched off.'

The taxi was loaded up, the villa's security alarms were set, and they left for the airport. CJ, who was catching an afternoon flight to Heathrow, had booked himself into the Connaught Hotel and would be spending Christmas Day with his friends Anna and Tom in Holland Park, followed by Boxing Day at a country house party in Kent. Mimi's plane, leaving an hour earlier, was due to land at Bristol at three in the afternoon and she was being picked up by Lois. The thought of arriving back in Goosebrook, where the weather was currently crisp and cold with the fairy-tale promise of snow, was giving her prickles of anticipation. Marcus might not be there, but the welcome would still be warm.

Belatedly remembering the message on her phone, she unzipped her bag to see who'd sent it. Hopefully there wasn't a problem with Lois being able to collect her from the airport.

But the message was from a number she didn't recognise. The opening sentence on the screen said: *Hi Mimi, this is Willa's mum here. Willa doesn't know I'm contacting you . . .*

Mystified, Mimi opened the rest of the message.

. . . but I just had to. I need to speak to CJ. Could you please call me back on this number so I can explain? As soon as possible, please. Thanks so much, pet.

More mystery. Mimi opened her mouth to tell CJ who the message was from, then saw that he was sitting back with his eyes closed, plugged into music and entirely oblivious to his surroundings.

Maybe it was easier to leave him that way for now.

She called the number and heard a breathy voice pick up on the second ring.

'Mimi, is that you? Oh thank goodness, I thought you

229

weren't going to call back. Hello, pet, it's Helen here, Willa's mam.'

'Hi. Is everything all right?'

'It's Willa, pet. The thing is, she's having a baby—'

'I know she is,' said Mimi.

'No, I mean she's having it now. It wasn't due for another month but she woke up with pains this morning and the midwife's just confirmed that she's in labour.'

'Oh, how lovely! And one month early won't be a problem, loads of babies are born early,' Mimi reassured her. 'I'm sure everything'll be fine.'

'I know, pet, but I needed CJ to know that it was happening. You see, Willa didn't want me to tell him but I just thought . . . well, it *is* happening and he really *should* know . . . so do you think you could pass the news on to him, just in case? I mean, Willa's so stubborn, but she's my daughter and I felt . . . Do you understand what I'm trying to say, pet? Could you tell him, would you do that for me? Because she says he doesn't want to know, but I just keep thinking, what if he *did*?'

Mimi was lost for words. Utter bafflement had turned to realisation, which in turn had morphed into a mixture of disbelief and dismay. Finally managing to speak, she said into the phone, 'Of course I'll tell him. And thank you for calling.' Feeling so sorry for both Willa and her worried mother, Mimi added, 'As soon as I've spoken to him, I'll message you back.'

She ended the call and looked over at CJ. His eyes were still closed but she knew he wasn't asleep; the fingers of his left hand were resting on his knee, tapping along to the rhythm of whatever music he was currently listening to.

She reached across and prodded his right arm to get his attention.

CJ took out one of his earbuds. 'What?'

'That message on my phone earlier? It was Willa's mum. She wanted to let us know that Willa's gone into labour.'

Silence. CJ assumed the expression of someone opening the front door to find a pair of bible-clutchers on the door-step.

Finally he said, 'And?'

'She's having the baby.'

'That's generally what going into labour implies.'

'OK, sorry. You don't seem to be getting this.' Mimi held his gaze. 'She's having *your* baby.'

This time his face reddened. He shook his head and looked out of the window. The deathly silence lengthened.

Her patience slipped. 'Oh my God, all this time and I had no idea. You didn't tell me *you* were the father.'

'Who says I am? Willa? Maybe she's just saying that.'

'Are you serious?' Mimi's voice rose. 'You slept with her and she got pregnant.'

'So that makes it my fault?' CJ shot back. 'How do you know there aren't other contenders?'

'She wouldn't do that.'

'You've never even met her.'

This was true, but Mimi had a strong sense of the person Willa was. She said, 'Did she have a boyfriend when she was out here working for you?'

'A boyfriend? What is this, some Disney movie? No, she didn't have a boyfriend, but you don't actually need to be in a relationship to get pregnant. Any old one-night stand will do.'

231

'And did Willa have a one-night stand?'

His jaw jutted. 'She says not. But that's what happens, isn't it? When people get caught out, they lie.'

'You don't know she lied.'

'I do,' said CJ. 'I saw her.'

'You mean you caught them together? Actually having sex?'

A memory of finding Rob and Kendra together on the rooftop flashed through Mimi's mind; she knew only too well how that felt.

'I saw them walking together on the beach,' CJ growled. 'Talking.'

'I don't think that counts as sex,' said Mimi.

'And the next day they had coffee in the square. They were sitting outside Plaza Uno. Still talking.'

'Still not having sex.' But Mimi's voice softened, because she could understand how his upbringing had affected his ability to trust people. And yelling at him, whilst tempting, wasn't going to do any good. 'Right, listen. The baby's on its way. Once it's here, you can get a DNA test done. Because you've spent the last six months telling yourself it might not be yours.' She leaned across and rested her hand on his forearm. 'But what if it *is*?'

CJ shook his head. 'What if I see it and think it's mine and then it turns out it isn't? Because if that happened, I just couldn't bear it.'

'OK,' said Mimi, 'think about it from the baby's point of view. Once children are old enough to ask about when they were born, they always want to know if their dad was there too. And it makes them feel loved and secure if he was.'

'You're clutching at straws now.' He scowled. 'Making it up.'

'No, I'm not. My dad was there with my mum when I was born and I know how I felt when I found that out. It matters.' Mimi shrugged. 'It mattered to Mum too.'

'I shouldn't think for one minute that Willa wants me with her while she's giving birth.'

'You're assuming that. Besides, even if you aren't in the room with her, you could be there at the hospital. Honestly,' Mimi willed him to understand, 'I think you'd really regret it if you weren't.'

CJ closed his eyes. The taxi had reached the outskirts of Palma and they'd soon be at the airport. He clearly needed time to think.

And then they were being dropped off at Departures. As they hauled their cases into the terminal, Mimi said, 'Well?'

'We're here. By the time I get there, it'll probably be too late.'

'Then again, it might not be.'

'I knew you'd say that.' CJ looked at her. 'I'm scared.'

'I know you are.'

He faltered, then said, 'Will you come with me?'

Mimi's heart sank like a stone. It was Christmas Eve and she'd been so looking forward to getting back to Goosebrook.

But she was the one who'd persuaded CJ to do this. How could she abandon him now?

'Please.' CJ cleared his throat.

'Of course I will.' She turned in the direction of her airline's flight desk. Now they just had to hope she could make it happen, before letting Willa and her mother know they were on their way.

Luck was on their side; Mimi was able to book CJ onto her flight. She arranged for a driver to meet them at Bristol and take them up to Sheffield. There was snow forecast for the north of England, but hopefully they'd have completed the three-hour journey by the time it arrived.

When she called Willa's mother to let her know they'd be there by early evening, Mimi knew they were doing the right thing. She heard Helen's sigh of relief before she gasped, 'Oh thank you, pet, thank you so much . . . I'm so glad I told you.' Her voice broke with emotion as she added, 'I knew it was the right thing to do.'

And the gods were with them. Their flight took off and landed punctually. The cases were unloaded in record time and their driver was waiting for them at the gate. Mimi experienced a wave of regret at having had to cancel Lois. Fingers crossed, the baby would be born within minutes of their arrival, enabling her to leave CJ basking in love and new fatherhood while she shot back down south . . .

Unless Willa flatly refused to see him. Or the baby came out looking exactly like the handsome dark-haired man CJ had seen her walking with along the beach.

Oh God, please don't let that happen.

They reached Sheffield as the first fat snowflakes began to fall. There had been no further texts since the one two hours ago from Helen saying: *Four centimetres dilated, all going well so far.* Which hopefully meant the baby hadn't popped out yet.

'I can't believe I bought this. I shouldn't have bought it.' CJ gave the stuffed toy giraffe he'd picked up in duty-free a fretful shake. 'What were you thinking, letting me buy something so ridiculous?'

'It's sweet,' Mimi protested.

'I look like an idiot.' He yanked free one of the giraffe's gangly hind legs as it got caught in the hospital's swing doors.

Mimi winced; hopefully he wouldn't do that if he were holding an actual baby. 'Are you nervous?'

'Terrified. And I need to find a bathroom before my bladder explodes.'

Spotting a sign to the men's toilets, Mimi pointed down the corridor to the left and found herself the recipient of the toy giraffe while CJ hurried off.

The next moment, as she was about to text Willa's mother, two women emerged from the maternity unit up ahead. One, in her fifties, was holding the door open for the other, who was younger, hugely pregnant and wearing a lilac dressing gown.

Mimi recognised her from the photos. Unable to tear her eyes away, she watched as the pair made their way slowly along the corridor towards her.

As the girl paused to massage her back, she in turn recognised Mimi, presumably from a recent photo posted on CJ's website.

'Oh, it's you. Is CJ here too?' Willa's chin lifted. 'Or has he done a runner?'

'He's here.' Mimi nodded and gestured behind her. 'He'll be back in a minute.'

'You must be Mimi.' Helen's voice was warm. 'Hello, pet. Thanks so much for doing this.'

'Can I just quickly ask something?' said Willa. 'And I need an honest answer. Are you and CJ . . . together?'

'Oh my God.' Startled, Mimi shook her head. 'No way. Absolutely not.'

235

'OK. Well, thanks. I didn't think so, but it's nice to know for sure . . . ow . . . *owww* . . .'

The next contraction was making itself felt. Helen, supporting her daughter while she breathed her way through the pain, explained, 'She's still only five centimetres dilated so the midwife said going for a walk might help to move things along.'

'Oh God, here he is.' Willa visibly braced herself as CJ appeared at the end of the corridor.

In turn, CJ did a double-take at the sight of her, before approaching as cautiously as if she were a cheetah baring her teeth.

'Willa.'

'CJ.'

'You're looking . . .' He floundered, searching for the right word. 'Huge.'

So much for being a writer. Mimi rolled her eyes.

'Thanks.' Willa finished exhaling and straightened up. 'You're looking old. And if you're wondering, it was my mum's idea to get you here, not mine.'

'I can leave if you want,' said CJ.

'Oh no,' Mimi blurted out. 'Please don't start arguing. We're here now. It's Christmas Eve. You're going to have a baby!' Her arms gestured wildly, managing to include both of them.

'She is,' CJ retorted. 'I might not be.'

'Do you still think that? *Seriously?*' Willa's shoulders stiffened.

'I saw you with that guy on the beach. You were talking. Then you both stopped walking and he hugged you. And you hugged him back.'

'What? I've never hugged anyone on the beach. Who was he?'

'Around your age. Dark hair, good-looking. He was wearing red shorts.' His tone meaningful, CJ added, 'And nothing else.'

'But I don't even know . . . Oh, you mean Stefano?' Willa's look of puzzlement cleared. 'He works at the dental surgery behind Pine Walk. His boyfriend's one of the chefs at La Scala. I used to see him every morning walking his little dog . . . and then one day I asked him where she was and he told me she'd just died. And he got upset so I comforted him and gave him a hug. Is he the one you thought I was seeing? Stefano, the gay dentist?'

CJ retorted defensively, 'He didn't look gay.'

'You should have said something before. I didn't know it was Stefano you had a bee in your bonnet about.'

'You told me you weren't seeing anyone.'

'That's because I *wasn't*,' Willa exclaimed. 'It's called being honest and telling the truth . . . Oh, here comes the next contraction . . . *oooh* . . .'

When it had passed, CJ said awkwardly, 'OK.'

'Do you believe me now?'

'About ninety-nine per cent.'

'Oh for crying out loud,' said Willa.

'What? I'm being honest. And I bought this for you.' CJ offered her the oversized gangling giraffe.

'No, you didn't.' Mimi gave him a nudge. 'You bought it for the baby.'

Willa leaned against her for support. 'I want to get back to my bed now. It's hurting more than before.'

'Can I come with you?' said CJ.

'Give me a bit of time to think this through.' Willa winced and clutched her stomach.

'But I came all this way.'

'Only because Mimi persuaded you to. You still aren't sure this baby's yours. It's four months since I last saw you,' Willa went on, 'and you haven't even said sorry yet for not believing me.'

'OK, I'm sorry,' CJ muttered.

Her voice rose. 'You don't get to say it when you still don't believe me. That means you don't really mean it! Oh—' She stopped abruptly and looked dismayed.

CJ frowned. 'What's happened now?'

But it really wasn't necessary for Willa to explain: a puddle of water was rapidly forming around her slippered feet. A midwife wearing Christmassy reindeer antlers popped her head out of a nearby room and said cheerfully, 'Whoops, spillage in aisle three! Can someone bring out a mop and bucket? Come on, my love, time to get you cleaned up and back to bed.'

Mimi had dozed off in the overheated waiting area at around eleven thirty. She woke up briefly at midnight, as church bells rang out in the distance and medical staff wished each other a chorus of Merry Christmases.

The next time she opened her eyes it was three in the morning and her arm had gone numb where she'd been sitting with her elbow on the arm of the chair and her head resting on her hand. The same breezy midwife was now giving her shoulder a gentle shake.

'Morning! You can come through if you'd like to. It's all been going on while you've been asleep!'

238

'Is it here?' Mimi followed her through the security doors and into the labour ward.

'Crikey, you really were out for the count. Since this one arrived, it's definitely been making its presence felt!'

She opened the door to Willa's room before Mimi had a chance to ask if Willa and CJ had called a truce. Thankfully, it seemed they had. Willa was sitting up in bed looking tired but happy, while her mother chatted excitedly on her phone. CJ was standing beside Willa with a look of utter besottedness on his face as he rocked from foot to foot, cradling the wrapped-up newborn in his arms.

'Congratulations!' Mimi gave Willa a hug. 'Is it a boy or a girl?'

And at that moment, something quite extraordinary happened: having opened his mouth to reply, CJ managed to contain himself and allow Willa to speak first.

'It's a girl,' said Willa. And she and Mimi exchanged a silent, significant glance, both of them only too well aware of CJ's habit of always needing to blurt out answers before anyone else.

'She's the most beautiful girl you ever saw,' CJ announced with pride.

'Can I see?' Mimi approached him and he held the baby towards her. She covered her mouth and said, 'Oh my goodness,' before starting to laugh. Because it was like she was looking at a miniature, wrinkle-free version of CJ. From the fine fair hair to the querulous eyebrows, from the challenging stare to the pursed lips and double chin, the similarity was inescapable.

'I know,' said Willa with a smile. 'Isn't it amazing?'

'How can she be so gorgeous *and* look exactly like CJ?'

'Hey,' CJ protested. 'I'm gorgeous too.'

Mimi smiled. 'So . . . is everything OK now?'

'It's better than OK. This is the best day of my life. I'm a father. We have a *baby*.' He turned to look at Willa. 'You were amazing. You *are* amazing. I'm so sorry I was such an idiot before.'

'You don't have to keep saying it,' Willa told him. 'I know you are.'

'I love you.' CJ choked up with emotion, stumbling over the words. 'I always did, but I couldn't risk telling you in case you were horrified and left. I'd had seven PAs walk out on me, remember, so I was terrified of losing you too. Then we accidentally did . . . well, *this*.' He indicated the infant in his arms, solemnly staring up at him. 'And you backed right off after that night.'

'You backed off first,' said Willa. 'I thought you wanted to pretend it had never happened. I was just trying to remain professional.'

'I saw you with the chap on the beach. Then the next thing I know, you were telling me you were pregnant. And that just triggered a massive reaction. I'm so sorry.'

'I know.' Willa nodded to reassure him that she understood. 'I know you are. We both flew into a bit of a panic. But it's OK, that's all behind us now. We just have to learn to trust each other.'

And tears welled up in CJ's eyes once more as he bent his head to kiss his daughter's forehead. Willa was dabbing her wet cheeks with the edge of the bed sheet. Even Willa's mum was surreptitiously wiping her eyes.

'My girl, my beautiful girl.' CJ stroked the baby's nose with an index finger. 'Hello, I'm your daddy! How about that, can you believe it? And today's your birthday.' He shook his head in amazement. 'I feel like a completely new person, as if my heart wants to burst out of my chest . . . Yes, that's your mummy!' He carefully transferred their daughter into Willa's arms and gazed at the two of them in wonder. 'This is the most incredible thing that's ever happened. I can't believe the difference it makes, having a baby.'

'And you aren't even the one who had to have stitches,' said Willa with a smile.

They stayed cocooned in the room for another thirty minutes, admiring the baby, examining her tiny fingers and toes and exclaiming over her defined eyebrows and the miraculous softness of the skin on the sides of her face. Then exhaustion set in for Willa, her eyelids began to droop and the midwife with the light-up antlers placed the infant in her crib beside the bed.

It was four thirty in the morning when Mimi, CJ and Helen left them to get some much-needed sleep.

'Bye! Merry Christmas,' said the midwife, waving them off.

'AAARRGHH,' bellowed a woman in the next room as her own midwives shouted, 'That's it, one more push!'

'Every day it's happening all over the world,' CJ marvelled. 'I never thought about it before, but it really is like a miracle.' He looked from Mimi to Helen, as overwhelmed as if he'd just had a spectacular religious experience. 'The miracle of birth!'

They were approaching the exit. Mimi said, 'D'you think there'll be any cabs outside?' Since that first eventful visit to Goosebrook, she'd never take taxis for granted again.

'If there aren't, we can call one,' said Helen.

'And we need to find a hotel.' There was a TV on in the reception area, with music playing at low volume. Chris Rea was apparently 'Driving Home for Christmas'.

'Oh you don't have to do that,' Helen protested. 'You must stay with me. I've got a spare room!'

'I'm not sharing a bed with Mimi.' CJ recoiled in horror. 'I'm a respectable man with a reputation to maintain.'

'Don't panic, pet. You can sleep downstairs on the sofa,' Helen reassured him.

CJ frowned. 'Or Mimi could, because she's smaller than me.'

'Look, it's Christmas,' said Mimi. 'And I'd really love to get home if I can, now that everything's sorted out here. There aren't any trains for the next two days, which means I'm going to have to book a taxi. Maybe I could head off now . . .' She hoped against hope that CJ would take the hint and offer to pay what was bound to be an extortionate fare.

But he was ignoring her, cradling the toy giraffe wrapped up in his discarded sweater in one arm and clutching his case in the other hand, whilst staring straight ahead. At that moment the glass doors at the entrance slid open to admit a man and his heavily pregnant partner, their heads and coats covered in fat snowflakes.

'Goodness, it's really snowing,' Helen exclaimed as the man helped the panting woman inside and a cab driver brought up the rear with a suitcase.

Mimi saw that beyond the sliding doors, the night sky was thick with tumbling flakes of snow. Alarmed, she said to the cab driver, 'If you're free now, can we grab you? I need to get down to Cirencester and we can drop these two en route . . .'

242

'You're havin' a laugh, darlin'.' He was already shaking his head. 'No way are you getting down to Cirencester. There's been a howlin' blizzard going on for the last six hours and the motorway's closed.'

Mimi gave a wail of dismay. 'Oh *no* . . .'

The cabbie was sympathetic. 'Sorry, not going to happen, not tonight. But on the plus side,' he added, indicating the wrapped-up bundle in CJ's arms and patting his own generous paunch before pointing to Mimi's flat stomach, 'if you've just given birth, I'm well impressed, love. Because you're looking great.'

Chapter 28

It was seven in the evening on Boxing Day, and as tradition dictated, everyone who was out was in the Black Swan.

Back in Goosebrook forty-eight hours after she'd originally expected to be, Mimi dumped her suitcase in the hallway of the cottage, then left again and made her way down the high street to where all the action was going on. She could already hear the music, even from here. The outside of the pub was lit up with strings of multicoloured fairy lights and the snow blanketing the village green lent a pale, ghostly air to the pervading darkness.

Much less snow here though than there had been in Sheffield. Just a thin layer that crunched beneath her boots. Reaching the Black Swan, Mimi paused and gazed in through the window. The inside of the pub had been enthusiastically decorated too, a real tree was up, and a lively fire burned in the grate. From out here, she could hear the babble of conversation and bursts of laughter as well as the music playing and the song currently being belted out by whoever's turn it was on the karaoke. Taking a step to the right, she saw that it was Eamonn from the village shop and Maria from the pub who were up on the stage, arm in arm as they sang 'Don't Go Breaking My Heart' with gusto.

There were plenty of familiar faces on the dance floor too, amongst them Paddy Fratelli and Felix and Lois, as well as plenty of other regulars complete with children of all ages and several dogs. Mimi spotted Cora and Charlotte, then moments later saw Della returning from the bar with fresh Cokes for them. Unable to help herself, she felt her heart sink a bit, because Della was looking so glamorous and beautiful. No sign of Cal, but he had to be there somewhere as well. Edging to the left to see if she could glimpse him at the back of the pub, she moved closer to the window—

'You know, they'd probably let you in if you asked nicely.'

She whipped round and saw Cal behind her, watching with amusement from the pavement.

'Oh! I was about to go in.' He had Otto with him, had presumably been taking him for a quick turn around the village.

'You look like the Little Match Girl, pressing your nose up against the glass.' He came and stood beside her.

Beneath her layers of clothing, Mimi felt the goose bumps rise on her skin simply because he was so near. 'It's my guilty secret. I love standing outside lit-up windows looking in. Not in a peeping Tom kind of way,' she added hastily. 'I just really like seeing people chatting and dancing, having a great time. They all look so happy.'

'It's OK, I know what you mean. Cora used to be obsessed with peering in through windows. She said it was like opening an old-fashioned Advent calendar, the ones with pictures instead of chocolate. Anyway, it's good to see you,' Cal went on. 'You made it down here at last. Lois kept me

245

updated with what's been going on.' His eyes crinkled at the corners. 'So, belatedly, happy Christmas.'

Mimi shivered, and not just from the cold. 'Thanks. You too.'

He tilted his head. 'And was it? Happy, I mean?'

'It was different.' As she spoke, the cloud of condensation from her mouth mingled with the one from Cal's and the intimacy of it made her feel quite giddy with longing. To distract herself, Mimi bent down and made a fuss of Otto, then glanced up at Cal again. 'How about yours?'

'Mine was different too.' He shrugged. 'Well, I suppose it was bound to be. Everyone has their own Christmas traditions, don't they, so when two families get together, they just have to learn to adapt. But it was fine, it was great. And first thing tomorrow we're off on our skiing trip.'

Of course they were. Bloody skiing trip. Aloud, Mimi said, 'Oh, it'll be brilliant. You'll have so much fun. And the girls will love it.'

'I hope so. You're shivering.' As the door to the pub opened from the inside and Otto lunged towards it, the hand clutching the lead brushed against hers and Mimi felt a spark of electricity dance up her arm. Cal said, 'You're freezing cold.'

But his own hand was wonderfully warm. For a mad moment Mimi longed to grab hold of it and press his palm against her cheek. Oh God, just imagine, how would he react if she actually *did* that?

'OK, Little Match Girl, let's get you inside before frostbite sets in.' Ushering her towards the open door, Cal called out above a lull in the music, 'Hey, look who's here, better late than never!'

And it was just the loveliest feeling, because heads turned and people seemed genuinely delighted to see her, and there was even some cheering, which made Mimi flush with joy. Because Marcus might not be around right now, but it didn't matter; there was a fantastic sense of belonging. She felt like a part of the village in her own right.

Then Lois was hugging her, and a big glass of Sauvignon Blanc was thrust into her hand. She kissed people she knew – not Cal, though – and wished everyone a belated happy Christmas before telling them about the unexpected adventure that had led to her spending the last two nights in snowbound Sheffield, sleeping on the sofa that belonged to her boss's girlfriend's mother.

'You did a good thing,' Lois declared. 'Honestly, if *I'd* been looking after CJ and he'd dug his heels in, I'd have bloody left him to it. You gave up your Christmas for that selfish prat.'

She didn't know the full story. Mimi said, 'Doesn't matter, it was worth it in the end. And I'm here now. Oh, thanks so much.' She took the glass of wine Cal had just bought for her and lined it up next to the first one. Tomorrow he might be off on holiday with Della, but at least she was able to look at him tonight, imprint every detail of his face in her memory and listen to his beautiful voice.

'Hi, you made it then!' Della joined them. 'Lois said you were coming back tonight. I bet you had fun though, didn't you? Oh, just the thought of cuddling a newborn makes me feel all broody . . . breathing in that incredible baby smell.' She wriggled her shoulders and quivered with ecstasy, then gave Cal a nudge. 'Remember when we were opening our Christmas presents yesterday morning and Cora said

247

her favourite smell was chocolate? And Charlotte said, "Mum's favourite smell in the world is little babies." But it's true. I just love it so much. Makes me swoon!'

'Uh oh, Mum's going funny over babies again.' Charlotte had come bouncing up with Cora. 'Mum, stop it, you're too old to have any more.'

'Cheek! Of course I'm not too old. I'm in my prime, I'll have you know!' Della bridled with mock outrage. 'Anyway, are you two having a good time? Don't drink any more Cokes after these, will you, or you won't be able to sleep. And we need to leave in . . . ooh,' she checked her watch, 'fifteen minutes.'

Mimi's spirits lifted. Was it really so wrong to hope that fifteen minutes from now, Della would be taking the girls home but Cal might stay here for a bit longer? Not because she wanted to do anything lascivious to him, obviously, but it was just so nice to see him. And after this evening, who knew how long it might be before it happened again?

Felix, who was running the karaoke, grabbed the microphone. 'OK, who's up next? Della, it's your name on the list and you've chosen one hell of a song. Come along then, let's see what you're made of!'

'Want to come up and sing with me?' Della reached playfully for Cal's hand, but he stepped back.

'Thanks, but I think I'll leave this one to you.'

Della took to the small stage and the emotive opening bars of the theme to *Titanic* began to play, prompting whoops of delight from the crowd. As everyone turned to watch, Mimi found herself next to Cal, her arm briefly brushing against his in the crush. The next moment they were squashed closer still, as a result of Cora wriggling in on her other side.

In the expectant second before Della began to sing, Mimi wondered if it might all go horribly wrong. Maybe she would miss the first note . . . get in a flustered muddle with the words . . . or turn out to be tone deaf, which would obviously be the best outcome of all.

Then Cora tugged at her sleeve and whispered up to her, 'She should be on *The X Factor*, she's a really brilliant singer,' and the brief fantasy splintered. Because of course Della would be a brilliant singer, of *course* she would.

Unlike me.

Also, wasn't it lovely that Cora was bigging her up like this and looking so proud?

Ashamed of herself for having entertained such uncharitable thoughts, Mimi guiltily moved her arm so it was no longer touching Cal's. If she couldn't be delighted that he and Della were now a proper couple, she could at least be happy for Cora and Charlotte.

'. . . My heart will go *ooooooooon aaaaand oooooooooon.*'

The song ended and everyone in the pub burst into wild applause, whistling and registering their appreciation because Della had absolutely nailed it. On either side of Mimi, Cal and Cora were clapping madly whilst up on the stage Della did a modest little curtsey and said into the microphone, 'Oh gosh, thanks so much, I'm just glad I didn't mess it up!'

The next moment, Mimi found herself being grabbed and hauled towards the stage, where Felix was setting up the next track.

'What are you doing?' She stared in horror at Lois, who was doing the hauling. 'I can't sing!'

'Everyone can sing. And I don't want to be up there on my own. Come on, it'll be a laugh.'

249

'For a one-legged woman, you're incredibly strong.'

Lois grinned. 'It's my secret super-power.'

Mimi felt the fear wash over her. 'No, please don't make me do this . . .'

But people were cheering and Lois was still determinedly dragging her, and now Della was handing over the microphone she'd just sung so brilliantly into, saying, 'Oh don't be shy! If I can do it, so can you!'

Oh God, it was a nightmare but she was going to have to plough on through it. Standing next to Lois, gazing down at the sea of familiar faces, she waited for the music to begin and knew the moment was fast approaching when anyone who might have fancied her even the tiniest bit was about to have their illusions well and truly shattered.

'Purple RAIN . . . purple RAAAAINNN . . .'

OK, the only way to do this if you were a terrible singer was to employ enthusiasm to make up for utter lack of talent. With Lois alongside her, Mimi flung herself into the performance with abandon. Each wrong note was accompanied by an air punch and worn as a badge of honour. And three minutes later, when it mercifully reached an end, she bowed deeply and said into the microphone, 'Thanks so much, I'm just glad I didn't mess it up!'

Which made everyone roar with laughter, thank goodness. At least they knew she knew how bad her singing voice was.

Paddy Fratelli, his eyes as electric blue as his shirt, helped her down from the stage and handed her a full glass of wine. 'Well done, here you go, you deserve this.'

'Thanks, but I've already got one over there somewhere . . . or two . . .'

250

'You were great.' He smiled his disconcertingly all-seeing smile.

'Oh, I wasn't—'

'Mimi, you were so *funny*.' Cora came bouncing up to them. 'We liked your dancing!' She executed some Jagger-style moves and waved her arms in the air in exuberant homage. 'Charlotte said it looked as if you were being electrocuted!'

Behind her, Charlotte beamed and nodded. They clearly hadn't meant it as an insult. Mimi said, 'Well thank you, because that was exactly the effect I was going for.'

'Right, girls, we need to make a move now.' Della's glossy hair swung past her shoulders as she made chivvying gestures. 'Go and collect your coats.'

'Oh, but can't we stay just a bit longer?' begged Cora.

'No, because we have to be up very early in the morning. We need to leave for the airport at three thirty. Well done up there, by the way.' Della turned to Mimi. 'Very disinhib-ited!'

Ouch.

'Dad hasn't finished his drink yet, though.' Cora was pulling out all the stops in an effort to delay their departure.

'He's going to finish it in twenty seconds. Cal?' Della beckoned to him. 'Time we were off.'

Cal nodded. 'I'll go and fetch the girls' coats.'

Damn, he was leaving. A thought belatedly struck Mimi. 'Oh, there's something I need to have a word with you about.' Briefly indicating Cora, she added, 'In private?'

'No problem, come with me while I get the coats.'

Grabbing her shoulder bag and excusing herself with a smile, Mimi said to Della, 'Sorry about this, won't be a second.' Then she followed Cal out through the side door and into the passageway where all the coats were hung up on a wooden rack.

Cal turned to look at her and frowned. 'Is everything OK?' He said it as if he really cared.

Mimi nodded, because of course everything wasn't OK but she could hardly blurt out that seeing him for twenty minutes just wasn't long enough. Instead, unzipping her shoulder bag, she showed him the large, festively wrapped parcel inside. 'The thing is, I bought Cora a Christmas present when I thought I'd be back by Christmas Eve, but obviously *that* didn't happen. So I brought it along with me tonight, but when I saw that Cora was here with Charlotte and you're all *together*,' she made a family-style gesture with her hands, 'I realised it'd be a bit awkward to just give a present to Cora. And now you're off and it's too big for you to hide inside your jacket, so I don't quite know what to do.'

'That's really kind of you.' Cal smiled and nodded, slowly understanding the dilemma. He thought for a moment. 'When are you heading back to Majorca?'

'Um, I don't know . . . it's up to CJ.'

'But he's in Sheffield and they've just had a baby. Look, we're only away for a week, so you'll probably still be here when we get back. You could give it to Cora then, when Charlotte isn't around. How about that?'

Mimi nodded, relieved. 'Good idea. Yes, perfect.'

'Hello?' The door opened behind them and Della appeared. 'Is this a private party or can anyone join in? Cal, can you pass me the girls' coats? We really do need to get them home.'

Her smile was charming. Cal said, 'No problem. We're

finished here,' and took the coats down from their hooks.

Back in the bar, the round of goodbyes and the many predictable break-a-leg jokes were made, and Mimi got stuck into her glass of wine. Up on the stage, Felix was belting out a surprisingly tuneful version of 'Back for Good'.

Whilst Cal was busy ushering Cora, Charlotte and Otto out of the pub, Della did a neat U-turn and came over to join her. Keeping her voice low and her face conspiratorially close to Mimi's, she said, 'By the way, just so you're aware, we do both know about your crush on Cal. I mean, it doesn't bother me at all but I do think Cal finds it pretty embarrassing, so you might want to try and dial it back a bit.' Her smile sympathetic, she gave Mimi's shoulder a consoling pat. 'I'm saying it for your sake rather than ours.'

The words sounded as if they were coming from far away. Unable to look at Della, Mimi stared blindly up at Felix instead and felt her entire body prickle with humiliation, horror and deep, deep shame.

It was already too late to protest that she was wrong. Della had turned and rejoined Cal and the girls as they left to make their way home ahead of tomorrow's crazy-early start.

Besides, Della hadn't been wrong, had she? It was the fact that she was spot on that made the situation so completely excruciating. Oh God.

Fifty times worse, *Cal knew.*

And he was such a nice person that he'd never once made it apparent that he was aware of the way she felt about him.

Whilst all the time, he and Della had been sharing the secret between the two of them; it had clearly been their own private joke.

Mimi took a huge gulp of wine. Up until now, discovering

her boyfriend and her best friend together up on that rooftop in Notting Hill had been the most mortifying experience of her life.

But this? This was worse by far.

'Hey! You OK?' It was Lois, bringing over the untouched glass of wine Cal had bought for her earlier.

Mimi took the glass. 'I'm great.' Because she couldn't even bring herself to confide in Lois; it was just too shameful to share. As Felix's turn on the karaoke came to an end and he basked in the burst of applause, she knocked back her drink and said, 'Up for another song? Come on, let's do it.'

Anything – *anything* – to get the memory of Della's words and the pity in her eyes out of her brain.

Chapter 29

The pub closed at midnight; the many strings of multi-coloured Christmas lights were switched off and the customers finally dispersed.

'I'll see you tomorrow.' Mimi threw her arms around first Lois, whose teeth were chattering like castanets, then Felix. 'Thanks, it's been a great night. Sorry if we hogged the karaoke.' As she said it, she marvelled at how well she'd done pretending everything was fantastic when in reality it had been one of the most agonising evenings ever.

'You were the life and soul of the party.' Felix grinned. 'Now, d'you want us to walk you home?'

'You mean all the way up the road to my front door, on the mean streets of Goosebrook? I think I can just about manage. You two get yourselves out of here before Lois gets frostbite.' Mimi shoved them in the direction of Fox Court on the other side of the green, and they left, crunching across the snow-crusted grass. She was glad that at least they'd had a good Christmas, without upsets, which was what Lois had been bracing herself for, courtesy of her mother-in-law. But at the last moment Henrietta had decided to spend

Christmas Day with friends in Cheltenham, and better still had taken Truman with her, which meant Lois and Felix had been able to relax and enjoy themselves without fear of barbed comments about undercooked sprouts or the wrong kind of cranberry sauce.

Mimi shivered and realised she was still filling her brain to the brim with Other Thoughts in order to distract from the ones that were the real problem. OK, once she was safely back inside the cottage, she could let her guard down, consider her options and decide what to do about Cal. At the moment, vanishing from the face of the earth seemed like the best plan.

Yet again, where were those giant sinkholes when you needed them?

Oof though, it was cold. After just a few minutes out here, her fingers were going numb. Mimi fumbled in her shoulder bag for the keys to Bay Cottage, waiting to make contact with the familiarly shaped objects and hear the welcome clink of metal.

She rummaged some more, felt wildly around in the bottom of the overfull bag, then tried each of the inside pockets in turn. Oh for heaven's sake, where were they? Come *on*.

The next moment, she heard an apologetic almost-but-not-quite-silent *woof* behind her, along with the sound of doggy breathing. She froze, her skin prickling with electricity and terror and embarrassment mixed with – despite everything – a soupçon of hope . . .

Because that was how relentlessly optimistic her stupid brain was.

'*Woof.*' Otto barked again in his muted late-night way and Mimi's heart broke into a far from muted gallop. She braced herself to turn and face him, just as Cal said, 'Hi, everything OK?'

Except it wasn't Cal's voice, which completely confused her. Swivelling round too quickly, managing to lose her footing on the packed-down snow, Mimi found herself making a comedy grab for the brass front-door knocker before missing it completely and landing on all fours.

Which was elegant.

'Whoa! Steady on, Bambi.' Paddy Fratelli came up the path and helped her back to her feet. 'There, got your balance now? Sorry, didn't mean to startle you.'

'You didn't startle me, I just slipped. I'm all right now,' said Mimi. Except she wasn't, was she? Quite apart from the disastrous Cal-and-Della debacle, she still hadn't managed to locate her house keys.

'Are you sure?' The motion sensor had caused the outside porch light to come on, enabling Paddy to study her with concern. 'Only I've been watching you try to find your keys for the last couple of minutes.'

'I don't know where they are. You have a look.' Mimi held her bag open to enable him to search. While he did so, she studied the top of his bent head, the way the glossy dark curls fell forward over his eyes. No sign at all of baldness, which had to be a relief for him.

'No.' He lifted his head. 'There aren't any keys in here.'

And she was getting colder by the minute. Mimi exhaled with frustration. 'Maybe I dropped them somewhere in the garden.'

Paddy took out his phone and switched on the torch app, throwing a beam of blue-white light over the snowy path, the dried leaves and tangled dead plants. 'Does Marcus keep a spare under a flowerpot?'

Not any more. Through chattering teeth Mimi said, 'If he d-did, I think I'd probably have used it by now.'

His blue eyes flashed with amusement. 'They could be somewhere in the pub.'

She looked down the deserted high street to where the Black Swan now stood in absolute darkness. 'Maria was shattered. I can't go banging on her door now.'

'What d'you want to do, then?'

There was Lois, but Mimi didn't want to disturb her and Felix on what had been showing signs of being a promisingly romantic night. She shook her head, suddenly overwhelmed with a build-up of emotions. 'Don't worry, I'll be fine.'

'Of course you will.'

Desperate to be rid of him, Mimi said, 'I mean it. Bye!'

Paddy raised an eyebrow. 'And where are you planning to sleep? On the doormat?'

'I'm OK. Really.'

'You're welcome to stay at my place.'

'No thanks.'

'Why not?'

'Just . . . because.'

'OK, two things.' Paddy counted off on his fingers. 'If you're worried I might try to seduce you, you don't have to be, because it isn't going to happen.'

Oh. Right. Startled, Mimi said, 'What's the other thing?'

He bent down to give Otto's head a reassuring pat before straightening back up and surveying her frankly. 'Well, beggars can't be choosers. And you can't really spend the rest of the night on your doormat.'

★   ★   ★

Thirty minutes later, Mimi was glad she hadn't said no. She was lying on a comfortably squishy red sofa in front of a roaring fire, with Otto curled up beside her and a glass of Barolo in her hand.

Not to mention a quite astonishing idea in her head, which, much as she attempted to dismiss it, was flatly refusing to go away.

She took a swallow of red wine and gazed at the TV screen without taking in details of the film currently playing. Otto's tail thumped contentedly against the sofa cushions. He was clearly at home here; it wasn't the first time Cal and Cora had gone away leaving him in Paddy's care.

Through the closed bedroom door Mimi could hear floorboards creaking and the wardrobe opening and closing as Paddy moved around. She'd spent the last ten minutes listening to him in the bathroom taking a quick shower before changing into comfortable clothes and making up the bed in the spare room.

It was picturing him in the shower that had set off the unexpected train of thought, possibly as a result of his blunt declaration that he had no intention of trying to seduce her.

In all honesty, the moment he'd said it her ego had popped up like an indignant meerkat wanting to know why not. What was wrong with her, hmm? He was a physically attractive man and she was a physically attractive woman. She wasn't some kind of repulsive troll, was she? No, definitely not.

Which was why it hadn't been the loveliest of feelings, especially following so closely on the heels of the Cal and Della humiliation, which in turn had followed the Rob and

Kendra kerfuffle. After a pretty rubbish few months, a girl could start to take this amount of rejection personally.

Mimi drank some more of the smooth red wine, and as the bedroom door began to open, she broke into a smile.

'Why are you smiling like that?' Paddy reappeared, his black hair still damp from the shower, his eyes seemingly bluer than ever in this living room with its whitewashed stone walls.

'I'm warm, I'm comfortable and I have red wine and a dog on the sofa next to me. Why wouldn't I smile?'

'You don't often, you know. At least, not when you're looking at me. I generally get the holding-back expression.' He half closed his eyes, mimicking her. 'The wary one, because you don't trust me an inch.'

He was teasing her now, and Mimi laughed because it was true. 'You can't blame me though, can you?'

'I suppose not. Ready for a top-up?' He reached for her almost empty glass and refilled it. Watching him while his attention was diverted, Mimi admired the lean lines of his body, the high cheekbones and black curly hair. From the start, it had been easy to maintain a distance from Paddy because her attention had always been so unerringly focused on Cal. But now she really did need to put a lid on that fantasy.

Maybe this was the answer.

Whilst it had come as a bit of a shock to find herself thinking it, why shouldn't Paddy be the one to provide the distraction? He had charm, he was single and he was rather beautiful to look at. Better still, he wouldn't be interested in anything more than a one-night stand or maybe a brief fling, which was all she wanted too.

Basically, he was perfect.

'You're still looking at me,' said Paddy.

'I was wondering if you wear coloured contact lenses.'

'I don't.' He sounded entertained. 'It's all me. No artificial enhancements.'

The way he said it seemed to hint at a double entendre. Mimi responded with a flirty smile and said, 'Well, I'm impressed,' before wondering if the smile had come out right and trying again, going more for sensual this time. Oh God, but it was difficult when you were so out of practice you'd completely forgotten how to do it.

'How about something to eat?' said Paddy. 'Are you hungry?'

Was she? Mimi mentally backtracked and realised she hadn't eaten anything since that sandwich back at the motorway service station around ten hours ago. She took another swallow of wine. 'I could manage something, what have you got?'

A glimmer of a smile. 'Well, food.' Which instantly caused Otto's ears to prick up and his tail to thump against the sofa cushions.

'Sounds good.'

'Let me have a look, see what I can offer you.'

Was he doing it on purpose? Was that another double entendre? Mimi raised an eyebrow. 'Am I allowed to look too?' she asked playfully.

Paddy hesitated. 'If you like.'

Right, progress. On to the next stage. She eased herself off the sofa, wagged a finger at Otto and murmured, '*Stay*.' After another slurp of wine, she followed Paddy into the compact kitchen and found him peering into the fridge.

261

'OK, we have bacon, we have chicken, we have eggs and mashed potato . . .'

He was wearing a pale grey sweatshirt with the sleeves pushed up to reveal his forearms. Realising she was now comparing his forearms with Cal's, Mimi forced herself to stop. 'Anything, I don't mind.' Then she added, 'What do you like best?' because it sounded a bit innuendoey and now that she'd made up her mind to distract herself with Paddy she wanted it to hurry up and happen.

'Well, we could make some bubble and squeak . . .'

Mimi blushed, was *that* an innuendo? 'Nothing like making someone squeak . . .'

Which instantly sounded wrong. *Aaarrgh.*

Paddy turned his attention away from the fridge. 'Sorry?'

'Forget it, didn't mean that.' Flustered, Mimi said, 'Slip of the tongue,' which definitely sounded like a double entendre. *Oh help.*

'If it was a slip of the tongue,' Paddy regarded her good-naturedly, 'what was it that you actually meant to say?'

Mimi threw caution to the wind. 'Look, I think I'm just a bit muddled because I'm nervous.'

'And why are you nervous?'

'I'm waiting for you to kiss me.'

He frowned. 'I'm not going to kiss you.'

'But I want you to!' Oh now listen to that, she'd just gone and blurted it out.

'You do?' He smiled slightly. 'Why?'

'Oh please, why do you think?' Mimi heaved a sigh and gestured in desperation. 'I've spent the last few months in Majorca working for the world's stroppiest boss. Before that, I found out my so-called wonderful boyfriend had been

262

cheating on me with my best friend. I was meant to be spending Christmas here in the village but that ended up not happening, and now tonight I've managed to lock myself out of my house. So all in all, the second half of this year has been pretty bloody disastrous and I just feel like I want something a little bit nice to happen, to cheer me up.'

There, now she'd *really* said it.

'Right. Wow.' The electric-blue eyes flashed with amusement. 'Well, I wasn't expecting this.'

'Oh dear, do you require twenty-four hours' warning?'

He hesitated. 'I wouldn't say that . . .'

'Good.' Moving forward and closing the fridge door, Mimi wrapped her arms around his neck and kissed him as if she meant business. Because she did, and Paddy was clearly in need of a bit of a kick-start.

And yes, hooray, he was kissing her back. It was a good kiss, skilled and perfectly executed, as you'd expect from someone with his wealth of experience. Eventually pulling away, she gazed into his eyes and murmured, 'That was nice. I'm impressed.'

'Thank you.'

'I think I've lost my appetite now.' As she said it, Mimi ran her left hand slowly, lightly – *significantly* – down the front of his grey sweatshirt. Beneath the soft material, his torso was taut and—

'We should have something to eat. I'm hungry. Why don't I do us a fantastic fry-up?' Paddy opened the fridge door again and took out bacon, mushrooms and tomatoes.

'Or you could do that later.' Mimi made her tone sultry, like a character in a soap, so he wouldn't be able to misunderstand. She smiled up at him. 'Much later.'

'Are you trying to seduce me?' said Paddy.

'Yes!' *Finally.* 'Yes, I am!'

His expressive eyebrows lifted a fraction. 'Are you sure that's wise?'

'Yes!' She moved towards him again, but he was shaking his head, backing away towards the sink.

Which, let's face it, wasn't the most promising reaction.

'Mimi, I'm not going to sleep with you,' he said seriously.

'What? Why not?'

'It wouldn't be right.'

'It would be! It'd be really right! Oh come on, you can't turn me down,' Mimi protested. 'You sleep with everyone!'

To add further insult to injury, a glance to the left revealed that Otto had now joined them and was standing in the kitchen doorway, observing the situation with interest. At least he couldn't rush to spread the word on Facebook. *OMG, you'll never guess what's happening here. Mimi just begged Paddy to have sex with her and he's turned her down flat LOL! Woof woof, embarrassing or what?!*

Paddy said, 'How long is it since you last slept with someone?'

'That's none of your business.'

'So, ages. Has there been anyone since that cheating ex of yours?'

Mimi looked at him and felt her palms prickle with perspiration.

'I'm guessing that means no.' Paddy shook his head in a dear-me kind of way.

'Why's it even relevant?' Honestly, talk about humiliating. 'What difference does it make? OK, it's been ages. Months and months. Which should be all the more reason for you to do the decent thing and *not* turn me down.'

'Mimi, listen to me. You're a lovely girl. Jumping into bed with someone like me just isn't *you*. I don't know why you've suddenly decided you want to do this tonight . . .' He paused, surveying her intently. 'But I might be able to hazard a guess.'

Oh God, please no, not again.

Mimi knew her face was reddening. She was going to deny it if it killed her. She said, 'You can't hazard a guess. I just want . . . to sleep with someone. Have some sex. That's all there is to it.'

Paddy's gaze was still unnervingly direct. 'Or you've decided the best way to get over a man you can't have is by distracting yourself with someone else.'

'That isn't true.' This was horrendous; did *everyone* in Goosebrook know about her crush on Cal?

His voice softened. 'You can talk to me about it if you want. I'm trustworthy. Discreet. I wouldn't breathe a word.'

'That's because there aren't any words to breathe.' It wasn't easy to speak when your mouth was dry and your tongue felt as if it had doubled in size.

'Look, you can't help the way you feel about people. There's no shame in it. You're allowed to be upset that you can't have him.'

Talk about sticking the knife in and twisting it. Mimi suddenly felt as if she might cry, because not only did the whole world apparently know, but Paddy was now refusing to help her take her mind off Cal *and* he was trying to be all kind and understanding.

'Hey,' he consoled her. 'It's OK. And of course I'd sleep with you if I thought it was going to help, but I'm being honourable here, doing the decent thing. Tomorrow morning you'll be glad it didn't happen.'

265

In a tiny, reluctant corner of her mind, Mimi knew he was right. She never had been any good at meaningless flings. She swallowed. 'Yes. I'm sorry I threw myself at you.'

'I deserve a medal for saying no.' Paddy was grinning now. 'I've never done that before.'

'You know you said you were discreet? You won't tell anyone about this, will you?'

'I promise. Cross my heart.'

'And you won't tell anyone why I did it?' Who knew if he'd keep his promise? But she had to at least ask.

'I won't say a word.' He drew her to him for a brief hug, the strictly-just-friends kind. 'Your secret's safe with me.'

Mimi hugged him back. 'Thanks.'

'It can't have been easy for you.'

She nodded in rueful agreement. 'It definitely hasn't been easy.'

'Can I just say one thing and then we won't mention it again?'

Mimi braced herself. 'Go ahead.'

'I think you should stop working for him. They've got a baby now. And I watched a couple of his TV interviews on YouTube.' Paddy grimaced slightly as he said it. 'I know he's loaded, but you could do so much better than him.'

Oh *thank goodness*. A tsunami of relief washed over her. On the verge of laughing out loud, Mimi hastily reined herself in and looked suitably brave. She nodded. 'You're right. I can.'

Mimi woke up the next morning in Paddy's spare room with a small hangover and a considerably larger sense of relief.

'Here she is.' Paddy, greeting her in the kitchen, was cooking the bacon and eggs they hadn't got around to eating the night before. 'How are you feeling?'

'Good, thanks.'

'Come here.' He beckoned her over and planted a brotherly kiss on her cheek. 'Was I right?'

'About what?'

'Everything. But mainly not letting you seduce me.'

If only he knew what he *hadn't* been right about. Mimi smiled and inhaled the scent of sizzling bacon. 'You were. Thanks for everything. Especially this breakfast.'

Twenty minutes later, they made their way back to Bay Cottage, which was looking impossibly festive in the morning sunshine with its coating of snow topped with Swarovski-style frost. After a brief search, Paddy located her lost key just off the front path, half hidden beneath a blanket of variegated ivy.

'It must have fallen out of my bag while I was looking for it,' said Mimi, relieved. 'I'm such a plank.'

'You're not, you're great.' Paddy regarded her with affection. 'You just need to have a bit of faith in yourself. I meant what I said yesterday,' he added. 'You deserve way better than CJ Exley.'

'I do.' Mimi nodded; at least that much was true.

'I actually read one of his books a couple of weeks ago.'

'You did? Enjoy it?'

Paddy shrugged. 'He knows how to tell a good tale. Kept me turning the pages. But it got on my nerves that the main guy kept looking at beautiful women and thinking their legs went up to their armpits. Because I'm pretty sure they didn't.'

Mimi laughed, because CJ might be a fantastic storyteller, but this was one of those clichéd lines he just loved to use; it made her cringe too. 'I know. I'll have a word with him, make sure it doesn't happen again.'

'I *never* want you to do anything like that again,' said Marcus.

Mimi hung her head. 'I'm sorry. I was just trying to help.'

'I know you were. But you didn't. It was . . . agonising.' He closed his eyes briefly and shuddered, clearly still haunted by the memory.

How could a plan that had been so well-intentioned go so badly awry? 'I promise I won't do it again,' Mimi said. 'I thought you might be ready.'

'Well I'm not. And I don't want to be ready. Sorry, darling, but they're never going to be your dad, so I'm really not interested. I'd rather stay single for the rest of my life.'

Oh how Mimi wished now that she hadn't put him through it. Last night had been New Year's Eve. Marcus, back from his trip to Newcastle, had stayed at home while she had joined Lois and Felix over at the Swan. Midway through the evening, having got chatting to a group of people from Cirencester, they'd discovered in passing that one of them was gay.

His name was Pierre, he was forty-four and an orthodontist. He'd broken up with his previous partner eighteen months ago. His hair was dark and neatly trimmed, his clothes were smart and fitted him well, and he had one of those quiet, intelligent faces that made him look calm and trustworthy. Mimi had thought what a perfect match he and Marcus would make. Then, as soon as Pierre excused himself to go to the gents, Lois had instantly exclaimed, 'Oh my

God, are you thinking what I'm thinking? We *have* to get him and Marcus together!'

It had felt like the best kind of fate, one of those magical moments when two people were so obviously right for each other that nothing could go wrong. But, aware that Marcus wouldn't willingly agree to being fixed up with a blind date, they'd formed a cunning plan instead. Lois would ask him to join her at the pub on New Year's Day to discuss her financial investments for the coming year, she would casually introduce him to Pierre, then Mimi would arrive to whisk her away, leaving Pierre and Marcus to get to know each other in peace.

It had been a flawless plan and Pierre had been happy to go along with it. So had Marcus, right up until the moment he'd realised what was going on and had found himself the unwilling victim of a fait accompli. Leaving him, Mimi had felt like a dog-owner waltzing off on holiday and dumping her startled, unsuspecting Labrador in kennels. But it had been with the very best of intentions. She and Lois had waved goodbye and left them to it, safe in the knowledge that Marcus's innate good manners would prevent him from abandoning Pierre and walking out. And it went without saying that within minutes in each other's company, Cupid's dart would have done its thing and the two men would realise how perfect for each other they were.

Except it hadn't happened. The expected explosion of chemistry hadn't materialised. After an excruciatingly awkward forty minutes, Pierre and Marcus had shaken hands and parted company, evidently both hoping they would never again have to endure such a mortifying experience in their lifetime.

Mimi looked at Marcus. She'd meant so well and it had ended up being disastrous.

Guilty and chastened, she said, 'I promise I'll never do it again.'

Chapter 30

Mimi was meandering along the beach when her phone began to ring. Dragging it out of her shorts pocket, she pressed answer and said happily, 'Hey! How are you?'

'You first,' said Lois. 'It's peeing down with rain here. Tell me it's not cold and miserable where you are.'

'I'm wearing a T-shirt and shorts,' said Mimi. 'And Ray-Bans, because the sun is so bright it's hurting my eyes.'

'Oh you lucky thing,' Lois sighed.

'I know.' It was the end of March and winter was over in Puerto Pollensa. The visitors were returning, the town was readying itself for the summer influx. 'Why don't you come over for a visit? I'd love that. You'd be so welcome, honestly. I can't believe it's been three months since I last saw you.'

'Well it hasn't been three months since we saw *you*.' Lois sounded cheerful. 'We see you every day. I mean, I know I've said this before, but it's just so brilliant. What have you started?'

Mimi said, 'I know, isn't it mad? I've turned a monster

into a national treasure without even meaning to. It was a complete accident.'

'But a brilliant one. And thanks for the offer, but I can't come out just now; I'm kind of busy here. Quite a lot going on.' Lois paused and took an audible breath. 'Actually, I'm moving out of Fox Court.'

'What? Why?' Shocked, Mimi stopped dead in her tracks. 'I thought you and Felix were doing OK. What's happened?'

'Oh God, it's going to sound so stupid, but I just really need a break from that place. And a break from Henrietta with her snarky comments and her disapproving stares. It's meant to be our home but it's still hers too, and if she was lovely everything would be fine . . . but she *isn't* lovely and nothing's ever going to be fine. And all Felix does is try to smooth things over, because he just wants an easy life. He's used to her being the way she is, and most of it goes over his head. I want him to stick up for me and tell his mother she's an evil old bag, but he won't. And that's what's getting to me.' Her voice rising, Lois blurted out, 'I can't put up with it any longer, I just can't. Last week that bloody cat of hers was sick in the hallway and I didn't see it. I slipped in it, fell over on the parquet floor and bashed my good leg. And d'you know what Henrietta said when she came to find out what had happened?'

'No . . .' Mimi braced herself; it clearly wasn't going to be good.

'She told me I should have jolly well looked where I was going. So I said if her cat was sick it was her job to clear up the mess. Then *she* said Truman was never ill so if he was sick now it was probably because he'd eaten something I'd left out. Meaning that it was basically my fault all along.

That was her answer. And then she stalked off leaving me flat on my back like an upturned beetle. Didn't even try to help me up. Seriously,' Lois wailed in frustration, 'I can't cope with her any more. And there's no way she's ever going to leave Fox Court, which means it's up to me to do the honours. So that's it, I've had enough. I'm off.'

'Oh no!' Mimi was shocked but not altogether surprised. 'I wish I was there to give you a big hug. What does Felix have to say about it?'

'Oh who knows? I can't bear to listen to him any more. He pretends to care, but does he really?' She exhaled noisily. 'Maybe he's secretly relieved, glad to be getting rid of me at last, what with all the trouble I cause. God knows, Henrietta must be over the moon. I'm surprised Fox Court isn't covered in bunting.'

'And how are you feeling?' said Mimi, because it was impossible to tell over the phone. Lois might be putting on a brave front, but this was her marriage they were talking about; she had to be upset.

'I don't even know how to feel right now. It might turn out to be the best thing ever. Maybe I'll be relieved too.'

'And where are you going to go? Oh no, will I even see you when I come back?' What if Lois was moving to London, or up to Edinburgh, where her parents lived? Mimi realised with a jolt how much she'd miss her if she were no longer there.

'Don't worry, you'll still see me. I'm only moving into the Latimers' place on Church Lane.'

Relieved, Mimi said, 'You're staying in Goosebrook?'

'Why not? It's easier. I know everyone.' Lois paused. 'When Nancy Latimer mentioned that they were spending the next

273

three months in New Zealand and were looking for someone to keep an eye on their house, it just made sense to volunteer. I can live there while they're away, and it'll give me and Felix a chance to see how things go. After three months we'll have worked out what has to happen next.'

'Oh, I hope everything does work out.' Mimi was also aware that the unspoken reason for staying in the village was because Goosebrook had become Lois's security blanket. Everyone who knew her was used to her scars and injuries, the way she now looked. Having to endure the stares and whispers of curious strangers was what she hated most.

'One way or another it will,' said Lois. 'Maybe having a break is just what we need. Apart from anything else, it's going to feel like a holiday getting away from Henrietta.'

She was bringing that line of conversation to a close. To change the subject, Mimi said, 'Well good luck. What else has been happening while I've been away? Anything exciting?'

'OK, let me think. Did Marcus tell you he's got himself a gorgeous new boyfriend?'

'*Whaaaat?*' Mimi almost dropped her phone. 'Are you *kidding* me?'

'Yes, I'm kidding.' Lois snorted with laughter. 'We keep hoping it'll happen, but no joy so far.'

'You got my hopes up there for a moment.'

'Sorry. Ooh, I know what else *has* happened. Cal and Della have broken up!'

Twelve hundred miles away, Mimi heard the words and felt her heart launch into a gallop. She watched two birds fly overhead in formation before veering away from the water's edge. Cal and Della, no longer together. Unless . . .

'Is this another joke?'

'Nope, it's the real thing. Cross my heart. All over. Heard about it last night. Which means Cal's back on the market,' said Lois. 'So that's a bit exciting, isn't it?'

'Why did they break up?' Did her voice sound normal? Mimi couldn't begin to tell. Had she even said the words in the right order?

'Oh, no one knows.' Lois put on her mysterious voice. 'That's what makes it so interesting. I can't wait to be nosy and find out!'

It was ironic that after months of working hard to present CJ Exley in the best possible light and conceal the less attractive aspects of his personality from the world, Mimi's greatest PR success had come about by reversing that plan.

And then, even more cunningly, by reversing that reversal.

It had all started completely by chance. Mimi had returned to Puerto Pollensa on 2 January, the day before Cal, Della and their two girls had flown home from their skiing holiday in Austria. A few days after that, having organised baby Alice's passport, Willa and CJ arrived at the villa along with Alice and an absolute ton of luggage, because CJ couldn't stop buying toys, clothes and baby paraphernalia for his beloved new daughter.

Mimi stayed put in her apartment, the one that had once been occupied by Willa. Willa and her belongings moved into CJ's master suite and decorators were hastily hired to turn one of the other bedrooms into a fairy-tale nursery. And now Mimi had to work harder than ever to keep CJ at his desk when he really didn't want to be there, because all he cared about was his newly formed family.

But contracts had been signed and needed to be fulfilled;

major publishing houses around the world were waiting impatiently for the next book and it had to be written. The only way to ensure it happened had been to turn Alice into her father's reward system. Each time CJ hit his targeted word count, he was allowed to see his daughter for ten minutes.

The first video had come about entirely by chance. With CJ in his office and the sound of muffled epithets leaking through the closed door, Mimi said to Willa, 'Take your bets, then. What's he going to say when I ask him how he's doing?'

Willa, who was cradling Alice in her arms, said promptly, 'He's going to call you an evil witch. And he'll probably threaten to sack you, too.'

'I think he'll tell me it's my fault it's all going wrong, and demand a bowl of Twiglets.'

They both knew him so well. Mimi took out her phone and crossed the living room. She knocked on the door of CJ's office, switched on video recording and said into the camera, 'OK, here we go, into the lion's den. Brace yourselves.'

'Bring me a whisky,' CJ barked as the door creaked open.

'How's it going?'

'I hate you. Nothing's right and it's all your fault.'

'Oh CJ, it can't be that bad.'

'It's worse. Get me some Twiglets too.' He glanced round at her finally. 'Oh for crying out loud, are you filming me? Whaddaya have to do that for? Go away.'

'How many words have you written?'

He held up a single foolscap sheet, covered in his terrible handwriting and multiple crossings-out.

'One page, so that's two hundred words. You need to do

better than that. Get yourself up to five hundred words,' Mimi said calmly, 'and then you can have your Twiglets.'

He shot her a murderous look. 'Get out. And don't you dare send that video to anyone or you're fired.'

The next day, having persuaded him to change his mind, Mimi had posted the clip on YouTube and linked it to his social media accounts, where it had promptly been shared and retweeted worldwide, evoking more responses in one day than all his previous posts had attained in total.

The grumpy, tetchy reality of CJ Exley had captured the attention of millions of people in a way that no carefully crafted interview portraying him in the best light ever had. Mimi began filming him daily, inviting viewers to guess in advance how many words might have been written and which choice new insult he might come up with, before posting the latest video on his website. The lucky winners would then have their names included in CJ's next tirade of abuse.

Everyone loved getting involved, the viewing figures for the videos continued to spiral upwards, and requests for TV interviews with the literary world's favourite curmudgeon came flooding in. When CJ was flown over to the US to appear on *The Ellen DeGeneres Show*, he shook his head at the audience and told them they were a bunch of hysterical shrieking harpies who needed to get a grip. Which just made them shriek all the more.

And sales of his books rocketed.

Was CJ effusively grateful to Mimi for all she'd done for him?

Of course he wasn't. Not one bit.

But she knew that deep down he was pleased it had happened.

And now the time had come for her to move on. Having inherited none of CJ's character traits, Alice was proving herself to be a smiley, placid baby who slept well and seldom cried. Willa, Mimi knew, liked to keep busy and had been increasingly eager to get back to work. The morning Mimi switched on her work laptop to type up the two thousand words CJ had written the day before only to find them already typed, she knew it was time to let go.

'Sorry.' Willa was apologetic. 'Couldn't help myself. I just miss doing it so much.'

'It's fine. We always knew I was only here for a while.' Mimi held out her arms to take Alice. 'Let me have a cuddle with this one. I'm going to miss her so much.'

'You can come out and visit us whenever you want. Can't she?' said Willa as CJ joined them in the kitchen.

'Does this mean she's abandoning us?' CJ mimed horror, but there was laughter in his eyes; they'd clearly already discussed the situation.

'I'm like Mary Poppins,' Mimi told him. 'My work here is done. I've sorted you out, turned you into a decent human being, and now I'm going to let you carry on without me.'

'More like that scary one with the giant tooth.' CJ ducked out of the way before she could hit him. 'Nanny McPhee.'

Chapter 31

That had happened a week ago. And now here she was, on a plane home, heading back to Goosebrook. As they began their descent, Mimi mentally replayed her last few minutes with Willa, Alice and CJ, who had come with her to Palma to see her off. Willa had hugged her and said, 'We're going to miss you so much.' Alice had tried to tug her hair. And CJ had launched quite unexpectedly into an impassioned speech, telling her that she'd changed his life and he could never thank her enough for everything she'd done. Then, in a voice husky with emotion, he'd clasped her hands between his own and asked her if she'd promise to come to their wedding when he and Willa married, because how could she not be there when they both owed her so much?

Unbelievably touched, Mimi had said of course she would, then Willa had pointed out that CJ hadn't actually asked her to marry him yet, which defused the emotional impact of the moment and made everyone laugh. 'I'll ask you tonight,' CJ assured her. 'But only if you promise to say yes.'

And when Mimi had turned to take one last look at them

before heading off into Departures, she'd seen them standing together, waving goodbye to her. The next moment, taking Alice in his arms, CJ leaned sideways and kissed Willa on the mouth, and Willa was lovingly kissing him back . . .

'You OK, love?' said the woman in the next seat, and it wasn't until that moment that Mimi realised a tear had just slid down her face and dripped onto the front of her T-shirt.

'I'm fine . . . oh, thanks.' Gratefully Mimi took the clean tissue being offered. 'How weird, I didn't even know I was crying.'

'Ah, I can guess what it's all about. You've been miles away.' The woman gave her a reassuring smile and reached down into the capacious handbag at her feet. 'Left your boyfriend behind, I bet. Not going to see him again for a while.'

'Actually—'

'Worried sick he's going to be getting up to mischief behind your back.' The woman nodded sagely. 'Now that you're on your way home, some new little tart in a bikini's going to get her claws into him and he'll forget all about you, am I right? Trust me, I've seen it all in my time. Here, you help yourself.' She offered Mimi an already opened packet of custard creams. 'It's just what men are like; all they care about is sex, sex, sex. You cheer yourself up, love. No point crying over some bloke who isn't worth it. Dry those eyes and have a few biscuits instead.'

After which, Mimi didn't have the heart to tell her there was no boyfriend in her life, faithful or otherwise. Once you'd eaten six of someone else's custard creams and accepted their sympathy, it just wouldn't have been right. Instead, she took out her notebook and added more notes to the plans she'd been making for the months – and hopefully years – ahead.

Forty minutes later, having hauled her cases off the carousel and loaded them onto a trolley, Mimi reached the arrivals gate and saw a pretty brunette with magenta streaks in her hair holding up a card bearing her name. She'd known that CJ had booked a car for her, but it wasn't until they reached the short-stay car park and she saw the bright red Bentley Continental that Mimi realised he'd arranged something quite so special.

The driver, whose name was Cleo, was delighted by her reaction. 'Oh, I'm so glad you love it. This car is my pride and joy!'

Reverently Mimi stroked the glossy paintwork. 'We were talking about favourite cars last week and I told my boss I'd always fantasised about being driven in a Bentley Continental. Elton John used to have one that was this exact colour, and it just seemed like the best car you could ever wish for.' Deeply touched that he'd remembered, she added, 'CJ must have chosen you specially.'

'He did.' Cleo grinned. 'He found my website and called me up a few days ago to make the booking. Which was pretty thrilling for me,' she continued whilst efficiently hauling the cases into the boot of the car, 'because I'm such a fan – I've read every book CJ Exley has ever written. And I told him I'd been watching the videos on his website every day too. He said if we send him a photo of the two of us together, he'll include it in his next blog. I just love how he can be all grumpy and fierce one minute, then so sweet and kind the next. The new videos of him with Alice are so heart-melting they make me cry.'

These had been Mimi's last idea before leaving, brief clips showing CJ being reunited with his daughter once the requisite number of words had been written each day. How the viewers adored seeing his face light up with love as he scooped Alice into his arms and called her his little pumpkin. 'It's been fun working for him,' she told Cleo. 'His bark's worse than his bite. Oh, do I have to go in the back?' Having closed the boot, Cleo was now opening one of the rear doors for her. 'Can't I sit in the front with you?'

They chatted non-stop all the way to Goosebrook. Mimi learned about the ups and downs of Cleo's job as a chauffeur, and also discovered that her husband created life-sized wire sculptures of horses for a living. Googling him on her phone, she admired the spectacular sculptures, then said, 'Oh I say,' because there was a photo of Johnny LaVenture himself and he was rather gorgeous too. 'Am I allowed to be nosy and ask how you two got together?'

Cleo laughed. 'Oh we knew each other at school. I hated him! Then he moved over to the States for ages. When he came back, we saw each other again and I hated him even more . . . but, well, gradually I changed my mind. And here we are now, happier than we ever imagined. It was kind of the complete opposite of love at first sight.' She pulled a *whoops* face, then added, 'Luckily it all seems to have worked out all right.'

'That's great.'

'And now it's my turn to be nosy. Ever had that love-at-first-sight thing happen to you?'

The lightning bolt, she meant. Mimi instantly thought back to the first time she'd clapped eyes on Cal. OK, maybe not the very first moments in that field when she'd thought

282

he was attacking a sheep, but within a few minutes of actually speaking to him there had definitely been a spark of attraction. More than a spark, in fact; a cheerful flame potentially capable of growing into a small bonfire. She'd been thrilled to discover he lived in Goosebrook and had been so looking forward to seeing him again later that evening . . .

Except, she belatedly remembered, Cleo was asking her about relationships that had actually happened in real life, not the kind that had only ever existed in her mind. Forcing herself to think of Rob instead – ugh, it now seemed like a lifetime ago – Mimi said, 'I've never had one of those moments where you absolutely know right away. When I was living in London I got into a relationship with my boss, but that one was more of a slow burn.'

'And how did it turn out?' Cleo sounded interested.

'Not brilliantly.' Mimi pulled a face. 'Which is why I escaped from London and moved down here.'

They were approaching the brow of the hill now. As Cleo braked slightly, Goosebrook appeared ahead of them, wonderfully familiar and bathed in golden afternoon sunlight.

'Well I can't imagine that was too much of a hardship. This place looks gorgeous. And I've grown up in a Cotswold village,' Cleo added, 'so I know what I'm talking about.'

Mimi found herself holding her breath as the car drove past Cedar Lane, along which Cal's cottage stood. She knew she'd be seeing him again before long, but a few hours to regain her bearings wouldn't go amiss.

'Oh my goodness,' she said as heads turned to follow their progress along the high street. 'This is amazing. I feel like the queen.'

Grinning, Cleo drew to a halt outside Bay Cottage. Within seconds, Cora and Lauren had abandoned their friends on the green and come racing over to join them.

'Mimi, is this your new car? Did you win the lottery? It's *really* cool.'

Climbing out of the passenger seat, Mimi said, 'It isn't mine, sorry. I wish it was. Cleo met me at the airport and drove me down here.'

'It's so cool.' Cora's eyes were wide as she admired the Bentley. 'My uncle in Wales has a red car but it's nothing like this and it's always covered in mud. Mimi, I really loved the hat and scarf you gave me for Christmas. I've worn them so many times, haven't I? The purple ones?' She turned to Lauren, who nodded vigorously.

'I'm glad you liked them. And I loved the thank-you card you sent me.' Mimi had been charmed by the fact that Cal had evidently prompted his daughter to make and send the card, which had arrived in the post the week after they'd returned from their skiing trip to Austria.

'OK, all done.' Whilst she'd been talking to Cora, Cleo had unloaded the cases. She looked at Cora and Lauren. 'Before I head off, would you two girls like a quick trip around the village green in a Bentley?'

With squeals of delight, they leapt onto the back seats. Mimi took photos of them as they beamed at her and waved through the wound-down windows, then Cleo made a slow circuit of the green so they could show off gleefully in front of their friends. Finally, having tumbled back out of the car, Cora took a couple of photos of Mimi and Cleo standing together in front of it, so that Cleo could send them to CJ.

When the red Bentley had disappeared from view, Lauren said, 'It's four o'clock, shall we go back to mine now?'

'Um . . .' Cora hesitated. 'I'll come over in a bit, OK? I want to . . . thank Mimi for my scarf.'

Lauren frowned. 'You already did that.'

'I know.' Cora stood her ground. 'I just want to say it again.'

Chapter 32

When Lauren had turned and left, Mimi reached for the largest of the cases on the pavement. 'You don't have to thank me,' she said. 'Is everything OK?'

'Not really.' Cora's voice was subdued.

'Oh sweetheart!' Mimi took out her front door key. 'Well, Marcus won't be home for a while, so why don't you come along inside and we'll have a chat. You can tell me what's on your mind.'

Together they hauled the cases inside the cottage. As she made a mug of tea for herself and found biscuits and apple juice for Cora, Mimi chatted about her time in Puerto Pollensa, about the tiny fish that darted through the shallows where the Mediterranean met the beach, and about the noisy birds she'd thrown crumbs to each morning on her terrace. Then they carried everything through to the living room and she sat down on the sofa, patting the seat next to her.

'Come on then, what's been happening? And you can tell me anything, you know. I won't breathe a word to anyone, not unless you want me to.'

Cora looked alarmed. 'I definitely don't want you to.'

Oh Lord, what was this about? 'Then it won't happen, I promise. And I'm brilliant at keeping secrets. You wouldn't *believe* how many incredible secrets I know.'

'About who?'

'Can't tell you. It's a secret.'

Cora smiled, and the tension in her skinny shoulders visibly reduced. She picked up one of the pink wafer biscuits that Marcus unaccountably loved and nibbled one end before pulling a face. 'These are a bit weird.'

'Yes, sorry about that. They're Marcus's favourites.'

'Dad and Della aren't seeing each other any more.'

Oh no, was that the problem? Mimi hesitated, then nodded. 'I know, I heard. How do you feel about that?'

Cora shrugged. 'All right. Della was OK, but I'm not upset they broke up.'

Well that was something. Mimi longed to know why it had happened, but she could hardly ask Cora. Instead she said, 'Has it made things awkward between you and Charlotte?'

Another shrug. 'A bit. But it was like, we were having to spend loads of time together before, and sometimes it felt like too much time, you know? Plus I wasn't getting to see Lauren so much, even though she was my real best friend, because Della said me and Charlotte were best friends now. Except we never were, not really. It was just like we had to pretend everything we did was more fun than it really was.'

'That can't have been easy.' Mimi's heart went out to her.

'But Della won't bring Charlotte over here any more, so it's better now.'

287

'OK, that's good!' Rather than bombard her with questions, Mimi took a swallow of hot tea instead, and waited.

Finally Cora said, 'I think Dad's got another girlfriend now.'

The words echoed through Mimi's brain like pebbles being dropped down a well. She had to catch her breath as they sank in. Because deep down, of course she'd been happy to hear that Cal and Della were no longer a couple. Deep, *deep* down, she'd fantasised that maybe she might stand a smidgeon of a chance with him after all.

Well so much for that idea. Cal was evidently wasting no time in moving on from one to the next; maybe the new woman in his life was the reason he'd broken up with Della. Mimi felt sick with disappointment, then a split second later sicker still, because this wasn't about her. She was being confided in because Cora clearly wasn't happy with the situation. And really, who could blame her? After years of mourning his wife and steering clear of the dating scene, Cal now appeared to be intent on making up for lost time.

'And?' Mimi saw the troubled expression in Cora's eyes and gently stroked the back of her hand. 'Do you think it's a bit soon?'

Cora nodded fractionally. 'Yes.'

'Have you met her? Is she nice?'

'She's OK, but not right for Dad.' Cora turned her head to look at Mimi. 'Do you know who it is?'

Mimi was taken aback. 'No, who?'

But Cora was shaking her head. 'I can't say.'

'Sweetheart, that's fine, you don't have to if you don't want to.' Mimi wondered if Cal was seeing one of Cora's teachers, which surely had the potential to be embarrassing.

'I do want to. It just keeps going round and round in my mind. But I'm scared in case you talk to someone about it.'

'OK, I one hundred per cent guarantee I won't breathe a word. Cross my heart. Hang on.' Mimi jumped up and collected the notepad and pen Marcus always kept in the kitchen for his beloved list-making, then returned and wrote: *I hereby promise one million per cent not to say anything to anyone about Cora Mathieson's secret. I will never ever talk about it. Signed: Mimi Huish.*

Cora took the sheet of paper from her. She folded it carefully and pushed it into the pocket of her navy-blue school skirt. 'You won't be cross with me, will you?'

'What? No, *never.*' Mimi placed an arm around her shoulders. 'And that's another solid gold promise.'

She felt the big shuddery intake of breath, then Cora clasped her hands together in her lap. 'It's Lois.'

Now it was Mimi's turn to be at a loss for words. *Lois?* More than that, she was knocked sideways. Was it true? Could it be? There'd never been any hint before that Cal and Lois might secretly be attracted to each other.

Then again, Cal had his morals; he would never have done anything to break up Lois and Felix's marriage. But now that she'd moved out of Fox Court, maybe those rules no longer applied.

Cal and Lois. *Oh God, Cal and Lois.*

To give herself a few seconds to assimilate this information, Mimi reached over for her cup and took a gulp of tea. How? When? Why?

Finally she said, 'Are you sure?'

'Well, yes.'

'Does your dad know you aren't happy about it?'

Cora shook her head so vigorously her curls jiggled. 'He doesn't know I know.'

'Does anyone else know? In the village, I mean?'

'I don't think so. I haven't even told Lauren. Because Dad hasn't said anything,' Cora explained, 'so it means they want to keep it a secret too.'

Poor Felix, he would be devastated. Cal was his friend. The fallout in the village once it became public knowledge would be major. No wonder Cal and Lois were so anxious to keep things under wraps.

'How did you find out?' Mimi asked cautiously.

'Dad was painting in his studio last week. I said I was going to take Otto out with Lauren, then we'd watch a film at her place. But Lauren had to go to the orthodontist with her mum, so I just took Otto for a quick walk, then we came home.' As she relayed the story, Cora edged closer to Mimi's side and absently pulled at the frayed sleeve of her school sweatshirt. 'Dad didn't know we were back because me and Otto just went up to my room. And it was only when I looked out of the window about five minutes later that I saw Lois coming into our back garden. She didn't ring the doorbell or anything, just came round the side and went straight over to the studio. Then she knocked on the door and Dad opened it, and they were just, like, standing there and really smiling at each other . . . then they went inside and closed the door.' She rubbed the flat of her hand over her chin and said reluctantly, 'They were in there for an hour.'

Hope rising, Mimi said, 'Maybe your dad's painting her portrait? They could be secretly doing it for her mum's birthday, or just as a general surprise . . .'

But Cora was already shaking her head firmly. 'I went over and checked, searched the whole studio. There wasn't any painting, or any photos or sketches either, anywhere inside.' She paused, scratched her bare knee, then blurted out, 'And when they came out of the studio together, Dad had taken off his jumper so he was just wearing his shirt. And they were both looking happy, and kind of hot and out of breath.'

Oh God.

'I'm not a baby.' Cora's cheeks flushed slightly. 'I know what goes on. And it's happened two more times since then as well. The exact same thing. The blinds in the studio are drawn and Dad's fitted a new lock on the inside of the door so no one can get in, and it's not that I *hate* Lois, because I don't, I just don't feel like she's right for Dad. Plus, it's too soon after breaking up with Della.'

'I know, I know.' Mimi gave her shoulders a reassuring squeeze. 'Oh you poor thing, no wonder you wanted to talk. It isn't easy, is it?'

Cora shook her head. 'I'm not being horrible, honestly. And I do want Dad to be happy. I used to imagine him with someone really nice. But this feels all wrong. I never thought he'd go for someone like Lois.'

Ditto. As she stroked Cora's tangled blonde hair, Mimi recalled the phone conversation she'd had the other week when Lois had first told her about Cal and Della splitting up. Lois had said brightly, 'Which means Cal's back on the market. So that's a bit exciting, isn't it?'

It hadn't crossed her mind at the time that Lois had meant it was exciting for *her*.

Aloud, she said, 'Look, maybe it won't last. Give them another couple of weeks and it might all be over.'

'I hope so. Ben in my class has a new stepmother he doesn't like, and he says having to live with her is awful.'

'If you ever need to talk, I'm here.' As she said it, Mimi recognised the sound of Marcus's car pulling up outside. 'We can chat about anything you want, any time you like.'

'Thanks. And for letting us have that ride in the Bentley.' Cora tilted her head, cornflower-blue eyes gazing up at her. 'I'm really glad you're back.'

Mimi smiled. 'Me too.'

Although deep down, she was beginning to wonder now if this was true.

Chapter 33

'Come on, *relax*,' Lois urged. 'Get it down you! We're celebrating you being home and me having my friend back at last.'

But there was no way Mimi could relax, nor did she trust herself to have any more of the Cloudy Bay Sauvignon Blanc, even though it was crazily expensive and tasted like angels dancing on her tongue.

'I'm fine, honestly. I have to start work early tomorrow.' She covered her glass before Lois could top it up, then gestured around the sitting room. 'Isn't this place great? Does it feel weird, living here on your own?' Was she sounding normal? To her own ears it felt as if everything she said held a subtext. At the same time, the house Lois was minding for Nancy and Simon Latimer was large and undoubtedly beautiful, but she now understood why Lois and Cal would choose to hold their secret trysts in the studio tucked away in Cal's back garden. This house, here on Church Lane overlooking the village green, simply wasn't somewhere you could sneak into unnoticed.

'It does feel weird, but it was just something I needed to

do. And like I said, it's bliss not having Henrietta sticking her nose in and being disapproving of pretty much everything I do, including breathing.' Lois plonked the bottle of Cloudy Bay back in the ice bucket and tore open a packet of cashews. 'Although she still has her personal private detective keeping an eye on me.'

'Really?' Jolted, Mimi wondered if Henrietta already knew about Lois and Cal's clandestine get-togethers. But how could a private detective possibly blend in here, in a village the size of Goosebrook?

'Oh yes. In fact he's watching us right now.'

What? The next moment, Mimi realised Lois was indicating the small window over to the left of the fireplace, and saw that Truman was sitting on the narrow windowsill gazing in at them with his unblinking, implacable stare.

'Got you.' Entertained, Lois added, 'Not that I wouldn't put it past Henrietta to hire someone, but it hasn't happened yet.'

'Unless it has and you just haven't noticed.'

Lois laughed and Mimi wondered if there was a smidgeon of guilt buried in the laughter before being hastily smothered by a handful of cashews.

'So, any other news since you moved in here?' Did *that* sound casual enough?

'Nothing to report so far. But it's only been a fortnight, so give me a chance.' Lois looked rueful and ran the flat of her hand over the scars across her throat and upper chest. 'Although it's all very well being single and ready to mingle, but who says anyone would want to mingle with me?'

Unless, of course, it was someone who already knew about the self-consciousness and the scars, and who wasn't shallow enough to be put off by them. Someone who was kind, fully grounded and a genuinely good person.

Was Lois's self-deprecating comment in fact a form of double bluff?

'Plenty of men would want to mingle with you.' As Mimi said it, a vision of the future ran through her mind and a shiver of dismay simultaneously crawled over her skin. Because up until now she'd been concentrating on Cora's dilemma. But Cora was an eleven-year-old child who might easily change her mind, just as her one-time passion for zebras had bloomed and faded and been replaced by a series of other fads. Who was to say that in weeks to come she might not decide that Lois was a brilliant person and a perfect match for her dad after all? And that the relationship between Lois, Cal and Cora might not flourish and grow? Six months from now, they could be the happiest family unit imaginable, with Cora finding it impossible to believe that she'd ever had her doubts about Lois coming into their lives.

And who wouldn't wish for this to come true, for Cora to end up with a wonderful stepmother to love and be loved by in return? She'd been through so much and it was what she deserved. Mimi swallowed, realising that if that were to happen, she would have to get over her own hidden feelings for Cal once and for all, plaster on a bright smile and *make* herself be delighted for them.

Would she really be able to manage that?

Then again, like it or not, she'd just have to. Since he'd never been hers in the first place, it was a matter of not having any other choice.

★　★　★

'Are you sure about this?' Marcus was about to leave for work the next morning. 'You don't have to do it, you know. I can get someone in.' Except they both knew he wouldn't, not until the situation was desperate and completely out of hand. Bay Cottage itself might be immaculate, but gardening was low on Marcus's list of priorities. When her dad had been alive, the garden had been entirely his domain. After his death, an elderly man from the next village had been hired to keep it in order, but since his retirement last September, nothing more had been done.

Until this morning. Spring was here, the sun was shining in a washed-blue sky, and Mimi had decided that the time had come to seize the day.

'Off you go.' She shooed Marcus, in his smart suit, out of the front door. 'I'm looking forward to this. By the time you get home, this place is going to look like Chelsea Flower Show.'

Well, it would look better than it did now, with all the new green shoots and unfurling petals struggling to be seen as they battled their way up through the winter detritus of dried leaves and weeds and drastically overgrown hedges.

Having waved Marcus off in his car, Mimi braved the musty, cobwebby depths of the garden shed and dragged out everything she needed to tackle the job. A startled spider ran across the wooden handle of the spade and galloped up her arm, and she had to force herself to be brave by pretending it was a task on *I'm a Celebrity*.

Right, time to get going. She was going to cut down everything that was dead, clear up as many weeds as possible and heap everything into a big pile at the far end of the garden.

Two hours later, the pile was growing, perspiration was trickling down Mimi's spine, and she was about to give her aching back a rest when the sound of footsteps on the pavement made her look up. From here at the side of the house she glimpsed Cal making his way with Otto along the high street.

As he turned his head in her direction, Mimi hastily jerked her face away and, heart clamouring, pretended to be thoroughly occupied with an overgrown bramble.

Of course it had to happen sooner or later. But please, not just yet.

The bramble was longer than expected, and over the course of the winter had woven itself into the lawn. Thank goodness there'd been heavy-duty gardening gloves in the shed. Grasping it in both securely protected hands at the halfway point, Mimi began to tear it away from its mesh of grass and weeds, then tugged with all her might.

The unexpected brush of a wagging tail against her bare ankle caused her to lose her balance just as the bramble freed itself. The thin, wiry end sprang up and came whipping through the air, and Mimi only managed to jerk her head back and squeeze her eyes shut in the nick of time.

She also just about managed not to land on Otto and squash him flat.

'*Aaaaarrrgh . . .*'

'*Woof!*' Still wagging his tail in delight, Otto did a little dance on his hind legs and scrabbled his front paws against her knees.

Was it ridiculous to be wincing with pain yet at the same time secretly thrilled that he was so pleased to see her?

'Hi. Sorry, I didn't have him on a lead,' said Cal, behind

them. 'He just took off like a mad thing and came racing over to see you . . . Oh God.'

Having turned and dropped her hand from her face, Mimi saw his look of alarm and glanced down at the smears of blood on her gloved fingers. She shook her head. 'No problem, it's fine.'

'You haven't seen it. Stand still and let me take a proper look. Otto, leave her alone. Sit down. Not you,' Cal added as Mimi began to edge towards the wooden seat on the patio. 'Unless you're feeling faint. Are you going to faint?'

'Of course I'm not going to faint.' Honestly, how much of a wimp did he think she was? 'It's only a couple of scratches.' If anything, at least the mishap had created a diversion from the awkwardness of seeing him again for the first time since Della's warning to her in the pub. Plus, thanks to two hours of energetic gardening, her face was already pink.

'Are you up to date with your tetanus jabs?'

Mimi nodded. 'I am.'

'We still need to get you cleaned up, though. You don't want it getting infected.'

Upstairs in the bathroom, Cal opened the cabinet and took out antiseptic cream and cotton wool pads.

'Sit,' he instructed once more, addressing Mimi this time and pointing to the rolltop edge of the bath.

'I can do it myself,' she protested, but he shook his head.

'I feel guilty. It was Otto's fault. Yes, *you*,' Cal added sternly as Otto's ears pricked up. 'You caused all this damage.'

Mimi perched and said with a twinge of alarm, 'How much damage?' Oh God, was it worse than it felt?

'Don't worry, it's only surface scratches. Nothing major.'

298

Entirely unrepentant, Otto leapt onto her lap and made himself comfortable, and Mimi's spirits lifted in an unattractively competitive way. Had he always been this affectionate with Della?

'Right, close your eyes.' Cal had run a couple of the cotton wool pads under the cold tap.

'Hang on, I don't even know what I look like.' Reaching to one side, Mimi grabbed the magnifying mirror from the windowsill then recoiled at the sight that greeted her. The way the bramble had whipped across her face meant the tiny, razor-sharp thorns had dragged through her skin from up in her hairline all the way down the side of her face to her chin. The blood was beading and dripping down her cheek. Putting the mirror back, she said, 'I look as if I've had a fight with a tiny chainsaw.'

Cal nodded in agreement. 'That's why I asked you to close your eyes.'

She remained perched on the side of the bath and stroked Otto's warm, curled-up body while Cal painstakingly cleaned her face and applied the antiseptic cream.

'You're good at this,' said Mimi.

'I'm a dad.' His tone was wry. 'I've had plenty of practice. There, all done. And sorry again about Otto.'

'You don't have to apologise.'

'If I'd had him on a lead, he wouldn't have been able to catch you by surprise. So it is actually my fault. But there won't be any scars,' Cal assured her. 'You'll be as good as new in a week.'

'Well, thanks for cleaning me up.'

'My pleasure. And it's good to see you again.'

If he only knew how fast her heart was beating. Mimi

299

nodded awkwardly and they headed downstairs, so much still unsaid. She knew what he must be thinking and it was agonisingly embarrassing that he *was* thinking it. But raising the subject would be even worse. If not mentioning her crush on him was the way Cal wanted to deal with it, she was more than happy to go along with that. Oh, but there were so many questions she was longing to ask him – about Della, about Cora, and most of all about whatever was going on between him and Lois.

'I'd better be getting back to the garden. I'm blitzing it while Marcus is out at work.' As they made their way outside, Mimi said, 'I want it to look fifty times better by the time he gets home.' She paused on the small patio and surveyed the amount of work still needing to be done. 'Well let's say a *bit* better.'

'You've made a start.' Next to her, Cal nodded. 'I could give you a hand if you like.'

'Really?' Her heart thud-thudded.

'Why not? My next project doesn't start till tomorrow, so I'm free for the rest of the day.' He shrugged casually. 'Let's do it.'

Mimi swallowed; he was so nice.

Oh God, why does he have to be so nice? It doesn't help.

Chapter 34

By two o'clock, the difference in the garden was noticeable. There was a skip-sized pile of dead branches at the far end, the weeds in the flower beds had been cleared and the grass had been cut. Cal had steered the lawnmower around the clumps of daffodils that randomly dotted the lawn, and now they swayed happily in the sunshine like mini desert islands.

'It looks fantastic.' If she'd been perspiring before, Mimi was really sweating now. She raked muddy, grass-stained fingers through the hair that was sticking attractively to the back of her neck. 'Thank you so much.'

'What are you, some kind of lightweight? We're just stopping for lunch,' said Cal. 'We haven't finished yet.'

In the kitchen, they made toasted cheese sandwiches and a chicken salad, then took the food outside to eat at the oak table on the patio. For the last three hours they'd been talking about the work they were doing in the garden, but now they were in danger of having to have an actual conversation about other stuff.

Cal cracked open the two cans of Lilt they'd taken from the fridge and handed one to her. 'Here you go. Cheers.'

'Cheers.' She clinked her can against his. 'If I hadn't been looking such a mess, we could have gone over to the Swan and I'd have treated you to a proper lunch.'

'This'll do me fine. And you don't look too horrendous.'

Mimi pulled a face, because she knew she did. 'Enough of a mess not to want to be seen in public.'

Cal took a bite of his toasted cheese sandwich. When he'd swallowed, he said, 'So what's the plan, are you back for good? Or will you be off again as soon as the next job comes along?'

Mimi glanced at him. She'd told Lois her plans last night, but Cal didn't appear to be aware of them. Unless he did know and was just pretending not to. Because that was the trouble with secret relationships: once you knew two people were seeing each other on the quiet, it made it hard to believe anything they said.

Then again, maybe he and Lois had more interesting things to talk about than Mimi's boring career plans.

Oh well, he'd asked now. 'I'm going to set up my own PR agency,' she said.

'You are? Wow!' He definitely looked surprised. 'I'm impressed.'

'Nothing massive. Just me, to start with. And I'll be working from home most of the time.' She took a gulp of Lilt. 'But CJ's videos going viral created quite a bit of interest. I was approached by a couple of big companies, one in Toronto and one in New York, but decided I'd rather go it alone. I've been contacted by individual writers and actors asking if they can hire me to promote them, so now seems like the best time to do it.' She shrugged. 'Have laptop, no need to travel.'

'Sounds brilliant. If anyone can make it work, it's you. And how great that you'll be staying here.' Cal's brown eyes softened; he had such a way of looking at you and making you feel like the most important person in the world. He sounded as if he really meant it, too. Mimi, her heart twisting with regret, reminded herself that he only regarded her as a friend, and by unspoken mutual agreement there would be no mention of the awkward one-sided crush.

She collected herself. 'Well it's only going to be great if the plan works out. We'll just have to see if it does.' And she popped a cherry tomato into her mouth to signal that the job talk was at an end.

Cal waited for a couple of seconds, then said, 'You haven't asked me about Della.'

Oh help, was this where things started getting embarrassing? Mimi chewed and swallowed. 'What about her?'

'We broke up.'

'I know.'

He smiled briefly. 'Everyone else has been desperate to know why. You haven't even mentioned it. I thought you might.'

The subtext being: *Seeing as you're the one who fantasises about taking her place.*

Mimi said casually, 'Whatever it was, it's between you and Della. Nobody else's business.'

'This is true.' He nodded in agreement. 'But I'll tell you anyway. Nothing terrible happened. Neither of us did anything awful. It was just a couple of small things that gradually became a few not-quite-so-small things . . . and at the beginning you think maybe you'll get used to those things and won't notice them after a while, but as time goes by you kind of realise that isn't going to happen. Do you know what I mean?'

On the surface, they were behaving as if they were just friends who talked about this kind of stuff to each other. Inside, a swarm of bees had invaded Mimi's stomach. If she hadn't bumped into Cora yesterday afternoon and heard the whole Cal and Lois story, imagine how excited the way he was speaking to her now would be making her feel.

But she had, and actually it was just as well, because who knows what embarrassing impulse she might have acted upon otherwise. It didn't bear thinking about.

'I do.' Mimi speared a piece of chicken with her fork. 'Like those sexy texts she used to send you.'

'Exactly.' Cal nodded.

This presumably meant Lois didn't do that.

Or hadn't done it *yet*.

'And she was very keen on hand-holding in public.' Cal pulled a face. 'I mean, *all* the time, even when it wasn't practical. I was trying to carry our Christmas tree back to the car in Cirencester and she still kept trying to hold my hand. When it's not what you're used to, it feels really strange.'

'PDAs,' said Mimi.

'What?'

'Public displays of affection. That's what it's called.'

'Public displays of awkwardness, more like.' Cal's smile was dry. 'And the selfies were a bit of a pain, too. It was like nothing had even happened unless it was on Instagram.'

'Except you didn't mind when she posted photos of your paintings online.' Mimi couldn't help herself; it was only fair to point it out.

'OK, touché.' He broke into a grin. 'Now I feel bad for

saying it. She did do me a big favour there. I shouldn't be saying these things about her now.'

Oh please, don't stop on my account.

'I won't tell anyone. You can trust me,' said Mimi. 'I'm discreet.'

Cal looked at her. 'Me too.'

Was he about to confide in her about his secret relationship with Lois? Mimi tried and failed to read his mind, before realising with a jolt that he was more likely to be referring to her giant not-so-secret crush.

'Good.' Her mouth was dry and her tongue had stuck itself to the roof of her mouth, so it came out as *ggd*.

'Just so we both know.' Cal nodded slowly, and this time there was an expression in his brown eyes that she really couldn't gauge. In a split second Mimi knew she had to say something, because if the look was pity she just couldn't bear it.

'OK, I need to say something,' she blurted out. 'I didn't want to, but it has to be done so we can clear the air. That thing Della talked to me about as you were all leaving the pub on Boxing Day . . . I know she'd have told you about it, but it's all in the past now. It was like one of those things that just comes whooshing up out of nowhere and then before you know it, it's gone again. And that was what happened – it went, and I'm so glad it did. But I wanted you to know. It's gone and it really is over, as if it was never there in the first place. It's like I just came to my senses. And it won't ever happen again, I promise.'

'Right.' Cal nodded as she came to a breathless halt. 'Well, I'm glad it's all sorted out. That's good to know.'

'It was pretty embarrassing,' Mimi admitted, the can of

Lilt creaking in her hand as her grasp tightened. 'Could we pretend it never happened? Is that OK?'

'Of course.' Cal sounded relieved. 'I really am glad you're over it now. Everything can get back to normal and we're never going to mention it again.' He finished his own drink and passed the last half-slice of toasted cheese sandwich down to Otto, who'd been salivating longingly at his side. With a glance at his watch, he rose to his feet. 'Right, let's get back to work on the garden, shall we? See how much more we can get done before Marcus arrives home.'

They worked together for the next hour and a half, and Mimi felt so much better knowing she'd seized the moment and addressed the subject, and that it wouldn't be referred to again. For now, at least, she could relax. She'd brought Marcus's radio outside and switched it from his beloved Radio 3 to a channel playing the kind of music they could recognise. As Cal tore clinging strips of variegated ivy from the dry-stone wall separating Bay Cottage from the Old Schoolhouse next door, one of ABBA's songs came on and Mimi saw Otto's ears prick up in recognition. Two minutes later, Cal glanced round and saw he was being watched. He straightened up. 'Are you laughing at me?'

'Laughing? Me? Nooo.' Mimi's eyes danced. 'I'm wildly impressed. You're word-perfect.'

'I don't have much choice. Two years ago, all I ever heard in the house was One Direction. Last year it was Prince and George Michael.' He paused to add a huge armful of ripped-away ivy to the overflowing wheelbarrow. 'And this year Cora's completely besotted with ABBA. It's quite hard not to learn every word to every song off by heart.'

'Could be worse,' said Mimi. 'Could have been Val Doonican.'

Cal grinned. 'Oh it could definitely be worse. ABBA aren't so bad – I quite like them really. Which reminds me, April the seventeenth. Save the date, you're invited to a party.'

'Really? I'll have to consult my packed social calendar. OK,' Mimi amended, 'my completely empty one. Whose party? Yours?'

He shook his head. 'It's Cora's birthday. My baby girl is turning eleven.'

'Well that's lovely. But . . . are you sure she'd want me there?' Mimi hesitated, because what eleven-year-old would want someone as ancient as herself to be asked along?

'I'm quite sure. She added your name to the list last night. And she took all the invitations off to school with her this morning to get them written during the lunch break. But you know what kids are like, could take a few days before it actually happens. Which is why I'm letting you know now, before you book something else for that night.'

'But is it going to be, like . . . a whole load of eleven-year-olds?' Mimi was still baffled as to why she would be included.

'Ah, of course, you haven't been to one of Cora's parties before.' Cal smiled at her confusion. 'We hire out the village hall. For the first hour, it's just Cora and her friends, then after that everyone else turns up and joins in, and we make a proper evening of it.'

'Well that sounds brilliant. I'd love to come along.' Mimi was relieved. 'What a great idea.'

'Stacey came up with it when Cora was six. She found out that it would cost sixty pounds to hire the hall for three hours, or for an extra tenner we could have it for the whole night. So we did it that way and invited everyone along, and Cora loved every minute. She said it was the best party ever. Then the next year the accident happened and . . . well, there was no party that time. But the following year, Cora asked if we could hire the hall again and do what we'd done before. So that's what we did, and it was good.' Cal nodded slowly as he spoke, remembering the occasion. 'For all of us, really. The kids were jumping around like kids always do, and everyone who'd helped us out since the accident came along, and it kind of made all of us feel as if we could get through what had happened and come out the other side. And since then, Cora's asked me every year if we can do it again.' He nodded and said simply, 'So we do.'

'That's so lovely.' In her head, Mimi added: *And so are you.*

'I know it won't last forever. Two years from now, she'll be thirteen and we'll probably get, "Oh God, Dad, no *waaay*, can't me and my mates just go off to an all-night rave instead?" But until that day comes,' said Cal, 'I'll carry on giving her the party she wants.'

Don't cry, mustn't cry. Mimi managed to maintain control. 'Of course you will.'

He shrugged. 'I do the best I can.'

Mimi wanted to say, *She's lucky to have you*, but under the circumstances it might sound wrong. Not to sound envious of Cora, she said instead, 'You're a good dad.'

Chapter 35

The next morning, there was a loud knock on the front door as Mimi was heading downstairs with her laptop tucked under one arm and her phone and empty tea mug clutched in her spare hand.

'Hiya, this is for you and Marcus.' Cora was standing on the doorstep in her school uniform. 'Sorry, I got carried away and made them too big to fit through everyone's letter boxes. I'm such a durr-brain!'

Mimi took the bright yellow envelope. 'How exciting!' she exclaimed. 'Is this our invitation to your party?'

Cora's blue eyes danced. 'Dad said he told you about it yesterday afternoon, but you were already on the list anyway. Go on, have a look!'

Mimi opened the envelope and took out the hand-made invite with *Cora's Party!* emblazoned across it in silver and iridescent purple, with green glitter liberally decorating the royal-blue card. 'It's beautiful,' she said admiringly.

'I like making them, it's my favourite thing. Will you both be there?'

'Definitely. Can't wait. Thanks so much for asking us.'

'You'll love it. I have the best parties. Uh oh, better go,' yelped Cora as the school bus trundled into view. 'See you!'

Mimi watched as she raced off down the high street with her blonde plait bouncing off her backpack. Then she opened the card and read the details inside, in Cora's swirly silver handwriting. At the bottom she'd added: *PS Dress code is . . . guess what? ABBA!*

Oh dear, poor Marcus. He wasn't going to be very happy about that.

The day of the party dawned clear and bright. Mimi, sitting cross-legged on her bed working her way through the to-do list on her laptop, glanced up every so often to observe the signs of activity happening around the village hall over to the left of the green. Cars and people were coming and going as preparations were made. It was a major event; the evening celebrations were due to start at seven and over two hundred guests were expected.

Mimi carried on working throughout the afternoon; for the last fortnight, almost every waking moment had been spent setting up the new company, building herself a fabulous website and getting her name out there to potential clients. It was, frankly, a bit of a miracle that her MacBook hadn't exploded, she'd sent out and replied to so many emails.

At four o'clock, she saw Paddy heading into the hall carrying crates of drinks, followed by Eamonn from the shop unloading boxes from the back of his van. There was a huge amount of work involved in putting on a party of this size. A twinge of guilt prompted Mimi to reach for her phone and call Cal's number.

When he answered, she said, 'Hi there. Look, I feel terrible for not offering before to help out. I've been busy, but I could come over now if there's anything I can do. Just say the word.'

'No, no need,' said Cal. 'Absolutely no need. Everything's under control here, we're bang on schedule.'

'But—'

'Thanks for offering,' he went, 'but we're fine. We have all the help we need. See you later, OK? Bye.'

And that was it, about as firm a refusal as anyone could receive. Mimi put her phone down on the bed and wondered what was going on. Oh well, it was none of her business, and at least if he was so keen not to have her there, it meant she'd be able to get another couple of hours of work in. At that moment a new email landed with a *ding* in her inbox, forcing her to stop thinking about Cal. It was an enquiry from a mystery writer colleague of CJ's, keen to raise his online profile and create more interest in his books . . .

At six, it was time to close the laptop and jump into the shower. When she emerged, Mimi could hear Marcus, home from his shopping trip to Cirencester, moving around downstairs. As predicted, he'd flatly refused to contemplate dressing up for the party. 'I'll wear my grey suit,' he'd declared. 'If anyone asks, I'm there as ABBA's accountant.'

By ten to seven, she was ready, even if it wasn't possible to view her full-length reflection in the little mirror on her dresser. Hopefully, though, the overall effect was OK. The outfit comprised a violet satin shirt she'd found in a charity shop, tightly belted at the waist and worn with narrow white trousers tucked into stiletto-heeled over-the-knee red boots.

She'd left her hair loose to fall over her shoulders, and basically piled on a lot more make-up than usual, especially sapphire-blue eyeshadow.

Across the landing, Marcus's bedroom door opened and she heard him call out, 'Are you ready?'

Mimi squirted her neck and wrists with scent and called back, 'Yes.'

But she wasn't.

'Oh my *God.*' Her hands flew to her face when she saw him. 'OH MY GOD!'

'How do I look?' Marcus said mildly.

And Mimi started to laugh, because he looked exactly like Colin Firth at the very end of the film *Mamma Mia!*, in a turquoise satin jumpsuit with flared trousers, high pointed collar and a shirt section that was slashed to the waist. Taking in the fact that he was looking taller than usual, she belatedly spotted the silver platforms beneath the extravagant flares.

Mimi threw her arms around Marcus. 'I love you so much. Where did you *find* this?'

'Online. I ordered it last week. You signed for the package when it arrived on Tuesday.'

She gasped. 'You told me it was a new cover for your golf bag!'

'I lied.'

'You said you were going to wear your grey suit!'

'That was the original plan.'

Together they made their way downstairs. In the kitchen, Marcus filled a glass with cold water from the dispenser on the fridge.

'So what made you change your mind?' said Mimi.

He took a drink. 'I was walking through the graveyard and found Cora sitting by her mum's grave with Otto. I stopped to say hello, and we ended up having a little chat. She asked me if I still missed your dad as much as before or if things were a bit easier now, and we both agreed that it was a bit easier but that sometimes it made us feel guilty.' Marcus shrugged. 'It's normal, of course. We all know that. It still feels weird, though, when it happens.'

Mimi nodded in silent agreement. Been there, done that. When you woke up and realised that the loved one you'd lost wasn't the first thing you'd thought of, your conscience kicked in and delivered a whole new kind of shame, slyly hinting that maybe you hadn't loved them that much after all.

'Anyway, then Cora said because her mum and your dad had died at the exact same time, did I ever wonder if they were in heaven together, like maybe because they'd arrived at the same moment and knew each other they'd stayed together and become really good friends? And then she asked me if I thought they were watching us from up there to see what we're doing and how we're getting on.' Another pause, then Marcus continued, 'And I said it sounded brilliant, just because I knew it was what she wanted to hear. But ever since then, I've kind of found myself thinking about it and realising that it really would be great if they were up there together. And no, I can't quite believe I'm saying that.' He gave Mimi a rueful smile. 'It's so much the opposite of everything I've ever thought before.'

Sensing he needed the reassurance, Mimi said, 'I like the idea too.'

Marcus nodded. 'So last week I bumped into Cora again

outside the shop, and she asked if I'd be dressing up for the party. And it was when I looked into her eyes that I realised I couldn't tell her I'd be wearing my suit. It just felt as if Stacey and Dan were watching us, waiting to hear what I'd say. So I told her I'd definitely be dressing up, and you should have seen the look on her face . . . well, you know what Cora's like when she smiles. She just lit up and said, "Oh hooray, they're going to be so pleased!"' He shrugged good-naturedly. 'So that was it, I knew I had to get online and find myself something ABBA-esque that would meet with her approval.'

Mimi gave him another hug and took the opportunity to let the tear in her eye be absorbed into the shiny turquoise satin of his jumpsuit. Then she held him at arm's length and broke into a grin, because the touching explanation had been so wildly at odds with his appearance.

'I love you, and you look fantastic.'

As he adjusted his steel-rimmed spectacles and ran a hand over his short light-brown hair, Marcus looked more than ever like Colin Firth at his most wary and diffident. The next moment, he smiled, as if determined to push the reservations away. 'Come on then, let's go. We'll just have to hope an incriminating photo of me in this outfit doesn't end up on the front cover of *Accountancy Today*.'

Together they made their way across the village green, along with other partygoers converging from different directions and wearing a variety of seventies outfits. A barbecue was up and running outside the hall, and dogs were racing around, tantalised by the smell of sizzling burgers and sausages.

Inside, ABBA music was blaring out, disco lights were swirling and the dancing had already begun. The interior of the hall had been decorated with dozens of multicoloured balloons, streamers and what seemed like miles of shimmering silver bunting. Metallic spirals hung from the ceiling, interspersed with strings of curled ribbons and stars. The DJ behind his decks was singing along to 'Mamma Mia' and encouraging everyone else to join in.

There were also more foil wigs on display than you could shake a stick at.

Cora was dancing with her friends in front of the DJ. Having spotted Marcus and Mimi, she beamed and waved at them across the crowded hall. Mimi's heart melted at the sight of her evidently having the time of her life. She and the other girls were wearing neon-bright outfits and coloured trainers, all the better to dance in. There were bangles jangling on their skinny arms and—

'You're here, hooray! And Marcus, oh my word, look at you! *Amazing.*' Lois greeted him with delight, then threw her arms around Mimi. 'And look at you too . . . oh, it feels as if I've hardly seen you lately.'

This was because she hadn't, partly because Mimi had been working her socks off to get the new company up and running, but also because she'd found herself less enthusiastic about the idea now that she knew what Lois was getting up to behind her back. Then again, the one time she'd texted her suggesting they meet up for a quick drink in the Swan, Lois had apologised and explained that she was too busy. Yet just twenty minutes later, Mimi had watched from her bedroom window as Lois left her new home on foot and headed off up the hill in a Cal-wards direction.

Mimi felt a clutch of sadness. It didn't feel great when a friendship began to fade, but sometimes these things just happened and there was nothing you could do about it. The mental images of Lois and Cal together were something she hadn't been able to get out of her brain.

But Lois hadn't done anything truly terrible. At least they could maintain an amicable relationship. Mimi said, 'You're looking brilliant.' Which was true: Lois was wearing a long swirly dress in ice-cream shades of pink and green, and necklaces to match. But even as she was paying the compliment, she was aware of Lois glancing past her with an expectant smile on her face. Before turning round herself, Mimi already knew she was looking at Cal.

'Isn't it a great party? Ooh, I must take a photo of you . . . smile!' Having whipped out her phone, Lois began snapping away, and Mimi wondered if she was deliberately angling the lens to capture Cal behind them. The next moment, Eamonn from the shop thrust a glass of wine into Mimi's hand and offered one to Lois, who shook her head. 'No thanks, I'm too hyped up, better not have another one.'

Hyped up? What was *that* supposed to mean?

Then other people joined them, exclaiming with delight over Marcus's outfit, and Lois said, 'I'll see you again in a bit,' before disappearing into the crowd.

Minutes later, over by the trestle tables containing the buffet, Mimi saw Cal talking to Maria from the Swan, but despite listening for all she was worth, she was only able to make out the words 'Oh don't worry, it's just a bit of a surprise, you'll find out soon enough.' But when she looked over again, she saw that whilst he was addressing Maria, his attention was actually on Lois, who in turn was gazing at him, unable to hide her little ooh-aren't-we-naughty smile.

With a sudden thud of alarm in her chest, Mimi wondered

if Cal had got it into his head that this evening would be an excellent time to announce to everyone that he and Lois were now a couple.

Oh God no, surely not, not in the middle of Cora's birthday party.

Chapter 36

Gazing around wildly, Mimi spotted Felix over to the right of the DJ's decks, fiddling with the little GoPro he'd been using on Boxing Day to film the karaoke over at the Swan. Felix would be devastated too. And as for poor Cora . . . surely Cal wouldn't land it on her like this, would he?

For that matter, where even was Cora? The other girls were still dancing energetically, but Cora and Lauren had now vanished. Mimi prevaricated; should she find them and discreetly warn Cora that something might be about to happen, or was her own overactive imagination running away with her? Oh God, what should she do? Because if it happened and Cora was left in a state of shock, her whole birthday would be spoiled. Maybe warning Cal not to do anything was the best way to go, if she could manage to say it without admitting that she already knew about his and Lois's—

'Mimi!'

It was like trying to drive off without realising the hand-brake was still on. As Mimi began to head over to Cal, a hand grabbed the back of her leather belt, halting the momentum and hauling her back.

When she swivelled round and saw that the human hand-brake was Cora, her first thought was that she'd somehow found out too.

'Oh Mimi, quick, can you come with me? Something so gross has happened and I need you to help!'

But it wasn't that kind of gross. In the ladies' loo, half the sink and most of the floor in front of it was smeared with sick. Away from the sink, Lauren was leaning against the tiled wall, looking pea green and embarrassed.

'She threw up,' said Cora, in case Mimi wasn't familiar with the concept. 'We tried to clean it up but it just keeps, like, kind of *spreading* everywhere. And Lauren's mum isn't here yet so I didn't know who else to ask, then I thought of you.'

It was the kind of compliment no one really wanted to be on the receiving end of. Mimi looked at Lauren. 'OK, first thing, why have you been sick? Are you ill?' Because the other night she'd watched an episode of *Casualty* and the vomiting teenager had turned out to be suffering from viral encephalitis.

'I ate eleven sausage rolls,' Lauren confessed shamefacedly. 'For a bet.'

'Plus all those orange Smarties,' Cora reminded her.

Lauren nodded and finished wiping her mouth with a paper towel. 'And three cans of blue lemonade.'

Well that explained the colour.

Mimi dispatched Cora to the utility room to collect a mop, bucket and spray cleaner, then made a start with the towels in the dispenser.

Cora returned with the cleaning equipment. 'Honestly, thanks so much for helping us. They're playing my favourite song now.'

'Oh, but Lauren's still looking a bit pale—'

'"Waterloo"!' bellowed Lauren, chucking a handful of mint Tic Tacs down her throat before darting around the sick on the floor with all the agility of Mo Farah. 'Quick, we're missing it!'

'Cora, just a sec, I wanted to say—' But Cora flung her a pleading look and allowed Lauren, no longer pale green, to bundle her out through the doorway. All Mimi had time to call out before the door swung shut behind them was, 'Don't jump up and down too much.' Which was a bit like returning home after six months away and asking your dog not to bark.

Out in the hall, the entire village now appeared to be singing and dancing along to "Waterloo". Alone in the bathroom, Mimi opened the windows and mopped and squeezed, then wiped and rinsed and polished until all the blue sick had been cleared up and the floor was so spotless and shiny you could . . . well, maybe not that.

Leaving the windows open, she returned the cleaning things to the utility room and made her way back to the party. The DJ had now moved on to 'Money, Money, Money' and everyone was bellowing the chorus as they bounced around the dance floor in their bright outfits and multi-coloured wigs. The revolving glitter balls bounced light off the heaving mass of sequins, and Otto was leaping like a ninja, desperate to reach the balloons two teenage boys were batting back and forth just above his head.

Mimi's heart lifted at the sight of Marcus dancing with Maria – a bit awkwardly, it had to be said, but it was good that he was joining in.

Right, this was a party; she needed to relax and join in

too. Spotting Lois standing on her own by the buffet, she made her way over. 'Come on then, are we going to show these kids how it's done?'

But Lois, barely glancing in her direction, murmured, 'No thanks, not just now,' and when Mimi followed the direction of her gaze, she realised that – surprise, surprise – all her attention was on Cal.

Again.

Moments later, Cal turned his head and winked – actually *winked* – at Lois.

Mimi felt sick. For God's sake, they were behaving like a pair of teenagers.

Suddenly the music paused. The DJ grabbed his mic and shouted, 'OK, everybody, if you could all move back a bit now and pay attention, the father of the birthday girl has a little something he'd like to say. Over here, Cal, step up and take the floor.'

Mimi felt sicker.

As Cal took the mic from the DJ, whistles and cheers filled the hall. He grinned around at everyone. 'Don't worry, it isn't going to be a long speech. I just wanted to thank you all for coming, and to say how lucky I am to have the best daughter in the world. And Cora might not remember this, but last summer she did tell me there was something she'd love to see . . . so I've done my best today to make it happen.' He turned to the DJ. 'Look, could you turn the music down? I'm trying to say something deep and mean-ingful here.'

The DJ raised his hands. 'It won't turn off. The button's broken.' As the opening chords of 'Voulez-Vous' filled the air, he shrugged helplessly. 'Sorry, mate, I can't make it stop.'

The music was getting louder and louder. Next to her, Mimi could feel Lois actually quivering. Cal did a few jokey experimental dance steps, then said into the mic, 'Nope, can't manage this on my own, going to need a hand . . .'

And as the music reached maximum volume, Lois left Mimi's side, threading her way through the crowd until she reached Cal. He grinned, placed one arm around her waist and swung her into a spin that caused everyone to erupt in shrieks of incredulous delight as they realised the DJ had been in on it all along. It also swiftly became apparent that this wasn't simply a case of two people dancing together and hoping for the best; every step, every turn and swirl had been choreographed, and they were moving exactly in time with each other to the music as everyone around them whooped and clapped, amazed that it was happening at all and blown away by the fact that it was so good.

Because Cal and Lois were putting on an impressive display; they'd clearly spent a lot of time practising the moves. Watching them, Mimi marvelled at the skill and determination this must have needed, especially for Lois, who had always been so painfully self-conscious about her leg. A lump formed in her throat, because Lois was looking transformed, like the vibrant, confident, beautiful girl she used to be before the accident, and it was just the most miraculous thing to witness. Which had come first, she wondered: had they started secretly seeing each other and *then* decided to learn the dance? Or, like so many of the contestants on *Strictly*, had dancing together for so many hours on end been the catalyst for their relationship?

But it was Cora's reaction that was the most unexpected. There she was, on the edge of the dance floor, clapping and laughing, seemingly thrilled by the surprise that had been sprung on her and completely unfazed by the fact that her father was dancing with Lois.

The dance came to an end and the applause was thunderous. Felix, who had filmed the whole thing, was clapping too and Mimi saw him furtively wipe a tear from his eye. Cora raced over to Cal, who lifted her into his arms and swung her round.

When he eventually put her down, he took the mic from the DJ again. 'So last summer, Cora showed me one of those surprise dances on YouTube and said how much she wished she could see one happen in real life. Which gave me the idea to do it. Oh, and massive thanks to Lois for agreeing to join in, so I didn't have to get up there on my own. Wasn't she brilliant?'

When the party and the general dancing had resumed, Cora came over to Mimi and led her outside. As they sat together on one of the wooden benches beneath the flowering chestnut trees, Cora took a slurp of cherry Tango and said, 'Lois isn't Dad's girlfriend.'

Mimi's stomach did a helter-skelter swoop. 'Really? How do you know?'

'I asked him this morning. I decided I had to, because it was my birthday and it was just killing me. I needed to know the truth, so I just came out with it, and he hugged me and told me she wasn't his girlfriend. So then I made him promise he wasn't lying and said he had to swear on my life, and he did. So *then* I told him I'd seen Lois going into his studio and he said he couldn't tell me why because it was a big surprise, but I'd find out this evening at my party.' Cora dramatically ran out of breath, then refilled her lungs with air, a beaming smile simultaneously spreading across her face. 'And that's it, that's what they'd been doing in the studio this whole time – practising the dance. They're just friends. I got it all wrong. So that's good, isn't it!'

Just a bit.

'Very good.' Mimi nodded and gave Cora's thin shoulders a reassuring squeeze.

'I meant to tell you earlier but I forgot,' Cora continued blithely. 'Because it was my party and I was just busy being happy and dancing . . . and then Lauren ate all those sausage rolls and was sick, so I didn't think of letting you know. Anyway, you know now.'

'I do.' Mimi smiled, because Cora could have no idea how great a relief it had been for her too.

'Here's Dad.' As Cal spotted them and made his way over, Cora called out, 'I was just telling Mimi about me getting it wrong. I talked to her about it last week.'

'Sweetheart, Felix wants to get some video of you with the cake before it's cut up, and Lauren's brother wants to FaceTime his gran so she can see you having fun. I said I'd find you and send you in.'

'OK, I'll do it now.' Cora jumped up and ran inside.

'Lauren's gran broke her hip, so she's stuck in hospital.' Cal took Cora's place on the wooden bench.

'I heard. Poor thing.'

He looked sideways at her. 'So, you've spent the last week thinking there was something going on between me and Lois.'

Talk about getting straight to the point. Mimi nodded. 'Well, yes.'

324

'That explains it then.'

'Explains what?' Her mouth was dry.

'The way you were when we were working in your garden. I knew there was something bothering you, but had no idea what it was.' He raised an eyebrow. 'You really thought we were secretly seeing each other?'

From here, Mimi could smell the citrus tang of his cologne. She shrugged. 'I was shocked, but all I had to go on was what Cora told me. And you and Lois *were* secretly seeing each other, to be fair. Just not for the reason we thought.'

'I can't believe Cora saw Lois coming into the garden and me letting her into the studio. We thought we'd planned everything so well. There was no music to hear because we wore headphones. It was like a silent disco.' Cal paused. 'But what I really can't believe is that you thought I'd do something like that to Felix. He's my friend.' He gestured with an upturned palm. 'I just wouldn't.'

'I know, and that's why I was so shocked when Cora told me. But it all added up and she made me promise not to say a word. I couldn't ask you. I couldn't ask Lois either. I thought the two of you were going to make some kind of big romantic announcement tonight . . . I'm so sorry,' Mimi blurted out, because he was looking more horrified by the second.

'You think I'd do that to my own daughter? On her birthday?'

'I didn't think you'd do that,' Mimi exclaimed helplessly. 'But it seemed as if it was going to happen anyway.'

'I would never do *anything* like that,' said Cal.

'You wouldn't.'

'Lois is a friend. There's nothing going on between us. Never has been, never will be.'

She nodded vigorously in agreement and with more than a bit of relief. 'I know.'

'The reason we kept the dance a secret was so that it could be a surprise for everyone. I told Felix this morning, just so he wouldn't think there was something up.'

'Right.' As she nodded, Mimi saw Lois coming towards them, her pink and green dress swirling around her legs as she walked.

'It was Lois who had the idea of me learning a dance,' Cal went on. 'And I was the one who decided she should do it with me.'

Lois arrived at the bench with a grin. 'And *I* was the one who said not in a million years, no way could I do that and no way would I even try it, not after that time I ended up flat on my back like a beetle.'

Mimi hadn't been there, but she'd heard about it from Lois, who had tried to dance at a wedding on the prosthetic leg she hadn't yet had a chance to get properly used to. So mortified had she been by her ungainly tumble that she'd vowed never to dance in public again.

Up until today, she never had.

'But Cal persuaded you,' Mimi said. 'And now you've shown everyone you can do it, and they've seen how brilliant you are.'

'Well, not brilliant, but I did OK. I'm proud I managed to get through it in one piece. All thanks to this one here.' Lois beamed at Cal, then turned back to Mimi. 'Did he tell you about Cora thinking we were secretly seeing each other?'

'I did.' Cal nodded.

'God, can you imagine?'

Cal said drily, 'Oh, she did.'

'*What?*' Lois stared at Mimi, her eyes widening in disbelief. 'Seriously? But how could you think I'd do that to Felix?'

It did seem unlikely now, but at the time it had felt so real.

'What can I say?' Mimi spread her hands helplessly. 'If it looks like a duck and quacks like a duck . . .'

Lois burst out laughing. 'We weren't quacking, we were dancing.' She stuck out her legs and waggled her feet, one real and one prosthetic. 'Dancing like ducks!'

Chapter 37

As April segued into May, the weather continued to improve and the holiday rental cottages in the vicinity of Goosebrook began to fill up with visitors and tourists. By and large, they divided up into two categories: quiet people in sensible clothes who enjoyed tramping for miles through beautiful country-side, admiring the scenery and visiting local pubs in order to enjoy ploughman's lunches and halves of bitter; and the party rentals, groups of exuberant City types who descended on the tranquil Cotswolds for a long weekend of carousing and drinking and being as ear-splittingly loud as possible.

Some of these visitors to the area were great fun, whilst others were a living nightmare.

Still, it ensured that a Saturday evening in the Black Swan was always interesting, if a little crowded. And noisy too, when multiple parties of visitors filed in and the alcohol consumption soared.

'I knew there was something I'd forgotten to bring along,' said Lois.

Mimi twisted her empty crisp packet into a knot. 'What's that then?'

'Earplugs.' As Lois said it, a nearby burst of laughter rattled the glasses on their table.

'If you wore earplugs you wouldn't be able to hear me.' Mimi indicated the braying ringleader of the group. 'He just needs a bit of volume control, like a dial in his chest that you could turn down when it all gets too much.'

'Felix always used to say the louder the bloke, the smaller the dick. Well,' Lois amended, 'he isn't dead, so he probably still does say it. But how would I know?' She shrugged and forced a smile, and Mimi felt for her. On the evening of Cora's birthday party, following Lois and Cal's magical dance, she'd wondered if a reunion between Lois and Felix might miraculously happen. But it hadn't, and the core issues between them were evidently still there. Felix had scarcely been seen in the village in recent weeks. Mimi knew Lois was missing him dreadfully, but was far too proud to say so.

'He's probably busy with work.'

'Oh, I don't think so. By all accounts, Henrietta's beside herself with joy that I've moved out and she's doing her damnedest to find Felix a more suitable replacement.'

It was so lovely having Lois properly back in her life; Mimi only wished there was more she could do to cheer her up. But the only way she could help right now was by listening and providing emotional support. They both knew that Henrietta had been contacting all her well-connected friends with available daughters, suggesting that they and Felix should meet up. The reason they both knew this was because Henrietta had been telling practically everyone she crossed paths with. From the sound of things, every remotely suitable single female in her late twenties was getting the intensive sales pitch.

'Just because she's doing it,' said Mimi, 'doesn't mean Felix is going to be interested.'

'It's like *Pride and Prejudice*.' Lois pulled a face. 'If you cross Mrs Bennet with a really tenacious wolfhound, you get Henrietta. Anyway, that's quite enough gloomy talk about my evil mother-in-law for one night. Have you spotted those two over there? What d'you reckon to his chances?'

Mimi followed the direction of her unobtrusive nod. Standing in front of the fireplace was one of the noisy City types who had taken over Hawthorne Lodge, deep in conversation with a member of the hen weekend currently staying in Owl Cottage. He was tall, and fairly good looking, with rugby player's shoulders and crumpled red chinos. She was the quietest of her group of friends and strikingly pretty in an understated way, with natural blonde hair and minimal make-up.

'She's beautiful,' said Mimi.

'Too good for him.'

'But she seems quite shy. Maybe she needs someone like that to bring her out of herself.'

'Well he's taking up too much space and he gives me the creeps. Then again,' Lois conceded, 'I think I don't like him because he reminds me of my horrible maths teacher at school.'

They carried on watching as the couple continued their conversation in the quietest section of the bar. Ten minutes later, Mimi said, 'He's definitely winning her over.' It was fascinating to observe the interaction and body language between two people who were learning about each other for the first time. Initially the girl had been leaning away; now she was touching his arm.

'Looks like I was wrong and you were right about him.'

Lois said. 'Ooh, he's off to buy her another drink. And her friend's dragging her outside for a girlie chat . . .'

They watched as the two girls made their way across to the back door of the pub.

'Seems a shame to miss out on the best bit,' said Mimi.

'Just what I was thinking.' Lois scooped up her bag and her drink in one practised movement. 'Let's go.'

Outside on the heated patio bordered with hanging baskets and ropes of white fairy lights, several other tables were occupied but the one next to the pretty blonde girl and her brunette friend was fortuitously free.

'OK, tell me everything.' Having lit up a cigarette and exhaled a plume of smoke, the friend leaned forward avidly. 'All the details. What's he like?'

'OK, his name's Baz and he works as a trader in the City, and at first I wasn't sure because he seemed a bit full of himself. But we carried on talking and I realised that isn't what he's really like at all. It's just a front he puts up to cover his real feelings. Honestly, he's so much nicer than I thought he was.'

Her friend wrinkled her nose. 'Red trousers, though.'

'I know. But . . . well, maybe I could get used to them. They're only trousers, after all.'

But they were still *red*. Mimi and Lois exchanged a doubtful glance.

At the next table, the brunette exclaimed. 'Oh my God, Deb, you've got it bad. Look at you, all lit up and excited!'

'I *feel* excited. He's just so sweet and thoughtful, and the way he was talking to me, honestly . . . You know how some people make you feel special, like you're the centre of their world? That's how it is with Baz. And he's been through so

331

much, too.' Deb lowered her voice. 'Two years ago, he lost his fiancée.'

'Lost her where? I once got totally lost in the Westfield shopping centre. Mind you, me and Candice had got through two bottles of Bolly at the champagne bar—'

'Nooo, not that kind of lost. His fiancée *died*.' Deb clutched her chest. 'She was killed in a car accident just three weeks before their wedding . . . can you imagine?'

'No way! God, that's awful!'

'*So* awful. He got all choked up when he was telling me. I mean, it happened two years ago but you never really get over something like that, do you? He thought he'd met the love of his life and then the next minute she was gone. It's so unbearably tragic . . . Oh, now look at me, I'm getting all upset just thinking about what he's had to go through. And it's taken him until now to get himself out of the house and start thinking about dating again.'

'Poor guy. Maybe you're the one he needs to help him. Meeting him tonight could be fate.'

Deb tucked a strand of blonde hair behind her ear and nodded. 'I thought that too. I mean, I never imagined coming out tonight and meeting someone I felt a real connection with, but somehow it's happened. And now I'm feeling all jittery and excited . . .'

The brunette stubbed out the cigarette she'd been energetically puffing her way through. 'Woo-hoo, this could be it, you need to get yourself back inside.' She gave her friend a triumphant smile. 'Tonight could be the night you change your life.'

The two girls headed back into the pub. Mimi and Lois looked at each other.

'Wow.' Lois exhaled.

Mimi nodded. 'I know. I feel bad that we made fun of his red trousers now.'

'I feel bad saying that thing about men who laugh loudly.'

'We're horrible people.' A lump had expanded in Mimi's throat at the thought of what Baz had been through.

'Poor guy.' Digging in the front pocket of her jeans, Lois pulled out a tissue and pressed it carefully beneath each eye.

'Poor guy? I hope you don't mean me.' Mimi jumped as a hand landed on her shoulder and Cal appeared behind them. The next moment, noticing the mascara-stained tissue in Lois's hand, he said, 'Oh God, sorry, what's happened?'

Lois gestured helplessly. 'I'm OK, everything's fine, we just . . .' She froze, in the process of stuffing the crumpled tissue back into her jeans pocket.

'What?' said Mimi, as Lois pulled an oh-no face.

'Zip's broken.' She leaned forward to look and Mimi caught a flash of white knicker. 'Bugger, nature's way of letting you know you ate too much dinner before coming out.' Levering herself upright, Lois held one hand over the gaping zip and tugged her short top down with the other in an attempt to cover it. 'Right, I'm going to have to get home and change. At least I don't have far to go.'

Cal took her seat. Together they watched as Lois, limping slightly, crossed the village green and was swallowed up by the darkness. 'She isn't fine, though,' he said. 'What happened to upset her? Has she heard about Felix?'

'No. What about Felix?'

Cal lowered his voice. 'He's gone out on a date with some girl Henrietta fixed him up with. If Lois doesn't know, don't tell her.'

'Oh no.' Except Henrietta would make sure the whole village heard about it before the weekend was out.

'So why *was* she upset?'

'We were inside earlier, watching two people meet for the first time.' Aware of the sensitivity of the subject, Mimi made sure the side of her leg didn't accidentally make contact with Cal's knee. 'He was wearing red trousers and seemed like a bit of a prat, and we couldn't understand why this really pretty girl was so smitten with him. But we just over-heard her out here telling her friend that the guy's fiancée died just before they were due to get married.' She paused. 'It was a car accident, three weeks before the wedding. So that meant we both felt awful for thinking bad things about him. When you see a stranger, you never know what they've been through, do you? This poor guy, Baz . . . well, he's doing his best to get his life together again, but it must be so hard. Sorry.' Mimi shook her head because this was Cal she was talking to.

'Hey, don't worry. And look on the bright side: if he's hit it off with this girl tonight, that's a good thing.' In the reflected glow from the strung-up fairy lights, his brown eyes softened. 'It happens to most of us sooner or later.'

Which probably wasn't meant to sound significant but in Mimi's head instantly felt as if it did. Shifting on her chair and recrossing her legs, her thigh brushed against Cal's knee. Although it had been a complete accident, at the same time it was utterly thrilling, but what if he thought she'd done it deliberately and was clumsily attempting to make a move on him?

To divert his attention, she blurted out, 'So anyway, how's the painting coming along? And when's the designer going to sort out that website of yours?' Because it was currently awash with annoying glitches and an absolute nightmare to navigate. Not wanting to sound horrible, she added, 'Sorry, I don't like to criticise, but it's really not that great. It's your website and you need it to work.'

'You don't have to tell me.' Cal grimaced. 'It's like whack-a-mole: he fixes two problems and four bigger ones pop up. I just don't have the heart to tell him I'd rather hire someone else to take over.'

He was giving her one of those looks again, the kind that made the tips of her fingers go all tingly. Mimi said, 'I'd be happy to do it, you know that.'

In all honesty, seeing as it was a speciality of hers, she was a tiny bit miffed that he hadn't asked her in the first place.

'Thanks. And I do know that, but it's a bit of an awkward situation. I'm the only client he has. It's Eamonn's son,' Cal admitted. 'He was desperate to set himself up as a web designer after leaving school, but no one else was hiring him. So Eamonn begged me to give him a chance. How could I say no?'

Well *that* explained the truly terrible website. No wonder Cal had kept so quiet about it up until now. Mimi wanted to kiss him; how could you not love someone who was simply too nice to tell a friend's shy teenage son that his services were no longer required?

OK, maybe she didn't mean love in quite *that* sense . . .

But her heart had begun to thud-thud-thud in panicky realisation.

Because what if she did?

Cal raised his arm in greeting and said, 'Here she is,' as Lois re-emerged out of the darkness in a different pair of jeans, looser black ones this time. He rose to his feet and gave her her seat back. 'Right, it's sounding pretty busy in there. Shall I go in and get us some drinks?'

As soon as Cal had disappeared into the pub, Lois pulled out her phone and said flatly, 'Look what came up on Instagram ten minutes ago.'

Mimi braced herself. Her first guess was right. The photo had been posted by someone called Clementine and was a selfie of four people in an extremely plush-looking bar. The caption said: *Hahaha, what a super night! Rory whisked me off to dinner at Colworth Manor Hotel and who should we bump into??? Only my gorgeous friend Arabella Playdell-Grey and her super-hot date Felix Mercer, whoop whoop!!!*

Out of loyalty to Lois, Mimi said, 'Well I wouldn't call her gorgeous. Her teeth are a bit rabbity.'

'I know. I thought that too. She does look like a rabbit.' Lois paused. 'A pretty rabbit, though.'

'Not that pretty.'

'Prettier than me.'

Mimi shook her head. 'She isn't.'

'Bet she isn't covered in scars. Bet she's got two legs.'

'Look, Felix is only there because Henrietta forced him into it. He's probably having a terrible time, hating every minute.'

'Unlike Henrietta, who's probably riding around on her broomstick having a good old cackle and breaking open the champagne.'

Mimi said sympathetically, 'Are you OK?'

'I'm going to have to be, aren't I?' Lois sighed and took one last look at the photo before switching off her phone. 'Horrible stuff happens and we all just have to get through it the best way we can. What I hate is feeling miserable about the state of my body, then having to tell myself that loads of people have had to go through so much worse. Like Cal, and red-trouser guy in there.' Her bracelets jangled as she waved an arm in the direction of the pub. 'So then I have to feel guilty as well, for being such a selfish, whiny cow.'

A few minutes later, Cal reappeared carrying their drinks.

'About time too,' Lois exclaimed, jumping up to give him a hand, but Mimi was immediately struck by the realisation that something had changed. There was tension in Cal's jaw, the easy laid-back demeanour had gone and he was no longer smiling.

'What's wrong?' she said.

'What's wrong is that we had to wait so long for our drinks.' Lois was back in let's-be-cheerful mode; she clinked her glass against each of theirs. 'But they're here now, so happy days! Cal, we pulled this chair over for you. Why aren't you sitting down?'

'It's OK, I'd rather stand.' He met Mimi's concerned gaze. 'I'm fine.'

But he wasn't, she knew it. And as Lois chattered on about the next quiz night and the epic cheating that had gone on during the last one, Mimi sensed that Cal was counting the seconds, waiting for something to happen. On the surface, he appeared calm, but beneath it she just knew he was . . . what? Simmering with anger? Why, though? Especially since he had never been the angry type.

And then it happened: a door crashed open and Baz appeared silhouetted in the doorway. When he spotted Cal out on the patio, he snarled, 'There he is,' and began to advance towards him.

Chapter 38

Lois swivelled round to see what was going on. 'Ooh, look, that's the guy who—'

'My God, what's going on? What are you *doing*?' The pretty blonde girl was right behind Baz, looking absolutely horrified.

'What am I doing? I'm teaching the interfering bastard a fucking lesson.' Baz spoke through gritted teeth as Cal turned to face him.

'Seriously?' Cal had already put down his drink. His tone icy, he repeated with derision, 'I mean, *seriously*?'

'What gives you the right to interfere with other people? How fucking *dare* you?' Baz's face matched his trousers as he spat the words out.

'You're despicable.' Cal stood his ground.

'It was none of your *business*,' roared Baz, completely losing it and aiming a wild swing at Cal's head.

Cal effortlessly sidestepped the swing with a pitying smile that enraged Baz even more. He yelled, 'Right, that's it, I'm going to *get* you,' and launched himself once more at Cal, who felled him with a single uppercut to the jaw.

Baz went crashing backwards, scattering chairs and tables and landing with a hefty thud on the floor. He let out a bull-like bellow of outrage and lay there on his back, clutching his face and swearing. Having heard the commotion, people began pouring out of the pub to see what was going on. The blonde girl, clearly mortified by what had happened, clutched Cal's arm. 'Oh God, you didn't just say that to me as a joke, did you?'

'Say what?' demanded Lois as Baz ordered his friends to call 999 and get the police over here right now. 'And tell them to send an ambulance too. The mad bastard's broken my jaw. He's going down for this, I can tell you that right now. He's going to get done for fucking GBH.'

'Mate.' One of his friends was shaking his head, looking doubtful. 'It's not worth it.'

'He's not getting away with this,' Baz shouted. He'd cut his hand on a smashed glass, and now blood was dripping onto his chest. 'Fuck, and this is my best shirt too. Phone the cops, Rupe. If you don't, I will.'

While they waited for the police to arrive, Cal went inside with Mimi and Lois.

'Right, tell us what happened,' said Lois. 'This is killing us.'

Cal spoke evenly. 'When I came in to get the drinks, I saw Baz with the blonde girl and recognised him from your description. I placed my order and went to the gents'. Baz came in a few seconds later with one of his friends, who asked him how things were going with the girl. Baz said it was a slam-dunk, she'd swallowed the story hook, line and sinker, and now all he had to do was reel her in. So then his friend said, "Jesus, Baz, are you still using the dead-girlfriend shtick?" And Baz said, "Hey, whatever it takes is good enough for me." His friend said, "Failed parachute?" and Baz said, "Nah, the last time I used that one, the girl tried to bloody google it. I'm sticking to car crashes from now on."'

Silence.

'Oh God,' said Lois.

Cal paused, every detail of the exchange clearly etched into his brain. Then he shrugged slightly. 'I didn't say anything, didn't even look at them. But on my way back to the bar, I passed the girl Baz had been talking to and told her the story about his girlfriend wasn't true, he'd just said it to get her into bed.'

Mimi felt hot with anger on his behalf. 'You know what you did wrong?' she told Cal. 'Didn't hit him hard enough.'

'Oh trust me, I wanted to.' He glanced down at his unmarked knuckles, opening and closing his right hand. 'I really did.'

Two police officers arrived twenty minutes later, one fat, one thin. The fat one said, 'Hey, Cal, how's it going?'

'Not the greatest evening of my life,' said Cal. 'I'm the reason you've been called here.'

'Are you now?' The officer lifted his eyebrows. 'That's a turn-up for the books. Someone hit you, did they?'

'Not quite. I hit them,' said Cal.

Mimi and Lois accompanied him outside, to where Baz and his four embarrassed friends were sitting. The chairs and tables had been righted by this time, the broken glass swept up.

'Where's my ambulance?' Baz demanded.

'I didn't ask them to send one,' muttered the friend who'd

340

been instructed to call 999. 'Your jaw isn't broken. You can't call an ambulance for a cut hand.'

Once the police officers had taken down all the relevant personal details, they listened to Baz's version of events. Then it was Cal's turn to give his side of the story, which he did concisely and without drama.

When he'd finished, the fat police officer sat back and nodded slowly. 'Right. Well, I think we've heard everything we need to hear.'

'God, this is taking forever,' Baz moaned. 'Just get on and arrest him, for crying out loud. Cart him off and give him a night in the cells, that'll teach him to stick his nose into other people's business.'

'OK, Baz, don't get worked up again,' warned his friend.

'Why the fuck shouldn't I get worked up?' Baz gestured angrily. 'I was all set to pull that bird until he saw fit to ruin everything.'

'Have you two ever met before?' The fat police officer looked at Baz.

'No, we haven't, and—'

'The thing is, *I've* met him before,' the officer continued steadily. 'I first met Cal five years ago.'

'Oh great, so he's a mate and you're on his side. Old pals' network, is that what I'm up against?'

The officer nodded at Cal. 'How's Cora? Doing OK?'

'She's good, thanks.'

Spittle escaped as Baz gave a splutter of disbelief. 'For fuck's sake! Who cares how his missus is doing? This is a stitch-up, it's police corruption. You people make me sick.'

'You see, you're jumping to conclusions now,' said the officer. 'Cora isn't Cal's missus. She's his daughter. And the

341

reason we first got to know each other was because Cal's wife died five years ago, not far from here.' He raised his bushy eyebrows at Baz. 'In a car crash.'

It was ten minutes past midnight and the last stragglers were leaving the pub.

'Oh come on, it's too early to stop now,' Lois protested as Paddy helped her into her jacket. 'Let's all go back to mine for a nightcap.'

Cal said, 'I can't.'

'You can! Cora's staying over at Lauren's, so you can stay as late as you like.'

He shook his head. 'I need to get back for Otto.'

'I have to get home too,' said Mimi. 'I've got a video-conference call at six, which means setting the alarm for five so I can stick some make-up on.'

'Honestly, you people. Paddy, will you come back to mine, just for one drink? Pleeeease.'

'OK, but something's up.' As usual, Paddy wasn't missing a trick. 'What's this really about?'

Lois exhaled noisily. 'Fine. If you *must* know, that girl Felix is out with tonight has posted three photos on Instagram now. Three! Showing off what an amazing time they're having . . . I mean, I could cope with the first one, but this is just rubbing my nose in it. So I thought I might post a couple of my own, of *me* having fantastic fun with someone else.'

'But you've had all evening to do that,' Paddy pointed out. 'We could have taken loads of photos in the pub.'

'Honestly, how can you not get it? We go to the pub all the time. Photos of us in there don't count.' Lois gave him a *duh* look. 'But ones of us having fun back at my place . . . well, that could mean anything at all. Oh please,' she begged, 'just to make me feel better. I promise you don't have to stay long.'

Paddy grinned. 'Come on then, let's do it. I feel so used, knowing you only want me for my body.'

The two of them headed off across the village green, leaving Mimi and Cal to walk home together.

'How do you feel about that?' Cal indicated the two figures melting into the darkness.

'I'm sure it'll be fine. Let's just hope he doesn't seduce her,' Mimi said. 'Anyway, more to the point, how are you feeling?'

'You mean about Baz? Oh, I'm OK.' He waited while she leaned against the wall and shook a tiny stone out of her shoe. 'I wonder if he'll stop doing it now.'

Mimi said, 'I think he will.'

The moment Baz had heard the police officer's explanation, he'd deflated like a pricked balloon. In an instant, all the bluster and fury had vanished.

'Shit. Oh God, it was only ever meant to be a joke.' He'd covered his shiny face in shame. 'I was just having a laugh, it's something we do to win the birds over, that's all. Gets you the sympathy vote, know what I mean?'

One of his friends, equally mortified, had said, 'We don't all do it, Baz.'

'Yeah, well. Look, I'm sorry. I didn't know, did I? It won't happen again.'

They'd slunk off then, their night in the Cotswolds not ending in quite the way they'd hoped.

Mimi fitted her shoe back onto her left foot. Cal watched

343

her. 'Well, they're heading back to London tomorrow, so I guess we'll never find out,' he said. 'Speaking of London, what's this I hear about a wedding at the Savoy?'

Mimi grinned. 'I meant to tell you, then everything else happened and I forgot. CJ and Willa are getting married, two weeks from now. Can you believe it?'

'How on earth did he manage to get the Savoy? Aren't those kinds of places booked up for years ahead?'

'There was a last-minute cancellation and CJ snapped it up. Still costing him a fortune, of course, but they didn't want to wait. I was asking Lois if she'd be my plus-one, but it's her mum's birthday and she's already arranged to fly up to Edinburgh and take her out to the theatre.'

'So who *is* going to be your plus-one?' said Cal.

Mimi levered herself away from the wall and adjusted her jacket. 'Haven't really thought about it. I mean, I suppose I could go on my own, but it's not the same. Especially when you hardly know anyone else there.'

'When's it happening?'

'Saturday the twenty-sixth. Gosh, look at the stars, aren't they amazing?'

They paused to gaze upwards. The earlier cloud cover had cleared and the inky sky now resembled black velvet scattered with tiny sequins.

'Cassiopeia.' Cal pointed out the constellation, tracing the lines with his outstretched finger.

'Andromeda.' Mimi raised her own arm. It was the only one she knew.

'Perseus.' His shoulder brushed against hers and she hoped he couldn't feel the effect it had on her, sending little zings of delight down her spine.

'Hippopotamus.' Mimi confidently drew a random shape in the air.

'Clavicle.' Cal nodded and did the same.

'Cauliflower.'

'Concertina.'

'Chlamydia. *Oh.*' Mimi winced. 'Not chlamydia. Why did I have to say that? Why do the wrong words just fall out of my mouth without asking my brain first?'

'Hey, don't worry, I love that this kind of thing happens to you.' Cal was laughing, but Mimi's heart was so busy leaping into her throat she could barely concentrate, because for a split second she'd thought he'd been about to say *I love you.*

Obviously it wouldn't have happened, but that was the way her brain functioned sometimes; it was too intent on finishing other people's sentences to her own satisfaction to wait and listen patiently to what they actually had to say.

'I'm a hopeless case,' Mimi said ruefully. She forced herself to get a grip.

'Look, this wedding in London. It's fine if there's someone else you'd rather take.' Cal paused. 'But if you really are stuck for a plus-one, I'd be happy to go along with you.'

Mimi looked at him, and now her chest was going like Skippy the Kangaroo, using up far more heartbeats than she could probably spare.

'Only if you want me to,' Cal went on. 'Feel free to say no. I won't be offended, I promise.'

Offended? *As if.*

Except he was a friend, offering to help her out, that was all. Although the way he was looking at her now was having even more of an effect than usual.

'That'd be great.' Mimi nodded. Because, let's face it, there was no way she was going to say no. 'Thanks.'

'My pleasure.' Cal's eyes glittered, a light breeze ruffling his hair as he smiled down at her. 'We'll have fun.'

Fun? What kind of fun? The good kind? Was he moving closer to her? Oh wow, what could be about to happen? She heard herself say, 'Well, it should be a good do . . . and you'll finally get to meet CJ and Willa . . . er . . . um . . .'

Cal sounded concerned. 'Are you OK?'

But Mimi's train of thought had gone, splintered. She was peering through the darkness at the ghostly outline of a figure moving towards them, a thin, pale figure with a translucent quality and a way of walking that seemed oddly familiar . . .

And oddly capable of making her feel quite sick.

Chapter 39

Turning, Cal studied the approaching stranger. 'Do you know who that is?' he murmured.

Mimi nodded, feeling the little hairs rise on her arms. 'It's Kendra.'

Kendra closed the distance between them. 'Mimi, is that you? I've been waiting for you to come home. Oh Mimi . . .' Her voice breaking with emotion, she held out her arms and stumbled forward. 'I've missed you so much.'

Mimi exhaled. Basically, if anything *had* been on the brink of happening between herself and Cal, it certainly wasn't going to happen now.

Oh well, chances were she'd only been imagining it anyway.

'What are you doing here?' As she said it, Mimi realised from the blast of alcohol fumes in her face that Kendra had been drinking.

'I needed to find you. I can't bear that we haven't talked for so long. I've dumped Rob . . . God, men are such bastards, aren't they? Oh Mimi, it's so good to see you again! Have you missed me as much as I've missed you?'

Mimi stood stock-still while Kendra threw her arms

around her. She could feel Kendra trembling as she tightened the hug. 'I don't understand why you'd just turn up like this. With no warning at all.'

'Well I couldn't call you, could I? You blocked my number. You blocked me *everywhere* online, so how could I let you know?'

'Maybe I did that for a reason.'

'Oh I know, but that was, like, *so* long ago, almost a year now. It's ancient history. You're my best *friend*.' Kendra's voice cracked again. 'The best friend I ever had. And I know you were upset when you found out about me and Rob, but it's not as if I did it for fun, like, just on a whim or something. I really did love him.'

'And what's happened now? Why did you dump him?'

'Because he cheated on me. On *me*! Can you believe it?' Kendra's smooth cheeks were wet with tears and she was taking big, gasping breaths. 'I found out he'd been sleeping with the girl he replaced you with at the agency, and she's not even as pretty as me. She has fat ankles!'

Oh Rob. Once a cheat, always a cheat. Mimi exchanged a glance with Cal and knew he was thinking the same.

'Men, they'll always let you down,' Kendra went on. 'But best friends are for life.'

Until they sleep with your boyfriend. Mimi couldn't deny herself a feeling of triumph that karma had caught up with Kendra. Aloud, she said, 'How did you get down here?'

'Drove.' Kendra gestured carelessly behind her. 'My car's over there, outside your house.'

'You drove down from London, *drunk*?'

'Oh come on, of course I didn't do that. I brought two bottles of champagne with me, got here an hour ago.

348

Someone saw me ringing your doorbell and told me you were over in the Swan. But I didn't want to go and find you in the pub in front of everyone, so I waited in the car instead and opened one of the bottles to pass the time. I drank half of it but there's still plenty left.' Kendra paused and peered at Cal for the first time. 'You're better-looking than Rob. Are you Mimi's boyfriend?' She turned back to Mimi. 'He's miles better-looking. See? I did you a massive favour. You have to admit it now.'

'He isn't my boyfriend.'

'No? He should be. Well, unless he's a cheating bastard too.' Kendra shivered dramatically. 'OK, I'm starting to get really cold. Can we go inside now?'

'No.' Mimi shook her head.

'Oh, but there's so much I want to say to you!'

'And so little I want to hear.'

'Mimi, *please*. I've made plans . . . so many plans. I'm going to make it all up to you . . . Look, sorry.' Kendra turned to Cal. 'Could you give us some privacy? It's a bit weird trying to talk in front of a stranger, and this is quite personal.'

'Up to you.' Cal addressed Mimi. 'I can stay if you'd rather.'

'Thanks, but it's OK.' Kendra was right: none of this was any of Cal's concern. 'I'll be fine.'

He briefly touched her arm. 'If you're sure. I'll see you soon.'

They both watched as he made his way across the green and up the high street in a homeward direction.

'He's nice,' said Kendra.

'I know.'

'Shagged him?'

'No.'

349

'You want to make your move before someone else snaps him up. Actually, don't. I've got a better offer for you. *Brrrrr.*' Kendra rubbed her arms and gave another exaggerated shiver. 'Let's get into the house and warm up.'

'You're not coming in,' said Mimi.

'Oh come on, don't be like that. It's me!'

'Still no.'

'Look, I'm *sorry*. But like I said, I did you a massive favour. You and Rob were never going to last. You got off lightly.'

Rather than say it again, Mimi silently shook her head.

'But I've been drinking. I can't drive back to London. I have to stay somewhere!'

Which was probably the reason she'd opened the champagne. Without speaking, Mimi began walking in the direction of Bay Cottage. When she reached Kendra's red BMW parked outside it, she stopped dead. 'You can sleep in your car.'

'Oh for crying out loud, why are you being like this? I've just had the most hideous week of my life. I came down here so we could make up and be friends again. I want to help you!'

'How? How could *you* possibly help *me*?'

'Because I want you back, and I know you need a job, so I've found you one.' As she said it, Kendra unlocked the boot of the BMW and rummaged through a tan leather holdall. Pulling an oversized navy sweater over her white shirt, she flung herself down on the verge and took another swig from the opened bottle of Moët that had been nestling in the grass before offering it to Mimi. 'I've been stalking you online, and it hasn't been easy, what with you having blocked me.'

'So how did you?'

'I got Jess to sign into Facebook on my phone.'

Jess, who worked on the reception desk at Morris Molloy, cheerful, clueless Jess with her elongated vowels and eagerness to please.

'It's been nearly a year,' Kendra went on, 'and you're back from Spain, living with your dad's boyfriend in this godforsaken place, setting up your own little business because you can't find a decent job and spending your evenings in the only pub in a village where nothing ever happens . . . I mean, *listen* to this place. Silence! Everyone's asleep! It's enough to drive any normal person insane. You can't waste your life down here . . . you're going to shrivel up and die of boredom!'

If only she knew.

But Mimi had already worked out where this was heading; she knew Kendra too well. Innocently she said, 'So what do you think I should do?'

'Come back with me.' Kendra's reply was instantaneous. 'Back to London, where you belong. You can move into your old room and we can carry on where we left off, having fun together. And guess who's on the hunt for someone to fill a vacancy for a senior PR exec? Only Carrick Payne!' Her eyes gleamed in the dim light; Carrick Payne in Soho were Morris Molloy's greatest rivals. 'I spoke to Josh Carrick yesterday and told him you were available, and I swear to God, he was over the moon. All you have to do is say the word and the job's yours.'

This was the thing about people: you could be friends with them whilst at the same time being aware of their various faults. Kendra had always been somewhat self-obsessed and ruthless, keen on getting her own way. Now that Rob had moved out of her flat in Notting Hill, she needed her old best friend back to keep her company whilst she negotiated being single once more.

She'd never had much of a conscience either. When Kendra wanted something, she tended to take it.

'I'm not coming back to London,' Mimi told her. 'I wouldn't want to share your flat again.'

'Look, you're just cutting your nose off to spite your face. I'm offering you everything!'

'How could I ever trust you?'

'You *could*. I wouldn't go after any of your boyfriends, and that's a promise.'

'Once was enough.'

'Oh Mimi, please can we go inside? We can't stay out here all night.'

Kendra thought she could wear her down, win her over. Mimi repeated, 'You aren't coming into the house. I'm not going to change my mind.'

'But I need a wee.' Kendra's voice rose.

'There are trees over there. Go behind one of them.'

'I NEED A WEE!'

'Shh,' said Mimi.

'WHY ARE YOU TELLING ME TO SHUSH?' bellowed Kendra. 'I'LL SHOUT IF I WANT TO. WHAT'S GOING TO HAPPEN IN THIS GODFOR-SAKEN BACKWATER? WILL I BE BURNED AT THE STAKE?'

'What's going on?' A male voice came out of the darkness and Kendra swivelled round on the grass verge to see who owned it.

352

'Who are you? Have you come to arrest me?' Peering up at him as his face was illuminated in the glow of the street light, she said, 'Actually, maybe I wouldn't mind being arrested by you.'

Paddy raised an enquiring eyebrow at Mimi.

'It's Kendra. I used to share a flat with her in London before coming down here.'

Without missing a beat, Paddy said, 'This is the one who slept with your boyfriend?'

'Yes.'

'Wow.'

'She wants me to move back in with her. I'm not going.'

'Not surprised.'

'I said *sorry*.' Kendra threw up her hands in despair.

'She's not staying at my place,' Mimi went on, 'but she's had two thirds of a bottle of Möet so she can't drive home.'

'And I need a *wee*,' Kendra wailed.

Paddy thought for a moment. 'I suppose she can stay at mine.'

'That'd be great,' said Mimi, relieved.

'I don't even know him. He could be anyone!'

'His name's Paddy Fratelli. He lives just up the road. You'll be safe with him.'

Kendra took a closer look at Paddy. 'But will he be safe with me?' She was nodding, smiling slightly; he'd clearly met with her approval.

'Come on then, if you want a roof over your head.' Paddy beckoned in businesslike fashion, and Kendra was on her feet in a flash, grabbing her overnight bag from the boot of the car.

She looked at Mimi. 'Have you slept with this one?'

Mimi shook her head, refusing to even think about the night Paddy had rebuffed her humiliating attempt to seduce him. Hopefully he wouldn't share that particular hilarious anecdote with Kendra.

'God, you're hopeless,' Kendra snorted. 'Or is there something wrong with him?'

'Nothing wrong with me,' said Paddy.

Kendra gave him her overnight bag to carry. 'I'll be the judge of that.'

Chapter 40

At five the next morning, Mimi rose and showered, then applied her make-up and conducted the video conference with a TV historian in New Zealand and his manager in Montreal. When it was over, she glanced out of the window – Kendra's BMW was still parked outside – then went back to bed.

When the doorbell rang at seven thirty, she ignored it, but the caller was persistent. After the third prolonged bout of rings, she slid out of bed and peered down at the front path. Kendra, still wearing last night's clothes, indicated that Mimi should open the window.

'Have you changed your mind?'

Mimi marvelled at her perseverance. 'Not even slightly.'

'Fine.' Kendra shrugged. 'Your loss. Good luck to you, stuck down here in the back of beyond.'

Mimi had already known she wouldn't take well to having her olive branch rejected. 'I love it here,' she said evenly.

'Well just so you know, I slept with Paddy last night. He was spectacular.'

Had she really? Or was she just saying that? 'Well done you.'

'Bet you're jealous.'

'He sleeps with everyone.' *Except me.*

'You should give him a go sometime. Anyway, I'm off.' Kendra shook back her hair defiantly. 'I don't suppose we'll bump into each other again. Enjoy living here with nothing to look forward to.'

'I shall. Bye.'

Mimi watched as the car disappeared from view. But Kendra was wrong; she *did* have something to look forward to. Very much indeed.

For the next three hours, she attended to a stream of business emails and made half a dozen phone calls, breaking off every now and again to check the website of her favourite dress shop in search of something perfect to wear to CJ and Willa's wedding. Maybe the canary-yellow strappy shift dress with the big bows on each shoulder, or the blue and white polka-dotted one with wide skirts and a little waist-length jacket to match . . . ooh, or if she went for the lilac and pink stripy jacket she could team it with her favourite pink shoes . . .

The doorbell rang, and this time she went to answer it in case Marcus was home from his business trip to Manchester and had forgotten his key.

This was a joke, obviously; Marcus would never forget anything, let alone a key.

In the moment before Mimi opened the door, she realised from the blurred outline through the rectangle of stained glass that it was Cal on the doorstep. Thud-thud-thud went her heart and she instinctively pushed her fingers through her hair in case it was looking flat.

And then the door was open and there he was, his own

just-washed blonde hair bright in the morning sunshine and his olive skin already developing a tan that was shown off by a turquoise polo shirt.

'Hi, I'm just off to Oxford but wanted to drop by and see how you are, make sure everything's all right.' He checked over her shoulder as he said it. 'Not here, is she?'

'No. Gone.' Mimi added drily, 'For good.'

'Thought so, when I saw the car had disappeared. What did she want?'

Cal followed her into the kitchen, turned down her offer of coffee and listened as she told him about Kendra's plan to get her back to the flat in Notting Hill.

'And you told her you weren't interested.'

'I did. I said I was happy here.'

Cal's expression softened. 'Glad to hear it. So did you let her sleep here in the end?'

Mimi shook her head. 'I wouldn't let her stay. Luckily Paddy came along and took her back with him to his place.'

'Luckily?'

'Well I didn't want her here, did I? She spent the night with him.' Unable to resist it, she added, 'They slept together.'

'Right.' Cal paused. 'And how did you feel about that?'

'What she does is up to her.' Mimi shrugged. 'I shouldn't think I'll ever see her again. She was a friend once and she betrayed me. I don't need people like that in my life.' As she said it, she leaned against the kitchen table and her hip knocked the edge of her laptop, bringing up the last opened page before the screensaver had kicked in.

'Just as well you aren't my boss,' Mimi said cheerfully as Cal glanced at the screen. 'At least when you work for yourself you can't get told off for googling dresses to wear to your ex-boss's smart wedding.'

'Ah—'

'Ooh, now you're here you could give me your expert opinion. Right, I've narrowed it down to a shortlist of three, so which do you prefer?' Tapping keys, she brought the outfits up.

'Actually, that's the other reason I dropped by.' Cal cast a distracted glance at the screen. 'I mean, I like the yellow one with the ribbony things . . . or the purple dress, although it looks pretty short.'

'It isn't purple, it's lilac,' said Mimi. 'And it isn't a dress, it's a jacket, so I'd wear it over a white top and trousers.' She was wondering if it was worth asking Cal what he'd be wearing, to make sure they wouldn't clash, when she saw the expression on his face. 'Oh, do you hate all of them?'

'No, no, they're great. It's not that,' said Cal. 'Look, I know I only suggested it last night, but I'm not going to be able to make it after all.'

'Oh.' This was bad news, not what she'd wanted to hear at all. Forced to pretend not to be disappointed, Mimi said as brightly as she could manage, 'That's a shame! Never mind, though, it's fine, I'll just ask someone else instead. Probably not Kendra!'

'I'm really sorry. I had a call an hour ago from a racehorse trainer who'd commissioned a portrait to be carried out next week, but he's been held up in Australia and has to reschedule, and the only date he can manage is the twenty-sixth.' He shook his head. 'I know, typical. Had to be that day, didn't it? I mean, I could have said no, but it was a bit of a coup to be asked.'

'It's a massive coup,' Mimi exclaimed, 'and of course you couldn't say no. Honestly, don't worry about it, you can't turn down a chance like that. And you mustn't apologise either, it's no problem, no problem at all.'

At the front door, as he was leaving, Cal turned abruptly. 'Look, I know it's none of my business, but I don't think you should invite Paddy to go with you.'

'To the wedding?' Mimi blinked. 'I hadn't even thought of asking him.' Well, this was almost true; it had very briefly crossed her mind. God, at this rate she was going to be left with a choice of either Old Bert who looked after the pigs on Hardy's Farm, or Eamonn from the village shop.

Cal studied her for a couple of seconds, almost-but-not-quite looking as if he didn't believe her and causing a warm flush to crawl up Mimi's neck. Then he tilted his head and said evenly, 'I just don't think it'd be a good idea.'

Chapter 41

The text that had just flashed up on Mimi's phone was from Lois.

Can you come over? Need some help.

Mimi had been working on a presentation for a possible future client. She texted back: *On my way.*

What had happened? Was it something to do with Felix? Since the other evening when the oh-so-casual battle of the Instagram accounts had taken place, Lois had been decidedly on edge and she and Felix had been avoiding each other.

But when she arrived at the house a couple of minutes later, she found Lois kneeling in the front garden, in the middle of a flower bed, clutching something black on her lap.

Mimi said, 'What's happened?'

'I just found him out here. Not sitting on the window ledge like he usually does. He was lying on the gravel path.' Lois gingerly stroked Truman's silky head, as if half expecting him to hiss like a snake and sink his teeth into her fingers. 'And he never lies on gravel. Then he crawled over here and climbed onto my lap, and he *definitely* never does that. I think he's been sick too. He's not right at all.'

Mimi crouched down. 'He doesn't look right.'

'I need to get him over to Henrietta. Will you come with me?' Lois grimaced. 'If I go on my own, she'll accuse me of tipping bleach down his throat or something and we'll end up in a slanging match.'

The last time they'd encountered each other, in the village shop, Eamonn had been complimenting Lois on her new shoes and Henrietta had eyed them with disdain before announcing how nice it was that Felix's new girlfriend possessed both style and class. It had taken all Lois's self-control not to pelt Henrietta, *Tom and Jerry* style, with the contents of her shopping basket.

'I suppose I could take him.' Mimi made the offer without enthusiasm. 'Or you could call Felix, see if he'll come over and pick him up?'

'I already texted him. He's at work. Come on, we'll go together. Safety in numbers,' said Lois as with Mimi's help and the cat safely supported in her arms, she managed to stagger to her feet.

Ivy-clad Fox Court was even more imposing at close quarters than it was from a distance. Most properties of this size in the Cotswolds had long since been turned into hotels, but Henrietta had flatly refused to countenance such a plan. Officially she occupied the south wing, but in reality the house was her domain and the lack of privacy was one of the things that had driven Lois to distraction.

Ringing the bell of Henrietta's separate front door got no response. 'Surprise surprise,' Lois muttered as they made their way back round to the entrance of the main house that until seven weeks ago had been her own home.

This time the door opened to reveal Henrietta, stiff-shouldered and wearing her sourest expression. Her gaze flickered from Mimi to Lois, and then down to Truman cradled in Lois's arms. 'Why are you carrying my cat?'

'He's ill. I found him in my garden.'

'What have you done to him? Did you run him over?' Henrietta held out her arms to take him and Mimi sensed Lois bristling with annoyance.

'I did not. He was lying on the gravel path and he'd been sick. The only thing I've done is bring him over here to you.'

Mimi held her breath. You could feel the tension crackling in the air between them.

'Have you been putting rat poison down in that garden? Because if that's the case, I'm going to make sure—'

'I haven't, OK?' Lois's eyes flashed. 'And I don't know what's wrong with Truman but I'm starting to wish I'd left him there.'

'Just give him to me,' Henrietta snapped. But Truman's body was so soft and floppy that attempting to complete the changeover without their hands touching proved impossible. Each time there was a risk of physical contact, both women veered away like repelling magnets.

'Look,' Lois said finally, 'let me into the house and I'll put him down on his bed. Then you need to call the vet and—'

'Don't tell me what to do.' Henrietta spat the words out like teeth. 'And *don't* pretend to care about my cat.'

'Are you worried that if you let me over the threshold I'll handcuff myself to the Aga? Trust me, I can't wait to be out of here.' Marching straight past Henrietta, across the polished oak floor of the wood-panelled hall, Lois headed for the kitchen. After a moment's hesitation, Mimi followed her.

'Thought so,' said Lois when she saw the cushioned cat bed in the kitchen that had until recently been her domain. She crouched down and carefully decanted Truman. 'Right, done, he's all yours.' But as she indicated to Mimi that it was time for them to leave, she stopped in her tracks and said, 'What's that smell?'

Chapter 42

Mimi sniffed the air but couldn't detect anything; there was no sign of any food having recently been cooked.

'What *is* it?' Lois repeated.

'I thought you were leaving,' Henrietta snapped back.

There was a moment of hostile silence, during which Lois lifted her head like a meerkat. Then she turned to the right and disappeared through a second half-open door. Within seconds she called out, 'Come through here.'

'For God's *sake*.' Henrietta's eyes narrowed, but she followed Mimi into the sunlit drawing room, where Lois was pointing to a heavy cut-glass bowl positioned on the polished walnut occasional table next to the sash window.

'What?' Henrietta demanded.

'Stargazer lilies,' said Lois.

'Well done. That's what they're called. And your point is?'

'Lilies are poisonous for cats. Just chewing a leaf or licking a bit of pollen can kill them.'

'Wh-what?' This time Henrietta's voice wavered; she shook her head rapidly and stared at them in disbelief. 'I've never heard of that. It can't be true.'

As if Lois might have made it up in order to scare her.

'It's true,' said Lois, 'and it's serious. If the poison's in their body for longer than a few hours, it causes kidney failure. How long have the lilies been here?'

'I . . . I bought them yesterday. Yesterday evening. Oh God, no . . . oh Truman.' Fumbling in the side pocket of her brown tweed skirt, Henrietta found her phone and pushed it into Mimi's hand. 'I'm shaking, can you do it? Call Felix for me . . .'

'We've already tried him,' Mimi said abruptly. 'He's in Melksham.'

Melksham was over an hour away. 'But . . . OK, call a taxi, there's a number in the phone book out in the hall. Of all the days my car had to be in for repairs . . . Hurry *up*, girl.' Henrietta's voice rose as she addressed Mimi. 'Tell them we need someone here right away to take us to Cirencester.'

Her tone was sharp but there was panic in her eyes.

'Quicker if I take you,' said Lois.

Henrietta was already shaking her head. 'No, that won't be necessary.'

'It is necessary.' Lois took a deep, steadying breath. 'If it's lily poisoning, every second counts.'

Lois hurried out of Fox Court and returned within minutes in her own car. Mimi went with them in case a fight broke out. Henrietta climbed into the back seat and cradled Truman on her lap. Truman's eyes were dull and half closed; he'd been sick again as they were leaving the house.

'I d–didn't know.' Henrietta's voice trembled with emotion as they took off down the gravelled drive. 'I had no idea. I saw the lilies in the supermarket yesterday and they'd been reduced to one pound fifty so I couldn't resist them.' She swallowed audibly. '*Why* didn't I know? If lilies can kill cats, there should be warning signs on them. Or they should be banned, full stop. Oh Truman, I'm so sorry . . .'

Tears were sliding down her face now. Seeing this in the rear-view mirror, Lois grabbed a packet of tissues from the driver's-side pocket and handed them to Mimi to pass back.

'I love him so much,' Henrietta sobbed as she opened the packet.

'I know you do.' Lois spoke gently.

'He's all I've got.'

Well, she also had a son, but Mimi knew what she meant; Truman was her constant companion. Lois glanced sideways at Mimi, clearly conveying the thought that was it any wonder, the way Henrietta carried on. But her voice was kind as she said, 'And he loves you too. Look, you can't blame yourself.'

'I can.'

'Well you mustn't. Everyone knows you'd never do anything to hurt Truman.'

Henrietta blew her nose noisily into one of the tissues. 'And I couldn't wait to get you out of the house. If you hadn't smelled the lilies, I wouldn't have known.'

Lois said, 'You'd still have taken him to the vet, though.'

'But I'd have waited until Felix arrived home. I wouldn't have realised how urgent it was. It would have been too late.'

Mimi exchanged another glance with Lois. It might still be too late.

'We're getting him there as fast as we can,' said Lois.

'Anyway, it could be something else entirely. I might not even be right.'

But Lois had been right. And she had supported Henrietta both physically and emotionally when the vet in Cirencester confirmed the diagnosis before warning them that although he'd do everything possible to save Truman's life, if the kidneys were damaged beyond repair, survival simply wasn't an option.

Henrietta, understandably, had been in bits. Mimi, taking a diplomatic back seat, watched as Lois consoled her formerly terrifying, now utterly terrified mother-in-law and took charge of the situation, making notes of everything the vet told them and placing a reassuring arm around Henrietta's shoulders when she broke down once more in tears of anguish.

The lovely vet, whose name was Drew, praised Lois for getting Truman there as soon as she had; if emergency treatment began within six hours of consumption of the toxin and before it affected the kidneys, he explained, the chances of recovery were good. Without it, kidney failure would develop in two to three days.

Emptying the gastrointestinal tract and setting up intravenous fluid therapy had therefore begun, and Henrietta had stayed with Truman whilst Lois and Mimi had left the veterinary hospital and headed back to Goosebrook.

When they reached the village, Mimi said, 'Shall we go over to the Swan, get something to eat there?' Her stomach was rumbling; she hadn't eaten for hours.

But Lois shook her head. 'Actually, I think I'll go back to Cirencester. It feels wrong leaving Henrietta there on her own.'

'Blimey,' said Mimi.

'I know. Mad, isn't it? I just never knew it was possible for her to *be* distraught. Not even after the accident when Felix's father died. But I just feel so sorry for her now.'

Mimi nodded.'Me too.'Although the very idea still seemed beyond surreal.

Lois unzipped the side pocket of her handbag and took out a key. 'I kept a spare to Fox Court in case of emergencies. I'm going to let myself in and pick up one of Henrietta's cardigans for Truman to lie on. It'll comfort him when she isn't able to be there.'

'Good idea.' Mimi was touched by her thoughtfulness.

'Oh God, I hope we managed to get him there in time.' Lois exhaled noisily and raked agitated fingers through her hair. 'I really hope Truman doesn't die.'

Chapter 43

And now it was three days later and the longed-for miracle had happened. Truman's kidney function was within normal limits. Thanks to Lois finding him and getting him to the vet in time, the potentially fatal organ damage had been avoided and he'd made a full recovery.

Over at Lois's house, Mimi listened to her on the phone to Henrietta and marvelled at the astonishing turn of events. Nor was she the only one to have been doing so; Henrietta was currently the talk of the village.

The call ended. Lois said, 'She's on her way over now,' and this time Mimi hid a smile because Lois had already begun plumping up cushions and clearing their empty plates from the coffee table as if she genuinely cared what Henrietta thought. This afternoon, Lois had driven Henrietta into Cirencester to bring Truman home. In the last seventy-two hours they'd spent more time together than they had over the course of the past five years. Even more incredibly, they hadn't scratched each other's eyes out.

Was it any wonder the inhabitants of Goosebrook were agog?

The doorbell rang and Lois went to answer it. Mimi heard her exclaim, 'Oh Hen, you really didn't have to do this,' followed by the crackle of expensive cellophane.

Hen. Imagine!

When they came into the sitting room, Lois was barely visible behind a vast bouquet of mixed roses, iris and lupins. 'They're so gorgeous, but you don't even approve of florists! You've always said why waste money when there are flowers growing in the garden for free.'

'I have always said that,' Henrietta agreed. 'And three years ago I overheard you telling Felix I was a skinflint for only ever giving people flowers from my garden.'

Lois clapped a hand to her mouth. 'Oh God, you actually heard that? I'm so sorry. I didn't mean it, I swear!'

'Of course you meant it. So I thought you'd prefer me to pay an extortionate amount for these.' Henrietta softened the words with a wry smile. 'And yes, I still think it's a shocking waste of money, but I wanted to get you something *you'd* like.'

'I do,' said Lois. 'I love them. Thank you so much.'

'Well, good. I'm glad you like them.' There was a moment's pause, then Henrietta said, 'Anyway, I'll be off now, leave you two in peace.' She glanced at the two clean glasses on the white marble coffee table, next to the unopened bottle of Sauvignon Blanc they'd been about to dive into.

'Stay and have a drink with us,' Lois offered impulsively.

'Oh no, it's fine, I don't want to intrude . . .'

'You wouldn't be intruding. Don't go.' Darting into the kitchen, Lois returned with a third glass. 'Truman's home and that's something to celebrate.'

An hour later, a second bottle was almost gone and

Henrietta had noticeably loosened up. Peering in surprise at her empty glass, she said, 'How many of these have I had?'

'Two. Well, two and a half,' Mimi fibbed. 'But only small ones.' It was actually more like four.

'Shall I tell you something? I'm sixty-seven years old and this is the first time in my life I've sat down and shared a bottle of wine with fr . . . Oh, I nearly said friends. Is that OK? Can I call you that?'

Mimi couldn't get over the fact that she was still here with them. Relaxed Henrietta was *so* different to uptight Henrietta.

'Of course we're friends,' said Lois. 'But I don't understand why you've never done it before.'

'I need to tell you something.' Henrietta nodded, reassuring herself. 'I think you deserve to know. It's just that it's been so long since it started; sometimes these things become . . . ingrained. Then before you know it, you've turned into a type of person you never thought you'd be.'

She wasn't drunk, merely helped along by the loosening effect of more alcohol than she was used to. Plus, of course, the massive relief of having Truman back at home, safe and well.

'You don't have to tell us,' said Lois. 'Not if you don't want to.'

This was a massive lie; she was clearly burning to know what it was.

Luckily Henrietta had made up her mind. 'I do want to. It's only right. You see, when I was your age I wasn't anything like you two. I worked in a research laboratory at a neuro-logical institute in Bristol. I wore a lab coat and spent my days carrying out investigations on patients alongside the

371

rest of the team. I was no great beauty, of course, but that was OK. We worked well together and the research was worthwhile.' She paused, her thoughts forty years in the past. 'There was a camaraderie amongst us. And one of the male doctors in particular, Laurence . . . well, let's say the friendship deepened as time went by. We grew closer. A relationship developed. It was the most wonderful thing that had ever happened to me. I fell in love with him . . . I mean, properly in love. But relationships between work colleagues were frowned upon, so we had to keep it a secret. I didn't mind, though. That was a small price to pay. If anything, it made the situation more thrilling, heightened the excitement. And we carried on our wonderful secret affair for quite a while. In fact, for nine years.'

Mimi's eyes widened. 'That's . . . a long time.'

'The happiest nine years of my life.' Henrietta pulled a handkerchief out of her skirt pocket and began twisting it between her fingers. 'Then guess what happened?'

Lois gasped, 'Oh God, did he die?'

A rueful head shake. 'I often wondered afterwards if that might have been easier. No, a new doctor joined the team. She was Danish, blonde, beautiful. And fun,' Henrietta added. 'Always laughing, singing, joking around. With all the male co-workers, but mainly with Laurence. Her name was Freja. And she decided she wanted Laurence, so she took him, simple as that. Within two months of arriving in Bristol, he'd finished with me and proposed marriage to Freja.'

Lois was outraged. 'What about no relationships allowed in the workplace?'

'It was only frowned upon, not banned outright. Once Laurence and Freja announced that they were getting married, it was pretty much a fait accompli. The institute didn't want to lose two brilliant research scientists in one fell swoop.'

'That's awful. So unfair.' Lois sounded appalled. 'You must have been devastated. Did you have to carry on working with them?'

Henrietta swallowed. 'I tried, forced myself to stick it out for a few weeks. But it was impossible. Everyone knew what had been going on. Our secret had never really been a secret, it turned out.' She hesitated. 'Apparently I'd been regarded as a bit of a laughing stock all along.'

'Oh *no* . . .' Lois winced.

A thought crossed Mimi's mind at that moment, but before she could articulate it, Henrietta continued. 'So I left the institute and came home to Goosebrook, where at least no one knew what had happened. And that's when my mother told me I needed to find someone else to settle down with pretty damn quick. I was the only child, the last of the line, you see. And Fox Court required me to produce an heir. When you're thirty-five years old, you can't afford to hang about.' She glanced at the bare bony fingers of her left hand as if picturing the rings that had once been worn there. 'So she set about finding a man who'd be happy to marry a heartbroken woman and provide her with a child, regardless of whether or not love was involved. Needless to say, she found Eddie Mercer. Who didn't love me in the slightest but enjoyed the idea of living a lavish lifestyle and spending my family's money.'

'Oh Hen, I'm so sorry, this is unbearable,' said Lois. 'I mean, obviously you and Eddie ended up living separate lives, but I had no idea you'd been unhappy from day one.'

'I never should have married him. Unhappy doesn't begin to describe it. My husband was unfaithful, work-shy, he drank far too much and didn't care one bit that I was miserable. Maybe women don't put up with that kind of behaviour these days, but at the time I just felt completely trapped. My mother had told me divorce was out of the question.'

'I can't imagine you letting anyone tell you what to do,' Lois marvelled.

'Well that's because I wasn't always like this.' Henrietta paused, examining her knuckles. 'I built a wall around myself. My life was horrible and I couldn't see the point of being a nice person, so I became horrible too. I think I wanted to punish everyone else for the fact that so much had gone wrong for me . . . Does that even make sense? Each time I said something unkind, it made me feel better. I found myself doing it again and again. It was addictive, almost like a drug . . . not that I've ever taken any drugs, of course. Sorry, should I stop now? Am I talking too much? Are you girls bored to tears?'

Was she kidding?

Mimi said, 'No!'

'Hand on heart,' said Lois, 'I think I can safely say this is the least bored I've ever been in my life. But it's just the saddest thing . . . All those years you were so unhappy, and you never found anyone to make you feel loved.'

Mimi tried to imagine what Henrietta's life must have been like, utterly devoid of a genuine emotional connection with someone who adored her in return.

'Oh,' said Henrietta, 'but I did.'

Lois boggled. 'Really? Who?'

Henrietta's expression softened. 'He was wonderful. His

374

name was Gianfranco. He came to work as our gardener at Fox Court when Felix was two years old.' She shook her head. 'I can't quite believe I'm telling you this. No one else has ever known. But Gianfranco was the love of my life and this time I knew he felt the same way about me. He also knew how dreadfully Eddie treated me. We had an affair and I've never regretted it. For once in my life I was truly, *properly* happy.'

Lois's own face was a picture. 'This is amazing. How long did it last?'

'One perfect summer. From May to September. He asked me to run away with him, back to Tuscany. And I was going to do it, I really was. I was going to take Felix with me and leave my life here in Goosebrook with my hideous husband and my bossy mother. Because this was my one and only chance. Nothing was more important than spending the rest of my life with Gianfranco. And he didn't just love me, he adored Felix too. Oh, I wish you could have seen them together . . .' Henrietta shook her head, lost in her memories, clearly picturing the two of them. 'The night before we were due to leave, Felix called Gianfranco *Daddy* by mistake, then laughed and said, "Will you be my daddy?" And it was as if he *knew*, although really it was only because Eddie was away so often. When you're nearly three years old, all you want is someone who's around to pay attention to you.'

She stopped then, and wiped away the tear that was trickling down her weathered cheek.

Lois said gently, 'What happened?'

'We'd arranged to leave at three in the afternoon. He didn't turn up. I thought he'd changed his mind but couldn't believe he'd do that to me. So I went to the gardener's cottage and found him there in bed.'

For a split second Mimi thought Henrietta had found him in bed with some other woman, or maybe a man.

'And he was ill, so ill. Barely conscious.' Henrietta's voice cracked. 'I called an ambulance and went with him to the hospital. It was a burst appendix. There was no phone in the cottage back then, so he hadn't been able to call for help, which meant it was too late to save him. By the time the doctors saw him, the poison had spread through his body. He died three days later of peritonitis. And that — oh God — that was the very hardest time of all.' She paused to swallow audibly. 'My whole world had collapsed but I had to behave as if everything was fine, because as far as everyone else was concerned, it was just a bit of bad luck that we'd lost a decent gardener.'

Mimi nodded gently; the parallels between Truman's illness and Gianfranco's were inescapable. 'And you've never talked about him before?'

'Never once. All this time, I've kept him here.' Henrietta pressed a trembling hand to her heart. 'My secret. The only man who ever truly loved me. If he hadn't died, can you imagine how different my life would have been?'

'And Felix's life too,' Lois reminded her.

'Of course. Oh dear, I've been awful to you, haven't I?'

'Well, yes. But you've been fairly awful to everyone, not just me.'

'I'm going to change. I need to change. Will you help me?'

Lois reached over and gave her hand a squeeze. 'Yes, we all will. You're already doing brilliantly. Everyone's so impressed.'

Henrietta took a shuddery breath. 'There's something else I need to explain. When I first met you, I thought you were all wrong for Felix. I was convinced you'd run rings around him and ruin his life. Just the sight of you made me feel sick. I'm sorry, I know that sounds terrible, but it's the truth.'

'Oh, right.' Lois was visibly taken aback. 'Well, I knew you didn't approve of me . . .'

'May I?' Henrietta pointed to the iPad on the coffee table, and in that moment, Mimi knew what she was about to show them. She passed the tablet across to her and watched as Henrietta tapped a couple of words into the search engine.

'I don't have any photos of Gianfranco,' Henrietta murmured. 'I wish I did, but there was never an opportunity to take a photograph. After he died, I was terrified I'd forget what he looked like.'

'But you didn't,' said Mimi.

'No, thank goodness. I can picture him as clearly as if he were still here in front of me. Although it's probably just as well he isn't.' Henrietta managed a brief smile. 'Seeing as I'm old now, and he'd still be young. Poor chap, he'd run a mile.' She paused again, then gathered herself and clicked on a link. 'Anyway, here's someone I *can* show you.'

Mimi and Lois both leaned in. The photograph had been taken in a science laboratory and featured a group of people engaged in conducting some kind of research on the brain of a patient lying on an old-fashioned-looking metal-framed hospital bed. Two men were examining a paper printout of what appeared to be masses of squiggly lines, a younger version of Henrietta was adjusting electrodes attached to the patient's head, and a second woman was pressing switches on the large, complicated-looking machine from which the paper had emerged.

'There's you,' said Lois.

'Yes. And there's Laurence.' Henrietta indicated the taller of the two men.

'And is that her?' Lois pointed to the woman at the controls of the machine. 'Is that Freja?'

Henrietta nodded; there was no need to say anything else. Together they studied the face of the attractive blonde doctor who had so effortlessly stolen Laurence's heart, and who so closely resembled Lois.

'Wow,' said Lois. 'No wonder you could hardly stand the sight of me.'

Chapter 44

Poor Marcus. Mimi could feel him mentally bracing himself. She was about to put him through an hours-long endurance test of the most agonising kind.

'Thank you for doing this,' she said. 'We can leave as soon as the speeches are over. The moment the dancing gets started, we'll sneak away, I promise.'

'You don't have to, though. I could disappear, but you can stay on if you're having fun.'

'Well, let's see how things go.' Mimi touched the sleeve of his immaculately tailored three-piece suit. 'You look fantastic, by the way.'

He cracked a wry smile. 'Flattery isn't going to persuade me to hang around here any longer than I have to.'

She sympathised. They reached the riverside entrance of the Savoy. Behind them, beyond Embankment Gardens, the Thames glittered in the sunlight. Ahead, Marcus faced the prospect of having to make inconsequential chit-chat with a roomful of complete strangers . . . or, alternatively, lurking by the enormous windows pretending to be utterly enthralled by the way the . . . er, sunlight was glittering on the Thames.

He knew no one here other than CJ, whom he'd briefly met that one time and hadn't much liked. He coped well enough in work situations, Mimi knew, because that involved meeting other accountants and at least they could make accountanty small talk. And he coped at home in Goosebrook because he knew everyone, which helped. But accompanying her here today . . . well, he'd done it out of the goodness of his heart, but no way was he going to find it enjoyable.

The decor in the River Room was sublime, the flower arrangements were spectacular and the exchange of vows went off without a hitch, which just went to show how much CJ had changed.

Willa was looking gorgeous in her stylish, understated way. CJ, puffed up with love and pride and wearing a multi-coloured silk waistcoat, was visibly ecstatic. When the service was over and the bride and groom had kissed, he took baby Alice into his arms and triumphantly announced, 'We've only gone and done it! And you can tell this is the best day of my life – it's costing me a bloody fortune and I don't even care!'

Everyone cheered and applauded. The MC announced that lunch would be served in thirty minutes. More trays of champagne began circulating, the rows of chairs were swiftly removed and an oversized woman in a tight *café au lait* dress and an enormous lace-trimmed hat tapped Mimi on the shoulder.

'You're Mimi! Hello, I'm Brenda! Helen's sister?'

Helen's sister, which made her Willa's aunt. Mimi said, 'Oh, hi,' and went to shake her hand, but Brenda, who appeared to be in her late sixties, had already turned her attention to Marcus.

'And you must be Marcus, how wonderful! We've heard *so* much about you!'

Bemused, Marcus found his own hand being seized and vigorously shaken. 'You have?'

'As soon as we found out Mimi was bringing you here today, we knew it was fate!'

Oh God. A sensation of impending doom began to unfurl inside Mimi's chest. Surely not . . .

'You must meet my son, Ewan. You have so much in common!'

Marcus grew visibly more tense. 'Is he an accountant?'

'No, he's . . . you know, *like you*!' Moving closer, Brenda enthusiastically mouthed the word *gay*. 'Look, there he is over there, blonde hair and emerald-green tie. He's forty-seven, keeps himself trim and—'

'Please don't do this,' Marcus blurted out.

'Oh but he's *such* a lovely boy, if I do say so myself! Now come on, don't be shy, why don't I introduce you to him now? Just a quick hello, you won't regret it!'

Mimi said hastily, 'Maybe later, OK? Once the speeches are over and everyone's a bit more relaxed.' By which time Marcus would have had time to skip away, back to their hotel in Leicester Square, out of danger. Because if there was anything more horrifying than attending a wedding full of strangers, it was discovering you were the victim of a pushy mother intent on setting you up with possibly the only other single gay man in the room.

'Did you know that was going to happen?' Marcus murmured when they were alone once more.

'God, *no*.' Mimi was so mortified she couldn't bring herself to look up in case she accidentally managed to catch Ewan's eye.

'This is even worse than when you set me up with that orthodontist in the Swan.'

Mimi winced. Eurgh, the dreaded Pierre from Cirencester. And to think she'd been so convinced he and Marcus were a match made in heaven.

Thirty minutes later, as they took their seats at their allocated table, a young waitress placed a folded note in front of Marcus. 'I was asked to give you this,' she said with a smile.

Marcus read the brief note before passing it to Mimi next to him.

A million apologies. My mother means well, but she's the worst. I had *no* idea she was planning to do that. Be assured that I shall keep my distance. By the time the speeches are over, I'll be gone.

Sorry again.

Ewan

It was a nice note, which meant he sounded like a nice person, but Mimi knew better than to point this out. She said, 'Well thank goodness for that. At least you don't have to worry now.'

Marcus nodded and gazed intently out of the window. He didn't look as if he planned to stop worrying any time soon.

Just over an hour later, the three-course meal had been cleared away and Mimi could feel Marcus silently counting down the minutes. The speeches began, and she risked glancing across the room to the table at which Ewan and his mother were seated along with other members of Willa's family. Ewan was facing in the opposite direction so Mimi could only see his back view. But he looked to have good shoulders.

The best man, a fellow thriller writer who'd flown over from Boston for the ceremony, gave a long speech and managed to lever in three separate mentions of his own books as well as a massive plug for the movie of his most recent novel, which was about to go into production starring Tom Cruise.

Then it was CJ's turn to speak, because as he'd already explained, it made sense to leave the best till last. Eyeing his best man – and greatest rival in the publishing world – he announced, 'And my next book has been optioned by Tom Hanks, who's going to direct *and* star it in, so I guess I win.'

But when the laughter had subsided, CJ grew serious and made an affecting speech that quite clearly came from the heart. He explained how lucky he was to have found someone to transform his life, how wonderful Willa was, and how the arrival of Alice had made both their lives complete.

He paused, then continued, 'Most of you know that I have my faults, although I generally prefer not to admit to them. Willa loves me despite them, and it's my job now to become a better person, to be worthy of that love.' His voice thickened with emotion. 'And to be worthy of our daughter's love, too. As you probably also know, Willa and I had a bit of a rocky start as a couple, but thanks to our friend Mimi, who basically sat me down and told me I was an idiot, I was able to be there at the hospital when Alice came into the world. Without Mimi, I doubt we'd be here now, celebrating the fact that I never knew it was possible to be as happy as I am today.' This time he needed to reach for

383

the white handkerchief in his breast pocket in order to wipe his eyes. 'Look at me, what a wuss. Anyway, thank you all for coming, thank you to Mimi for making me see sense, thank you to Willa, the only woman I've ever loved . . . and if anyone takes a photo of me blubbing like a baby, you'll end up in the Thames.'

Once the tumultuous applause had died down, music began to play and people rose from their seats in order to mingle, visit the loo, greet friends or make their way onto the dance floor.

Marcus, more relieved than most to get to his feet, said in a low voice, 'I'm going to head off now, is that OK? Will you be all right on your own?'

'I'll be fine. Come on, I'll see you out.' Since he was keen to slip away without being noticed, Mimi didn't want to give him a goodbye hug in front of everyone else. Leaving her jacket over the back of her chair, she followed him out of the room and down the staircase. Once they reached the stunning foyer on the ground floor, she wrapped her arms around him. 'Thank you again. And you can relax now, it's over. I'll explain to CJ and Willa that you had to leave early—'

'What are you *doing*?'

Mimi swung round and saw Ewan standing behind them. Viewing him for the first time at close quarters, she was struck by the openness of his face; he looked like a good person, an honest one.

'I'm leaving,' said Marcus, but Ewan shook his head vehemently.

'No, no, you don't have to. I told you I'd leave. I'm going now.'

'But there's no need,' Marcus replied. 'You can stay. I'm the one who's leaving.'

'*I* will,' said Ewan. 'Really, I insist.'

They stared at each other in dismay, until Marcus exclaimed, 'But I *want* to go.'

'Not as much as I do.' Ewan grimaced slightly. 'I've been counting down the minutes.'

Mimi said, 'Trust me, so has Marcus.'

Was there ever such an utterly British situation? The next moment a loud Australian herding three enormous suitcases on wheels bellowed, 'Outta the way, you guys, I gotta get these into a cab. Whoops, sorry about that, aaargh, and again. Sorry, mate, I'm a *tirrible* driver!'

The man and his cases were helped out of the hotel by two bellboys, leaving Marcus and Ewan to dust the wheel marks off their highly polished shoes before resuming their mutually uncomfortable conversation.

'Social events are my worst nightmare,' Ewan ventured.

Marcus nodded. 'Mine too.'

'I really am sorry about my mother.'

'Don't worry. She means well.'

'I know. She wants me to be happy.' Ewan smiled slightly. 'Just goes about it the wrong way and ends up giving me palpitations when I find out what she's been up to.'

Mimi said, 'I did the same thing to Marcus not long ago. It's a wonder he's even speaking to me after what I put him through . . . Oh, sorry.' She stepped aside as a porter trundled past pushing a loaded brass luggage cart.

Ewan looked at Marcus. 'What did she put you through?'

And now it was Marcus's turn to smile, because at least it was behind him now. 'Only the worst blind date in the world. I made her promise never to do it again, otherwise she'd be out on the streets.'

'Look,' said Mimi, 'we're getting in people's way. Tell you what, why don't we get out of here? There's a nice place just across the road . . . right now I could really do with a cup of coffee. Then you can tell Ewan all about the disastrous date I forced you to go on.'

Amazingly, incredibly, it worked. The relaxed atmosphere of the family-run Mediterranean restaurant opposite the Savoy wove its magic too, and because it was mid afternoon, they were able to get a table by the window. Once their coffees had arrived and the conversation was safely flowing, Mimi rubbed her bare arms and said, 'Brrr, this air con's efficient! I'm going to nip back and pick up my jacket. Won't be two minutes.' Pushing back her chair, she amended, 'If I *am* longer than two minutes, it means CJ has forced me to dance with him. OK, if I'm not back in fifteen minutes, you need to give me a call and rescue me. I'll pretend it's a client with some kind of PR emergency. Don't forget!'

She left them in the restaurant and made her way back to the wedding reception. CJ was too busy showing off his beloved daughter to ask her to dance, but Mimi wasn't distraught. Having helped herself to another glass of champagne, she spent a happy half-hour chatting to Willa's mum Helen and various other friends and relatives.

No call had come through from Marcus. Just as well she hadn't needed rescuing.

After another hour, Mimi retraced her steps and, lurking like a secret agent, surveyed the restaurant from across the road. But there was no need to be furtive; frankly, the chances were that Marcus and Ewan wouldn't have noticed if a squawking pterodactyl had been circling above their heads.

Oh, but just look at them.

Mimi felt her heart expand with love for shy, gentle Marcus, who so deserved to be happy again. And of course – *of course* – it was far too soon to be getting her hopes up, but at least the first tricky hurdle had been overcome. He and Ewan were talking non-stop, utterly engrossed in each other's company. All she could do now was leave them to it and keep everything crossed, because wouldn't it be wonderful if something could blossom as a result of this most serendipitous of meetings, and after such an unpromising start?

A text pinged up on Mimi's phone at midnight. Her pulse began to race when she saw that it was from Cal.

Hi, just wondered how the wedding went. All OK? Did you have a good time? (How about Marcus??) Sorry if you were asleep and this has woken you up x

He'd put a kiss. Well, an x. Mimi gazed at it and felt her stomach flip. She typed back: *I'm not asleep! And today went brilliantly. I'm in my hotel room and guess who isn't back here yet?!*

She hesitated, savouring the moment, then added an x. As she did it, she realised she was imagining planting a fleeting flirty kiss on Cal's mouth.

Just as well he couldn't see her doing it. She pressed send.

As she'd hoped, her phone rang seconds later.

'You can't text something like that and not tell me what's going on.' Cal sounded as if he was smiling, and the intimacy of his voice in her room – in her *ear* – sent a quiver down her spine.

'The most amazing thing happened.' From her bed, Mimi was able to gaze down at the bustle and lights of central London. As other people's lives played out beyond the uncurtained window, she told Cal the whole story and was touched that he was as delighted for Marcus as she was.

'I checked on them twice and they were still there in the restaurant. At six, Marcus gave me a call to let me know they were going for a walk along the Embankment before finding somewhere to eat. Then an hour ago he texted to say he'd be back here soon.'

'And you're still waiting.'

'Like a stern Victorian father sitting in the parlour, checking my pocket watch for the millionth time.'

Cal laughed. 'I'm home now, but Cora stayed at Lauren's today while I was up in Lambourn. I gave her a call this afternoon and as a joke asked if she was missing me. She said, "Oh Dad, don't be so needy."'

'She's growing up.' Through the window Mimi had been idly observing a scene unfold. 'No, *stop*,' she blurted out. 'You're ruining it!'

Startled, Cal said, 'Ruining what?'

'Sorry, not you. My room overlooks Leicester Square and I was watching a couple standing together under a street lamp. He was just plucking up the courage to kiss her when this group of lads went past and one of them yelled out something rude. And now they've run off but the guy's too embarrassed to try again. Honestly, what a bunch of animals. *Animals.*' Mimi raised her voice as the lads raced past beneath her window, then heard barking at the other end of the phone. 'Oh sorry, did Otto hear me say that?'

'No, he's gone tearing upstairs; sounds like something's woken Cora.'

In the background, Mimi made out a high-pitched wail and a loud crash, followed by Cora calling out *Daaaaaad* and the scrape of chair legs on the tiled floor. She heard Cal carry the phone up the stairs, push open the bedroom door and say, 'What's happened?' followed by the sound of Cora yelling, 'Get it out of here, Dad! Get it *out*.'

And now Cal had started to laugh. 'It's a bat,' he told Mimi. 'A pipistrelle. It's flown in through the window and now it's doing circuits of her bedroom, and Cora's jumping up and down on her bed like a jack-in-the-box . . . Sweetie, calm down, you know it isn't going to hurt you.'

'But it's flapping its wings so fast and . . . *aaaargh*, Dad, get it away from me, I don't want it in here! MAKE IT STOP.'

Shortly after ending the call, Mimi heard the lift opening, followed by the sound of Marcus's gentle throat-clearing as he paused in the corridor outside the room next to hers. She leapt up and opened her door as he was swiping his key card.

'Oh, hi.' He blinked at her from behind his spectacles. 'Did CJ mind that we left early?'

'Not one bit. He was delighted.' Mimi smiled, because Marcus was looking – there was no other word for it – *radiant*. 'Oh Marcus, this is the best thing . . .'

He said mildly, 'You haven't even asked me how we got on.'

'Do you want to take a look at yourself in the mirror? I

don't need to ask.' She hugged him. 'And no one deserves this more than you.'

Once they were back in their respective rooms, Mimi sent Cal another text to keep him updated: *Marcus is back, and so so happy. Just think, if you'd been my plus-one, he and Ewan would never have met. It's all thanks to you x*

Cal's reply pinged onto her phone screen a minute later: *I know, I'm brilliant. Also, managed to get rid of the bat. Go me. xx*

Two kisses! Two!

Smiling to herself, Mimi sent: *You see? Sometimes your little girl does still need you after all. xx*

There, now she'd sent two back to him. What a wanton floozy! Oh, but it was so exciting, flirting by text. Would Cal reply with three kisses? And if he did, would she send three more back to him? How long could they keep it going?

Mimi held her breath, giddy with anticipation, waiting for the next *ping* to arrive.

Then she took a few more breaths and held them too.

But there were no more pings, or texts, or kisses. So much for getting her hopes up.

Oh well.

Chapter 45

Eamonn's son Sam had been left in charge of the shop while his dad was playing cricket. Mimi, having popped in to buy chewing gum, said, 'How's the web-designing coming along?' and saw the boy's ears redden.

'Not so bad.'

'Are you enjoying it?'

Sam looked a bit panicked. 'It's OK.'

'I was having a look at Cal's website last night,' Mimi said gently. 'I noticed a few of the links aren't working all that well.'

The ears grew redder. 'I know. I'll get them fixed. I've just been busy.'

'Well, I've sorted out a few websites in my time, so if you ever need a hand, just say.'

Hope flared in Sam's pale eyes. 'Really? That'd be good. I wouldn't mind.'

'Websites can be tricky, can't they?'

He nodded vehemently. 'More difficult than I thought.'

'OK, now this is just a suggestion,' Mimi looked at him, 'but if you ever decide you'd rather not be in charge of Cal's site, I'd be more than happy to take it over . . . you know, at some stage in the future—'

'Or now?' Sam blurted out. 'You could take over doing it straight away. That'd be better.'

'I can. Of course I can,' Mimi said sympathetically. 'Or if you prefer, I could just give you a hand, show you how to get things fixed—'

'No.' Sam was shaking his head vigorously. 'I think you should do all of it.' His ears were glowing like embers. 'I like working here in the shop; making websites isn't really my thing.' Clearly relieved to have been handed a get-out clause, he admitted, 'My dad thought it'd be good because I'm always on my computer, but I don't know how to fix things when they go wrong. All I really like doing is playing Runescape.'

'Seriously?' She could hear the delight in Cal's voice. 'Oh my God, that's fantastic! You are a *star*.'

Mimi wished he wasn't a hundred-odd miles away at the other end of the phone. If she could have given him the news face to face, there was a good chance he'd have hugged her, which would have been even more fantastic. But he had taken Cora to his sister's place on the Gower coast to celebrate her cousin's birthday, so telling him this way would just have to do.

'Poor Sam, he was so out of his depth but too embarrassed to admit it. He asked me to tell his dad, so I've just been over to the pavilion and spoken to Eamonn. He's fine with it too.'

'Relief all round,' said Cal. 'You're brilliant. Really, thanks so much.'

'If only all takeovers were as easy to sort out.' His words made her feel all warm and glowy inside. 'Anyway, I just wanted to let you know. I'll make a start on the website tonight, but I need to get back to Lois now.' Having cleared the situation with Eamonn, she was making her way around the perimeter of the cricket pitch. 'Felix and Arabella are here.'

'Ah, tricky. How's she doing?'

'Not great.'

'I'll let you go,' said Cal.

I wish you wouldn't, thought Mimi.

'They're still there,' said Lois. 'Not that I'm looking.'

'I know.' Mimi rejoined her on their bench outside the pub, deliberately positioning herself between Lois and the spot where Felix and Arabella Playdell-Grey were seated at the edge of the pitch watching the cricket.

'Now you're in the way.' Lois peered to the left of her, then to the right.

'Just ignore them.'

'I *am* ignoring them.' Two seconds passed. 'Have you seen that picnic hamper she's brought along? Four different kinds of sandwiches! Cupcakes *and* cakes. And I bet you any money she made everything herself.'

'How can you even see it all from here?' said Mimi.

Lois patted her shoulder bag. 'I may just happen to have a small pair of binoculars with me.'

'Well that's a good look. Let's hope they don't catch you spying on them like a lunatic.'

'They won't. I'm discreet. Oh don't look at me like that,' Lois wailed. 'I know, OK? I've messed up big-time. I left my husband because I couldn't stand my mother-in-law. Now that's all sorted out and I actually like her – even if I still can't believe it myself – and you'd think that'd make everything wonderful, except it hasn't, because my husband has found himself a new girlfriend who just happens to have *two* legs and *no* scars, and to top it all she can make cakes as well.'

'You don't know that for sure,' said Mimi.

'Maria told me she'd heard that Arabella was nearly picked for *Great British Bake Off*.'

'She wasn't *on* it, though, was she?'

'Yeah, but she was almost good enough.' Lois moved her bag to one side as Paddy approached their table.

'If you wanted to learn to bake, you could do it.' Mimi gestured towards Felix and Arabella, who were now packing everything back in their hamper and rolling up the picnic rug. 'Look, they're going now.'

'Probably off to have wild sex,' Lois said gloomily. 'And the last time I tried to bake a cake I forgot to add the eggs. It ended up being a frisbee instead.'

Paddy put down his drink and sat beside her. 'Could this be anything to do with Arabella, by any chance?'

'Don't start making fun of me,' Lois warned.

'I'm not. I was over there just now, right behind them.'

'I know you were. I saw you through my binoculars. Did she make those cakes herself?'

'Actually, she did. And she offered me some too.' Paddy's blue eyes glittered. 'The lemon drizzle sponge was out of this world.'

'You're a monster,' said Lois.

'She's a sweet girl.'

'I know, I know she is. Everyone keeps telling me, as if that's somehow supposed to make me feel better.'

They watched in silence as Arabella and Felix carried their picnic paraphernalia across the grass to where Felix's car was parked.

'You were the one who left him,' Paddy reminded her with a what-can-you-expect shrug.

'I know that too,' Lois sighed. 'But at the time I thought something needed to happen. I suppose I hoped it would make Felix realise he did love me after all.' She gestured in despair. 'And then everything would be all right. I didn't know he was going to meet the perfect girlfriend, did I?'

A butterfly landed on the wooden table. Mimi said, 'Why don't you tell him how you feel?'

'Because then I'd look like even more of a loser than I already do. I can't beg him to take me back, not when he so clearly isn't interested.'

'What if he *was* interested, though?' said Paddy. 'You couldn't expect *him* to beg *you*. Not after you moved out. That would just be wrong.'

'I suppose.' Lois nodded sadly.

'Oh dear.' He gave her arm a companionable nudge. 'You haven't played this very well at all, have you?'

'Do you think I don't know that? You're not helping, you know.' A tear splashed onto the front of her T-shirt and she hurriedly wiped her cheek.

'Are you crying? Don't cry! God, don't do that.' Horrified, Paddy grabbed a paper napkin from the dispenser on the table. 'Here, before your make-up runs. Sorry, I thought you were OK from the way you've been joking about it.' As he spoke, he was reaching for his phone.

'It's called putting on a brave face, pretending to be fine.'
Lois pushed the phone away. 'And don't even *think* of taking
a photo of me looking like this.'

'I'm really sorry. And I wasn't going to take a photo,'
Paddy told her. 'The only reason I was teasing was because
I've got something to show you.'

'Well I don't want to see it,' said Lois. 'What did they
give you, an invitation to their wedding?'

He broke into a smile. 'Come on, cheer up, you're going
to like this. Although I probably shouldn't be showing you.'

Mimi saw Lois give herself a mental shake. 'Fine, go on
then.' She leaned sideways to get a look at the screen and
her expression changed to one of dismay. 'Oh what, are you
serious? A video of a cricket match? Do you want me to
die of boredom?'

'You're an actual nightmare. Be patient,' Paddy ordered.
'Let me find the bit I'm looking for.'

Lois shrugged, mystified. 'I don't understand why you'd
even video a cricket match in the first place.'

'You heard about Old Bert from Hardy's Farm, did you?
Slipped over in the pigpen on Thursday and broke his pelvis.
He's stuck in hospital recovering from surgery.' As he spoke,
Paddy was searching at speed through the footage. 'And he
was upset about missing the match, so I said I'd record it
for him. OK, here we go. Pay attention.'

'To a game of cricket?' Lois looked pained.

'You don't have to watch.' He tapped his ear. 'Just use
these.'

Mimi and Lois both leaned in to listen to the sound of
cricket being played whilst birds sang overhead and someone
snored gently in the background. On the screen, a corner

396

of tartan rug and the edge of a plate of sandwiches were visible.

'. . . But if we don't book soon, all the best places will be gone.' The female voice was light and extremely elocuted. 'We really should choose one now.'

Next to her, Mimi felt Lois's shoulder tense up.

'There's no hurry.' This time the voice was instantly recognisable as belonging to Felix. 'Something'll turn up.'

'Holidays don't just turn up, though. You have to arrange them and book them.' Arabella sounded frustrated. 'Which is why I've drawn up this list. All you have to do is pick one, then we can get it done.'

Mimi couldn't help it; she reached across and paused the video. 'Who's that doing the snoring? It's getting on my nerves.'

'That's me,' said Paddy.

'Oh. Sorry.' Wow, who'd have thought it? Paddy Fratelli, the great seducer, snored like *that*.

'You sound like a warthog,' said Lois.

Paddy looked proud. 'I don't really snore. Once things started getting interesting, I had to make sure they thought I was properly asleep.'

Chapter 46

Mimi pressed play again. After a few seconds of silence, broken only by another snore, they heard Arabella say, 'It took me ages to put together that list and you're not even looking at it. Felix, is there some kind of problem here?'

'No . . . I mean, er . . . the thing is . . .' Felix had never sounded more pained and Hugh Grant-like.

'You don't want to go away on holiday with me, do you.' Arabella said it flatly, a statement rather than a question.

Another long pause, then Felix sighed audibly. 'No.'

'Oh.' She sounded crestfallen.

'Sorry. I'm so sorry. It's just . . . I mean, I don't know quite how to say it . . .'

'Shall I do it for you?'

'It's not you,' Felix blurted out. 'It's me!'

'Oh Felix, you're wrong. It isn't you. It isn't me either.' Arabella's tone was sad but at the same time heartbreakingly upbeat. 'And it's no one's fault. You still love your wife and there's nothing any of us can do about it.'

Lois had covered her mouth and was inching closer to the screen.

'True,' said Felix. 'Sorry. Guilty as charged.'

'You two should get back together,' said Arabella.

'Lois left me.' He sounded resigned. 'She doesn't want me back. But that's irrelevant right now. I'm sorry about us. You're a wonderful girl. I've messed you around and I didn't mean to.'

'Felix, it's fine. I've been single for the last thirty-three years. It might break my mother's heart,' Arabella added with a rueful air, 'but trust me, I'm used to it.'

Mimi looked at Lois, who was trembling all over. Lois reached for her glass of wine and found it whisked away by Paddy.

'Don't drink it.' He showed her the wasp flailing furiously on the surface.

Mimi slid her own drink over to Lois, who took a hefty, grateful gulp, then another.

'So that's as far as I got,' said Paddy. 'The cricket stopped for tea and I pretended to wake myself up with an extra-loud snore. Felix and Arabella were starting to pack away their picnic when I left. And I wasn't sure whether it'd be a good idea to let you know what I'd overheard.' He paused, then winked at Lois. 'But on balance, after coming over here, I thought it might.'

Arabella, they knew, lived just a few miles away, in Missingham. If Felix took her home and dropped her off before driving straight back, Mimi calculated he'd be here in ten minutes.

'What if she was all calm and sensible while she was here and there were other people around them,' said Lois, 'but now she's crying her eyes out and clinging to him like a limpet, begging him to change his mind?'

'He's still going to say no,' said Mimi.

'If she needs a bit of cheering up,' said Paddy, 'I could always give her a call, offer to show her a good time.'

His electric-blue eyes were glittering, his tone playful. He was, Mimi thought, a far nicer person than he liked to make out.

They waited, pretending they weren't. Time slowed to a crawl. A fresh round of drinks was ordered and delivered to them, and a trickle of perspiration slid down Mimi's sun-warmed spine.

After twenty minutes, Lois said abruptly, 'I feel a bit sick. Maybe I should go home.'

'Stay,' said Paddy.

'I don't even know what I'd do . . . what I'd say to him, if he did come back. I ought to have a plan. I think it's better if I just leave it for now, then—'

'Here he is,' said Mimi.

Felix's bright-green MG had come into view. As they watched, it crossed the hump-backed stone bridge and approached the high street.

'Now I'm feeling really sick.' Shaking, Lois turned visibly paler as she tracked the car's progress. 'I don't have a plan, not even the beginnings of one . . .'

To calm her down, Mimi said soothingly, 'It's OK, you don't have to do anything today if—'

'Are you *kidding* me? Of course I do!' Lois was already lurching to her feet, knocking into the table as her prosthetic leg got caught under the bench. Then, regaining her balance, she was limping off across the grass, heading as fast as she could towards the road, waving her arms wildly in the air to attract Felix's attention.

He braked as she launched herself off the edge of the pavement and yelled, 'STOP!' at the top of her voice. The car slowed and came to a halt and Lois, hyperventilating, gasped, '*Stop!*' again.

The driver's door opened and Felix climbed out of the car looking bewildered. 'I have.'

Lois stared at him. 'I know. I didn't know what else to say.'

Silence. Mimi held her breath and waited. Next to her, she heard Paddy murmur, 'Uh-oh. Stage fright.'

The sunlight caught the blonde stubble on Felix's jaw as he said, 'Is everything OK?'

'Not really.' Lois swallowed.

'Why not? Has something happened?'

'I don't know.' Her voice wavered. 'Has it?'

'Come *on*,' Paddy exclaimed. 'Spit it out!'

Hearing him, Lois glanced over at them, then looked at Felix and blurted, 'You and Arabella. Are the two of you still . . . you know?'

'Together?' Felix supplied the missing word and shook his head. 'No.'

'Why not?'

'It wasn't working.'

'Are you upset?'

'No.'

'Is there anyone else you'd rather be with?'

Felix glanced around, then rubbed his hand over the top of his head, ruffling his already ruffled hair. 'Yes.'

Mimi jumped as a round of applause broke out behind them, but it was the spectators welcoming the teams back onto the pitch following their break for tea. Apart from herself and Paddy, no one else was within earshot.

'Is it me? Oh Felix, is it?' Lois's hand was pressed to her sternum.

Felix said cautiously, 'Do you want it to be you?'

'Yes! Yes, I do, more than anything . . . Sorry, my heart feels as if it's about to burst out of my chest. Felix, I want it to be me because I love you so much.'

He took a few steps towards her. 'Really?'

'Really. I thought you were only with me because you were stuck with me.'

Felix looked appalled. 'You seriously thought that? Never.'

Mimi saw Lois's eyes fill with tears and her heart went out to her. The accident had scarred Lois both physically and mentally. It had robbed her of her confidence and of her perceived ability to be enough for her husband.

Felix closed the distance between them. 'I love you. I don't find it easy to talk about, you know, feelings. I think things, but it's hard to say them out loud. But I'm saying it now. I love you more than anything. I only went out with Arabella because she asked me and I didn't want to embarrass her. I just didn't know how to say no. I'll never stop loving you.' His voice lowered as he wrapped his arms around Lois, and now she was half laughing, half sobbing as he murmured something else in her ear.

'Well this is annoying.' Mimi gave a sigh of impatience. 'I can't hear what they're saying now.'

'I think they're happy, and that's all that matters.' Paddy turned to look at her. 'What are you doing?'

Mimi had her phone in her hand. 'We should be filming this.'

'Pervert,' said Paddy with a grin.

'It's romantic,' Mimi told him.

'It's private.'

Lois was now hugging Felix as if she would never let him go. Mimi pressed the video button and said, 'Not if it's happening in the middle of the road.'

Chapter 47

Cal had come home to Goosebrook and now he'd just told her he was leaving again. It was hard, feeling poleaxed with disappointment whilst having to pretend everything was fine.

'How funny.' Outwardly cheerful, Mimi poured coffee into two cups and pushed one across the table to him. 'You've been here while I was in Jersey, and now I'm back it's your turn to be flying off.'

Unless he'd deliberately planned it that way, in which case it wasn't funny at all.

'But you're definitely home for the next week?' said Cal.

She nodded. 'Yes, why?'

'I need to ask a favour.'

'Of course, anything. No problem!'

'It's a big one.'

Mimi blinked.

Cal amended. 'I mean, you should never say yes until you know what the favour is.'

'But you wouldn't ask me to do something I couldn't manage. Anyway, fire away.'

'The sheikh who saw the portrait I did of the racehorse

trainer wants me to fly over to Dubai to paint him and his brother.'

'Well you have to go,' Mimi exclaimed. 'That's brilliant!'

'It is. But I'd need to leave tomorrow. And normally Cora and Otto would go to Lauren's, but Lauren's grandmother's staying with them and she's allergic to dogs, so I can't do that.'

'Well, it's—'

'And I know I could put Otto into kennels, but he hates it, he wouldn't be happy.'

'That's—'

'So it was Cora who wondered if maybe you'd be able to help out, but you can say no if it's too much to—'

'Cal! Can you stop interrupting? It's fine, I'd love to help.' Mimi raised a hand. 'I'll do it. Problem solved.'

'Are you sure? OK, thank you.' He sat back, relieved. 'You were a star last week when you rescued my website from Sam. This time you're a superstar. You've saved the day again. Now, do you want them to come here, or . . .?'

'It's easier if I stay at yours. Otto will be happier.' *And so will I!* But Mimi kept that thought to herself; instead she said, 'And I can work anywhere, so it doesn't bother me at all.'

Cal was nodding. 'The only problem is, I've got a ton of furniture stored in the spare room, but I can get that cleared out tonight.'

'Don't worry about it, I can sleep anywhere too.'

'If you're sure.' He was evidently thinking through everything he needed to do. 'It'd be great if I could put you in my bed.'

Ooh. Time stopped and Mimi's fingers tightened around

her coffee cup. The expression in Cal's clear brown eyes as he realised what he'd said was the kind that was hard to look away from. She saw the beginnings of a smile tugging at the corners of his mouth and felt breathless with—

DRRRRINNGGGGG. Cal's phone broke the silence.

Time started again and the moment slid away. He looked at the screen. 'It's your new housemate.'

Mimi smiled. 'Better answer it then.'

She listened as Cal told Cora everything was arranged, and heard Cora yell *Hooray!* with eleven-year-old enthusiasm.

'I think she's happy,' Cal said with a smile when he'd hung up. 'She's just getting off the bus now. I'd better go.' He finished his coffee and rose to leave. 'Come up to the house around ten tomorrow, OK? And thanks again. You don't know how grateful I am.'

That's nothing, thought Mimi as she showed him to the front door. You don't know how much I'm looking forward to sleeping in your bed.

Six nights later, the novelty still hadn't worn off. Outside, the wind whistled through the trees and rain was spattering against the windows like gravel, but inside Cal's bedroom all was warm and dry and welcoming.

Well, it would be even more welcoming if Cal were here too, but never mind that for now. Mimi, stretched out on top of the thick blue and white striped duvet in her pyjamas, gazed at the framed photo on the bedside table. It was an informal snap of Cal, Cora and Otto on a sweeping curve of beach in west Wales, and every time she looked at it, it made her smile. The photo had been taken last year by Cal's sister, and Cora had already told her the story of how, on that one eventful afternoon, Otto had managed to get himself tangled in a sprawl of seaweed, chased along the sand by an irate seagull and finally pinched on the nose by a crab.

Never mind cats and their nine lives; Otto appeared to have more like twenty.

Mimi had been hearing stories about the Mathieson family all week. During the day Cora had gone to school and she had worked, but the moment Cora arrived home, the non-stop chatter had resumed. They never ran out of things to talk about. Mimi now knew enough about the family to be pretty confident she could pass an A level on the subject.

And it was all good. *All good.* She ran her hands over the crisp cotton duvet cover. Cora had already related the story of how she and Cal had bought it last year from Cavendish House in Cheltenham. She'd wanted him to buy the orange and purple one but he'd gone for blue and white stripes instead, then they'd had pizza afterwards and he'd accidentally left the carrier bag behind in the restaurant. A waitress had come running after them, Cora had explained to Mimi with great relish. And *then* the waitress had tried to give Cal her phone number in case he wanted to meet up for a drink sometime, and he'd had to say no and pretend he couldn't because he was married.

Everything in the house had a story, and Cora loved to tell them.

Speak of the devil, here she came now. The sound of footsteps racing up the stairs grew louder, the bedroom door crashed open and Cora burst into the room with Otto at her heels, a DVD in one hand and a giant bag of sweet-and-salted popcorn in the other. In one bound, they both landed on the bed.

Mimi pointed at Otto. 'Off.'

'Oh let him stay, just for a bit. It's our last night.'

'Your dad said we mustn't encourage him.'

'We aren't encouraging him; he's already made up his own mind. And he likes being up here with us. How would you like to sit on the floor all the time while everyone else was comfortable?' Plumping up the pillows, Cora wriggled alongside Mimi and got herself settled. She was wearing white pyjamas covered in purple stars and her hair smelled of apple shampoo.

'What are we watching?' said Mimi.

'*Mamma Mia!*'

'Cal says you've seen it eighty-seven times before.'

'More than that.' Cora grinned and stroked Otto's ears as he crawled onto her lap, eyes averted in case they noticed he was there and tipped him off the bed. 'But it's nicer seeing it again with someone else. When I watch it with Dad he always ends up falling asleep. I mean, at least he doesn't snore, but it's still annoying.'

Mimi nodded in agreement. 'It is.'

Doesn't snore. Big tick. Excellent.

'Who was your best ever boyfriend?' Cora tilted her head to look up at Mimi with interest.

Initially, these random out-of-the-blue questions had caught her off guard, but Mimi was used to them now. She thought about it for a few seconds. 'I suppose it was a boy called Marco at school. We were friends for a couple of years, then we got together . . . and he was really nice.'

This wasn't nearly enough information for Cora. 'What kind of nice? How long were you together? What was he *like*?'

'Well, he was good fun to be with. Not one of those moody, stroppy types. We played a lot of tennis. And I suppose we lasted for about a year. I left school,' Mimi explained, 'and he stayed on to do A levels. There was no big bust-up. He was studying for exams, I was working hard and then his parents moved to the other side of London. We just kind of drifted apart. But while we were together, he was a really lovely boyfriend.'

'Do you wish you were still with him now?' Cora's eyes were wide.

'No, not at all. It was all so long ago.'

'Was he good-looking?'

'Pretty good-looking, yes.' Mimi nodded.

'What colour was his hair?'

'Um . . . dark brown.'

'Eyes?'

'Kind of greeny-grey.'

'What ones are your favourite?'

Mimi said tactfully, 'I don't mind. I think what the person's like is more important. Are you going to open that bag of popcorn or are we just going to admire it from the outside?'

Cora promptly pulled open the bag and popcorn fountained out onto the duvet. 'Whoops! Don't worry, I won't tell Dad you spilled popcorn in his bed.' She giggled at Mimi's look of mock outrage. 'What time's he coming back tomorrow?'

'Flight's landing at five.' Mimi's stomach tightened at the thought of seeing Cal again. 'He's hoping to be home by seven. Have you missed him?'

'Yes, but it's been great having you here.' Cora leaned her

head against Mimi's shoulder. 'Are you looking forward to him coming back?'

Mimi said, 'Open your mouth,' and tossed a piece of popcorn into the air so that Cora could catch it like a seal. To change the subject, she went on, 'How about we cook something really nice for him tomorrow night? You can be in charge of the menu. What would be his favourite meal?'

Cora had caught the bus to school and Mimi was taking Otto for his morning walk when she bumped into Lois coming out of the shop with milk, croissants and a bag of oranges.

'You look like a honeymooner.'

Lois beamed; her mascara-smudged eyes were shining and her hair was messed up. 'I feel like one. Honestly, everything's so great. I can't believe how happy I am.'

'That's brilliant.' Mimi was genuinely thrilled for her.

'Oh, and wait till I tell you.' Lois clutched her arm. 'You won't believe what happened last night.'

'You don't have to give me all the gory details . . .'

'No, I do have to! Remember in Puerto Pollensa when CJ asked me if Felix had ever kissed my bad leg?'

Mimi nodded. 'I remember. And you said he never had.'

'I told Felix about it last night and he said he'd never done it because I was always so self-conscious he thought I'd be horrified if he tried anything like that. Which was when I realised he was right, and he said of course he'd kiss the scarred bit at the end if I wanted him to . . . and then he did, and he said it was a part of who I was, and it was so lovely I cried.'

'That *is* lovely,' said Mimi.

'Don't tell CJ, though.' Lois pulled a face. 'You know what he's like, he'll put it in a book.'

By six thirty, the dinner was ready, Cora and Otto were ready, and Cal had called to say he was on his way home. Mimi, who wasn't ready, was wondering why her shampoo wasn't foaming and belatedly discovering that it was because it was conditioner.

But by five to seven she was dressed in jeans and a light green T-shirt, and her hair – shampooed *and* conditioned – was more or less dry. Having resisted the urge to spray herself with scent, she'd also kept the make-up to a minimum because only a complete try-hard would do themselves up like a dog's dinner when someone who was *just a friend* was coming home after a week away.

Then a car pulled up outside the house, Otto burst into a volley of hysterical barking and Cora yelled, 'Hooray, Dad's here!'

Mimi, upstairs in Cal's bedroom, watched from the window overlooking the lane as Cal emerged from the driver's seat – oh God, just *look* at him, all golden-skinned and laughing and gorgeous. The next moment, Cora was racing down the path, throwing herself into his outstretched arms.

Maybe some eleven-year-olds would regard themselves as too cool for such a display of affection, but Cal and Cora were a tight unit; what they'd been through together had created an unbreakable bond between them. Mimi, observing the way Cora wrapped her skinny arms around Cal's neck, felt a tumult of emotions welling up and realised she loved them both.

Damn, now she was going to have to redo her mascara.

411

Chapter 48

'Well, that was the best meal I've ever had in my life,' said Cal.

'That's because I chose all of your favourite things,' Cora told him, 'and Mimi made the dinner.'

'We made it together,' Mimi reminded her.

'Yes, but you're better at cooking than me.'

Cal said, 'Every single bit of it was perfect.'

Mimi said, 'You were lucky, you got me on a good day. Sometimes my food's a disaster.'

'I don't believe you.' He shook his head.

'No, Dad, she's telling the truth. We had to throw away the first gravy,' Cora said gleefully, 'because Mimi made it with sugar instead of salt.'

'Hello?' Mimi protested. 'At least I found out before it was too late.'

But they were laughing with her, not at her. It was one of those moments, she realised, that you wished you could capture in a jar and preserve forever. Here they were, seated together around the kitchen table, utterly relaxed as they finished a bottle of duty-free Sancerre. The table was littered with plates, bowls and – at Cora's insistence – a dozen flickering tea lights. Cora was still giggling at the earlier mistake with the gravy and Cal was playfully tweaking the multicoloured charity bands on her left wrist. His week in Dubai had deepened his tan and he was looking more irresistible than ever. Mimi swallowed; this, being here now, was what absolute unalloyed happiness felt like. If only it could go on forever.

'You forgot to remind me.' Cal raised his eyebrows at Cora and tapped his watch. 'It's nine thirty.'

'Oh Dad, no. Can't I stay up a bit later? It's a special night!'

'You've got school tomorrow.'

'I'm not tired, though. I'm excited you're home!'

Cal said good-naturedly, 'You might not be tired, but I am.'

Of course he was tired. Mimi realised she was outstaying her welcome. 'I must go too.'

'No need to rush off this minute. You can stay and finish your drink.'

'You're so strict,' Cora grumbled. 'Mimi always let me stay up until midnight.'

'You wish,' said Mimi.

Five minutes later, changed into her pyjamas and smelling of toothpaste, Cora came downstairs to say goodnight. She hugged Mimi and stage-whispered, 'Thank you for staying here and looking after me and letting me stay up really late every night.'

Then she kissed Cal and said, 'Night, Dad. Love you. Bye, Otto!'

Otto wagged his tail. '*Woof.*'

When Cora had headed back upstairs, Mimi said, 'I didn't let her stay up late.'

'I know.' The glimmering light from the candles was reflected in the golden brown of Cal's eyes. 'How's she been this week?'

'Wonderful.' Mimi spread her hands; it was the truth. 'She's such great company. Honestly, I've loved every minute.'

'And how many times did you have to watch *Mamma Mia!*?' His expression was grave.

'Only twice. I think I got off lightly.'

'You did.' Cal divided up the last of the wine in the bottle, then clinked his glass against hers. 'Anyway, thank you.'

'My pleasure.' Mimi felt her pulse quicken because all of a sudden the atmosphere in the kitchen seemed to be changing. Was it just wishful thinking on her part? She took a gulp of wine, then instantly realised her mistake, because once it was gone it would be time to leave. Oh, but what would Cal do if she were to lean across and kiss him now? Would he be OK with that, or completely horrified? Plus he'd already told them he was shattered after his flight. Imagine how grim it'd be if she tried it and he shrank away, muttering, 'Oh dear, I don't think that's a good idea . . .'

As if to save her from herself, his phone chose that moment to receive a message. Taking it out of his pocket, Cal looked at the screen for a couple of seconds.

Finally he glanced up. 'Sorry, I need to just . . . deal with this.' And there was a faint edge to his voice that made Mimi wonder what could be about to go wrong this time.

Because something did always seem to crop up when she least wanted it to, so why should this evening be any different?

'No problem!' Pushing back her chair, she grabbed the pudding plates. 'I'll just clear up a bit . . .'

But as she switched on the hot tap and squirted washing-up

liquid into the sink, she heard the front door close and realised that Cal had stepped outside. Clearly he needed to have a conversation with someone that couldn't be overheard by her.

A cold sensation crawled through Mimi's intestines, because this kind of implied it was something *she* wouldn't want to hear either. She could hazard a guess as to what it might be too. Cal had met someone in Dubai, someone beautiful and incredibly glamorous who had captured his attention, and since she was as confident as she was irresistible, she'd seduced him on the first night of his visit, which meant they'd spent the last week having wild sex at every opportunity . . . She was probably messaging to let him know that her plane had landed at Bristol and she was on her way over to Goosebrook right now.

Mimi blinked; she could even picture her, the epitome of elegance with luxuriant black hair and flashing dark eyes, her body swathed in the kind of outfit Amal Clooney would wear— *Oh, oww.*

The front door opened and closed once more, heralding Cal's return, and Mimi winced at the cut on her finger from the razor-sharp vegetable knife she hadn't realised was in the bottom of the washing-up bowl. Hastily she grabbed a wodge of kitchen paper and wrapped it around her finger. As Cal reappeared in the kitchen, she plastered on a bright smile – *Look at me, busy doing the washing up!* – and said casually, 'Everything OK?'

But Cal wasn't smiling. The expression on his face was unreadable. He crossed the kitchen and held his phone out to her. 'There's something here I want you to see.'

Mimi took the phone with her good hand and saw that

415

the message had been from Cora. It said: *Dad, look at this. But NOT in front of Mimi.*

Oh God, had she done something awful without even realising it? Inadvertently said something terrible? Was it to do with the teaspoon she'd dropped into the waste disposal . . . had it been Cora's all-time favourite spoon?

Or, oh please no, the last one Stacey had used before she died?

Without looking at Cal and with apprehension tightening her chest, Mimi pressed play, and the image of Cora on the screen came to life.

'Hi, Dad, it's me, and I promise I'm going to sleep now but there's just something I need to say to you first.' Sitting cross-legged on her bed in her pyjamas, she was gazing earnestly into the camera lens. 'OK, I know you felt bad about upsetting me when you broke up with Della, but I honestly wasn't upset about that. And then I thought you were secretly seeing Lois, which just felt wrong from the start so I was really glad when I found out it wasn't true. And I know you've hardly been out with anyone at all since Mum because you don't want me getting confused and wondering how long any of them are going to last, which can't have been much fun for you.' She paused to take a deep breath. 'So I'm just going to say this now, in case you were wondering. Because if you think you might really like Mimi . . . well, that would be amazing, and if you two got together it would honestly make me so happy. OK, maybe you aren't interested or Mimi isn't, but I just wanted you to know that if it did happen I definitely wouldn't be upset, because this week we've had the best time ever and if Mimi was your actual girlfriend it'd be *so* great. Anyway, if you aren't interested you can delete this, but I just had to say it.

And now I'm going to sleep, I promise. Night!' Still beaming, Cora waved madly with both hands into the camera, then the screen went blank.

Mimi realised she'd been holding her breath since the message had begun. Her heart was banging and she still couldn't bring herself to look at Cal, because it was just the most heartbreakingly wonderful message, but what if he thought she'd begged Cora to send it?

'Can I just ask one question?' said Cal.

'I didn't know she was going to say that,' Mimi blurted out. 'I didn't ask her to do it!'

'What?' Cal shook his head slightly. 'That wasn't the question. I just need to know . . . are you completely over him now?'

Struggling to think straight and in need of physical support, she leaned back against the sink. 'Over him? Of course I am. It's been almost a year since I last saw Rob . . . I don't even *think* about him—'

'Not Rob,' Cal cut in. 'I'm not talking about Rob.' He frowned. 'I meant Paddy.'

It was one of those completely surreal moments. '*Paddy?* Why would I need to be over Paddy?'

'Because you were crazy about him.'

'WHAT?'

'OK, let's call it a massive crush . . .'

'Who told you this?' Mimi stared at him in disbelief. 'Because it just isn't true!'

'You told me,' said Cal. 'Well, you told me you were over it, you *insisted* it was all in the past. But sometimes people say that because they want it to be true . . . they're just trying to convince themselves . . .'

'Oh my God,' Mimi gasped as realisation rolled over her like a wave. 'When I told you that, that wasn't who I was talking about. What made you think it was Paddy?'

It was Cal's turn to be taken aback. 'Della told me. She said she'd had to warn you that he was trouble, and that for your own good you should steer clear of him, not get involved.'

Now Mimi understood everything. Della had warned her off Cal, but it had been without his knowledge. In all likelihood, she hadn't told Cal in case the idea roused his interest. Which meant he hadn't been laughing at her, and had completely misunderstood her stumbling, agonisingly awkward explanation, the one she'd begged him never to mention again.

And he hadn't. Until tonight.

Nor had he deleted Cora's video message. Instead, he'd shown it to her.

He hadn't spent the last week in bed with a glamorous Amal Clooney lookalike either.

Well, let's hope not.

Cal said, 'So who was it, if it wasn't Paddy?'

Mimi's mouth was dry. The time had come to be brave. Could she do it?

She swallowed and said simply, 'It was you.'

Now she was able to witness Cal mentally scrolling back through time, slotting into place those pieces of the jigsaw that had never fitted together before.

Finally his expression cleared. 'And you thought I knew all along?'

Mimi tilted her head in acknowledgement. 'I did.'

'Hang on.' He frowned. 'You told me you were completely

over your mad crush. And you weren't talking about Paddy, you were talking about me. So does that mean . . .?'

'I was lying. Through my teeth. I wasn't over you at all.'

Cal stopped frowning. 'Well that's good to know.'

Mimi ventured a smile. Butterflies were taking flight inside her ribcage. As she pressed her hand against her chest, she saw the look on Cal's face turn to one of horror before belatedly realising why.

'What have you *done*?'

She gazed down at her hand, wrapped in blood-soaked kitchen paper. Having stained the front of her T-shirt, the blood was dripping onto the floor. Honestly, Amal Clooney would never be so careless with a vegetable knife.

Nor, probably, would she wear a T-shirt that had cost three pounds fifty in a charity shop.

'There was a knife in the sink. It's nothing, I'm fine.' It was the least important injury she'd ever sustained, but Cal was already unpeeling the kitchen paper and inspecting the wound.

'Sorry,' said Mimi as blood dripped onto his fingers.

A slow smile tugged at the corners of his mouth. 'Are you apologising for having cut yourself whilst doing my washing-up?'

'Don't get your hopes up – I only managed to wash one plate.'

Cal went into the utility room and returned with the first aid box. He ran her hand under the cold tap, patted it dry then efficiently began dressing the wound. And Mimi discovered that it was no longer the least important injury she'd ever sustained. Every time their hands touched, it felt like magic, and she half expected stars to appear, Disney-style.

Cal might be concentrating on the task, but all she was concentrating on was Cal.

Finally he said, 'There, done,' and raised his gaze to meet hers. And there it was again, that swooping, time-slowing-down sensation overtaking her senses. It was like an out-of-body experience.

Mimi swallowed. 'Thanks.'

'No problem.' He was observing her with interest. 'So, what do you think? About Cora's message.'

'I think . . . it's lovely that she's trying to help you.'

'All this time,' Cal nodded slowly, 'I've wondered how you felt about me.'

'Have you? Really?'

'Oh yes. But I was scared in case it was just wishful thinking on my part. Because making a mistake would have been . . . well, awful. And it was too important to risk messing everything up. Every time I thought maybe it could happen, something went wrong. I couldn't bear it when I thought you and Paddy might get together.'

'I couldn't bear it when I thought about you and Lois.' Mimi felt as if someone else was in charge of sending the words out of her mouth.

'On the afternoon of Cora's party, Paddy asked when you were coming over. That's why I said we didn't need any help when you offered.'

'Oh, there's something else I need to tell you.' Suddenly remembering, Mimi blurted out, 'I was so mortified on Boxing Day when Della said you were embarrassed by my crush on you. And then I lost my front door key and Paddy let me stay over at his place, and I threw myself at him. But only because my love life was a complete disaster, a barren

420

wasteland of nothingness, and I was so ashamed by what Della had told me. I didn't fancy him at all, I was just desperate to get over you and I thought it might help.' It was a terrible thing to have to confess, but she had to say it. Cal needed to know.

'You tried to seduce him? And did you?'

'No. He turned me down.' More shame. 'He said I wasn't that kind of girl and I'd regret it in the morning.'

Cal half smiled. 'Well, I'm impressed with Paddy. And do you think you would have regretted it?'

'God, yes!'

'Did you . . . kiss him?'

'Only once. For about two seconds, before he stopped it.' Mimi shrugged. 'Then we both went to bed in separate rooms.'

Cal shook his head thoughtfully. 'If it had been me, I don't think I'd have done that.'

'I'm just glad he did.'

His smile broadened. 'What are you looking at?'

'Your mouth.'

'Why?'

'Just wondering what it would be like to kiss it.'

Oh my life, listen to me!

Cal said, 'I've wondered what it'd be like to kiss you ever since you moved down here last summer.' He moved closer, and Mimi felt her skin tingle with anticipation. As he slid his hands over her shoulders then lifted her face up to meet his, he said in a low voice, 'I was beginning to think I'd never find out.'

Oh, the sheer bliss of the moment. Finally, it was happening. The adrenalin rush reached every inch of her body as she

421

gave herself up to the culmination of all those months of longing and wishing and waiting. Nothing – *nothing* – had ever felt so right.

The kiss went on and on. At last they came up for air and Mimi discovered she couldn't tear herself away.

'Well, now I know,' said Cal.

'That's a coincidence. Me too.' Her eyes were locked on his. His arms around her were all that were keeping her upright.

'Is it too soon to tell you I love you? It's probably too soon. I won't say it yet.' Cal ran his index finger over the curve of her upper lip. 'I'll just think it.'

Mimi kissed him again, and this time when they finally drew apart, Cal murmured, 'Is it OK to say it now?'

The patter of small paws behind them heralded Otto's entrance into the kitchen.

'Basket,' prompted Cal, but Otto wagged his tail and did a polite throat-clearing *woof*.

'Has he actually learned to tell the time?' Mimi marvelled, because according to the clock on the wall, it was two minutes to ten. 'I know you told me about this, but every night he gets it spot on.'

'The joys of the bedtime routine. Come on, we won't get any peace until he's sorted.' Cal clasped her hand in his and walked with her to the front door. Otto had always refused to go for his last wee of the evening in the back garden, preferring instead to explore the lane at the front of the house before using the grass verge just beyond the front gate.

Leaving the door open, they waited on the narrow path while Otto darted around, busily inspecting his favourite nooks and crannies as he always did.

All was silent around them until the church clock chimed the hour. The stars were out, the night was warm and still, and the scent of new-mown grass hung in the air. Cal said quietly, 'I'm still thinking it,' then kissed Mimi again, and this time the kiss seemed to go on for ever because neither of them wanted it to end, and if there was anything more amazing than the way she was feeling right now, Mimi didn't know what it could be . . . OK, well maybe apart from—

'*Woof woof!*' said Otto, and it wasn't until then that they realised they were no longer alone; the outlines of a figure and another dog were emerging from the darkness. But whereas they couldn't identify the new arrivals, Mimi knew that she and Cal were clearly illuminated in the light from the hallway beyond the open front door. Whoever it was couldn't have failed to spot them.

Then the second dog gave a gruff answering bark and Cal, recognising the sound, said, 'That's Bongo.'

The straggly-haired mongrel, who closely resembled his owner, belonged to Old Bert. During Bert's prolonged stay in hospital, Bongo was being looked after by Paddy.

Now close enough for them to see him, Paddy said in conversational tones, 'I usually just take him for a walk around the green, but it turns out this way's far more interesting.' His teeth gleamed white in the darkness at the sight of Mimi and Cal with their arms wrapped around each other. 'Well done.'

'Thanks.' Cal was smiling too. 'I love her.'

With a shiver of joy, Mimi blurted out, 'And I love him.'

She heard Cal's intake of breath as he turned to look at her. 'You do?'

'Oh yes.' She nodded and squeezed his hand. 'Definitely. I have done for ages.'

423

'It never was CJ, was it?' Paddy sounded amused.

'It was *never* CJ,' Mimi agreed.

'I can't believe I got that so wrong. Although I did manage to figure out the real story at Cora's party.' He was making his way past the front gate now, with Bongo loping along at his heels. 'But it's nice that you finally managed to work it out for yourselves.'

'It's taken a while.' As Otto rejoined them, Cal's arm tightened around Mimi's waist. 'But we got there in the end.'

An owl hooted nearby. Still fizzing with exhilaration, Mimi murmured, 'We should be getting back inside.'

'Well don't go counting on getting any privacy,' said Paddy.

Mimi was startled. 'Why not?' Surely he wasn't planning to invite himself in for a drink.

But Paddy was grinning now, pointing past them and above their heads before leaving them to it and making his way back down the hill into Goosebrook.

When they turned and looked up, there was Cora, doing a victory dance and waving madly at them through the open bedroom window.

'Oh God.' Cal spluttered with laughter. 'She's going to be wide awake for hours.'

'Doesn't matter,' Mimi murmured back. 'We've got plenty of time.'

Cal dropped a kiss on her forehead. 'All the time in the world. But I still wish she was asleep right now.'

Above them, beaming with satisfaction, Cora proudly called down, 'See? I knew my idea would work. I'm always right!'

Jill Mansell

MAYBE THIS TIME is Jill Mansell's thirtieth fabulous, feel-good novel. Jill's novels have sold an astonishing eleven million copies around the world, bringing joy to readers for over twenty-five years.

Jill started writing fiction when she read a magazine article that inspired her to join a local creative writing class, and she has never looked back. She writes her novels by hand, in a series of notebooks. On their pages she creates characters who become friends to readers, making them laugh and cry, and compelling them to turn the pages as fast as they can to find out what's going to happen next.

Jill lives with her family in Bristol, where she is already working on a new novel for 2020.

Mimi isn't looking for love when she spends a weekend in
Goosebrook, the Cotswolds village her dad has moved to. And
her first encounter with Cal, who lives there too, is nothing like
a scene in a romantic movie – although she can't help noticing
how charismatic he is. But Cal's in no position to be any more
than a friend, and Mimi heads back to her busy London life.

When they meet again four years later, it's still not to be.
Cal is focusing on his family, and Mimi on her career. Then
Cal dives into a potentially perfect new romance whilst
Mimi's busy fixing other people's relationships.

It seems as if something, or someone else, always gets in
their way. Will it ever be the right time for both of them?

The joy of Jill's novels

'The queen of w
feel-good
Red

'Should be prescribed reading for anyone
feeling down in the dumps'
Veronica Henry

'One of my favourite writers'
Katie Fforde

www.headline.co.uk www.jillmansell.co.uk
@JillMansell /OfficialJillMansell

UK £7.99 CAN $15.99

ISBN 978-1-4722-4846-6

Also available in
ebook and audio

FICTION

FSC